COUNTDOWN TO
KILLING
KURTIS

USA Today bestselling author
Lauren Rowe

Chapter 1

Hollywood, California, 1992

20 Years Old
1 Day Before Killing Kurtis

My head bangs against the wall as Kurtis has his way with me, groaning and grunting all the while. I can sense he's reaching his limit and can't hold out much longer.

"Baby," he moans, his voice straining.

I turn my face into his ear and exhale sharply, making sure my breathing seems ragged and desperate, as if, despite my best efforts at maintaining my composure, I just can't control myself. Of course, my dear husband, only you bring out the wide-eyed little girl in me, the girl who believes in happily ever afters and soul mates. I roll my eyes, even as my skull bangs against the wall with a loud thud.

The vast majority of the time, something as simple as panting in Kurtis' ear does the trick and sends him over the edge. But not this time.

Bang, bang, bang. My head continues its assault on the wall of our hotel room.

"Oh, Kurtis," I blurt loudly, taking great care to infuse my voice with breathless excitement. And then, because Kurtis absolutely loves it when I talk Texas, I bring my lips right to his ear, blow out a puff of warm air, and whisper, in my most exaggerated twang, "Goodness gracious, sugar."

1

That ought to do the trick.

I wait.

He's moaning and grunting like a hog in slop, but undeniably hanging on. Well, hells bells. Looks like I'm gonna have to work a little harder than usual to lead my blind pig of a husband to an acorn tonight. I make a noise like my insides are being split in two by pleasure so intense, it hurts—and then, just because I like wearing belts *and* suspenders, I bite his earlobe, too. Hard.

Yep, that does it. Hallelujah. Kurtis lets out a mangled cry of release and relief, and I respond with my trademark I'm-just-so-in-love-with-you sigh. Just for the heck of it, since this is my final performance, after all, and I'm a big believer in "leaving it all out there," I follow all of it up with a little shimmy—something I've only recently learned I'm supposed to do at times such as this—and then I arch my back with apparent pleasure like I'm finally, deliciously scratching a hard-to-reach itch.

I smirk. I should have been an actress. Oh wait—I *am* an actress. And a damn good one, too—destined to be seen by audiences in cineplexes all over the world.

Kurtis becomes still. His body goes slack. Beads of sweat cover his brow, his chest, his cheeks. If I didn't hate my husband so much, I might actually think he's handsome—quite handsome, indeed.

I smile dreamily at my dear husband, thinking about tomorrow—when he'll finally be dead.

"You're amazing, baby," Kurtis says, grinning like a possum with a sweet potato.

"Oh, Kurtis," I squeal. In a sudden and unexpected fit of genuine glee, I throw my head back and laugh with abandon. Tomorrow is finally Killing Kurtis Day, and I'm bursting at the seams about it.

Kurtis kisses my nose. "I love you, baby."

"I love you, too, Kurtis," I reply. And it's true. I *do* love Kurtis—that is, if you define love as that hard-to-pin-down sensation of anticipation and longing you get as you count down the days, then hours, and then minutes until your loved one is cold and dead as he so richly deserves to be. What a thrill—a turn-on, even, if I'm being honest—to be so very close now, so very, very close, after waiting a tortuous year minus one day for his well-deserved fate to come. Being on the eve of his one-way departure from planet earth, I feel somewhat hot and bothered, actually. Hey now, being so close to Happy Killing Kurtis Day is getting me hotter than a stolen tamale. I suddenly and enthusiastically kiss my husband's mouth, and he plunges his tongue into mine in reply.

"Oh, baby," he murmurs, his brawny body instantly responding to my surprising invitation. "Again?"

"Again," I mutter.

Might as well send the fucker off with a smile on his stupid, lying face.

Chapter 2

Kermit, Texas, 1982

10 Years Old
3,552 Days Before Killing Kurtis

"You're so pretty, Buttercup," Daddy says to me, brushing my hair out of my eyes. "You could sit on a fence and the birds would feed *you*." Not a single day has gone by in my entire ten-year-old life that Daddy hasn't said these words, or some variation of them, to me. He's sitting on the edge of my cot, tucking me in for the night. Momma's already passed out on her mattress down the hall, stinking of whiskey, as usual. "You're the prettiest little girl in the whole wide world," Daddy coos, emphasizing each word with a fingertip pressed to my forehead. "Never, ever settle for anything but the very best in this life, Buttercup. If someone would've given me that advice when I was ten, maybe my life would've turned out a whole lot differently."

Does that mean he regrets having me, I wonder?

Daddy must see the look of worry in my eyes because he touches my cheek tenderly and says, "But I wouldn't change a goddamned thing, Buttercup, 'cause the Lord gave me you. And you're all I ever need to be happier than a tornado in a trailer park."

I smile broadly.

"You deserve nothing but the best."

Whenever Daddy makes the "Charlie Wilber's Daughter's Gonna Be Somebody" speech, which is often, I know it's my cue to fist-pump the air as a sign of unwavering solidarity and shared vision—and I never miss my cue.

"Nothing but the best for Charlie Wilber's Daughter," I declare.

Yes, if I've heard it once, I've heard it a thousand times from Daddy: "Just 'cause Charlie Wilber got stuck living in a trailer with a drunk, soul-sucking, good-for-nothing wife who doesn't have an ounce of class, doesn't mean Charlie Wilber's *Daughter*'s gonna follow him to hell. No sir, Charlie Wilber's Daughter's gonna get herself educated and be somebody."

Daddy used to have big plans for himself, not just for his daughter—specifically, Daddy used to dream of becoming a world-famous mini-golf-course designer. But, sadly, things just didn't work out as planned, thanks to the limitless supply of dumbasses in the world. "I used every penny of my inheritance from dear old Uncle Ray, may he rest in peace, to buy a premium piece of land right along Route 291—you know, that long stretch in the desert?—and I was gonna build the best mini-golf experience the world has ever seen." But thanks to the Napoleon-types at the Department of Planning who were every one of 'em as dumb as a bag of hammers and just itching to lord over someone, Daddy's mini-golf course designs got bogged down in red tape until he finally had to face the hard truth that he wasn't ever gonna get out of Kermit, Texas—population eight hundred forty-three.

Whenever I look sad about how Daddy's life maybe hasn't turned out the way he always dreamed about, he quickly reassures me it's all in God's plan. "If a trip around the world cost a dollar, I couldn't get to the Oklahoma line," he always says. "But that's okay, Buttercup, because my biggest invention in this life is just gonna have to be you."

Right at this part of Daddy's story, I usually suggest that maybe it's not too late for Daddy's dreams to still come true?

"No, Buttercup," Daddy always replies, "when I nailed the hottest chick in Winkler County at age seventeen, right behind the eighteenth hole at Walt's Mini-Golf, I found out the trajectory of a man's entire life can change with one little ejaculation." Daddy always laughs at that punch line and I join him, even though I don't know what a trajectory is. Or an ejaculation, for that matter.

When Daddy first heard about sixteen-year-old Momma's unexpected bun in the oven, he rejoiced, believe it or not, because he instantly realized that the tadpole inside Momma's belly was gonna deliver him his first-ever chance at happiness—an actual family he could love and call his own and shower with expensive gifts like gold-plated watches and modems and jetpack-backpacks that make you fly through the air like an astronaut. "I figured, heck, as long as I'm gettin' started having kids so young, I might as well have twelve and create my own army for when we get nuked by the Russians." Daddy always laughs when he says that last part about us getting nuked by the Russians, and I laugh, too, even though, honestly, it makes me feel as scared as a cat left behind at the dog pound.

Tonight's bedtime routine is no different than every other night. After Daddy tells me how pretty I am and reminds me how the dumbasses of the world have thwarted him at every turn, he asks me about my day, just like he always does.

"Well," I reply, "you know that scruffy little dog that lives with Mrs. Miller and her dopey little grandson in the trailer with the rusty screen door? Well, that crazy dog got out and was runnin' around like a squirrel in a forest fire so I gave him some water on account of it being hotter than a fur coat in Marfa today and played with him for a while." I sigh at the warm memory—I sure do love puppies and kitties and everything furry. "But after a while," I continue, "I heard Mrs. Miller's dopey grandson calling to him from their trailer, so I brought the little guy to him—and, gosh, that boy sure was grateful to get his dog back." I blush, remembering how that little boy looked at me like I was pretty as a picture. "And, Daddy, that boy said I was the prettiest girl he'd ever seen in his whole dang life."

"Well, of course, he did," Daddy says. "There ain't nobody prettier than you, Buttercup."

I let out a long sigh. I know I should be happy to have made that dopey boy's day by bringing his dog back to him (and, even more so, by being so dang pretty), but all I can think about is how I've always wanted a little puppy or kitty of my own so I won't feel so dang lonely around here all the time. But we can't have any kind of pet on account of Momma's allergies.

Speak of the devil, Momma shuffles into the nearby kitchenette. She's still wearing her waitress uniform from earlier and her hair looks like it's been through a flood in a Fizzies factory.

Momma stares at Daddy and me for a minute, leaning against the counter and not saying a word, and we stare right back. Finally, Momma yawns so big I can see clear to the inside of her panties, grabs her whiskey bottle off the counter, and pours herself a tall one. When her glass is full and almost overflowing, she grunts like a mad monkey and shuffles back to the bedroom with her drink.

When Momma's out of sight, Daddy and I bust a gut laughing.

"Damn," Daddy says through his laughter, "she looks like she fell out the ugly tree and hit every branch on the way down."

I bring my hands up to my mouth to stifle my laughter, but it's no use. Daddy's just too funny.

"And drunk as a fiddler's bitch to boot," Daddy adds, still laughing, and I nod like a bobblehead doll. "Your momma sure has changed since I nailed her ten years ago behind hole eighteen. Back then, she was like a pearl in a fur cushion."

"Poor Daddy," I say. "Momma sure did pull the old switcheroo on you."

7

"Ain't that the truth."

"It sure is."

"And, holy hell, can that woman complain," Daddy says.

"That woman would complain if Jesus Christ himself came down and handed her a five-dollar bill."

Daddy throws his head back and guffaws. "Yes, indeed, I reckon she would."

I beam at him. Making Daddy bust a gut from laughing is my favorite thing.

When Daddy finally gathers his senses and wipes the laughing-tears from his eyes, he gazes at me like I'm a snow cone on a summer day. I know he's thinking "we're just two peas in a pod," and it makes my heart sing a happy tune.

"So, what'd you read for your education today?" Daddy asks.

Since Daddy has taken it upon himself to homeschool me, I usually tear through an entire book in a day. Even though Daddy's hardly ever around during the day to look after my education, he always makes sure to check on my progress every night at bedtime (which is more than I can say about Momma).

"Today's book was *In Cold Blood,*" I answer.

Daddy's face perks up. "Ah, Truman Capote. That's a good one, isn't it?"

"Yes, sir."

"Did you know that book single-handedly created the entire 'true-crime' genre?"

I shake my head.

"Well, if you like that one," Daddy says, "then let's have you read *Helter Skelter* next."

I nod enthusiastically, though I've never heard of that book. I like the title, though—it sounds kinda like "higgledy-piggledy."

"I want you to walk on down to the library tomorrow and get it," Daddy says.

"I will, Daddy."

8

"You've always gotta keep educating yourself, Buttercup."

I nod. "Yes, sir."

"It's up to you to maximize that big ol' brain of yours—to fill it with big thinking instead of standardized, small-minded crap."

I nod again and scrunch up my face to show him just how carefully I'm listening to what he's telling me. "Yes, Daddy."

"That's why I'm homeschooling you. Because the schools are all about telling you what you can and can't do and brainwashing you to think like everyone else. But you and me, we're not like everyone else. How do you think I've learned anything of any value whatsoever?"

"You taught yourself."

"Damn straight I did. I've never needed some small-minded teacher stuck in a classroom to tell me how to do something. If a teacher could invent a teleportation configuration system or design the world's greatest mini-golf course, don't you think that's exactly what he'd be doing, and not sitting around in a classroom handing out multiple-choice tests?"

I nod and say, "Pfft" so Daddy knows I'm nothing like any ol' small-minded teacher sitting in a classroom handing out multiple-choice tests.

"You can do anything you set your mind to, anything at all."

"I sure can, Daddy."

"Never let anyone tell you what you can and can't do."

"I won't, Daddy."

There's a groan from the back room. "Charlie!" Momma groans. "Bring me the bottle." Daddy rolls his eyes at me, and I roll mine back at him. Momma is our mutual cross to bear. When Daddy gets up to tend to Momma, I roll over onto my side with a huge smile on my face. I'm the luckiest girl in the world to have such a handsome and smart daddy who loves me so dang much.

Chapter 3

18 Years, 6 Days Old
735 Days Before Killing Kurtis

The secretary in the front room of Kurtis Jackman's office is old as dirt and sounds like she smokes two packs a day. The woman doesn't look the least bit impressed when I say, sweet as pie, "I'm here to see Mr. Kurtis Jackman." But when I add, "Johnny from the club sent me," she immediately replies, "Mr. Jackman will see you in a few minutes."

Ten minutes later, I'm standing right in front of the man himself in his cluttered office. He's seated behind a big, mahogany desk, talking on the telephone, looking out a large window. He's about twice my age, probably just about Daddy's age, but taller and brawnier than Daddy ever was, and he's dressed in a slick black suit with a purple tie that probably cost him a pretty penny.

Kurtis' face is actually handsome, to tell you the truth—with a strong jawline and piercing dark eyes—but the minute I look at him and notice the way he's fidgeting and bellowing into the phone, almost like he's *pretending* to be big and important, I instantly know that, deep down inside, Mr. Kurtis Jackman doesn't think he's big and important or handsome at all. In fact, I'd even go so far as to bet the farm that, way down underneath that fancy black suit and purple tie, Mr. Kurtis Jackman believes he's small and nobody and ugly as homemade sin.

Kurtis' entire office is bursting from floor to ceiling with videotapes and *Casanova Magazines,* framed movie posters featuring big-busted women, and photographs of himself with what I reckon are famous and important people, though I don't recognize a single one of them. The décor of his office, like the appearance of the man himself, all but screams, "Please like me!" Just looking around at everything, there's no doubt Kurtis is a man desperate for the pretty people to like him. Well, thank God I'm so damned pretty.

I decide to ready myself for the moment when Kurtis' eyes are gonna feast on me for the very first time. With an arch of my eyebrow and a purse of my lips, I contort my facial expression into one of extreme boredom. I even go so far as to sigh in frustration, like "When the hell is this damned yahoo gonna get off the phone and stop wasting my precious time?"

Of course, just two minutes ago, before I'd laid eyes on Mr. Kurtis Jackman, I would have bet dollars to doughnuts my best strategy would have been to adopt a demeanor of extreme humility. But one look at Kurtis and how he's strutting just sitting down, and I know faster than a bell clapper in a goose's ass that humility isn't my best strategy here.

"Well, hello-*hello.*" Apparently, Mr. Kurtis Jackman is off the telephone and he's talking to me. Of course, I didn't notice his phone call had ended because I'd been looking out the window at something far more interesting than him. But since this is his office and all, and since I'm here anyway, and since Johnny from the club *did* send me to meet Kurtis right away, I deign to lay eyes on him. And when I do, he's already looking at me like I'm the Lord's special gift to him, sent straight from heaven and wrapped up in a "Light Blonde Number 5" bow.

"Well, hello there, honey," Kurtis coos at me like he's talking a kitten down from a tree. "I'm Kurtis Jackman." He stands up and extends his hand to me.

I politely take a step forward and put my hand in his.

11

"Pleased to meet you, Mr. Jackman, sir." I'm surprised at the jolt I feel when my skin presses against his. I pull my hand back, making a point of sliding my palm along his as I do. "Johnny from the club asked me to hightail it over here to meet you right quick," I say, "but I'm sure I don't know why." I let loose one of my brightest, most alluring smiles, as if I'm remembering how Johnny fawned all over me yesterday.

"Please, have a seat." He gestures to the chair across from him.

I seat myself, all the while taking great care to keep my chin up and my eyelids low—because I've noticed I'm particularly beautiful when I position my features this way. I sigh, just a little bit, trying to paint the picture of a girl who's utterly and completely unimpressed, yet who has the good manners not to show it.

"Can I get you some water?" Kurtis asks.

"No, thank you. Aren't you sweet."

"So how long have you been dancing down at the club?"

"Oh, goodness, no, Mr. Jackman," I say, laughing and shaking my head. "I'm not a *dancer* at your club. *Of course not.*" I wave my hand like he's just suggested eating fried chicken for breakfast.

"Well, then, what do you do?"

"I'm an actress," I say. "And a damned good one, too. It's my destiny to become a legendary actress for the ages, seen by audiences in cineplexes all over the world."

A wide smile unfurls across his face. "Is that so?" He leans back, assessing me.

"Yes, sir," I say. I jut my chin. "You can take that to the bank."

Kurtis leans forward, looking at me like I'm a fancy steak supper. "What's your name, sweetheart?"

I put my elbows on his desk and lean forward, flashing him a conspiratorial grin, and then I say, very quietly, as if I'm sharing a juicy secret with him and only him, "My name is Buttercup."

Kurtis' eyes drift to my mouth. *"Buttercup,"* he repeats, letting it turn over on his tongue. "That's quite a name. What's your last name, sweetheart?" He licks his lips like he can't wait to taste whatever I'm serving up next.

Well, he's going to like this. During the long bus ride to Hollywood, I thought long and hard about what my new movie-star name should be. Whenever the passenger seated next to me wasn't jabbering in my ear about their hopes and dreams or their best friend Ned's cousin who's a real-life movie extra in Hollywood, I read a biography about the most elegant woman who ever lived, Jacqueline Bouvier Kennedy—and the minute I saw her full name on the page of my book, I yelped like I'd fallen face-first into a sticker patch.

I lean into Kurtis and lick my lips just the way he did a moment ago. "Bouvier," I whisper, drawing out each syllable like molasses to make it sound particularly alluring and elegant: "Boo-vee-yay." This is the first time I'm saying my new movie-star name out loud, and it's exhilarating. I sit up extra straight and bat my eyelashes at him. "My name's Buttercup Bouvier."

Kurtis' eyes lock onto mine and an undeniable heat passes between us—and into my panties. I look away from Kurtis, trying to regain my composure, but gosh dang it, that throbbing in my panties is pretty hard to ignore.

"Well, Mr. Jackman," I say. I can feel my cheeks flushing crimson. "I mean no disrespect to you, but I don't see how the owner of a *gentleman's* club would have any use for an *actress* like me." I stand to leave.

"Whoa, hang on. Johnny didn't tell you?"

I look at him blankly, making my eyes as big as saucers. "Tell me what?"

"All about me? About my other *ventures* besides the club?"

Looks like I've got a fish on a line here, folks. I suppress a smile. "I reckon I should have asked Johnny more questions, sir. All I know is that you own a *nudie bar.*" I say "nudie bar" like I'm saying *leper colony*.

Kurtis pauses, apparently trying to figure me out. "How long have you been in Hollywood, honey?"

"Since yesterday."

Kurtis bursts out laughing. "Fresh off the bus."

I bristle. "Well, sir, if you aim to *mock* me..." Without another word or even a glance, I march straight out the door.

Kurtis follows me. "No, no. Hang on, Buttercup."

I march right past Kurtis' old-lady secretary and out the front door of the building, into the blinding sunlight.

"Hang on," Kurtis says behind me. I can't tell if he's distressed or laughing at me.

"My daddy raised me too well to let anyone make fun of me," I call out over my shoulder.

"Wait, wait," Kurtis says, catching up to me—and now, yes, it's plain to see he's laughing at me. In fact, he's amused as hell. "I wasn't making fun of you, honey, I promise," he says, but he can't hide his amusement even as he says it.

"Maybe y'all aren't used to someone like me out here in Lah-de-Lah Land, Mr. Jackman, but I assure you, I do not suffer someone planting his crop before he's built his fence." I whirl around and gaze at him with as much ferocity as I can muster. "I will *not* be made a fool by *anyone*."

There's a long beat, during which it seems Kurtis has been rendered speechless.

"So... then," I stutter. Gosh, I kinda expected Kurtis to say something right there. "Well, um, goodbye, then." I begin stalking away again.

"Buttercup, wait," Kurtis calls after me. His tone is so commanding, I stop dead in my tracks and give him my undivided attention. By now, we're well on our way up the sidewalk in front of his office. "Please forgive me," he says, his voice softening. "I didn't mean to insult you." He lets out a loud exhale. "My goodness, you're a feisty little thing, aren't you?"

I squint my eyes at him, but I don't reply.

"I tell you what," Kurtis continues, a grin spreading

across his face. "Why don't you let me take you out to lunch and make it up to you? It's the least I can do for being so horribly, hideously rude to you." His eyes flicker at me like he's thinking something naughty.

I pause for a ridiculously long amount of time, acting like I'm thinking good and hard about whether I'm going to allow this unworthy man take me to lunch—but the truth is, I'm trying to get a grip on myself. I'm not sure why my heart is racing and my crotch is on fire right now, but there's no denying either. "Well..." I say, suppressing a smile.

Kurtis clutches his chest, like he's begging me to give him a chance. "Have mercy on me."

I twist my mouth, trying not to smile.

Kurtis yelps in victory, but I quickly interrupt his celebration. "Don't get too excited. I'm only *half*-inclined to say yes." I bite my lip. "*Half*."

But Kurtis isn't paying me any mind—he knows he's got me right where he wants me, and then some. "We'll consider it your 'Welcome to Hollywood' party, honey."

I reckon I could try to string him along a little more, but what's the point? We both know where this is headed on a nonstop bullet train. "Darn you, Kurtis Jackman," I blurt, laughing. "I suppose there can't be any harm in having *lunch* with you—*if* you promise you're gonna behave yourself?"

He crosses his heart and holds up three fingers into a Boy Scout pledge.

I feel my cheeks flush. "I must admit I'm feeling a bit wooed by you, Mr. Jackman."

He laughs. "Please, call me Kurtis. Now don't move, okay?" He sounds genuinely excited. "I'm just going back inside to grab my wallet." He makes a big show of holding my shoulders down, forcing me to stay put.

"My oh my, Kurtis Jackman, you're just as sweet as molasses, aren't you? All right then, I'll stay put, honey. But hurry up now—I'm so hungry my belly thinks my throat's been cut."

15

Chapter 4

11 Years Old
3,197 through 3,196 Days Before Killing Kurtis

"You're so pretty, Buttercup, you could make a hound dog smile," Daddy says, brushing the hair out of my eyes. He's sitting on the edge of my cot, tucking me in for the night. When he sees tears pricking my eyes, threatening to pool and fall down my cheeks, he's instantly distressed. "What's wrong, honey?"

"I went over to Jessica Santos' trailer today to play with her brand new kitty," I say, my lower lip trembling. "I was lonely and wanted to talk to someone. I didn't mean to hurt it." My voice warbles at that last bit, so I stop talking.

Daddy puts his finger under my chin and tilts my face to the side. "You've got a scratch on your cheek."

I bite my lip, trying to make the tears stop flowing, but I can't. I'm just too darned sad. The truth is that Momma was sleeping, as usual, and Daddy was out at who-knows-where again; I was tired of reading my latest book for my education; I didn't have any money to go down to the 7-Eleven for a Slurpee; and there's never anyone to talk to around here. So when I saw Jessica just sitting by the big rocks behind her trailer with that cute little black-and-white kitty, I just wanted to talk to her and maybe get to hold her kitty for a while.

Well, how did I know that Mrs. Miller's dopey grandson

was gonna walk by with his scruffy dog on a leash at that very moment and scare the bajeezus out of that kitty with his barking? All I was trying to do was hold the kitty extra tight so he wouldn't run away on account of that crazy dog, that's all. But I can't explain any of that to Daddy or else he might get mad at Jessica for getting mad at me—or, worse, feel bad about how I'm always so lonely. "Jessica said I was too rough with her kitty, that's all," I say. Tears begin streaming down my cheeks in big, soggy droplets. "She said I'm not allowed to hold him ever again."

Daddy grunts and curls his lip. "She said you're not allowed to hold her kitty, did she? That girl with the frizzy hair and dime-sized eyes thinks *she* can tell *you* what you can and can't do?"

I'm shocked to hear Daddy say those mean things about Jessica—I think Jessica's curly hair is awfully pretty and her eyes are as sparkly as diamonds. But Daddy looks so worked up, I don't dare tell him what I'm thinking.

"Christ Almighty," Daddy huffs, "has that girl looked in the mirror lately? That girl's so ugly she'd make a freight train take a dirt road."

I nod, but only because it's what Daddy wants me to do.

"She's so ugly," Daddy continues, "her momma had to tie a pork chop around her neck so the dogs would play with her."

Well, that one makes me smile, even though it's mean.

"She's so ugly," Daddy says, "the doctors slapped her *momma* when she was born."

Now I burst out laughing. My daddy's always got the cleverest ways to call someone ugly.

Daddy pauses, staring at me, and I know exactly what that look on his face means. He's waiting on me to say something clever, too, because he's Charlie Wilber and I'm Charlie Wilber's Daughter.

I clear my throat. "Jessica's so dang ugly she has to sneak up on breakfast," I mumble, but I feel kinda bad saying something so mean about Jessica, even if she did say I was too rough with her kitty.

"That's the spirit," Daddy says. He looks at me thoughtfully. "Is Jessica's trailer the one with the green awning out front?"

I nod. "Yes, sir. Next to the big rocks."

Daddy grunts. "She probably lives next to the big rocks so her nose don't look so damned big."

I nod again, even though, honestly, I think Jessica Santos' nose is perfect.

"That girl's as ugly as homemade soap," Daddy says. He grins at me briefly, but then he glances away.

Oh no. I don't like it when Daddy glances away like that. "She sure is," I say, hoping to catch Daddy's attention before he slips away. But Daddy doesn't respond. "She sure is, Daddy," I repeat, hoping to reach him before his eyes glaze over.

But, shoot. It's no use. Daddy's gone, even as he's sitting here with me—as surely as if he's stepped into one of those teleportation configuration systems he's always talking about.

I've learned to wait patiently for Daddy to come back from one of his daydreams. But, gosh, Daddy remains lost in his thoughts, his jaw muscles pulsing in and out, for what seems like forever this time. "Daddy?" I finally mutter softly. He looks at me, but it's like his eyes aren't seeing me. "That girl's so ugly," I say, "even the tide wouldn't take her out."

But Daddy doesn't react.

"Daddy?" I smile hopefully at him. "Even the tide wouldn't take her out."

All of a sudden, Daddy's eyes sparkle again and his face softens. He's back. I breathe a huge sigh of relief. I hate it when Daddy leaves me like that.

"That's right, baby," Daddy says softly. "That's a good one." He smooths my hair out of my eyes. "So, okay, enough about that." He beeps my nose with the tip of his finger. "Tell me about what you read today to get your mind good and educated."

Chapter 5

11 Years Old
3,195 Days Before Killing Kurtis

Momma's in bed and Daddy's out, as usual, so I sneak out of our trailer with a bologna sandwich and head straight over toward Jessica Santos' trailer. I don't care what Jessica said yesterday about me not getting to hold her kitty ever again—I reckon if I'm really nice to her, if I tell her how pretty I think she is—how much I wish I had long, curly hair just like hers—she'll let me hold her fuzzy kitten today, especially if I promise to be extra careful and gentle with him and make sure Mrs. Miller's dog is nowhere in sight.

I rap on the door of her trailer. I wait, but nobody answers. Gosh, I really want to hold that cute little kitty today.

I wait.

I kick the dirt.

Nobody's home.

Shoot.

I amble over to the big rocks. A warm wind's blowing like perfume through the prom. I climb to the top of the biggest rock and look around. I have a good view of the entire trailer park from up here. I wonder when Jessica's coming home. I think about what I'm going to say to her to convince her to let me hold her fuzzy little kitten or at least let me pet him while she's holding him.

Hey, I wonder if Jessica's inside her trailer right now? Did she hear me knock but ignore me, maybe, because she's still so mad at me? I stand up on the rock, peering over at her trailer. I don't see any movement in the trailer. But ... wait a minute. What's that? I squinch my eyes, trying to make out the black-and-white blob I reckon I see on the ground, just to the side of Jessica's trailer. Is that...? I continue squinting and squinching my eyes. Could that black-and-white blob in the dirt be the kitty? With that last gust of wind, it sure looked like the surface of that blob rippled a bit, like it was covered in fur. But if that blob down there is Jessica's kitty, why isn't he moving?

I get up and move slowly toward Jessica's trailer, toward that little mound on the ground, clutching my bologna sandwich. With each step I take, my stomach twists tighter and tighter and my heart pounds harder in my chest, until I'm just about ready to worry the warts off a frog. When I'm finally standing over the blob, I throw my bologna sandwich down on the ground and my hands over my face and burst into tears.

"What happened, Buttercup? Did Chevrolet stop making trucks?" Daddy asks, sitting down on the edge of my cot for bedtime. I've been lying here for hours, crying buckets and buckets into my pillow.

"Jessica's kitty," I whimper. "I went to pet it today, and—"

"Shh, now," Daddy soothes. "There's no call for crying over that kitty anymore." He wipes my tears. "What's done is done."

"But, Daddy, I went to pet the kitty, and..." I can't choke out the rest.

"Aw, honey. That girl, Jessica Santos? She's just a big bully is what she is—an ugly bully. Don't you waste any more tears on her."

I can't get the picture of that poor little mound of black-and-white fur out of my head. "But, Daddy, the kitty was *dead*."

Daddy's eyes narrow to slits. "Is that so?" A smile curls up on one side of his mouth. "I reckon Jessica Santos won't be telling Charlie Wilbur's Daughter what she can and can't do anymore, huh? Well, ain't that a funny coincidence."

My mouth hangs open.

"Serves her right."

Is Daddy saying he...? My mind won't finish the thought. I sit up in my cot, my fingernails digging into my cheeks. "Daddy?"

"I reckon it was that kitty's destiny to teach Jessica Santos, and the whole world, that nobody tells Charlie Wilber's Daughter what she can and can't do."

"Daddy," I choke out. I clamp my hands over my mouth to keep myself from screaming. I can't believe my ears. I know Daddy wants me to fist-pump and shout "Nobody!" right now, but all I can do is lie back down and cover my face with my hands. I can't stop picturing that poor little kitty, dead and bloodied in the dirt. How could Daddy have harmed a hair on his cute little head?

"And don't forget that kitty scratched you, Buttercup," Daddy says. "He was a bad kitty, anyway." Daddy pulls my hands off my face and makes me look at him. "He was a very *shitty* kitty." He smiles at his own joke.

I don't return Daddy's smile. That little kitty was soft and cute as a button, with a teeny-tiny pink nose. His whiskers tickled my nose. His itty-bitty tongue felt like sandpaper on my skin. His little "meow" was the sweetest sound you ever did hear. I didn't tell Daddy about Jessica so he'd do *this*—I was just trying to explain why I was crying. How could he think this is what I wanted him to do?

"Buttercup, I sure do love you," Daddy says, pushing my hair away from my wet face.

I don't respond.

"I love you bigger than the sky full of stars, you know that, right? I sure do hate to see you cry. I'll do just about anything to keep you from crying, honey."

I bite my lip. I can't speak. It ripped my heart out to say

goodbye to that fuzzy little kitten today, to see his tiny body, mangled in the dirt. Dang, that kitty was as big as the little end of nothing—he wouldn't have hurt a fly on top of a cornbread muffin.

"Okay, then," Daddy says. He stares at me with hard eyes, waiting on me to say something, but I can't think of a single thing to say. "Buttercup? You hear me?"

Daddy looks different to me all of a sudden. I'm having a hard time looking at him.

"Come on, now, Buttercup. Say it."

Gosh dang it. For the first time ever, I don't want to say it.

"Say it," Daddy repeats, his eyes twinkling.

I exhale. "Nobody tells Charlie Wilber's Daughter what she can and can't do," I mumble.

Daddy smiles. "Good girl." He pats me on the head. "Now, no more crying, you hear? It's time to get your butt off your shoulders." Daddy pulls my blanket up to my neck and kisses me on the forehead. "'Nighty-night, Buttercup. Don't let the bedbugs bite."

I try to smile at him, but I can't. Trying to smile just makes me feel like crying. I close my eyes, forcing my mind to imagine something besides that poor, bloody kitty in the dirt. *My daddy loves me,* I tell myself. *My daddy loves me and that's all that matters.*

Daddy begins shuffling toward the back room.

My daddy loves me and that's the most important thing.

"I love you, honey," he says, turning out the lamp near the little table. "Sleep tight."

"Daddy?" I say softly.

He turns around, his face illuminated by the moonlight.

I reckon getting a black-and-white-and-red valentine from my daddy is more important than nuzzling a cute little kitty's soft pink nose. "I love you."

Daddy winks and flashes me his biggest movie-star smile. "I love you, too, sugar—bigger than the sky full of stars."

Chapter 6

18 Years 1 Week Old
734 Days Before Killing Kurtis

The nurse nods at me and says, "Dr. Ishikawa will see you now."

I'm sitting in a cramped waiting room, if you want to call it that—it's more like a broom closet with two chairs—and, at the nurse's instruction, I get up and follow her through a small door into another tiny room, a room crowded to bursting with a small desk, a scale, and an examination table.

"Sit down there." She motions to the table. "Take off your shirt. The doctor will be with you in just a minute." The nurse leaves the room.

Well, I'm sure "take off your shirt" is a real "ho-hum" phrase to her, maybe like "pass the Tabasco" is to anyone else, but those words are jarring to me. I've never taken off my shirt in front of a man before, and though I've been to the doctor once or twice in my life, the last time was long before I'd grown actual boobs. Even if my boobs are on the small side, even if they're flat as a fritter, they're still mine, after all, and I'm not in the habit of showing them off to every Tom, Dick and Harry, whether a doctor or not. And, anyway, every doctor I've seen in the past has always given me a little paper gown to wear. Why the heck didn't Dr. Ishikawa's nurse give me a little paper gown to wear?

I wish I didn't need to be here at all, to tell you the truth, but I could wear my bra backwards and it'd still fit. Bigger boobs aren't gonna just shoot out of my chest like bottle rockets out of nowhere, no matter how hard I hope and wish and pray they would. Wishing for things to happen, instead of going out there and *making* them happen, is as useful as wishing a bullfrog had wings so he wouldn't bump his ass when he jumped.

Slowly, I unbutton my shirt and remove it. But then, once it's off, I hold my shirt up against my chest. Damn, this room is chilly. The door opens suddenly, without warning, and a short man with tiny hands and jet-black hair enters.

"I'm Dr. Ishikawa," he says. He extends his tiny hand and I shake it.

"Hi, Doctor," I manage, pressing my shirt tightly against my chest.

"How can I help you today?"

"Bettie sent me. She said you do all the girls?"

Bettie's name doesn't seem to ring a bell with Dr. Ishikawa.

"Bettie from the Casanova Club? With the long black hair and bangs?"

"Ah, yes. Of course. Bettie *Paigette*." He chuckles to himself, probably picturing Bettie Big Boobs with her shirt off. "Yes, her breasts certainly turned out well."

Breasts? Is that what he calls those things? I would have used a thousand other words before I got to "breasts," if ever. Hooters. Balloons. Melons. Maybe even knockers. But definitely not *breasts.*

"So, I assume you dance at the Casanova Club with Bettie?" the doctor says.

I blanche. "You assume wrong." I flip my newly blonde hair back and the wax paper on the examination table crinkles beneath me. "I'm an *actress.* I'm going to be a legendary actress seen by audiences in cineplexes all over the world. "

He grins at me. "Very nice. I'm sure you will." His smile

turns into a bit of a leer, and then into another chuckle, though I'm not quite sure what's prompting his laughter. "Well, then, let's take a look, shall we?" He motions to my chest, obviously wanting me to pull down my shirt.

I know in my head this moment is a necessary part of achieving my destiny, that I've got to be brave like the first man who ate an oyster, but I reckon I just didn't think how uncomfortable it would feel to show a strange man my boobs, destiny or not. Shoot. I take a deep breath, ignore my racing heart, and slowly drop my shirt into my lap.

"Sit up straight," the doctor instructs, staring at my chest.

I sit up straight, looking away.

The doctor bends down a bit, I reckon to bring his sightline even with my chest. "Good shape. Good symmetry," he says. "Ah, but size. Yes, I see why you came to me." He chuckles again.

Oh, for cryin' out loud. This is the first man who's ever been graced with the sight of my naked boobs and that's all he's got to say to me? I grit my teeth. I might have come to this doctor asking for new boobs, it's true, but the least he can do in this first-of-its-kind moment is tell me how pretty I am, just the way I am, and try to turn me away. "You're perfection," is what he *should* be saying to me right now, giving *me* the opportunity to say, "Well, now, hang on a minute there, Doc. Yes, I'm perfection, it's true—*if* I just want to be a normal girl—but I'm an *actress*, you see, and I've got a destiny to fulfill—a destiny to pick up the torch lit first by Lana and handed off to Marilyn and to carry it ever-farther into the catacombs of history—and, unfortunately, the boobs the Lord gave me are just too dainty for a job that big and mighty." Man, oh man, this here doctor's got a lot of nerve telling me I need new boobs, even if I'm here asking him for them in the first place. I glare at him, friendly as a fire ant.

Dr. Ishikawa continues staring at my boobs like he's choosing a pork chop from the butcher. "Hmm, we just have to decide what size. Let's see how much you weigh." He points to the scale in the corner of the room. And even though I'm this close to punching this dumbass doctor right in the teeth, I do as I'm told and slide off the examination table. While the good doctor peers down at the number, I cross my arms over my chest. Sweet Jesus, it's freezing in here.

Dr. Ishikawa motions for me to return to the examination table. "With your frame, which is on the petite side, the question is whether to give you Mansfields or Monroes."

My heart leaps out of my flat-as-a-pancake chest. Does everyone in Hollywood classify boobs as Mansfields or Monroes, or is this a sign from above that I'm barreling in the right direction towards my sacred destiny? Before I can reply to the doctor's comment, though, he adds, "Are you familiar with Jayne Mansfield and Marilyn Monroe?"

Does this man think I just fell off the turnip truck?

"Actually, with your platinum hair and the structure of your face, you quite resemble Jayne Mansfield." He smiles like he's just given me an enormous compliment.

"Gosh, thank you, Dr. Ishikawa," I say sweetly, even though I'm imagining myself whacking his head clean off with a baseball bat, "but I have *blue* eyes, like Marilyn. Jayne had *brown* eyes." Fool. All this dumbass doctor has to do is look at me to see I'm the spitting image of Marilyn Monroe. In fact, we could be twins.

"Well, given your *profession*," Dr. Ishikawa prompts, "I think you'll go a lot further with Mansfields..."

"Give me Marilyns, please," I say stiffly. "Big enough for a legendary Hollywood actress, but not so big that no one ever listens to a word I'm saying."

Dr. Ishikawa snorts, plainly thinking, *No one's ever going to listen to a word you're saying, either way.* When I squint at him with hard eyes, he purses his lips. "Okay, I'll make them closer to Marilyns. But standards have changed since the days of Marilyn Monroe. We'll need to go a bit bigger than hers, relative to your frame, just to comport with present-day industry standards."

I pause, trying to decide what to do. I don't know anything about "present-day industry standards"—it's the truth—but whatever they are, I sure as hell plan to "comport" with them. "Okay," I agree. "So long as you're not thinking anything along the lines of Bettie's boobs. I don't want anything even spitting-distance from Bettie's boobs, you understand? I'm an *actress,* not a *stripper.*"

"I understand." Doctor Ishikawa sniffs. "Now, let's talk about my fee."

He tells me how much these two fancy boobs of mine are going to cost me, and I about fall off the examination table. I had no idea two Marilyns would be so expensive. You'd think a girl could get ten Marilyns plus a nose for that price. I've never bought anything—or even *imagined* buying anything— so damned expensive. But, of course, I have to do it, no matter what the price. My destiny awaits me, and I can't get to it without fancy new boobs, even if those damned boobs are gonna cost me an arm and a leg. The good news is that I've got enough cash in my pocketbook to cover the good doctor's fee and then some, thanks to my dear friends, The Yankee Clipper and Mr. Clements. "That's not a problem," I say. "I can pay you in cash. All of it." I pat my pocketbook.

Dr. Ishikawa's face lights up. "Wonderful. Well, then, in that case, why don't we do the procedure tomorrow morning? Eight o'clock?"

"Wonderful."

"Be prepared to be off your feet for a full week."

Back at the motel where I'm renting a room—thanks to the generosity, yet again, of my buddies Joe DiMaggio and Mr. Clements—the desk clerk in the lobby flags me down.

"Buttercup, right? You got three phone calls while you were out," he says. "All from the same guy." He looks down at the message slips in his hand. "Kurtis Jackman?"

Yesterday, during my three-hour-lunch-turned-early-supper with Mr. Kurtis Jackman, I quickly surmised Kurtis likes The Chase more than whatever he happens to be chasing. When we said our goodbyes in front of the restaurant, I pointedly turned my cheek when he moved to kiss me, figuring it'd be best to leave the man wanting more—and, much to my surprise, when I turned my cheek, Kurtis complied without a peep, gracing me with a soft and gentlemanly peck, even though his eyes were burning like hot coals.

And an even bigger surprise than that was this: When I felt Kurtis' lips pressing against my skin, and I smelled the scent of his cologne floating up into my nostrils, and when I felt his big hand slide down my back and rest just above my bottom, lord have mercy if that heartbeat didn't start throbbing inside my panties again, but this time raging like a galloping stallion.

I find a payphone out on Sunset Boulevard and dial the number scrawled on the messages.

The line picks up after one ring. "This is Kurtis."

I'm startled. I expected Kurtis' secretary to pick up the phone. "Oh," I stutter, "well, hello there, Kurtis. It's me, Butter—"

"Hello-*hello*. I'd know that sexy little drawl anywhere. How're you doing, honey?"

"I couldn't be better. How're you doing, sugar?"

"I'm losing my mind, thank you very much. I haven't stopped thinking about you since you left me yesterday, standing all alone in front of the restaurant, needing a cold shower."

"Oh my," I breathe. No one's ever said anything quite like that to me before.

"I need to see you," Kurtis says, his voice low and intense.

I purposefully keep my voice light and bright, in direct contrast to the husky urgency of his. "Oh, Kurtis, you're as sweet as lemonade on a sunny day, aren't you? I've never met anybody quite like you."

I'm telling Kurtis the truth about that, actually. I was

genuinely surprised at how quickly and pleasantly time passed with Kurtis in that hoity-toity restaurant with the red leather booths. True, he laughed so loud he nearly made my ears bleed once or twice, and, true, his arm nearly broke from patting himself on the back. And, yes, I was slightly disappointed when he only briefly mentioned his movie production company (which was the one thing I was dying to hear about), and instead blabbed on and on about his stupid girly magazine.

But none of that mattered the minute Kurtis leaned forward, his eyes wild, and glared at me like he was an axe murderer I'd picked up hitchhiking. For a split second there, I wasn't sure if the man was fixin' to kiss me or kill me—but, in that moment, either one would have done me just fine. Right then, Kurtis raised his martini glass in salute to me and said, "To the most fucking gorgeous creature I've ever laid eyes on." And, as if that wasn't enough to make a girl ooze like a banana pudding parfait left out on a hot sidewalk, Kurtis didn't stop there. "You're so gorgeous," he said, "you make a man wanna sit and stare at you all day, every day—for the rest of his fucking life." Holy hell. If I'd stood up just then, I reckon there'd have been a snail track on the leather booth.

Kurtis exhales loudly over the phone line and I'm jolted back to the here and now.

"Why didn't you return my calls sooner, Buttercup?" Kurtis asks. "Are you trying to torture me?"

The tone of his voice makes my cheeks flush and my chest tighten, just like they did when he called me gorgeous during last night's lunch-turned-dinner.

"Torture you?" I say, smiling into the phone. "Well, gosh, honey, you know I'd never do that. I wouldn't hurt a fly taking a nap on top of a black bottom pie."

Kurtis hoots with laughter.

"I just had a few things to take care of, seeing as how I'm new in town, that's all. But I'm calling you now, aren't I, so you can't be *too* upset with me, can you?"

Kurtis makes a sound that reminds me of a bear waking up from a winter's hibernation. "You just keep talking with that sexy drawl of yours," he groans out, "and I'll never be upset with you as long as I live."

I feel heat rising in my cheeks.

"You could do nothing but read the phone book to me in bed," Kurtis continues, "and I'd die a happy boy."

I giggle. I don't mean to do it, but I do. I can't stop myself.

"Come to my house tomorrow," Kurtis says. "I want to show you something."

His house? The very idea makes me nervous and excited all at once. "Oh, honey, that sounds like a little slice of heaven," I manage to say, "but I've got something I've got to do tomorrow. And, actually, it's gonna keep me tied up for a full week."

"A week? What the hell are you doing for a whole week? I want to see you tomorrow."

I laugh, but this time, it's a full-throated laugh, not a giggle. "Patience, Kurtis," I coo. "The best things in life are always worth waiting for."

Kurtis laughs a naughty laugh. "I wouldn't know. When I want something, I never wait for it. Ever."

There's no mistaking his meaning. "Well," I say, swallowing hard, "then, I reckon there's a first time for everything, isn't there?"

I can hear Kurtis smiling devilishly across the phone line. "You know what? I do believe there is."

Chapter 7

12 Years Old
2,926 Days Before Killing Kurtis

Momma and Daddy are fighting. This is nothing unusual. I just keep reading my book. *Fatal Vision.* It's a good one. I'm not quite done with the book yet, but I know the guy killed his family. I'm sure of it. He fooled everyone at first, because he's a smart one, that one, and the world is full of dumbasses. But I'm even smarter than he is. If it were *me* in the book killing *my* family, then I wouldn't have gotten caught. I feel like telling the guy in the book, "Listen here, sir, if you wanna kill your family that's all well and good—it might even be perfectly understandable, depending on your situation—but just don't be a dumbass about it and get caught." I tell you one thing, if it were *me* who killed my family, no one would be able to write a damned book about it, you can bet on that.

Daddy's screaming in the back bedroom, "You sleep all day. You're worthless as a screen door on a submarine."

"I work all night," Momma yells back.

I roll my eyes. *I work all night.* That's Momma's go-to excuse for everything. But working the night shift at a diner certainly doesn't explain the fact that she does absolutely nothing around here, or the fact that she's drunker than a pissed mattress all the time.

"Oh wow, you work all night, huh?" Daddy screams.

31

"Working the night shift at a diner doesn't explain why you do absolutely nothing around here or that you're drunker than a Baptist preacher at a high school dance all the time," Daddy seethes.

I smile. Daddy and I really are two peas in a pod.

The woman is worthless.

"You're worthless," Daddy screams as if he's heard my exact thoughts.

"*I'm* worthless?" Momma shrieks. "I'm the only one bringing in a paycheck so's we have something to eat 'round here. What the hell do *you* do every day?"

"Shut your mouth," Daddy growls. "I've got something big coming down the pike—"

Momma whoops with angry laughter. "Oh, yeah, Charlie? What's it gonna be this time? You gonna build a mini-golf-course for the Queen of England? She gonna come play pitch-and-putt on your fancy course and make you a knight?" Her laughter is wicked.

I don't like listening to the sound of Momma and Daddy fighting, so I focus my attention back on my book to drown out the noise. I've been reading all kinds of good books lately for my education. Last month, I read one of my all-time favorite books so far—*Lana,* about movie-goddess Lana Turner from the Golden Age of Hollywood—and ever since then, it's been my dream to go to Hollywood and get discovered just like she did.

When Lana was sixteen, she ditched school one afternoon to go to a malt shop in Hollywood, and, just like that, Lana got herself discovered by a movie-man who happened to be standing there, buying himself a root beer float or whatnot. Just from being in the right place at the right time—and, of course, also thanks to her pretty face and blonde hair and big boobs, too—destiny found Lana that day in the malt shop, and she became a huge star overnight. And that's what I want to happen to me, too. Just like Lana.

As gorgeous as Lana was, life should have been sweet as

honey for her, all day, every day, right? But it wasn't. Because for some reason I can't understand, she took up with this rat-turd named Johnny Stompanato who used to grab Lana and shake her and whack her upside the head. So, one night, Lana's fourteen-year-old daughter grabbed a big ol' butcher knife and stabbed Johnny dead right where he stood—or so the daughter said. In my heart of hearts, I know it was Lana who did the deed herself and let her daughter take the fall for her—which was the right thing to do, of course, seeing as how Lana was a big movie star and all. That's what I'd do if I were a big movie star, anyway—just like Lana.

I reckon it just goes to show, people will always do what the pretty people tell them to do, even if it's killing someone—or, in this case, taking the blame for killing someone. And it also goes to show this, too: if some piece of shit man is gonna whack a glamorous movie star upside the head, then he best not be surprised when he looks down one night and sees a big ol' butcher knife poking out of his chest, that's for damned sure.

"I'm warning you, woman, shut your mouth," Daddy seethes in the back bedroom.

"You make me sick," Momma retorts, practically spitting the words.

I hear a loud slapping noise, and Momma's laughter abruptly stops.

"Buttercup," Daddy suddenly yells.

I snap my head up from my book. I clear my throat, intending to holler that I'm sitting right here at the table by the sink, but my voice doesn't work. I'm afraid to say anything. The hair on my arms is standing on end, but I don't know why.

Daddy bursts out of the back room, his nostrils flaring like a fire-breathing dragon. "Buttercup," he says again. His face is red and his eyes are hard, but when he sees me, his mouth twists into what appears to be a smile.

I half-smile back, but my stomach's doing somersaults.

Daddy's eyes aren't twinkling like they usually do. His jaw is clenched. Daddy rummages into his pocket and hands me three whole dollars—and in paper money, too, not even in coins. "Go on up the road to the 7-Eleven and get yourself something to eat," Daddy says. "Your momma and I are gonna have a little talk." He glances over his shoulder toward the back room. "In private."

"Yes, sir." I take the dollar bills into my fist, tuck my book under my arm, and wordlessly scoot out the front door.

It's hard to read and walk at the same time, but I manage it okay. I'm kind of an expert at it, actually. The 7-Eleven is right up the road about a mile away and it's hotter than blue blazes today. Whew! I couldn't have asked for a better day to get some money from Daddy to buy myself a hot dog and a Slurpee. I'm so hungry I could eat the south end of a northbound mule. Gosh, my daddy's always doing nice stuff for me at exactly the right time.

By the time I reach Main Street, I've finished my book, so I decide to get a new one at the library before hitting the 7-Eleven.

"Hi there, honey," the librarian, Mrs. Monaghan, says to me when I enter the front door. "Is it still hot enough out there to peel the paint off your house?"

"Yes, ma'am. It's so hot, I saw two trees bribing a dog on my way here."

Mrs. Monaghan smiles and little lines pop up around her eyes when she does. "Well, honey, you ready for a new book?" she asks.

"Yes, ma'am." I hand her my finished book.

"*Fatal Vision,*" she murmurs, reading the front cover. She scowls. "That's an interesting selection. Why don't I help you find a more appropriate book, hmm?"

I nod.

Mrs. Monaghan brushes past me and I catch a whiff of her pretty perfume. It smells like flowers. She leads me to the children's section and I bite my tongue. I've never read a book from the children's section before, but, okay, I'll see what she's got for me because I sure do like Mrs. Monaghan an awful lot.

"Maybe we should find you a classic, hmm?" she says. "Oh, how about this one? This is a good one." She hands me a book with two dogs on the cover called, *Where the Red Fern Grows*.

I read the blurb on the back cover. It seems like a book for little kids. "No, thank you, ma'am," I say politely. "I don't think that's right for my reading aptitude."

Mrs. Monaghan smiles really big at me, and I bite my lip in return.

"Do you maybe have a movie star biography for me, ma'am? I sure do like those."

"Hmm," she says, scanning the shelf. She runs her finger across the spines of several books. "Ah, this one." She hands me something called *The Secret Garden*. It looks just like the one about the dogs. But I like that it's about a secret. That sounds kinda interesting. And I sure don't want to disappoint Mrs. Monaghan.

I nod. "Thank you, ma'am."

She winks at me. "Let's go get it checked out, my dear."

I take the long way home past the oil derricks over by the highway, sweating in the hot sun. By the time I return to our trailer, I'm already four chapters into my new book, which isn't half bad, actually, though it's definitely beneath my reading aptitude, and my belly's crammed full of one extra-long hot dog and one extra-large cherry Slurpee. I'm full as a tick and feeling fine as wine.

I stand outside our trailer for a few minutes in the blazing heat, straining to hear whatever's going on inside, but it's really quiet in there. I wish I could have heard whatever Daddy said to Momma after I left. Whatever he said—or did—to her, I reckon she deserved it. She's worthless. And small-minded, too, just like those high-and-mighty Napoleon-types at the Department of Planning and teachers in classrooms handing out multiple-choice tests.

Gosh dang it, I can't hear a thing inside the trailer, not even the sound of Daddy's boots on the linoleum. I wait a while longer, sucking up the last of my Slurpee and then sticking out my tongue and looking cross-eyed at my red-stained tongue.

After a while, I put my ear to the door of our trailer again, trying to hear any sound at all. Nothing.

I finally decide to head on inside.

Daddy's sitting at the little table by the sink, hunched over an amber-colored drink. That's unusual. Daddy normally doesn't drink anything but water. "Don't touch that stuff," Daddy always preaches about alcohol. "You gotta stay dry as dirt and keep your mind clear at all times. You never know when you'll need to make a snap decision that might affect the trajectory of your entire life."

When I shuffle in, Daddy looks up at me and motions to the other chair at the table. "Sit down, Buttercup," he says softly.

I look around. Nothing looks out of place or amiss. Where's Momma? I glance toward the back room.

"She's not here," Daddy says, reading my thoughts. "Sit down."

I do as I'm told.

I reckon Daddy told Momma how the cow ate the cabbage. Well, whatever he said or did, she sure as heck deserved it.

Daddy takes a giant swig of his drink. It smells like Momma's whiskey.

"Every man is born free and equal," Daddy mutters. "If he gets married, that's his own damn fault." He sighs and takes another swallow of his drink. He looks me up and down. "You're so damned beautiful, Buttercup." His eyes flash with something I don't understand. "And bright as a new penny, too."

I shift my butt in my chair.

"Never settle for anything less than the best in this life."

"Nothing but the best for Charlie Wilber's Daughter," I declare, but I don't shout it with my usual glee.

Daddy smiles, but his eyes don't crinkle when he does it. "I'm going away for a while."

I'm instantly panicked.

"Calm down, sugar—*for a while,* I said. Just a while."

I'm slightly calmed by these words—but only slightly.

"I met a guy who knows a guy in California."

At the word "California," my eyes light up.

"In Hollywood."

Now my eyes are ablaze. *Hollywood.* Just like Lana.

Daddy puts his glass down on the little table and it makes a clunking sound.

"I've got the chance of a lifetime waiting for me out there in Hollywood, Buttercup," he says. "My buddy's cousin's best friend's brother-in-law knows a guy out there that's so rich, he buys a new boat when the other one gets wet. And when I go out there to California, I'm gonna get this Mr. Moneybags to invest in my mini-golf courses and maybe even my teleportation configuration system, too."

I lean back in my chair, taking this all in. This is amazing and horrible news, all at once. I want us to be rich, of course. But even more than that, I want Daddy and me to be together.

"When this Mr. Moneybags invests in my mini-golf courses," Daddy continues, "we're gonna be so rich, I'm gonna buy us a big ol' Hollywood mansion. It'll be so big, we'll need jetpacks to go from one end of it to the other. Shit, we'll have a pool and a Jacuzzi in our backyard, too, and even a fountain with naked ladies and cherubs and a little cupid with wings."

All of that sounds really exciting. But why can't I go, too? I want to go to Hollywood—but, mostly, I just want to be with Daddy.

"I'll go out there and get everything situated," Daddy continues. "And the minute I get the mansion, I'll come back for you, even before I've got the pool built or the furniture bought. That way you can help me decorate and decide what fancy curtains should go where and whether we should build a tennis court or a bowling alley, or both, and—"

"Why can't I go with you now, Daddy?" I blurt.

"Oh, come on, Buttercup. I can't homeschool you while I'm putting the deal together with Mr. Moneybags—I've gotta have laser-sharp focus. You gotta stay here with your momma, just while I get everything squared away. I'll come back for you the minute I've got everything situated."

I exhale sharply and cross my arms over my chest. Of course, I'm bursting with excitement that we're gonna live in Hollywood in a big ol' mansion with a fountain with naked ladies and cherubs and even a little cupid with wings, but right now I can't see past the fact that I'm going to be stuck here, all alone, with my drunk-ass mother. I don't care if it's only a week or two; being alone with Momma's gonna be torture. She's small-minded and lazy, nothing like Daddy and me, and dumb as a box of rocks, too. I can't even talk to her about my books. She's so dumb, if you put her brains into a bumblebee, it'd fly backwards. Dang it, I want to go with Daddy *now*. I try a new tactic. "If you let me come with you, I can be your personal assistant. I'd be as handy as a pocket on a shirt."

Daddy shakes his head. "You can't come."

"But I can go to a malt shop out there in Hollywood and get discovered like Lana Turner, and then I'll give you all my movie-star money. You can have it all, Daddy, every last penny."

"No." His tone leaves no room for negotiation.

I begin to cry. "But, Daddy, I thought *I* was your greatest invention. I thought *I* was your purpose in this life."

Daddy brushes the hair out of my eyes. "You *are,* baby, you are. Don't you see? You're the reason I'm doing all this. You deserve the very best of everything, and I'm gonna get it for you. How're you gonna have the very best in this life, living here in a trailer? Hmm?"

I shrug my shoulders and look down at the table.

"This is my ticket to make a life for you, the kind of life you deserve." He puts his finger under my chin and tilts my face to look at him. "Charlie Wilber's Daughter deserves nothing but the best. You deserve a fountain with naked ladies and cherubs and a little cupid with wings. Getting that for you is my biggest dream." He puts his hand back down on the table. "And nothing's gonna stop me from making that dream come true."

I sniffle, but I don't respond.

"Because I love you bigger than the sky full of stars," he says.

"I love you, too, Daddy. Bigger than the sky full of stars."

"Good girl."

I blink the last of my tears out of my eyes. "Okay, Daddy," I mumble. "I'll wait."

"Good girl," Daddy says again. "Nothing dries as quick as a tear." He softly beep-beeps my nose with the tip of his finger.

I reckon, if I put my mind to it, I can do just about anything to get to live in Hollywood with my handsome daddy—even wait a whole *month* for him to come back and get me. Because I love my dear, sweet daddy just that much. Bigger than the sky full of stars.

Chapter 8

18 Years 2 Weeks Old
727 Days Before Killing Kurtis

Kurtis laughs when he opens his front door and sees me. Maybe it's the expression on my face that's amusing to him because, holy hell, his house is a downright mansion. I'm not talking about a *big* house. I'm talking about a gen-u-ine Hollywood *mansion,* the kind of house you need a jetpack to get from one side of the house to the other. I'm literally speechless when Kurtis opens the door and I see the endlessness yawning behind him like the Great Plains.

The minute Kurtis sees me, he steps forward and wraps his big arms around me, grunting and hooting with joy. "Oh my God, come here," he shouts, squeezing me. "This has been the longest goddamned week of my life."

I back away slightly, creating some distance between our bodies, because my one-week-old boobs are still pretty sore. "Is this your *house?*" I ask, incredulous. "It's as big as all hell and half of Texas."

Kurtis laughs. "I'll give you a tour."

Kurtis takes me through each room of his house, and my jaw drops lower and lower 'til I swear he's gonna have to scoop it off the ground with a spatula. The ceilings in Kurtis' house are crazy-high, like I'm gonna get vertigo just looking up at them. And there's a "foyer," and a "laundry room," too, and even a dining room with enough room to sleep six, if that's what you wanted to do. And, best of all, there's a huge backyard with a pool *and* a Jacuzzi and, even a "veranda" overlooking it all.

"Well, what do you think?" Kurtis booms with excitement when the tour is finished and we're standing in what he calls his "home theater."

"It's a *bona fide* mansion," I manage.

"Have you ever seen anything like it?"

I shake my head. "I most certainly have not." And, boy-howdy, that's the truth. "Oh, Kurtis, you've got everything a girl could ever dream about 'cept a fountain with naked ladies and cherubs and a little cupid with wings."

Kurtis chuckles. "Honey, you make me laugh more than anyone I've ever met."

"That's 'cause I'm a laugh riot."

Kurtis takes a step toward me and his eyes turn smoky with desire. "I haven't stopped thinking about you all week long." He presses up against me, and it's easy to surmise just how happy he is to see me.

I take a small step back.

Kurtis smirks. "Have a seat, baby." He motions to one of the chairs facing the movie screen. "I've got a big surprise for you."

"You do?" I'm hoping his "big surprise" is something more than what I just felt poking at me through his pants.

"I sure do." He pauses for effect. "I'm about to show you my favorite movie of all the ones I've ever made..."

"Oh," I say, deflated. "Isn't that nice."

He beams at me like he's spilling a big secret. "So that I can explain the kind of movie I'm gonna make—starring *you*."

I hold my breath and look at him, not sure I heard him correctly. Am I just imagining those two words—"starring" and "you"—in the same sentence because I want to hear them so badly?

"Buttercup," Kurtis says, flashing me a toothy grin, "I'm gonna put you in one of my movies."

Tears instantly squirt out of my eyes and shoot across the room. I knew Kurtis was meant to discover me like Lana Turner in the malt shop. I *knew* it. I leap out of my chair and smash my body into his, my sore boobs be damned. "Oh, thank you, Kurtis." I throw my arms around him and nuzzle my nose into his neck.

Without asking for permission, Kurtis swoops right into my face and kisses me deeply—holy hell, does he ever. Goodness gracious, this is one heck of a damned kiss. This man is kissing me like he owns me. I've never been kissed like this before. *Woo-wee!* When Wesley used to kiss me, he was a hungry little squirrel looking for an acorn—and, don't get me wrong, I loved it. But Kurtis? He's a ravenous lion tearing the flesh off a gazelle—and, damn, he leaves me breathless.

To be honest, I'm thrilled by the mechanics of Kurtis' kiss, maybe because I've never kissed anyone but Wesley before—and certainly never a man twice my age. The stubble on Kurtis' chin is rough and scratchy and masculine, and the feel of Kurtis' tongue inside my mouth is making my knees go weak. Sweet Jesus, kissing Kurtis is more exciting than a roller coaster ride.

When I used to kiss Wesley, I always kind of knew whose tongue was fixin' to go where. But with Kurtis, when I think he's going to go left, he goes right, and when I'm sure he's going to close his mouth and pull away from me, he opens wider and demands more. His arms around me are big and strong, too, enough to make me swoon like a ninny—and when he presses his body into mine, and I feel his erection poking me in the crotch, begging me to let him in—well, hell on a biscuit, I *want* to let him in. Truth be told, I want to take this man's body into mine like a Hoover sucks up a shag carpet.

I slowly pull away, sighing. "Well, hello there and

howdy do," I breathe. I smooth my dress with my hands, not knowing what else to do. At the movement of my hands down the front of my dress, Kurtis' eyes snap right to my chest, and I can see unadulterated appreciation flicker in his eyes. Maybe he's thinking, "I don't remember them being that big." Or maybe his expert eye instantly knows my boobs have gotten a little man-made boost since he first laid eyes on me, and he's thinking, "So *that's* what she was doing this past week." Whatever he's thinking, his eyes tell me he approves of how I'm filling out the top of my dress.

Kurtis looks back up at my face, and his intensity surprises me. Damn, the man looks like an axe murderer again, just like he did in the restaurant during our lunch-turned-dinner date—and, oh my, I *like* it.

And just that fast, I suddenly realize I'm walking a tightrope here. This is a grown man, not a boy, and one who's plainly accustomed to getting everything he wants, when he wants it. Just one look at his house and his fancy suit tells me Kurtis is as big as life and twice as natural. Sooner or later, and I'm guessing sooner, this grown man is going to become awfully tired of chasing a little girl who doesn't do much of anything but kiss him and bat her eyelashes, and yet, on the other hand, I reckon he's gonna grow equally tired, if not more so, of pursuing a little girl who jumps right into his bed with no chase at all.

I reckon I'm gonna have to figure out a push-and-pull strategy here, if I'm ever gonna get this man to stay interested in me long enough to make a movie starring me—no matter how much my body's already itching to make like a vacuum. "Tell me more about your big movie idea," I say, licking my lips from our kiss.

Kurtis' face is flushed. "Sit down." He motions to one of the seats in the theater.

I sit.

"I'll be right back." Kurtis bounds to the back of the room to set something up and then returns and takes the seat next to mine. "I'm gonna show you my favorite movie so I can explain the film I'm gonna make with you."

The screen flashes "Casanova Productions," and then, *"Suzy Gets Hammered and Nailed,"* followed by "Rated XXX."

My eyes go wide. I haven't seen too many movies in my life, and certainly not one with the rating "XXX." My stomach convulses and I leap out of my chair.

"Lord have mercy, Kurtis. I can't be in a *porno.* "

Kurtis looks shocked at my reaction.

The movie casts flickering light throughout the room.

"I've never done any of that stuff in *real life*," I sputter. "I'm not gonna do it for the first time in front of a *camera.* " The minute I blurt out these honest but mortifying words, I wish I could recall them and stuff them back into my mouth. I never should have admitted this truth to Kurtis before finalizing my tight-rope-walking-strategy. Surely, I've just blown any chance I had of Kurtis discovering me like Lana Turner in the malt shop.

But, hey now. Wait. One look at Kurtis' beaming face and I know everything is fine as snuff and half as dusty. I need only look at Kurtis' glowing face to realize my blabbering just now has *helped* my standing in his eyes, not *hurt* it. Because Kurtis is looking at me like he's just captured a genuine unicorn—and promptly discovered three fistfuls of diamonds stuffed up its ass.

"What do you mean, you've never done *'any of that stuff'?* " he asks, his excitement bursting out of his pores.

Up on the screen, a woman with enormous boobs takes off her clothes while a man in a tool belt and hardhat (and nothing else) stands by, watching her. I turn my back. I don't want to see what happens next.

Kurtis bolts to the back of the room and turns the movie off, and I sigh with relief. When he returns to me, he's panting. "What do you mean you've never done 'any of that stuff'?" he asks again, his voice urgent. When I blush and don't respond, he asks, "*None* of it?" When I remain silent, he adds, "Nothing at all?"

"Well, no, not *nothing at all,*" I finally shout, crossing my arms defensively. "I mean, I've *kissed* a boy before, and..."

He smiles broadly at me, happier than a fox in the henhouse. "And...?"

Boom. My brain clicks into place and I realize what's just fallen into my lap. Kurtis' whole world is strippers and naked girls and pornos, so I must be something close to a mermaid juggling flaming bowling pins on top of a barn to him. Going into this conversation with Kurtis, I had no idea how I was going keep this hunting dog on the porch, but I sure as hell know now. For once in my life, the near-truth is gonna be my best friend.

"And, well, holy smokes, Kurtis," I add, exasperated. "That's it, okay? All I've ever done is kissing and not a whole lot of that. Don't embarrass me about it."

Kurtis' face makes it clear he's happier than a two-peckered dog.

"And I've actually only kissed *one* boy before." That's the God's truth. "*One time.*" Not at all true. I've kissed Wesley thousands and thousands of times under the big oak tree. For a fleeting second, I think about how much I always enjoyed kissing sweet, puppy-faced Wesley with the heart of gold, and my heart twists and pangs. "You only just now gave me my second kiss in my whole life. And my first kiss with tongue." Not even close to true. Wesley and I have swapped enough spit to fill the Rio Grande. "Gosh, now that I've kissed you, Kurtis, I realize I've never been kissed good and proper before." I'm not sure if this is true or not—because I sure did enjoy kissing Wesley all those times. But, holy heck, kissing Kurtis just now sure did set my panties on fire in a whole new way. I lower my eyelids to half-mast and part my lips the way I've seen Marilyn do it in the photos in her biography. "What you just did to me might as well have been my first kiss, ever," I whisper softly.

Kurtis' eyes light up like a Christmas tree.

I turn my head, feigning embarrassment. "I'm sorry, Kurtis. I'm sure you're accustomed to girls with lots and *lots* of experience, and I just don't know how I could ever compare to any of them."

Kurtis lunges at me and grabs my shoulders roughly. "You're better than all of them combined—they can't compare to *you.*" He looks me up and down. "Just look at you, baby. Oh my God, you're sexy as hell. And now, to find out you're a *virgin?* I mean, like, a total and complete virgin?" He throws his head back and guffaws. "You're a four-leaf clover, baby. You shouldn't exist, but you do. And I'm the luckiest bastard in the world, 'cause I'm the one who found you." He rubs his hands together. *"I found you."* He grabs my face and kisses me firmly on the lips yet again, like he's claiming a treasure trove, and, yet again, my knees wobble and my crotch ignites. When we pull apart, his eyes are ablaze and I'm sure mine are, too. "Tell me, how did this happen?" He motions at my body, gaping in amazement.

I have no idea how to answer this question. I'm certainly not going to tell him my entire life's story. But before I can say anything at all, Kurtis blurts, "Oh my God—you're a preacher's daughter, aren't you? Am I right?"

Oh, thank the Lord. That's a great explanation, and I can plainly see how titillating the idea is to Kurtis. Of course, my background didn't come up during our three-hour lunch a week ago because Kurtis used his ten-gallon mouth to yammer about himself and his magazine almost the whole time.

I nod my head furiously. "You guessed it—I'm a preacher's daughter."

"I knew it."

"Is it that obvious?"

Kurtis buckles over chuckling. "Yes, it's that obvious."

We laugh together at the obviousness of it.

"You just can't hide that country-preacher's-daughter thing you've got going on, especially from a connoisseur like me."

I feign offense. "But goodness gracious, Kurtis. I'm not *country*. I'm cos-mo-politan."

Kurtis throws his head back and guffaws, yet again. He's slurping me right up. "No, you're not, but that's your charm, honey. I just knew you were a preacher's daughter last week during lunch, but I decided not to say anything." He winks. "Didn't want to embarrass you or anything."

I look down, blushing like a mail-order bride. "And here I thought I was putting one over on you."

He laughs again. "Tell me more."

"Well...yes..." I say, collecting my thoughts on how to proceed here. "My daddy was a holy-roller. Fire and brimstone, that sort of thing? Woo-wee! He sure did beat back more than a few boys, I tell you what."

Kurtis laughs a full belly laugh at that one. The man is positively giddy.

"My daddy absolutely forbade me from going out with anyone, not even on a single date, ever, not even to the 7-Eleven for a dang Slurpee, and he made sure I was homeschooled to keep me away from boys, and he just kept me under lock and key."

"Oh my God, the world's gonna gobble you up."

"But then, bless my daddy's heart, during a Godly mission to feed the starving children of Africa, Daddy met his maker in a tragic incident with a hippopotamus, may he rest in peace." I look up to the heavens and tears spring into my eyes, right on cue. "Before he left for Africa, though, my daddy made me promise—no, he made me *swear*—to always keep myself pure in the eyes of the Lord."

"Holy fucking shit."

"God bless his soul, my daddy always told me I'm just too beautiful a creation to give myself away to just anyone. He made me swear to wait for someone"—I can physically feel Kurtis holding his breath, waiting for my next word—"*special.*"

If I blew on Kurtis ever so lightly, he'd tump over like a

sleeping cow. He nestles his mouth into my hair and murmurs right into my ear, "Am I special, Buttercup?"

I lean back and gaze at him, as if I'm considering his question with utmost seriousness. "Kurtis Jackman, you're sweet as sugar-cane candy." I touch his face gently. "And I already know you're unlike anyone I've ever met." I shake my head like I'm trying to gather my senses. "If you want to know the truth, your kiss makes me wanna forget my solemn vow to my daddy for the first time in my life."

Kurtis pulls me into him and presses his body into mine—and, howdy-do, his hard-on against my hip makes me shudder with desire.

"You've got me hotter than a two-dollar pistol, Kurtis," I say, trying to catch my breath.

"Buttercup," he groans, swooping in for another kiss.

I pull back suddenly. "But I made a solemn oath to my daddy, and I've got to stay true to it."

Kurtis looks like he's going to burst out of his skin. "Come here." He grabs my hand and leads me back to the chairs. He's deep in thought for a moment. "You're blowing my mind right now. Someone like you only comes along once in a lifetime, and I've got to handle it just right."

"Kurtis, I told you—I'm not gonna have sex for the first time in a *porno*." On this, I'm firm, my melting panties and sacred destiny be damned.

"Oh God no," Kurtis quickly agrees, sounding alarmed. "You're not gonna have sex for the first time in a *movie*." He chuckles like I've just said the funniest thing in the world. "No, no, no, you're gonna have sex for the first time with *me*."

Every hair on my body stands on end.

His eyes suddenly devour me. "And, trust me, baby, when we have sex for your first time, it'll be just you and me, all by ourselves."

I'm sure my face registers my shock, despite my usual expertise at keeping a poker face.

Kurtis leans toward me, within an inch of my face. "And trust me, I'm gonna do it right." He leans in and kisses me ever so gently.

I'm flooded with relief at the softness of his kiss and soothing words, though it kind of feels like he's just told me he's gonna execute me by beheading rather than a slow blood-letting.

"I've been wanting to make a legitimate movie for a long time," Kurtis says, "something people *respect.* You know, branch out from the adult movie industry." He runs his hand through his hair, his thoughts clearly going a mile-a-minute. "Maybe you walking through my door at this point in my life, and looking like you do, and being who you are, maybe it's just a sign from God it's time for me to make that mainstream feature I've been dreaming of making my whole goddamned life."

My heart's gonna bang right out of my chest. "What kind of mainstream feature have you been dreaming of making, Kurtis?" My voice isn't working properly. It's catching in my throat.

Kurtis grins. "A movie about a small-town girl who becomes the biggest sex symbol the world has ever known."

I'm sitting on the edge of my seat, intently watching Kurtis' mouth as it moves and holding my breath.

"It would be a fresh retelling of a certain mythology," Kurtis says. He opens his hands like a magician revealing a white bunny in a hat. "A movie-homage to Marilyn Monroe."

I knew it. Kurtis is here to deliver me to my destiny. I'm in very real danger of hyperventilating right now. But hang on, I tell myself. I've got to handle this just right. How the heck am I gonna keep this lusty porno-king interested in me long enough to get a movie-starring-me made? My brain clicks and clacks and suddenly locks onto a book I read last week while recuperating from my boob surgery, all about King Henry VIII and his second wife, Anne Boleyn. I reckon I'll just have to take a page out of Annie B's playbook.

You see, Annie B knew it was her sacred destiny to become queen one day—which, back then, was the same thing as being destined to be seen by audiences in cineplexes all over the world. But when King Henry wanted to get his junk inside Annie without promising her a kingdom in return, she wasn't having it. "I'm just too special to be one of your tramps," she told her lusty king—and she said it with a straight face, too. Well, goodness gracious, that girl was placing a tall order, seeing as how King Henry already had himself a queen and all. But that genius-woman stuck to her guns, by God, and damn if Henry didn't finally do whatever the hell she wanted, just so he could get in her pants.

Now, granted, the end of Annie's story is a real tearjerker, bless her heart (and her neck)—but the point is that Annie B had a plan; she stuck to it, and it worked like gangbusters. So that's what I'll do, too—I'll make a plan and stick to it.

How long could it possibly take? I reckon if an *actual* king could be lured into tossing a queen and a church aside to get with a girl, it ought to be a piece of cake to coax a *porno* king into doing something as simple as making a goddamned movie to get with me.

Chapter 9

13 Years Old
2,561 Days Before Killing Kurtis

It's been a year and nineteen days since Daddy left. And exactly one year since I received Daddy's one and only letter to me. All I wanted to do from the moment I held that unopened envelope in my hand a year ago was sprint right out the door of our trailer, right to the front gate of the trailer park, and wait for Daddy to pick me up. But before darting out the door as my body was itching to do, I quickly tore open the envelope, just in case Daddy had asked me to pack something in particular or meet him at a particular spot.

"Yes, it's true," Daddy wrote in his swirling script. "Hollywood is sunny all the time. And there are movie stars and mansions on every corner, too." I could barely breathe as I read Daddy's flamboyant handwriting for the first time. My eyes could scarcely focus on the words, so I just sort of absorbed them in large chunks and blocks rather than actually reading them: ". . . working really hard... miss you terribly... Nothing but the best for Charlie Wilber's Daughter... prettiest dress you ever saw... always deserve the best..."

Finally, towards the very bottom of the page, just above the big, bouncy heart Daddy had drawn with my name printed smack in the center, my eyes finally locked onto a full sentence: "It's going to take a bit longer than I thought to talk to Mr.

Moneybags," Daddy wrote. "But don't worry, I'll come back to get you just as soon as I've got myself situated in our mansion."

I dropped the letter onto the floor, my head spinning and throbbing.

And I haven't heard from Daddy since.

Every night before I go to sleep, I read and re-read Daddy's letter, and then I tuck it under my pillow for safekeeping. And just before I turn off my flashlight for the night, I say to myself, out loud, "I love you bigger than the sky full of stars."

Most nights, I dream of Daddy. And in every single dream, he's big as life and twice as natural, too. In some of my dreams, I'm in Hollywood with Daddy, in the backyard of our mansion, and we're laughing and laughing in the sun, right next to our fountain with the naked ladies and cherubs and the little cupid with wings. Sometimes, dream-Daddy comes to me and sits on the edge of my cot in the trailer, just like old times. "Nothing but the best for Charlie Wilber's Daughter," he always says. I hug him close and ask him, "Why'd you leave me, Daddy?" And he always says, "Because you deserve the very best in life." Every single time, I reply, "But, Daddy, I just want *you*."

Other times in my dreams, though not very often, I'm stabbing Daddy in the heart with a large, pointed butcher knife, and his blood is gushing all over my cot and all over the floor and onto my bare toes, and Daddy's eyes are bugging out in shock and pain and regret and apology as my knife burrows deeper and deeper into his chest cavity, and I lift the blade out of his chest and thrust it back in again and again. He's screaming as I shove the blade back inside him with all my might—so deep I can feel the warmth of his ragged and bloody flesh around my clenched fist—and then I rotate the handle of the blade back and forth like I'm hollowing out a big hole in Daddy's chest for some cornbread stuffing.

But no matter which Daddy-dream I had the prior night, no matter which book I might have read during the daytime to educate myself while Mother was sleeping or working at the diner, no matter how much I've imagined I'm a fancy lady living in a big ol' mansion in Hollywood with a fountain with naked ladies and cherubs and a little cupid with wings, no matter how many times I've walked to the 7-Eleven for a Slurpee or a hot dog or gone climbing on the big rocks, one thing always stays the same. I miss my daddy. So bad, it hurts. If Daddy doesn't come get me soon, then I'm going to get myself to Hollywood, come hell or high water, and I'm going to find him myself.

This whole year, I've had to live with Mother, all alone, and it's been hell. That woman could start an argument in an empty house. She barely speaks to me unless it's to scream at me for one thing or another—usually for something as stupid as leaving the closet door open in the back room. "When you leave the damned door open," she always screams, "I bang my head going to the bathroom in the middle of the night!" I hate how much Mother screams at me about that dang closet door—it's not like I'm *trying* to give her a big ol' bump on her forehead. Jeez. Everybody makes mistakes now and again.

"Hey there, Charlene," Mother says one day, out of nowhere, like she's trying to start a casual conversation about the weather.

I hate it when she calls me Charlene. I'm reminded that Daddy's not here when she says my name. Daddy and I are like salt and pepper. Peanut butter and jelly. Charlie and Charlene. Without Daddy here to be Charlie Wilber, there's no point in me being Charlene Wilber, is there? God, I hate it when Mother calls me Charlene. All it does is remind me that I'm missing my other half. And, anyway, no one but Mother calls me by that name. Even Daddy himself calls me Buttercup or Charlie Wilber's Daughter.

"Charlene," Mother says again when I don't respond the first time. But I don't look up from my book. *The Stranger Beside Me.* It's about Ted Bundy. Man, oh man, did he fool everyone—just because he had a pretty face.

When I don't look up from my book, Mother finally gives up and stomps out of the trailer. The front door creaks and slams behind her. I look up at the clock. Six o'clock. She's probably headed to work at the diner. Good riddance, Momma. When Daddy finally comes back to get me, I won't mind if I never see her again.

Chapter 10

15 Years Old
2,015 through 1,922 Days Before Killing Kurtis

I'm sitting at the little table in our trailer, reading a book. It's called *A Separate Peace,* one of the "classics" Mrs. Monaghan's always recommending to me, bless her heart. In the book, Gene shakes a tree branch when his best friend, Finny, is standing on it so that Finny falls off and shatters his leg. Gene shakes that tree branch on purpose—Gene actually *wants* Finny to fall—just because he's jealous of Finny for being so good lookin'. Well, all that's just fine and dandy, but the whole rest of book is about how Gene feels so gosh-dang guilty about shaking that tree branch, he can't find any peace and *blah, blah, blah.* Jeez, I wish Gene would stop whining about it. What's done is done, Gene.

The screen door slams. I look up.

"Hey there, Charlene," Mother says, clearing her throat. "This here's Jeb."

Mother's standing next to a mountain of a man in a flannel shirt. I'm guessing this guy's dark, curly hair hasn't encountered a pair of scissors in over a year and his belly threatens to pop open the last button of his shirt.

"Hey there, Charlene," the guy says. "I'm Jeb." His voice is softer than I'd have guessed, considering his size. He takes a step toward me and extends his hand.

I stare at his hand, but I don't take it.

Jeb nods and retracts his hand. "Nice to meet you," he says quietly.

Mother's smiling really, really big, like she just won a lifetime supply of biscuits and gravy. "Jeb's gonna be staying here with us for a while," she says, bubbling with enthusiasm. "Whenever he's in town, that is. Jeb's a trucker, so he's in and out, but whenever he's in town, he'll be here with us, helping us pay the bills and whatnot. Taking care of us." Mother and Jeb exchange googly-eyed smiles. "Being the man of the house."

I don't say a word. Daddy's gonna blow a gasket when he finds out about Jeb. The wooden table feels hot under my palms. I clench my hands into fists in my lap. This is not going to end well.

"Well, okay," Mother says, "why don't you come on back here with me, Jeb. I'll give you a fourteen-second tour of the palace." She giggles, and it occurs to me I've never heard Mother giggle before this very moment.

"It was nice to meet you, Charlene," Jeb says again. He tips his imaginary hat and turns to follow Mother into the back room.

That night, as I lie on my cot, I can hear Mother and Jeb giggling together—and groaning and flopping around on the mattress, too. I cover my ears with my pillow, my stomach turning over. When the sounds from the back room finally dissipate, when it's been a good thirty minutes since I've heard a peep from back there, I creep into the room with my flashlight and stand over Mother and Jeb's motionless bodies on the mattress. Jeb's arm is flopped over Mother's shoulder. His mouth hangs open.

I can hear Daddy's voice in my ear: "Oh hell no."

I tiptoe out of the room, flinging open the closet door as I go. Might as well give Mother a nice big howdy-do on her forehead to make her think twice about giggling and flopping around with anyone other than her husband ever again.

56

I'm sitting at the little table, eating a bowl of Cheerios and drinking my sweet tea. Jeb comes out of the back room and sits at the table with me. He's so big, he's gotta sit down in shifts. His hair's a rat's nest on top of his head. His belly hangs over the top of his pajama pants and peeks out the bottom of his Lynyrd Skynyrd T-shirt. Without even asking, Jeb pours himself a bowl of Cheerios and goes right ahead and pours himself a glass of sweet tea, too.

"So, Charlene," Jeb begins, munching on his Cheerios. "What do you like to do?"

I don't say anything.

"Do you like to fish?"

I remain silent.

"I really like fishing. I could take you fishing sometime, if that's something you'd like to do."

I say nothing.

"Or do you like ice cream? Because I was thinking of getting an ice cream cone later today, if you'd like to join me."

I continue staring, not saying a word, even though I love ice cream.

"My favorite flavor is strawberry. I know most people like chocolate, but I like the fruity flavors best. How about you?"

I decide to throw the dog a bone and say something. "Jeb, I'm fifteen. Not five."

Jeb smiles, apparently excited I've finally said something to him. "Well, you can still like ice cream at any age, can't you? I'm a whole lot older than fifteen, and I still love ice cream."

"I don't like ice cream." It's not true, of course. I adore it. But I'll be damned if I'm going to betray my daddy and get ice cream with another man.

"Okay, well, we don't have to get ice cream, then," Jeb says. "We can do whatever you want to do."

I don't reply.

Jeb clears his throat. "So, your mother says you love to read?"

I don't react in any way whatsoever to this question; though, if I were going to respond, I'd tell Jeb I don't "love to read." Does a bird love to fly? Does a spider love to make a web? Does a fish love to take in oxygen through its gills? If I were going to speak, which I'm not, I'd say, "I'm educating myself so I can fulfill my sacred destiny." But, of course, I don't say any such thing. I just stare at Jeb and let him hold up the conversation from his end.

"What are you reading lately?" Jeb asks.

I relent. I can't resist talking about my books, even to Jeb. "A biography of Jayne Mansfield," I say.

"Oh, wow. Hubba-hubba. She was a real looker, huh?"

It's funny the way Jeb's eyes have lit up at the mention of Jayne. I'm sure right now he's picturing her enormous boobs and tiny waist and platinum-blonde hair. I reckon he's not smiling like a wolf because he's thinking about her sharp mind and sense of humor. If I were going to speak right now, which I'm not, I'd say, "Actually, Jeb, Jayne Mansfield was Twentieth Century Fox's alternative to Marilyn Monroe, a knock-off, if you will, who came to be known as the 'Working Man's Monroe.'" But I don't say that. In fact, I don't say a thing.

"It didn't end well for poor Jayne Mansfield," Jeb observes.

"It never ends well, Jeb."

There's a short silence while Jeb regroups. "You like movies?" Jeb finally asks.

"I don't know. I read."

"Well then, maybe that's what we can do sometime. We can go to the movies."

I don't respond. I'm not going anywhere with Jeb. Unlike Mother, who apparently doesn't care that she still has a husband who's coming back any day now, I would never betray Daddy.

When I don't respond to Jeb's movie invitation, he focuses his gaze on his bowl of Cheerios, inhales every last "O," and quietly pours himself a second bowl.

For a solid three months after our first breakfast together, Jeb is a fixture in our trailer. Practically every day, he's there, just hanging around, even when Mother's sleeping or at work. Occasionally, Mother and Jeb go out bowling or to attend an AA meeting, which is something brand new for Mother—and occasionally they go in the back room to do exercises with the dumbbells Jeb bought her to help her "get her mind and body right." But mostly, there's just a lot of talking and giggling and playing dominoes and, of course, muffled sounds from the back room. And just about every day, whether Mother's there or not, Jeb tries to engage me in conversation or invite me to go bowling or fishing or to a movie or to play dominoes or toss a baseball or some other father-daughter-type-bonding activity he must have read about in *Parents Magazine*.

For the first two months, I ignore Jeb when he speaks to me, not even looking up from my book. With each and every rejection, Jeb snaps his fingers and says "Aw!" with a darn-it-I-thought-I-had-her-this-time-expression on his face, like, gosh, he almost cracked the code this time but missed victory by a hair.

Each time Jeb snaps his fingers and smiles, I find it harder and harder to turn him down, though I always manage to do it by the skin of my teeth. About a week ago, Jeb snapped his fingers and flashed me a wide smile, and I almost forgot to scowl at him. A couple days after that, I actually smiled back at Jeb when he snapped his fingers; and, yesterday, I not only smiled back at Jeb, I laughed out loud at the silly expression on his face. And when I laughed, Jeb joined me, and we both giggled for a solid two minutes. That's when a strange kind of happiness flooded me—the same kind of feeling I get from reading one of my favorite books, only maybe even better. But then I quickly looked down and that weird happy feeling went away.

"Your momma's been sober a full month now," Jeb says one day when Mother's at work. We're sitting at the table in the kitchenette, eating the tomato soup and grilled cheese sandwiches he's made for us. "I'm thinking I'm gonna bake her a cake to celebrate."

Holy heck. I hadn't really thought about it, but come to think of it, Mother hasn't been passed out on her mattress in the back room in a coon's age. And what the hell? She hasn't slurred her words or reeked of whiskey in forever and a day, either. In fact, I can't remember the last time I even saw Mother taking a sip of anything other than a coke or water. And about a month or so ago—or was it longer?—she even started working days at the diner so she could flop around on the mattress at night with Jeb.

My stomach flips over. I put my spoon down on the table. I feel ill. When Daddy comes home and sees how Jeb's taken over his wife and daughter—fixing me tomato soup and grilled cheese sandwiches and turning Mother into Suzy Bright Eyes—Daddy's gonna fly off the handle. Good lord, he's gonna think I've replaced him with Jeb.

My heart is racing.

I can't let Daddy see how I've been smiling and laughing with Jeb. If he sees that, he's gonna figure out just how much I've started enjoying having Jeb around.

"Your momma's gonna be home in a couple hours," Jeb says. "I'd better go get the ingredients for the cake. You wanna come to the store with me?"

I shake my head. "I've gotta get myself to the library to see if Mrs. Monaghan's got a new book for me."

"Oh, well, I'll give you a lift, then."

"Thanks, Jeb," I say. "That would be lovely."

Jeb grins. "Lovely." He laughs.

Usually, I'd laugh with Jeb right now, seeing as how he just did that silly thing with his face that makes me giggle. But I can't laugh. My heart is pounding in my ears and my stomach's in my toes. "But, hey, Jeb, I could bake that cake with you after the library—maybe you could teach me how." My stomach twists like it's in a vise.

A wide smile spreads across Jeb's face. "I'll go get my keys." He practically skips to the back room, happy as a puppy with two tails.

Oh lord, my chest feels tight.

Mrs. Monaghan greets me warmly at the library, as usual. "Well, hello, honey," she says. "What can I help you find today? Another movie star biography?"

I wring my hands and shift my weight anxiously. I look to the left and right, like I'm worried someone might overhear what I'm about to say. Mrs. Monaghan looks at me expectantly and then glances from side to side, clearly sensing I'm about to disclose a juicy secret. A shadow of concern crosses her face as I continue to fidget and fret, but she waits patiently.

"I... I don't know if I should say..." I begin.

"Say what, dear? Is there something wrong?"

"Oh no," I reply, a little too quickly. "No, there's nothing wrong. It's just... I... um... I have to do a... *report* on something."

Mrs. Monaghan knows I'm homeschooled. I'm sure she's wondering what report I'm doing and for whom. "A report?" she asks.

"Yes, ma'am, a report. On...um..."

"On what, dear?" Mrs. Monaghan looks worried.

I exhale loudly. "Battered Woman Syndrome?" I say meekly.

Mrs. Monaghan's face darkens. "Oh," she says. She knits her brows.

Tears spring to my eyes. "I never should have said anything. I... Mrs. Monaghan, please don't tell anyone I told you. Please don't tell *Jeb* what I just said, especially." I throw my hands over my face. "Please, forget I was ever here!"

I sprint out the front door of the library and streak down the block and around the corner to the side of Herb's

Laundromat. When I'm safely out of sight, I lean my back against the brick wall and burst into tears.

It's clear Jeb's enjoying teaching me how to make a congratulations-you're-not-a-drunkard-anymore cake for Mother. I wish we were making a congratulations-you're-not-a-whore-anymore cake for her, but no such luck.

"And that's all there is to it," Jeb says, putting the cake pans into the oven and closing the door. "Now, we just wait for the buzzer to beep." He winks at me. "This is gonna be a good one—made with extra love."

My stomach is flip-flopping. My chest is clanging. I try to reply, but my voice doesn't work.

Apparently, Jeb's used to me not talking—because he doesn't seem to notice I've gone speechless. He hands me a batter-covered spoon to lick. "Go ahead, Charlene—this is the best part."

I take the spoon from Jeb and take a tiny lick of the chocolate batter. "Thank you," I say, my voice wobbling.

He flashes me a smile that could melt the polar ice caps. "It's my pleasure, honey. The way I feel about you, it's like you're my daughter, Charlene. My very own."

I want to burst into tears like I did earlier today outside the library, but I hold myself at bay. "I..." I start to reply, and quickly close my mouth. Good lord, I was about to blurt, "I love you, Jeb!" What the hell is wrong with me? If Daddy ever found out the mushy feelings I've got for Jeb, he'd never forgive me. In fact, I reckon he'd even go so far as to refuse to let me live with him in Hollywood. Oh good lord, this is not a good situation. In fact, it's very, very bad.

Jeb, Mother and I are sitting around the little table in the kitchenette, all three of our bellies stuffed with Jeb's chocolate cake—which, I must say, was the best dang cake I've ever tasted. Momma's crying her eyes out because Jeb has just broken the sad news that, tomorrow, he's gotta leave for a job.

"It's just for four or five days," Jeb assures Mother. "Don't worry—I'll leave y'all with some emergency cash to tide you over while I'm gone."

Mother wipes her eyes and takes a deep breath.

Jeb stands and grabs his wallet out of his pants. "Here's fifty bucks, honey." He drops some bills into the empty coffee can in the cabinet.

"Thank you, Jebby," Momma says, "but it's not the money I want—it's *you*. I'm not sure I can keep on the straight and narrow without you."

Jeb flashes Mother a sympathetic face. "Aw, Carrie Ann, you've already made it through the first month, honey, and that's the hardest part. You know I've got to make us some money. I've burned through all my savings these past months, hanging out here with y'all."

"I know, I know," Mother replies. "Thank you, darlin'. But I don't know if I can stay strong without you here. Every single day, it's a struggle not to take a drink." Her lower lip begins to tremble and she looks down, ashamed.

"You can do it," Jeb says earnestly, pulling Mother up from her chair and into an embrace. "I'll be back before you know it." He puts both hands on her cheeks and kisses her gently. "And when I get back, maybe we'll start planning ourselves a wedding, making things official." He smiles at her. "How does that sound?"

"Oh, Jebby," Momma says, her face lighting up. "That sounds mighty fine."

I feel dizzy. My stomach is squeezing. This cannot be happening.

"And until I get back," Jeb continues. "Charlene will be here the whole time, keeping you on track." He turns to me. "Isn't that right, sweetheart?"

My heart is pounding in my ears. Daddy's gonna blow a gasket when he hears another man talking to *his* wife about making things official and calling *his* daughter "sweetheart." And, worst of all, I reckon Daddy's gonna be fit-to-kill when he finds out how it's making my heart go pitter-pat to hear Jeb say all of it.

I nod at Jeb. "Yes, sir. I'll be right here."

Mother's face melts with emotion. "Thank you, Charlene." She steps over to me and sweeps me into her arms for just about the first time I can recall in my whole dang life.

Jeb joins us, wrapping his big arms around the two of us at once.

I'm suddenly overcome with the desire to cry a river of tears. I step away from our three-way embrace and sit back down.

Mother and Jeb look at each other and something passes between them. Mother nods, as if she's encouraging Jeb to say something and then sits back down at the table across from me. She's fidgeting like a long-tailed cat in a roomful of rocking chairs.

Jeb clears his throat and sits back down. "Charlene, honey," he says tentatively. "I was thinking—well, your mother and I were both thinking, actually—you really should be going to school."

My stomach drops along with my jaw.

"You're so darned smart, honey—just as smart as a whip. There's no limit to what you can do. I don't understand why you haven't been getting a real education all these years." He looks over at Mother, and she crosses her arms across her chest, apparently thinking Jeb's last comment was meant as a jab at her so-called parenting. "When I come back from the road, I want to get you enrolled right quick down at the high school, okay?"

I close my gaping mouth and try to regain control of my face.

"How does that sound, honey?" Jeb persists. "If you get yourself educated, there'll be no stopping you in life."

I purse my lips as if I'm considering Jeb's suggestion. "Hmm," I begin softly, trying to quell the raging storm brewing inside me. I can feel heat rising in my cheeks and tears pricking my eyes. "Well..." I mumble. I'm shaking like cafeteria Jell-O. I take a deep breath, trying to calm myself, but it's hard to do. Holy hell, I've got to get myself under control. I inhale and exhale several times. "I'd really like that, Jeb," I declare with all the enthusiasm I can muster, but my voice is quavering. I try my darnedest to smile gratefully, but I can't. I don't want to do it, but I burst into tears.

Jeb looks like he's gonna cry right along with me. He gets up and covers me in a bear hug from behind, right where I'm sitting.

I want to lurch out of my chair to escape Jeb's arms and scream, "If dumb was dirt, you'd be covered in an acre!" But I don't. Instead, I lean back into his warm chest and lose myself to wracking sobs.

"There, there," Jeb says softly, stroking my hair. "Everything's gonna be all right, honey." He kisses the top of my head. "We'll get this all straightened out right quick."

The next morning, after a quick breakfast of Cheerios, it's goodbye-and-can't-wait-'til-you-come-home time for Jeb. Mother's a blubbering mess during the whole, long farewell. Of course, Jeb hugs her and tells her he'll be back before she knows it.

"Hey, Jeb," I say, my voice trembling, "how 'bout I bake you a welcome-home cake when you come home?"

Jeb's breath catches. He steps forward and puts out his arms, and I go to him, letting him envelop me in yet another hug.

"I'll bake it just the way you taught me to," I murmur into his burly chest. When I pull back from Jeb's embrace, he's smiling like a dead pig in the sunshine, and when I glance over at Mother, she's got tears in her eyes.

"Don't worry. I'll be back before you know it," Jeb assures us.

Mother nods, apparently too choked up to speak.

After kissing Mother one final time and patting my cheek, Jeb climbs into his rig, starts his noisy engine and pulls away, waving and blowing kisses to us girls as he goes.

It's been three days since Jeb left.

Mother went to bed over an hour ago.

And I've finally managed to pick my butt off my shoulders.

I sneak into the kitchenette, put on the yellow rubber kitchen gloves, and creep outside.

Yesterday, while I was sitting at the kitchen table reading a biography of Marilyn Monroe—which, by the way, is the best dang book I've ever read in the history of my life—I overheard our next-door neighbor, Mr. Oglethorpe, talking to Mother outside.

"Yeah, the rats are getting to be a problem," Mr. Oglethorpe lamented to Mother. "Have you seen any in your trailer?"

"No, thank goodness," Mother answered, "knock on wood. I'd probably have a conniption fit if I saw a rat inside. I saw a big one scoot past me the other night when I was taking out the trash, right over there, and I screamed like a banshee."

"Yeah, some of 'em get pretty big," Mr. Oglethorpe said. "I hollered like a Dallas debutante at a race riot when a big one scurried across my kitchen floor last night."

Mother squealed then, and Mr. Oglethorpe chuckled heartily at her reaction.

"I'm gonna get those suckers," he continued. "I'm putting out a bunch of traps, right over there and there, and I just put a big box of poison right under my front steps, too."

"I sure hope that does the trick," Mother said, sounding squeamish. "But if you get one of 'em, good lord, don't show it to me. I faint at the sight of anything dead."

And now, thanks to Mr. Oglethorpe's conveniently timed rat-vendetta, I'm down on my hands and knees in the middle of the cold, dark night, shivering and shining my flashlight under Mr. Oglethorpe's steps. Gosh dang it, it's colder than a well digger's butt in January tonight and as dark as a black cat in a coal bin.

Sure enough, when I lay my cheek onto the gravel and

shine my light under the steps, I see it—a box of rat poison sitting in the dirt, right where Mr. Oglethorpe said it'd be. I grab the box and tiptoe back toward my trailer, shaking like a leaf the whole time, either from the cold, my nerves, or both.

I slip back inside our trailer and creep into the back room where Mother's snoozing soundly on the mattress. Still wearing my yellow rubber gloves, I reach out with a shaky hand and gently press Mother's fingertips onto the box of poison. She doesn't even flinch.

Back in my cot, I pull my covers up to my neck, trying to stop myself from shaking, but no luck. My nerves won't stop zipping and zapping. I reckon I need to read—reading always calms me down. I pull out my Marilyn book and my flashlight from underneath my pillow, and the minute I open the book, I feel calmer.

I adore the way Marilyn closes her eyelids halfway when she smiles. I can't get enough of the way she manages to look sexy and innocent at the same time. And I love how Marilyn let the world think she was exactly who they wanted her to be, and all the while, on the inside, she was something else entirely.

I keep turning the pages of my book, studying every detail of every photograph.

Gosh, looking at photos of Marilyn is like looking at photos of myself, if I had blonde hair and big boobs. When I'm older, once I've dyed my hair and my boobs have finally sprouted to their full size, Marilyn and I are gonna be just like twins. The two of us are the same in every way—and not just how we look, either, but everything else, too, from A to Z, right down to our crazy mothers.

The only difference between Marilyn and me, as far as I can tell, is that poor Marilyn never knew her daddy, unlike me, so she wound up in a foster home after her momma went crazy. As much as I love Marilyn and want to be just like her, I'm actually glad for that one difference, to tell you the truth. I reckon not knowing your daddy and living in a foster home would be a fate worse than living in this trailer with Momma.

My eyelids are getting heavy. The pages of my book are starting to blur.

Poor Marilyn. I feel so sorry for her not ever knowing her daddy.

My mind wants to keep reading, but my body says it's turn-out-the-lights-the-party's-over time. I shove my book and flashlight under my pillow, and slowly, ever so slowly, drift off to sleep.

Chapter 11

Odessa, Texas

16 Years Old
1,613 through 1,585 Days Before Killing Kurtis

"Ladies and gentlemen of the jury," the prosecuting attorney says, "the State of Texas will prove to you, beyond a reasonable doubt, that this woman, Caroline McEntire"—and here she points at Mother, who's sitting feebly next to her Court-appointed lawyer at a small table—"committed first degree murder on October tenth of last year, when, with chilling premeditation, she poisoned and killed her live-in boyfriend, Jeb Watson."

I admit it was a shocker to find out Mother's legal last name isn't Wilber, after all, on account of her and Daddy not technically being married all these past years, on account of Mother being so young when she had me and not knowing for sure, at first, which boy was the lucky fella. I found all that out when I first became a ward of The State. Yeah, that part was a doozy of a shocker, too. I've had a lot of shocks to my system since the police first arrested Mother all those months ago—and all of it has made me feel lower than a snake's pecker every goddamned day of my life.

Maybe the biggest shock of all, the thing that kicked me in the teeth the hardest, was finding out Wilber's not legally my last name, either, because it turns out Daddy's name isn't listed on my birth certificate. Nope, the only father listed on my papers is some yahoo named "Father Unknown." Of course, Mother figured out who my rightful daddy is right quick after I was born, but I reckon she didn't go back to my papers and fill in the blank. Of course, I don't care what that gosh-dang piece of paper says. I'm Charlene Wilber and Charlie Wilber's Daughter. And that's a fact, Jack. But I reckon the folks at Child Protective Services don't give two squirts about who I really am, because all those small-minded Napoleon-types care about is what the legal papers say. I've begged them to find Daddy out in Hollywood a hundred-million times, but I swear, those people must be trying to scratch their ears with their elbows.

How hard can it be to find a guy living in Hollywood in a fancy mansion with a tennis court and a bowling alley and a fountain with naked ladies and cherubs and a little cupid with wings? My biggest fear is that Daddy came to the trailer looking for me, but I wasn't there. My heart aches to think about Daddy walking into our trailer, a big smile on his face, and finding me gone without a trace. Why would Daddy think to look for me in some run-down foster home in Odessa? He'd sooner think Mother had kidnapped me to Mexico than go looking for me in a sad-sack facility for teens without parents.

I'd bet anything Daddy came back to Kermit for me while I've been stuck in Odessa. I betcha when he came back to the trailer, he figured I must have gone off to California to find him. Lord have mercy, I could cry a deep river thinking about Daddy coming back for me and me not being there. But then again, almost everything makes me wanna cry a deep river these days. Goodness gracious, I didn't know it was even possible for a girl to cry this many tears.

It's clear to me I've got to take matters into my own hands and get my butt out to California as soon as possible. Unfortunately, however, before I can do that, I've got to wait and bide my time at the stupid group home for a little while longer. Now that the police know my name, and everyone at Child Protective Services thinks they've got the God-given right to tell me what I can and can't do simply because my only legal parent in this world has been locked away in a prison cell, and since I've got to show up at this gosh-dang trial every goddamned day so I can play Good Daughter for the jury, I reckon I've got no choice but to cool my jets and let this whole situation play itself out.

I steal a glance at Mother at the defense table. From my seat in the gallery at the back of the courtroom sitting next to Mrs. Clements from the group home, I can only see the back of Mother's head and her occasional profile when she whispers something to her baby lawyer. For cryin' out loud, that lawyer can't be much older than me, and I've only just turned sixteen—the boy looks like he stole his granddaddy's suit. And Mother? Well, bless her distilled heart and fermented liver, she looks guilty as homemade sin. The two of them together look like Tweedledee and Tweedledum.

"For our first witness, the State calls Detective Mark Carter," the prosecutor says. Mrs. Clements from the group home squeezes my hand, and I squeeze right back. I'm glad for her show of support, actually—my stomach's turning over like a plucked chicken on a spit.

Detective Mark Carter is a slightly rotund man with salt-and-pepper hair, bushy eyebrows, and pointy-toed boots. I remember him from when he came to our trailer on The Horrible Night of Jeb's Murder.

After swearing to tell the truth, the whole truth, and nothing but the truth so help him God, Detective Carter with the bushy eyebrows proceeds to tell a rapt courtroom about what he encountered when he first came to our trailer that night. He describes finding Jeb, dead as a doornail on the floor in the middle of the kitchenette, blood and froth and cake chunks and unspecified bodily fluids gurgling down his chin and staining the front of his plaid flannel shirt.

Detective Carter further describes finding a half-eaten

chocolate cake on the table and Mother passed out drunk as a skunk in the back room. He goes on to describe finding me, sitting in the corner of the trailer, rocking back and forth, sobbing, my hands wrapped around my knees.

In response to the prosecutor's questioning, Detective Carter describes his masterful detective work. He tells us how he found an empty box of rat poison in the Oglethorpes' trash bin outside their trailer, and he confirms, with a sparkle in his eye, that Mother's fingerprints were all over it. I'm sure the jury's thinking, "Wow, that's some brilliant detective work right there."

When Mother's attorney cross-examines Detective Carter, it becomes abundantly clear that boy's aiming to be a half-wit, but he's not gonna hit the mark—because everything that pipsqueak asks the detective seems to put yet another nail in Mother's coffin. Isn't the defendant's lawyer in a murder trial supposed to make his client sound *less* guilty, not more? I swear, if you put that boy's brains into a boxcar, it'd rattle around like a bee-bee. It's all I can do not to run up there, knock that twelve-year-old lawyer onto his butt, and start cross-examining that detective myself, just to give poor Momma a fighting chance.

For two solid weeks, I sit with Mrs. Clements in the courtroom gallery, listening to the testimony and alternately crying, hanging my head, looking defiant, confused, heartbroken, and/or shocked—sometimes all of them at once. Occasionally, Mother turns around to look at me, her eyes vacant and lifeless. I can't for the life of me figure out what she must be thinking—and, honestly, I probably wouldn't want to know.

"The State calls Bernard Oglethorpe to the stand."

Mr. Oglethorpe describes his conversation with Mother about the rats. "No, I didn't tell anyone else about the box of poison under my steps.... No, I never handed Carrie Ann the box of poison.... No, she didn't handle the box in my presence, nope.... No, I didn't remove the box of poison at any time.... No, I did not throw that box of poison away into my own trashcan."

"The State calls Margaret Monaghan to the stand."

Mrs. Monaghan describes how she's known me for years, how I used to come into the library often, and that I've always been a "voracious reader." She smiles at me when she says the "voracious reader" part—and coming from a librarian, I reckon that's high praise, indeed. "Charlene's always been an extremely shy and polite and curious young lady," Mrs. Monaghan confirms, but, she adds, glancing at me, "I must admit I've often wondered about her 'homeschooling' and what seemed to be a complete lack of parental supervision in her life." A scowl crosses her face when she says "complete lack of parental supervision," and at the same time, I notice several jurors' faces mirroring her disapproval.

Mrs. Monaghan tells the courtroom about the unforgettable day I came into the library, not too long before The Horrible Night of Jeb's Murder, anxious and fidgety and flustered—which was so unlike me she'll never forget it. After she gently prodded me, she says, I admitted to her that I desperately needed information about ... *dum-dum-dum!*... Battered Woman Syndrome.

Several jurors gasp when Mrs. Monaghan says "Battered Woman's Syndrome," and when Mrs. Monaghan further describes how I pleaded with her not to tell Jeb about my outburst—and says she'll never forget the look of fear in my eyes when I cried "please don't tell Jeb!"—a couple of the jurors just about slide off their chairs.

Mother's genius of a baby-lawyer tries to create doubt that the "alleged" conversation between Mrs. Monaghan and me ever happened, by asking, "Why on earth, if this girl had made such an 'unforgettable' cry for help, as you say she did, didn't you take *any* action at all to help her or her mother?" But instead, contrary to the stupid lawyer's presumable intentions, all this question does is open the door for Mrs. Monaghan to say, "I keep asking myself the same question. If only I'd done something— *anything at all*—to help this poor girl, maybe she wouldn't be without a mother now, and without a soul in the world to watch over her. I keep thinking if I'd done something different, maybe I could have prevented Charlene's mother from killing that man."

Well, turn out the lights. I can't even look at the jury right now—I don't trust my face.

Mother's fool attorney is apparently as shocked as everyone else in the courtroom right now, because he doesn't even move to strike any portion of it. Has that boy even gone to law school—or, jeez, at least read a single true-crime book? I swear, that boy is as smart as a soup sandwich.

I'm not sure why the Prosecutor even needs to call any more witnesses, but she does, anyway.

"The State calls Officer Ronald Frampton," she says.

Officer Frampton ambles to the witness stand. He's so large, it'd be easier to go over the top of him than around him.

"You were the first law enforcement officer on the scene, correct?" the prosecutor asks.

"That's correct."

"And what did you observe as the initial responder on the scene?"

Officer Frampton describes the same scene already painted by Detective Carter, except that in Officer Frampton's version of events, I was draped over Jeb's body, crying like a newborn, when he arrived.

"And where was the defendant during this time?"

"Passed out drunk in a bedroom in the back."

"Did you notice anything unusual about her?"

Officer Frampton answers that, yes, when he first saw Mother, he noticed two things: One, she'd soiled herself; and, two, she had a particularly nasty bruise on her cheek. When the prosecutor asks for more details about Mother's bruise, Officer Frampton says it looked to him like it had been inflicted fairly recently.

Officer Frampton identifies various photos from the scene

of the crime, including pictures of Mother taken on The Horrible Night of Jeb's Murder. In all the pictures, Mother looks battered and bruised and as wasted as a wino in a back alley.

While Officer Frampton is talking, I notice the jury looking carefully at the photos of Mother, and I can plainly see them comparing the human pile of rubble in those pictures to the cleaned-up version of Mother sitting at the defense table in a cheap suit. As they look back and forth between the sorry-ass pictures and the edited version sitting in the courtroom, I can hear their innermost thoughts as surely as if they were screaming them into a megaphone: *"You can't fool me, lady. I know what you did."*

The prosecutor looks awfully confident right now, like she thinks she's got this thing all wrapped up. The woman's not gifted with E.S.P. or anything, though—anyone with a half a brain can see the way the jury's glaring at Mother like she's a calf at the rodeo.

"Your honor," the prosecutor says, "the State rests its case."

The entire courtroom exhales.

"All right then," the judge says, "does the Defense plan to put on a case?"

All eyes are on Mother's pre-pubescent lawyer.

The fool stands and clears his throat. "Yes, thank you. Your honor, the Defense calls Dr. Irma Rodriguez to the stand."

"Battered Woman Syndrome is a physical and psychological condition that sometimes occurs when a woman suffers persistent emotional, physical, or sexual abuse from another person, usually her spouse or significant other," Dr. Rodriguez says, looking at the jury like she's teaching a class.

I can't believe it, but Boy Wonder has actually called Dr. Rodriguez to the stand to explain the phenomenon of Battered Woman Syndrome to the jury. By doing that, isn't that dumb lawyer basically admitting the fact that Jeb abused Mother? And that Mother killed him for it?

"The unique etiology of this syndrome explains why an abused woman might stay with her abuser, may not seek assistance from others or fight her abuser, or leave the abusive situation," Dr. Rodriguez continues, obviously enjoying how she gets to teach us all a thing or two. "It's very common for sufferers to have low self-esteem and believe that the abuse is their fault."

"Is it common for a sufferer of this syndrome to believe the only way out of her predicament is to *kill* her attacker?" Boy Genius asks.

"Why, yes," Dr. Rodriguez confirms. "That's a commonly-held thought process. Sometimes, that thought process will lead a victim to killing her abuser in what she perceives to be her only means of self defense against future attacks."

I can't believe this. If I understand the situation correctly, Mr. Baby Lawyer is admitting Mother's the one who took that rat poison from under Mr. Oglethorpe's steps and baked that poison into a chocolate cake. Good lord, Baby Lawyer's not trying to convince the jury Mother's innocent, he's trying to convince them that, even though Mother did the deed, she shouldn't fry for it. Lord have mercy, that lawyer couldn't pour rain out of a boot with a hole in the toe and directions on the heel.

On cross-examination, the prosecutor tears Dr. Rodriguez a new one, getting her to admit "there's absolutely no consensus in the medical profession that abuse results in a mental condition severe enough to excuse a killing."

At this point, the judge admonishes the jury, "Ladies and gentlemen, I will instruct you on the law pertaining to the Battered Person's Defense at the close of evidence. At that time—and only after I've instructed you on all applicable laws—you'll decide whether the evidence you've heard supports a claim of self defense. Or *not*."

Maybe I'm imagining it, but it sure sounds like the judge was giving that jury a secret winky-winky code when she said the word "not." And, frankly, I don't blame the judge for

COUNTDOWN TO KILLING KURTIS

having doubts about what Mother's lawyer is selling here—I reckon it'd be pretty hard for anyone to bake a rat-poison-cake in "self defense."

"The Defense calls Wanda Doshinsky to the stand."

"Yes, I've known Carrie Ann for years," Wanda Doshinsky confirms to Mother's baby-lawyer. "We've worked together at Uncle Jimmy's Diner, over on Route 271, for years." Wanda goes on to say that, yes, she's seen Mother covered with bruises throughout the entire time she's known her. "Yeah, for years and years, from way back, ever since I've known her."

"And what about during the time period when she was with Jeb Watson?"

"Yes, then, too. Carrie Ann's always had bruises. During the time with Jeb, mostly on her face."

Well, I'll be damned. Who knew all those times Mother accidentally got whacked in the face by that damned closet door would come back to bite Momma in the ass? I reckon she was right to yell at me so much about it, after all.

Of course, I was counting on the jury figuring Jeb had beaten Mother like a no-count fool—because, according to my true crime books, juries always want a motive for murder, even if the prosecution's not technically required to prove one. But I didn't expect Mother's lawyer to jumble everything up and use the *motive* as an *excuse*. If brains were leather, that lawyer couldn't saddle a flea.

After what seems like a month of Sundays, the day I've been simultaneously dreading and waiting for finally arrives.

"The Defense calls Charlene McEntire to the stand."

You could hear a pin drop in the courtroom.

Mrs. Clements from the group home squeezes my hand and quickly releases it. I rise from my seat in the court gallery and make my way, shakily, to the witness stand, my pulse pounding in my ears.

Chapter 12

16 Years Old
1,583 Days Before Killing Kurtis

"Charlene Ann... *McEntire*," I say into the microphone when Mother's adolescent attorney asks me to state my full name. Dang it, I hate saying anything other than Charlene Wilber, but I reckon I've got no choice in the matter.

I inhale and exhale deeply, trying to calm my jangling nerves. I glance over at the jury. Every single one of them is sitting on the edge of their seat, their eyes fixed on me.

"Can you tell us what happened on the evening of October tenth?"

I nod, but then, yet again, need to take a few deep breaths in and out before speaking. "Well, I... I was reading a book over on the big rocks in our trailer park, like I always do—well, like I always *used* to do." I look down at my hands for a moment. Life sure can surprise you. All those years living alone with Momma in the trailer, I thought I had it so bad, and now, all of a sudden, with the way things have been for me lately, I suddenly miss those days something awful.

"Charlene?" Baby Lawyer prompts me. "Can you tell us what happened next?"

"Yes, sir. Well, after a while," I continue, "I started to get hungry, so I decided to go back home to our trailer..."

"And what happened next?" Mother's baby-lawyer asks me.

"I... I came inside the trailer... and I saw Jeb lying on the ground. He was, you know, on the ground, shaking and thrashing around." I don't use the word "convulsing" because I reckon the phrase "shaking and thrashing around" sounds more natural.

"And what else did you notice?"

"There was a cake on the table, a half-eaten cake." A picture of Jeb smiling just before he bit into that cake pops into my mind and I begin to cry.

The judge hands me a box of tissues. "Do you need to take a break, dear?"

I nod, and squeak out, "Yes, please, ma'am—if y'all don't mind."

I sit with Mrs. Clements on a wooden bench in the hallway. Mrs. Clements puts her arm around my shoulder and I lean into her and let her stroke my hair. She's saying something or other to me, trying to soothe me, but I'm not listening. I'm lost in my thoughts.

It wasn't hard to get Mother back on the sauce. All I had to do was head down to the 7-Eleven with Jeb's emergency-cash in my pocket, and the very first drunkard I encountered in front of the store was more than willing to buy me a big bottle of whiskey, just as long as I gave him double the money so he could buy his own bottle, too. It was just that simple.

Despite Mother's thirty days of sobriety and her newly discovered lease on life, Mother just couldn't resist that damned bottle sitting on the counter calling her name. "Just one sip," I heard Mother whisper to herself, just before she dove headfirst into the bottle. By the time Jeb came home to my welcome-home cake on the table, Mother was practically drowning in whiskey in the back room, blitzed out of her mind and pissing her pants—as worthless as a steering wheel on a mule.

"You ready to resume?" the judge asks when I'm back on the witness stand.

"Yes, ma'am," I answer.

Mother's dumbass attorney looks down at his notepad for

a minute before asking his next question. "When you entered the trailer, what else did you notice besides Mr. Watson on the ground?"

"Well, um, I saw a half-eaten cake, and Jeb had all sorts of gross stuff coming out his mouth and down his shirt." I wipe at my eyes with a tissue. I don't like remembering how Jeb looked right after he ate that rat-poison cake. I've only just stopped having nightmares about that horrible twisted look on his face and I don't like reminding myself about it.

"Anything else?"

I look pointedly at Mother, like I'm afraid she'll be mad at me if I say anything more. I reckon it's probably best to let the prosecutor pull this part out of me on cross-examination. I shake my head. "No, sir."

Baby Lawyer moves on. "Did you ever see Jeb Watson physically hit your mother?"

I look again at Mother. She's glaring at me like I'm the devil herself. I look at the judge, my eyes wide. "Do I have to answer these questions, ma'am?"

"Yes, you do. And, remember, you're under oath."

I nod at the judge. "Yes, ma'am." I turn back to Boy Genius. "Yes," I whisper into the microphone. "Many times." Again, I start to cry. It's not hard to do. Saying a mean-spirited lie about poor Jeb is harder than I thought it'd be. But I'm taking comfort in the compassionate expressions on the jurors' faces. Each one of them wants to leap out of their chairs to hug me. It feels like flying with a jetpack to hold an audience in the palm of my hand like this.

"Did Jeb hit your mother on October tenth?"

"I don't know—I was outside reading my book on the big rock. I only know what my mother told me after I came into the trailer."

Baby Lawyer shifts his weight uncomfortably. Apparently, he's not sure what I'm going to say here. Should he ask the question or shouldn't he? Oh my, that boy couldn't find his butt with a flashlight in each hand. "What did your mother say to you then?" Boy Genius finally asks, barreling ahead with a blindfold on. I reckon he's decided a daughter wouldn't ever say anything to send her momma up the river.

"Hearsay," the prosecutor objects.

"Your honor, it goes to the defendant's state of mind," Baby Lawyer says.

"I'll allow it," the judge says matter-of-factly. She turns to me. "Go ahead and answer the question."

"Yes, ma'am," I answer. I clear my throat. "Well, when I came into the trailer, Jeb was on the ground, like I said, and Mother was standing there in the kitchenette, and she had a big ol' *bruise* on her face, on her cheek..."

I close my eyes, remembering how, that morning, Mother looked like she'd fallen facedown in a cactus grove (and then got trampled by a herd of cattle), thanks to an unfortunate closet door left open the night before. I reckon a certain set of dumbbells placed strategically on the floor didn't help poor, drunk Momma avoid that dang closet door in the dark, either.

"What did your mother say to you then?" Boy Genius asks.

I look at the judge, as if I'm hoping she'll excuse me from answering this particular question.

"Answer the question," the judge instructs me.

"Yes, ma'am." I clear my throat. "She looked right at me and she said..." Tears have started squirting out of my eyes and I wipe them with a tissue. I shift in my seat and steal a glance at the jury. They're enraptured. "She said..." I pause again. I can feel their attention on me and it makes my skin sizzle and pop, even as my stomach twists and somersaults at the whopper of a lie I'm about to tell. "She said, 'That motherfucker just hit me for the very last time.'"

The courtroom collectively gasps.

The prosecutor smirks, like she wasn't expecting that answer at all, but she's damned glad to hear it.

Mother, who'd been looking down at the table during my testimony, suddenly snaps her head up and looks me right in the eye. For just a split-second, the thought crosses my mind that she's about to leap up, point her finger at me, and holler, "It was Charlene!" and my stomach clenches. But then, when I see the look in Mother's eyes, like the life is draining out of her as surely as it whooshed out of poor Jeb, I know Mother's not going to do any such thing.

I feel a pang right now, a horrible pang in my chest, to tell you the truth. I didn't expect to feel quite this bad about this whole situation.

Before this very minute, I reckon Mother held out the slightest doubt about the truth. She'd probably created all sorts of cockamamie scenarios in her mind to explain how Mr. Oglethorpe's box of rat poison made its way into a cake and then into Jeb's mouth. But now, Momma knows the truth—she knows what I did to poor Jeb—and I suddenly realize I can't stand her knowing.

Tears begin filling Mother's horror-stricken eyes as water simultaneously starts gushing out of mine, too, and then Mother hangs her head down low and begins weeping like she's standing at my grave—or, more to the point, I reckon, her own.

Baby Lawyer sputters and stutters, clearly at a loss about what to do with this newest bit of information. Have I helped his client or hurt her? He clears his throat and looks around at the jury, at me, at the judge—and by the time he looks back at Mother sitting behind him, she's already got her head down on the table, her shoulders shuddering with violent sobs.

From my perch on the witness stand, I glance at the top of Mother's head, her face buried in her arms, praying she'll look back up at me. I need her to look at me, dang it, so that my eyes can tell her I had no choice. I was only doing what Daddy would have demanded—I was only doing what I had to do. But Momma doesn't even glance back up. She just keeps sobbing on the table, her face covered by her arms. I keep on staring at Mother's head, anyway, silently begging her to look at me. I can feel my insides twisting and curling and straining, aching for her to understand. *I had no choice.* But Mother still won't look at me.

I've got a storm raging inside me. I only did what had to be done. Daddy was coming back any day, I was sure of it, and God only knows what he would have done if he discovered Jeb taking over his family and making Mother into Suzy Bright Eyes and me into his daughter. He told me he loved me like his daughter! He said he was gonna send me to school! And, worst of all, he made my heart ache and pang for him when he left, almost as much as it did when Daddy left so long ago.

And, anyway, it was only a matter of time before Jeb was gonna leave us. Why doesn't Momma understand that part? Jeb wasn't gonna stick around forever, no matter what he said. No matter how much we might have enjoyed having him around.

I can't stop the tears from squirting out my eyes and gushing down my face.

The judge says something about a five-minute recess, but I don't leave my chair. I keep staring at the top of Momma's head through my tears, waiting for my chance. Momma's attorney grabs her by the arm and pulls her to standing like she's a rag doll.

I'm shaking with my sobs, aching to explain everything to her with my eyes so she'll understand. But she doesn't look up at me. She just covers her face with her hands and stays that way.

My heart pangs violently inside my chest.

Why won't she look at me, just once? Am I so horrible, so worthless, she can't even look me in the eyes and let me explain? After all these years of her lying on her mattress, drunk as a skunk, leaving me to scrounge up a bologna sandwich to eat, if I was lucky, she can't do this one thing for me? Just this one little thing?

Well, she can go hug a root, then. She's in no position to judge me. She might not have killed Jeb exactly the way I'm telling it here on the witness stand, but she sure as hell had a hand in killing Jeb just the same. She might not have baked the cake that actually did poor Jeb in, but she sure as hell killed him by making my life so miserable that I had to do it myself—by making *Daddy's* life so miserable that he had to leave me and go to Hollywood and not take me with him, just leave me here in Texas all by myself, sitting in the trailer with no one to talk to every single day of my life and nothing to do but amble over to the big rocks and play with goddamned dirt! Gosh dang it! Maybe if Mother hadn't been such a sorry excuse for a wife, Daddy would've stayed in love with her—and if he'd stayed in love with her, then maybe all three of us would be in Hollywood, together, right this very minute, soaking up the sunshine and feeling fine as wine, and I wouldn't have been all alone without my daddy all these years, living with a drunk-ass mother and just waiting and waiting for my sweet daddy to come get me like he promised to do but never did and I don't know why! I throw my hands over my face, but it's no use—I can't stop the waterworks from shooting out of me like a geyser.

Mother can refuse to look at me all she likes, if that's how she makes herself feel better about what she did to me all these years, but I know the truth: Mother might as well have killed Jeb herself.

Chapter 13

18 Years 4 Months Old
598 Days Before Killing Kurtis

"Point your chin up a bit, Buttercup," the photographer says. "Yeah, just a little more. Perfect, just like that."

The camera shutter clicks rapidly.

"That's too much, baby," Kurtis interjects. He's standing right behind the photographer, his eyes like laser beams. "Put your chin down."

I tilt my face down and raise my eyes. My nerves are jangling like spurs, but I just keep reminding myself that Marilyn herself did a bunch of nudie pictures before her acting career took off. When Kurtis suggested we do a "preacher's daughter" photo spread for his stupid girlie magazine three months ago, I said I'd do it—but that doesn't mean I'm not sweating bullets about it. Of course, I had two conditions before I'd agree to the photo shoots. "First," I said, "I'll only do nudie-cuties if the pictures are gonna make me into a legendary actress, Kurtis."

"Yes, baby, 'a legendary actress seen by audiences in cineplexes all over the world,'" Kurtis responded, smiling. "Trust me, these pictures are just the first step toward making you a star."

I squinted at him, trying to decide if I believed him.

"What's your second condition?" Kurtis asked, his eyes sparkling at me.

"I'll be a nudie-cutie—*on top only*—but I'm not gonna let my titties flap in the breeze like they're hanging on a line to dry. You've gotta promise the photos will leave something to the imagination."

Kurtis twisted his mouth and looked thoughtful for a moment, like he was considering his options. "Well, you can't totally cover up—I mean, this is for *Casanova,* after all. We've got standards."

I remained immovable, staring at him.

Kurtis continued thinking about the situation for another moment. "But I suppose we can make your shyness a selling point," he finally declared, and I could see the gears in his brain turning. "Yeah, we'll make it a monthly series for three or four consecutive issues—a 'good girl' series, starting with you as a buttoned-up preacher's daughter and moving on from there." Now his juices were really flowing. "Yeah, you can keep your bottoms on the whole series, honey. That's fine. And we'll keep you semi-covered on top—at first. With each installment of the series, we'll get more and more revealing. It'll be a long tease." His eyes devoured me. "Because everyone loves a good tease."

And so it was.

A month later, when my first "preacher's daughter" pictures finally came out in the magazine, Kurtis proved himself to be some sort of porno-genius. People did, it turned out, love a good tease, and then some. Even though my praying arms modestly covered my boobs in all the shots and my pictures were tucked away in the back of the magazine, that issue went flying off the shelves.

"You got twice as much fan mail as the spread-eagle-centerfold did," Kurtis hooted. "You're every man's fantasy, baby. We're on to something here."

The following month, for my second pictorial in the magazine, I reckon the preacher's daughter grew up to become a topless Sunday school teacher. And yet again, even though I covered my lady lumps with my hands that time, too, that issue was an even bigger success than the last one.

For my third photo shoot, the preacher's-daughter-Sunday-school-teacher apparently went away to college and joined a sorority—a sorority that's not all that fussy about its members wearing shirts, I reckon. With Kurtis looking on from behind the photographer, just like he's doing today, I posed for the camera, looking studious (and hot and bothered) while keeping my arms crossed over my bare chest. But that time, unlike the two prior photo sessions, Kurtis started cooing at me from behind the photographer to uncross my arms and put 'em over my head.

Of course, my first instinct was to say no. But then, when I saw the way Kurtis was looking at me, like he was waiting on me before taking his next breath, I felt a kind of electricity surge into my body—a delicious kind of zap that hit me right between the legs and vibrated throughout my sacred places—and I suddenly *wanted* to do it. Wordlessly, without taking my eyes off Kurtis, I pivoted my body away from the camera—away from Kurtis' blazing eyes—and brought my forearms to rest on top of my head. And even though the photographer was there, clicking away furiously at my side-boob, it suddenly felt like Kurtis and I were the only two people in the room.

I stared at Kurtis, silently, my chin straining over my shoulder, my body humming with that delicious electricity and the bull's-eye in my panties tingling like crazy—and I felt like a magnet to Kurtis' steel. When I licked my lips with my tongue and then bit my lower lip, Kurtis blinked slowly and practically convulsed on the spot. It was then that I knew Kurtis wanted me so bad, he'd stop at nothing to get me. If Kurtis had been married right then, his first wife would have been burnt toast—and if he'd belonged to a church, he gladly would have been excommunicated to get inside me. And, hot damn, the crazy part was I wanted Kurtis just as badly, too. I wanted nothing but to be his queen.

Of course, the side-boob shots were a sensation when they finally came out in *Casanova.* Apparently, every pervert who reads Kurtis' stupid magazine gets his rocks off watching a good girl slowly turning bad.

And now, here I am, at yet another good-girl photo shoot—my fourth and, hopefully, final one— wearing nothing but a little white hat, a stethoscope, and itty-bitty white panties emblazoned with a red cross on the front (because apparently, our now-famous preacher's-daughter-Sunday-school-teacher-sorority-girl furthered her education at nursing school.) I'm standing in front of the photographer guy and Kurtis, arching my back, trying to make my face look like I'm one matchstick away from a forest fire—and all the while, covering my boobs with my forearm. Gosh dang it, it's cold as a frosted frog in here.

"Pucker your lips a little, Buttercup," the photographer suggests.

I pucker.

"Yeah, that's good—"

"But keep an innocent look in your eyes," Kurtis interrupts.

"Like this?" I make my eyes wide and innocent, yet sultry.

"Yeah, baby," Kurtis says. "That's good. Make it sexy—but keep it sweet."

"Okay." I try to look simultaneously pure as the virgin snow on the faraway hills and yet hotter than a billy goat's ass in a pepper patch—all while freezing my titties off in this cold studio. The whole exercise is like trying to pick up a cow patty by the clean end.

"That's good, baby," Kurtis says. "Real good." He turns to the photographer. "What aperture are you set on?"

The photographer rolls his eyes. "It varies with every angle." He winks at me. "How 'bout a little smile, Buttercup?"

I give him a little smile.

"More of a smirk, baby," Kurtis says. "But keep your eyes innocent. Just let the corner of your mouth slide up, slightly. Yeah, like that. Oh, baby, yeah, just like that." Kurtis looks at me like I'm a needle and he wants to poke his thread through my eye. "You're something else, baby." He grunts like a gorilla. "You're a fucking knockout, you know that?" He leans his head toward the photographer. "How are you metering this?"

"Both in-camera and manually. I got it, Kurtis." The photographer smiles at me. "Buttercup, why don't you try—"

"Hey, honey," Kurtis interrupts. "Do me a favor. Look away for a second and then back at me."

I do as I'm told and the camera clicks away.

"Yeah, that's good. Just like that. Good. One more time. Yes. Now straighten your back."

"How's this?" I ask, straightening my back, taking great care to keep my bare chest covered with my forearm.

"Nice. Now, honey, look right at the camera the way you always look at me right after I kiss you." His voice is husky now. "Look at the camera how you do when we're all alone—when it's just me and you and I'm doing that thing you like so much. Oh, God, baby, yes, that's it. Holy shit, yes, that's it." Kurtis practically growls that last part. The thing he's referring to, the thing I like so much is when Kurtis kisses me between my legs. Holy hell, yes, I sure do like that a lot.

Right quick after Kurtis licked me for the very first time, I knew I had to find me a caveat to my preacher-daddy-vow of chastity lickety-split (pun intended)—so I explained to Kurtis that letting him kiss and lick me on my sacred places was allowed, believe it or not, every single day, in fact, if he was willing, because Kurtis' pecker stays in his pants and outside of me when he does it.

Kurtis just laughed when I said that. "Ah, so you've found a loophole, have you, baby?" He winked at me. "Well, good for you, baby—good for you."

"Kurtis," the photographer says, motioning for Kurtis to lean in and listen to him.

Kurtis looks annoyed at the photographer's interruption, but he peels his eyes off me, anyway (which seems to takes a Herculean effort), and gives the photographer his ear. "*What?*"

"Can she put her arms behind her?" the photographer asks softly, but loud enough for me to hear. "Can we get a full topless with an arched back this time?"

Kurtis considers. "Not showing everything is what makes her different. She's shy. She's"—he looks back at me, his eyes blazing—"*pure*."

I smile at Kurtis. That's right, honey. I'm pure.

And, actually, it's the truth. When Kurtis (and the photographer) glimpsed my side-boob at the last photo shoot, it was the first time any man had ever seen any part of my naked boobs. (Dr. Ishikawa doesn't count 'cause he's a doctor and he only got to see my old boobs, anyway—and even when I've let Kurtis lick me and kiss me between my legs under my skirt, I've adamantly kept my clothes on.) The truth is nobody's seen me fully naked, ever. Even through months of increasingly hot and steamy hanky-panky with Kurtis, I've managed to keep my clothes on my body while we've pretty much performed every variation of third base we could think of—except for me sucking on him—I've steadfastly refused to do that. "No, Kurtis," I explained. "'No sex' means your pecker's gotta stay out of me—no matter what opening."

Of course, after all these months, Kurtis has tried his mighty best to get me to change my mind about that sucking thing and about sex in general, of course, or, at the very least, about me taking my clothes off for him. But I've refused on all counts, citing my solemn vow to my daddy. But frankly, it's getting harder and harder to resist Kurtis, especially ever since I started letting him kiss and lick me between my legs. Good lord, when he does that to me, it makes me want to spread my legs afterwards and let him burrow deep, deep, deep inside me. Shoot, the way I scream and whimper when he's doing it to me, I'm surprised Kurtis hasn't just ripped my clothes clean off me and barreled right in anyway.

But he hasn't. In fact, although he begs and coaxes me every single day to let him finally slide his junk inside me, nice and deep, Kurtis is always the perfect gentleman when I turn him down. It's almost like a small piece of him likes me telling him no (though, of course, a much larger piece of him—namely, the rather large and hard piece of him that's straining up from between his legs—desperately wants to hear me say yes, yes, yes).

By now, after all the fooling around we've done, I reckon I actually want Kurtis to finally plow me as badly as he does. So bad, in fact, I'm starting to not trust myself to keep saying no. But the thing is, no matter how fierce my body's own urges have become, my brain knows my only card in this poker game with Kurtis is my V-card—a rare and irreplaceable commodity. Even if my crotch is ready to scream, "Come to Momma!" my head doesn't wanna lose my most valuable bargaining chip without the promise of a kingdom in return. I reckon keeping Kurtis outta home base, at least 'til our Marilyn movie's rounding second base, is the only way to keep my lusty porno king focused on fulfilling my destiny. But I don't know how much longer either of us can hang on. Especially me.

The photographer fidgets. "She might be pure, Kurtis," he concedes, treading carefully, "but *pure* ain't gonna sell magazines forever. We've gotta get the money shot sooner or later."

The muscles in Kurtis' jaw pulse in and out. He's thinking. After a minute, he exhales and walks past the blazing lights over to me. He puts a hand on my cheek. "Baby—"

"I didn't come to Hollywood to be a centerfold star," I whisper, keeping my chest firmly covered by my forearm. "I came here to be a movie star."

"I know," he says softly, dropping his hand. "But you gotta trust me. This is all part of the plan."

"Kurtis Jackman, I came here to fulfill my destiny to pick up the torch lit first by Lana and handed off to Marilyn—"

"—and to carry it ever-farther into the catacombs of history. I know, honey," Kurtis interrupts, smiling broadly. "And you will."

I scowl. I don't like being interrupted, especially when I'm talking about my sacred destiny.

Kurtis sticks out his lower lip, mocking my scowl, and when I twist my face up even more, he smiles broadly. "Baby, you're the cutest little thing ever, you know that?"

"Kurtis," I say, chastising him, "I'm not a centerfold. I'm an *actress*."

"Baby, listen. Marilyn herself did a whole bunch of full-frontal shots, and now, those pictures are part of her mythology. Back in the day, those pictures were what made her an 'It' girl."

"I don't need any help becoming an 'It' girl, honey. I'm already an 'It' girl. Just look at me, for cryin' out loud; you can't get any more 'it' than this."

Kurtis chuckles. "That's for damned sure." He touches my cheek again.

There's a beat as I consider the situation, biting on the inside of my cheek.

"Buttercup, will you just trust me, for Chrissakes?" Kurtis says. "All I'm trying to do is make you a star. Don't you know that?"

I'm surprised at the earnestness in Kurtis' eyes. He rubs my cheek with his thumb. "I know exactly what I'm doing, baby," he whispers. "You gotta trust me."

I glance over at the photographer. He's staring at us, blatantly eavesdropping. Now my eyes go back to Kurtis. Once again, the sincerity in his eyes surprises me. I look at him sideways. "So lemme see if I understand the situation correctly, Kurtis Jackman. You want me to put my naked boobies on full-frontal display in the presence of a mortal man *for the very first time in the history of the world* right here and now, in front of you—*and* this photographer-man?"

Kurtis' eyes ignite like someone just turned his gas barbeque onto high. He abruptly turns to the photographer. "Take a break, Phil," he barks. "*Outside*."

Kurtis' chest heaves up and down as I stand before him in nothing but my tiny undies, my arms crossed over my chest. We're standing four feet apart in a crowded supply closet at the back of the photo studio.

"I've never done this before," I whisper, my voice trembling.

Kurtis nods, apparently too overcome to speak. He lets out a shaky breath. Even from here, I can see his erection bulging in his pants.

"You're about to become the first man, ever, that's gonna see me in just my skivvies and a smile—head-on, in all my glory, both boobs at the same time."

Kurtis grunts and nods again. His nostrils flare.

"Because you mean just that much to me, Kurtis Jackman."

Kurtis' eyes are trained on me like he's a heart attack and I'm CPR.

"I'm glad it's you, Kurtis," I say. "I wouldn't want it to be anyone but you."

He groans with anticipation.

My crotch feels like it's filling up with warm Jell-O. I exhale and drop my arms to my sides. My nipples instantly harden under his gaze. I can barely stand still, I'm tingling so much between my legs.

Kurtis groans as he takes in the grandeur of my naked torso and boobs. "Oh, baby," he murmurs, "you're gorgeous." His eyes are blazing hotter than a two-dollar whore on nickel night. He continues appraising me with a kind of reverence and awe for another seven seconds or so, and then that's it— he's on me like a cheap suit, a sudden flurry of fingers and lips and wet tongue and voracious puffs of warm air all over my bare skin.

I throw my head back and jolt as his lips find my erect nipples and cry out when his wet tongue swirls around and around. He slams me into the wall of the closet, kissing me, attacking me, inhaling me, pressing himself into me, and before I can even think about what I'm doing, I wrap my leg around his waist and smash myself into him, feverishly rubbing my crotch against that bulge in his pants, aching for him to penetrate me and scratch my voracious itch. Kurtis responds to my fervor by moaning and grinding into me, right into the spot where I'm yearning for him the most.

His fingers reach inside my panties, busy as a bee in a tar barrel, and I shriek at the outrageous sensation. When his fingers slip inside me, my body ignites like a matchbox lit with a blowtorch and my shrieks turn to guttural moans. And when his fingers begin massaging the exact spot that's throbbing uncontrollably for him, I jolt and buck violently in his brawny arms. "Wes—" I scream, and quickly bite my tongue.

Holy motherfucking shit-on-a-stick, I almost shouted Wesley's goddamned name. Good lord, that would have been catastrophic—the death knell to my sacred destiny. "What's..." I say, trying to camouflage the name that almost shot out of my mouth. "What's happening to me?"

Holy hell. That's just the kind of higgledy-piggledy thing that happens when you let body parts besides your brains lead you out of the barn—you wind up with an ejaculation that'll fuck up the trajectory of your entire life.

But Kurtis hasn't heard a word I've said, anyhow. His hand retreats quickly from my wetness and fumbles desperately with his fly. I open my legs wider and jerk my pelvis into him, desperate for him to finally, *finally* plunge his hard-on inside me and rip me in two—oh God, yes, please—I want him deep, deep, deep inside me—but then I suddenly lurch back to my senses and leap out of his arms, even as my hips are jerking and thrusting like a dog humping his owner's leg. "No!" I shriek, my knees wobbling.

"Aw, fuck!" Kurtis shouts, his voice ragged. "Come on! I'm losing my fucking mind over here!" His cheeks are bright red.

I take a giant step back from him and cross my arms over my chest, panting, my crotch throbbing mercilessly, my knees barely able to support my weight. Oh good lord, I'm in physical pain between my legs.

Kurtis looks as pained as I feel. "I've never waited this long for a woman, ever," he pleads. "*Please,* Buttercup."

I'm breathless, yearning, aching. Oh God, I want him. I feel physically sick with this intense ache. "I've told you a million times," I sputter, gasping for air, "we can't eat supper before we've said grace." I tighten my arms across my chest, and cross my legs, trying to quell the pounding inside my crotch. "And anyway, do you want my very first time to be like this?" I look around the small storage closet. "Is that all you think of me?" My tone is scolding, verging on angry—but it's an act. Oh good lord, I'm giving the performance of a lifetime. Because the truth is I want him—in a storage closet, on the floor, in a bed, in a car, in a back alley, anywhere—I don't care where we do it, as long as we just do it already.

"No, that's not all I think of you." He puts his junk away and zips back up. "I think you're a goddamned fucking angel; that's what I think of you." He moves to me and grabs my shoulders, his eyes burning into mine. "I think you're gorgeous. And pure. And so goddamned *good.*" His voice quavers a bit. "You're *good,* Buttercup, and I'm so, so bad." Now his voice catches with a flood of emotion. "Before I met you, I didn't even know I wanted to be good—I thought I was happy being bad." He pulls me into a fierce embrace and talks right into my ear. "I just wanna get inside your goodness, baby, that's all, deep inside you, so you can save me from myself." His voice is suddenly low and intense. "I just wanna be good like *you.*"

My mouth hangs open.

Kurtis inhales and exhales deeply for a moment, his breathing ragged and shaky, apparently trying to collect himself. Finally, he pulls away from our embrace, his face set in resignation. "You're right. Your first time can't be in a fucking closet. You're too good for that." His voice is thick with emotion. He swallows hard. "You're too good for *me.*"

There's a beat, neither of us apparently knowing what to say or do.

Finally, I nod in agreement. That's right. I'm good. And pure. And my first time can't be in a fucking closet. That's right.

"I'm sorry," he says.

I nod again. If I speak, I'll surely tell him to forget everything I just said and take me now, right here on the floor—to hurry up and get inside me, deep inside me, and make this painful throbbing finally go away.

"I'm gonna make you a big star, baby," Kurtis says.

I don't respond for a long beat. "I don't wanna be a centerfold star," I finally manage to say. "I wanna be a movie star."

"I know. And you will be."

"But I still haven't set foot on a movie set since coming to Hollywood."

Kurtis lets out a deep sigh. "I keep telling you, baby. One thing leads to another. I'm still putting all the pieces together. I'm working hard to get investors lined up for our movie—but first things first: I gotta get everyone buzzing about you. Trust me."

I scowl.

"Let's go back in there and make history, huh? Let's take these pictures and give the world something it's never seen before. When everyone finally sees you in all your glory like I just did, holy fuck, you're gonna give the world a global orgasm."

"Can't we just do side-boob again? The world seemed to have a pretty big orgasm over that."

Kurtis puts his finger under my chin and tilts my face up to him. He leans in and kisses me softly, tenderly. His kiss is so sweet, so full of reverence, in fact, it actually makes me swoon a little bit, if you want to know the truth—not just in my panties but in my heart, too. "No, the world's got a global *hard-on* for you, baby," he whispers. "What I just saw is gonna give them the fucking *orgasm*."

I can't help but smile.

Kurtis smiles back at me. "Baby, if you go back out there and drop your arms for the camera the way you just did for me, these photos are gonna be *legendary*." He bites his lip, considering something. "I have something for you," he finally says. He pulls a little black velvet box out of his jacket pocket. "I was gonna give this to you at dinner tonight, but it makes more sense to give it to you now so you can wear it in the photos."

My heart is clanging in my chest as Kurtis hands me the little box.

I open it with shaky hands.

There's a necklace inside. A cross, inlaid with sparkling diamonds. And at the top of the cross, there's a singular diamond the size of Kermit, Texas, set in the middle of the star of Bethlehem. I look up at Kurtis, speechless.

"Because you're my Preacher's Daughter—and I'm going to make you the biggest star this world has ever seen."

My heart is exploding right now. I've never felt quite like this before, the way I feel with Kurtis in this moment. This is the happiest moment of my entire life.

Kurtis laughs. "Well, aren't you gonna say something, honey?" Tears spring into my eyes and Kurtis laughs again. "Aw, honey. Don't cry. I got this for you to make you smile."

"I'm so happy," I squeak out. "Oh, Kurtis."

"I got this for you so you understand how I feel about you." His eyes sparkle at me and I blush. "Let me put it on you, baby," Kurtis coos. I turn around, trembling with the adrenaline surging through me, and he secures the clasp under my hair. He turns me back around to face him and grips my shoulders firmly. "I'm gonna make you a star, baby. You just have to trust me."

I nod.

"Okay?"

"Okay, Kurtis."

He exhales, obviously relieved. "So, are you ready to go out there and take those legendary photos now?"

I wipe my eyes and nod. The way I'm feeling right now, I'd agree to do just about anything Kurtis asked of me, any little thing—no matter how naughty—even let him take my body all the way to home base and back again, any which way—if only he'd promise on a stack of bibles never to leave me all alone in this world. Suddenly, in this unexpectedly heart-stopping moment, I don't care about showing my titties off to the entire world—I don't even care about fulfilling my sacred destiny. All I care about is being with Kurtis—being safe and warm in his arms and letting him love me and take care of me and make my heart and my panties explode. Forever and ever. Maybe *that's* my sacred destiny, after all. I wipe my eyes again.

Kurtis hugs me to him and nuzzles into my hair. "You're so good, baby. So pure and good. I just wanna be good like you."

I melt into him. My heart is exploding in my chest like fireworks on the Fourth of July. I like being good for Kurtis. I've never wanted to be bad—it's just that I've had no choice in the past. Maybe, now, with Kurtis, this is my chance to start fresh and become the good and sweet girl he thinks I am. The good and sweet girl I've always wanted to be.

"I'm gonna give you the world, baby," Kurtis coos.

"Oh, Kurtis," I say, tears pricking my eyes. I squeeze him tight, bursting to tell him I'm ready to give him the world, too—a sky full of stars—that I don't care about anything except making him happy for the rest of my life. I touch the cross around my neck and shudder with excitement. It's my most prized possession—the best thing I've ever owned. I'll wear it forever and ever, every day of my life, and remember this moment as I do.

Kurtis kisses me and the sensation zings me right between the legs like he just shocked me there with a cattle brand. Oh good lord, I'm ready—he can take me now. He can have all of me, every square inch, inside and out. I don't care about the kingdom. I don't care about audiences seeing me in cineplexes around the world. I just want Kurtis to love me and never, ever leave. I disengage from our kiss and look at his handsome face. "Kurtis, I have something important to tell you." My cheeks are blazing with heat—with the *love* I feel for this beautiful man. "I want—"

"Yes, I know what you want," he says, his eyes twinkling. "And, honey, I'm gonna give it to you, I promise."

I hold my breath in anticipation of whatever he's gonna say next.

"You're gonna go out there and pose for these legendary photos for me, and then I'm gonna give you the world— something I've never given anyone else before." His eyes light up at what he's about to say next. "Baby, I'm gonna make you next month's cover girl, centerfold, and *'Casanova cutie'—all at the same time.*"

Chapter 14

16 Years Old
1,575 Days Before Killing Kurtis

I'm lying on my side on my cot at the group home. It's time for chores, but Mrs. Clements is letting me off the hook, just this once. "Just stay in bed and rest for a while, dear," Mrs. Clements tells me when we get back from the courtroom.

As expected, the jury convicted Mother of Jeb's murder after only two days of deliberations, but, based on all the abuse Mother apparently suffered at Jeb's hands, they went with second-degree murder instead of first—even though, if you ask me, baking a rat-poison cake for your boyfriend is pretty dang good evidence of "premeditation" and "malice aforethought." But it's okay. All second degree murder means is that Mother's going to spend the rest of her life in prison instead of sizzling in the electric chair—which, I must admit, I was actually relieved to hear.

I'm confused right now. Even though everything's gone exactly according to my well-thought-out plans, other than the fact that I'm stuck here in this group home, of course, and even though I should feel downright celebratory today—seeing as how I've done the right thing in light of the totality of the circumstances—I actually feel as low as a toad in a dry well right now, just as sad as the ocean blue—and I can't understand why.

I turn on my other side. That jury bought everything I was selling to them, and then some. I was a star up on that witness stand. Mother never stood a chance. I exhale a long breath. And neither did poor Jeb. When I handed Jeb that fateful cake, the look of gratitude mixed with elation on his face was downright heartbreaking, if you want to know the truth. He just looked so touched, so gosh-dang touched, that I'd taken the time and effort, it made me want to reach out and swat that poisonous cake out of his hands. *But I didn't.*

"No one's ever baked a cake for me before," Jeb gushed, his face aglow. "I'm always the one baking cakes for everyone else."

"Well, not anymore you aren't, Jeb," I somehow managed to reply, even though my stomach was twisting and turning.

And that's when Jeb hugged me with such unfiltered joy and gratitude, I almost broke down and cried. But I didn't. I kept myself together and hugged him back, squeezing him as tight as my arms could muster. But then I heard Daddy's voice whispering in my ear, and I pulled back from our embrace. "You've gotta eat a huge slice, Jeb," I said, hopping back, my voice quavering. "Seeing as how this is the first cake anyone's ever made for you and all."

"And it's the first cake you've ever made all by yourself," Jeb added, "so I'm gonna eat an extra-large slice."

My stomach dropped into my toes, but I kept talking anyway. "Yeah, I'm not sure I did it right, but you'll eat it all up, right? Even it's awful?" I'd put in twice as much sugar as the recipe called for to mask any telltale poison flavor, if any—I have no idea what rat poison tastes like—but I figured it couldn't hurt to prime Jeb to ignore any weird aftertastes, anyway.

"You bet I will," Jeb replied, looking around. "Where's your momma? Is she in the back room?"

"Nope, she's still at work," I said, even though, yes, she was passed out like a hobo in the back room. "But, Jeb, I just can't wait for you to try my cake. Let's have a big piece now, even before you put your stuff away, and then we'll have another one when Momma gets home."

"Gosh, lemme think about it," Jeb responded, but his expression made it clear he was pleased as punch. And then, without further ado, he dug right into that cake, a huge smile on his face.

I flip onto my back on my cot and cross a forearm over my face. I feel like I'm gonna throw up—just like poor Jeb did after eating that big slice of cake.

There's a noisy bustle of activity downstairs in the main room where the other kids are doing their chores before supper.

The way Jeb's eyes bugged out and his body started convulsing, it's no wonder I was screaming and crying when I called 911—no acting required.

There's a clatter of silverware downstairs. I reckon they're setting the table for supper. I roll onto my side, my back facing the door. I sigh. That day in court, when Mother figured out it was me who baked Jeb's deadly cake, I didn't like the way she looked at me right then, like I'd just served her up a big piece of rat-cake, too. It was like the life siphoned out of her in that very instant, exactly the same way the life had drained so horribly out of Jeb. And I especially didn't like the way Mother looked at me like I'm evil. I'm not a bad person. I'm really not. In that one particular instance, I might have done a bad thing. But I was just doing what had to be done, that's all.

I hear footsteps behind my cot. A hand gently touches my shoulder. "Charlene."

I don't turn around. There's no need. I already know who it is. *Wesley*. It's always Wesley, staring at me and following me around like a lost puppy. The very first day I arrived at this hellhole and walked through the front door, Wesley's dopey face lit up like a Christmas tree at the mere sight of me, almost like he'd been dreaming of me his whole life, or maybe even praying to God for me, and here I finally was. "Charlene," I heard him say softly after Mrs. Clements introduced me to all the kids. "Thank you, Sweet Jesus."

I feel a tap on my shoulder. "Hey, Charlene?" Wesley's voice says. "Mrs. Clements told me to come get you for supper."

I roll over and face him. Wesley's a year younger than me. His face is riddled with pimples and his ears are too big. He's so damned skinny, he's got to stand up twice to cast a shadow. If he stuck out his tongue, he'd look like a zipper. I'm about to speak, about to tell him I'm not hungry, but then, much to my surprise, I begin to cry. These aren't planned tears. What are these tears? These are tears of ... I have no idea. But once they come, they won't stop.

"Oh, hey," Wesley says softly. He sits down on the edge of my cot and brushes the hair out of my eyes. "Hey, now, sshhh," Wesley says tenderly. He caresses my cheek. "Don't you worry, Charlene. Everything's gonna be all right." He brings both his hands to my face and wipes my tears with his thumbs. He looks into my eyes. "I'm gonna take care of you, Charlene. I promise. Okay? I'll always take care of you, 'til the end of time."

I don't know why I do it, but I suddenly sit up and kiss Wesley right on his mouth. When my lips touch his, he lets out a sort of a yelp, and I feel his body jerk with delighted surprise as he leans into my face and kisses me right back.

It's my first-ever kiss, and I'm surprised at the softness and warmth of it, and especially at how much I like it.

When we pull away from each other, Wesley's eyes are on fire.

"Don't call me Charlene," I say flatly, heat rising in my cheeks.

He licks his lips. "I'll call you whatever you want."

I bite my lip, assessing him. I can still taste him on my mouth.

"What do you want me to call you, Charlene? I'll call

you whatever you want," he repeats, his voice shaky and spiking with urgency. When I don't reply, he leans forward and lowers his eyelids, clearly hoping I'll kiss him again.

But I don't lean in. "Buttercup," I whisper, my heart aching. "I want you to call me Buttercup."

Chapter 15

16 Years Old
1,294 Days Before Killing Kurtis

"Later?" Wesley mouths at me as I brush past him in the kitchen. I don't know why, after all this time, Wesley even bothers to ask if I'll meet him later. Just about every day, during free time at the house, right after homework and chores, I meet him over yonder at the big oak tree near the ridge. And there, I let him kiss me. Over and over and over. What's suddenly gonna be different about today? Nothing, that's what. Every day is Happy Kissing Wesley Day as far as I'm concerned. That dopey boy should know that by now.

And, anyway, there's no reason for Wesley to wonder if today might be different from the last, because every day around here is same-ol', same-ol'—just one long, blurry waiting game. And the thing that irks me the most is that, according to Mr. and Mrs. Clements, all that sameness is on purpose. As Mrs. Clements likes to tell me, it's her "God-given mission" to "instill" a sense of "predictability" and "stability" and "structure" into the lives of us kids "*whom* the world has forgotten."

Mrs. Clements always makes a point of saying *whom*, like she's super proud of herself for knowing when to use *whom* instead of *who*, like it makes her some kind of genius or something. I swear, that woman has her nose so high in the air, she could drown in a rainstorm. Well, let me tell you, Mrs.

Clements can gussy up her "God-given mission" all she likes, but I know the simple truth. She just plain likes to tell us kids what we can and can't do.

Honestly, every day around here is a special kind of hell. I can't wait to get my butt out to Hollywood to find Daddy and live like a queen. But I can't go yet, not when I'm only sixteen. If I leave now, Mrs. Clements would undoubtedly report me as missing or tell the police I'm a runaway. And I don't want anyone, least of all the police, knowing who I am and looking for me and snooping into my business.

No, as hard as it is, I've got to wait to make my move 'til I age out of the foster care system. I've only got a year and change to wait, and then I'm heading out west. Once I age out, I'll be free as a bird and no one will be able to tell me what I can and can't do, ever again. But until then, I've got to bide my time and wait patiently like any diligent and rule-following young lady would. And it sure does help that I've got Wesley to keep me company while I wait to age-out.

But the sameness of everything, the routine of it all, the fact that I've got to do as I'm told every single day of my life? It makes my blood boil. Every single morning, at the exact same time each day, I've got to get up and get my butt over to an actual school. Daddy would be furious, but there's no way around it, at least for now.

At least it's not a real school, though. It's a "continuation school" for "at-risk kids" and "kids with special problems." I'm not quite sure how I fit into that rubric, seeing as how the only thing I'm "at-risk" for is losing my mind from boredom, and my "special problem" is that I'm trapped in a classroom with small-minded teachers handing out multiple-choice tests. But whether I like it or not, it seems my lack of formal education before now makes me "special" in the eyes of the deep thinkers at the school district.

My saving grace in all this sameness and rule following, besides getting to spend time with Wesley, of course, is that school's only a part-time endeavor for me, since I tested through the roof in reading and writing and problem-solving and "analysis," whatever that is. Even though I've got to go to school in the mornings to listen to dumbass-teachers talk about useless things like the Pythagorean Theorem and cell mitosis and the War of 1812, Mrs. Clements agreed to a home study program for me for everything else. Thanks to that small mercy, for a few hours each day, when everyone else is out of the house at school or work, I get to stay at the house, all by myself, and lie on my cot and read and read and read. If it weren't for that time alone with my books, I'd probably go a little bit crazy, to tell you the truth, what with Mrs. Clements always wanting to chat me up and make sure I'm "doing okay." But even though I'm about to blow a gasket at any given moment, I never let anyone know it. I let them think I'm everything they want me to be—just like Marilyn did.

Sometimes, though not very often, I lie in my cot when I'm all alone, and I cry buckets of tears. I'm not sure exactly why. I reckon it's because I miss Daddy. I can't even remember exactly what he looks like anymore. I try to picture the exact curve of his lips, or the slant of his sideburns, or the particular twinkle of his eyes, but I just can't bring it to mind. And that makes me cry big, soggy tears.

Sometimes I think about how Jeb looked at me just before he fell to the ground, convulsing. And I feel awfully bad about that. I don't feel bad that he's dead, of course, because there could be no other ending to poor Jeb's story, I'm sorry to say, but I don't like to remember how Jeb looked at me in that very last instant, like he knew it was me who sent him to meet his maker. I reckon I just liked it better when Jeb thought I was good and kind, just like how Mrs. Monaghan thought about me, too. And how Mrs. Clements thinks of me now. I like it when people think I'm good. Because, honestly, I am. I just had to do one bad thing, that's all—because I had no choice. I reckon the bottom line is I don't mind Jeb opening himself up a worm farm in the ground so much as I don't like him knowing he opened it up on account of me.

As I throw my banana peel into the trash can in the kitchen, I nod almost imperceptibly at Wesley—really, it's more of a conscious blink of my eyes in his direction—to confirm that, yes, I'll meet him later today during free time for our usual round of kissing and talking. Of course, I will. Meeting with Wesley's the only good thing I've got in this whole, wide world and I wouldn't miss our time together for anything.

After I'm sure Wesley's seen my subtle nod to him, I march straight out of the kitchen without another glance so that Mrs. Clements doesn't suspect a thing about Wesley and me. Mrs. Clements watches all of us kids like a hawk, and me in particular ever since we got "so close" at Mother's "tragic" trial almost a year ago, and there's no doubt in my mind she'd have a problem, a *big* problem, if she ever found out about all the kissing Wesley and I do (and especially how much I enjoy it). I mean, Wesley and I live under the same roof, after all, so she'd probably think we're doing a whole lot more than kissing, even though we aren't, and I'd like to keep Mrs. Clements thinking I'm good and pure, if I can. Keeping her thinking that way about me let's me keep thinking that way about myself, I reckon.

And, anyway, no one, not even me, could ever understand Wesley and me. Since I'm a full year older than Wesley, and since girls tend to develop earlier than boys, I look like a full-blown woman while Wesley still looks like a gawky boy. And it's not just the age difference and uneven development that make us a higgledy-piggledy pair. Even if we were the same age and developed equally, we'd nevertheless be an affront to the natural order of things, him and me. I mean, Wesley's just... *Wesley*.

Sometimes, when Wesley and I are kissing, I suddenly think to myself, *this is like Marilyn Monroe kissing Scooby Doo*. Or, better yet, we're like a sports car kissing a wheelbarrow, or a cheetah kissing Goofy. Or, I reckon most accurately, we're like Marilyn kissing Goofy. Because Wesley really is just a big, dopey, cartoon-like puppy, and I'm a legendary beauty for the ages. And yet, I never feel so darned good as I do as when I'm kissing Wesley under the big oak tree and he's telling me his stories and promising to take care of me forever and ever—oh, and, of course, telling me I'm the prettiest girl in the whole wide world, too.

Of course, Wesley's right about that last thing. I'm damned pretty. Actually, over the past year, I've watched myself blossom into the most stunningly gorgeous creature I've ever seen, just as jaw-droppingly gorgeous as Lana when she walked into that malt shop and got herself discovered in Hollywood, just as awe-inspiring as any picture of Marilyn I've ever seen, even the one of her in the billowing white dress.

All I need is platinum blonde hair and I'll be a ringer for Lana and Marilyn. Well, and some big boobs, too. My boobs aren't quite as big as I'd like them to be, to be perfectly honest. But my skin is clear; my eyes are big and blue; my cheeks are high; and my lips are as full and pouty and luscious as can be. I'm stunning to look at is what I am—it's an objective fact. Whenever Mr. Clements is watching his baseball on television, I can plainly see in no uncertain terms that I'm as beautiful as any of the models in the commercials, even the ones in bikinis selling beer.

Mrs. Clements knows I'm pretty as a picture, too. A million times, she's said to me, "Charlene, you are just the most beautiful thing. One day, honey, you're going to have the world at your feet." And every time she says that, I always say the same thing back to her: "Why, thank you, Mrs. Clements. I sure do hope so."

Chapter 16

18 Years 6 Months Old
559 Days Before Killing Kurtis

"Oh... hello," Kurtis' crusty old secretary says when I waltz through the front door of his office. She looks nervously back at Kurtis' closed door. "Um, is Mr. Jackman expecting you?"

"Hello, Mildred," I purr. "No, Kurtis isn't expecting me today. I'm here to surprise him." And, of course, to tell him I'm sick and tired of waiting for my final "good-girl-who-conveniently-forgot-her-shirt" photos to come out in his stupid girlie magazine—the ones with the full-frontal boob shots he says are gonna make me a star.

When Kurtis saw those pictures come back from the photographer, I swear he lost his marbles. "These are even better than I thought they'd be," he said, his voice dripping with desire. "These pictures are gonna be bigger than anything we've ever done before, baby."

Right after that, Kurtis got right to work planning some sort of "special double issue" featuring me, but it's been taking forever and a day. "Soon," he keeps telling me. "Be patient. It's going to be worth the wait." But I'm tired of waiting. If this photo spread's gonna make me into a legendary movie star like Kurtis keeps promising, then let's get crackin' already.

It's quite obvious Kurtis thinks he can distract me by throwing wads of cash at me for endless shopping sprees, and sending flowers to me all the time, and buying me new books to read out by his pool, but honestly I don't care about any of it. What he doesn't realize is I've been waiting around for one thing or another my entire life, and I'm done waiting. I begin marching toward Kurtis' office door. "I'll just go in and surprise him," I flutter brightly.

"No," Mildred shouts, much too loudly for the small room. She leaps up, her eyes bulging with panic. "Mr. Jackman's in a meeting. He said no interruptions." She looks like I've threatened to toss her favorite puppy out a thirty-story window.

Mildred's agitation has the opposite effect on me than she intends. In a heartbeat, I lunge toward Kurtis' office door and fling it open. Kurtis instantly snaps his scowling face toward the suddenly wide-open door, clearly ready to berate whoever has dared interrupt his "meeting," but when he sees me, his face instantly contorts into an expression of faux-happy surprise.

Lord have mercy.

Kurtis is standing face-to-face with a buxom brunette. They're both standing together on *his* side of the desk, which isn't a natural sight.

Damn, this woman's got the biggest boobs I ever did see.

His face is flushed. So is hers.

The woman smooths the front of her dress. Holy hell, it's clinging to her curves so tight and short, I can see all the way to Christmas.

Kurtis pushes that big-boobed, dark-haired hussy out of his way and strides across his office to greet me, tucking his shirt into his pants as he goes.

I clench my jaw. Kurtis is never unbuttoned or untucked.

"Baby doll," Kurtis booms, reaching for me. "What are you doing here?"

I stand stock-still, my eyes fixed on that woman, the

gears in my mind click-clacking away. I've seen this woman before. I'm sure of it. A sparkling heart-shaped pendant around her neck catches my eye, and, instantly, I remember where I've seen her before. This woman is Bettie Paigette—Bettie Big Boobs.

I turn my gaze to Kurtis, anti-freeze and molten lava simultaneously filling my veins.

Kurtis clears his throat. "Bettie, I think that about covers everything," he says stiffly. "Just tell Johnny to get you whatever you need."

"Sure thing, Kurtis." She looks at me, suppressing a smirk. "Uh... *Mr. Jackman,* that is. Thanks." She touches the pendant around her neck and smiles at me.

Kurtis clears his throat again. "Okay, then, that's all," he mutters.

Bettie passes Kurtis on the way to the door, swinging her hips and flashing him a mega-watt smile as she goes—but Kurtis doesn't return Bettie's smile. His face remains etched in stone, even as his cheeks are turning beet-red.

And that does it. Even if I were dumb as a box of rocks and somehow hadn't figured out what was going on before now, Kurtis just gave himself away by not returning Bettie's smile. Because Kurtis Jackman never fails to return a smile, especially from a woman. He's a back-slapping, belly-laughing, wide-smiling, never-met-a-stranger kind of a guy who'll do just about anything to get people to like him, especially the pretty people. If Kurtis and Bettie Big Boobs had honestly been engaged in some sort of "business meeting," then Kurtis sure as hell would have returned that woman's smile with ease. But he didn't. And, therefore, they weren't.

Bettie Big Boobs shuffles past me toward the door, not even gracing me with a glance, and Kurtis, yet again revealing the depth of his duplicity, lets her leave without even an introduction.

The moment Bettie's gone from the room, Kurtis wraps

me in a bear hug. I can smell her on him. "Hello, baby. Did you get the flowers I had delivered to the house today?"

Yes, I got his flowers, the same as always—red roses surrounded by buttercups. I'm sure that man single-handedly keeps Hollywood Flowers in business the way he keeps sending them to me. But I don't give a crap about flowers right now. I stare him down. "Kurtis Jackman, what the hell's going on between you and that *woman*?" If I were being true to myself, I would have used words with a little more backbone than "hell" and "woman," but Kurtis thinks I'm as sweet as a bee's behind, and, even in my current state of rage, I'd like to keep him thinking that way.

"What are you talking about? Bettie *works* for me, baby. *Down at the club.*" His face flashes indignation, but I'm not buying it for a second. Clearly, this man would piss on my leg and tell me it's raining.

I don't speak for a long moment, letting Kurtis squirm in the silence. "Kurtis Jackman, don't you lie to me," I finally whisper, suppressing tears.

Kurtis actually looks like he's considering confessing his sins to me, but then, in a heartbeat, his expression makes a U-turn and it's clear he's decided to stick with his story. "We were having a business meeting," he declares.

"A business meeting about what?"

He pauses, apparently wondering if the answer to this question is gonna help him or hurt him. "Um, Bettie's gonna be in one of my films."

I slap Kurtis across the face. Hard. "You're making a movie with *her?*" Tears instantly spring out of my eyes. I turn to leave the room.

Kurtis grabs my arm. "Baby, no." His cheek is blazing red where I slapped him. "I mean, yes, I'm making a movie with her—but not a legitimate movie, not like the movie I'm making for you. She's gonna be in one of my *adult* films." He grins like this explanation makes everything all better. And, honestly, if all these two were up to was making a porno together, it actually would make everything all better because I couldn't care less how many pornos Kurtis makes or with *whom*. The man spends money like it's water, and I reckon it's gotta come from somewhere.

But a porno's not all that's going on here. No, what's really going on here is Kurtis is screwing Bettie Big Boobs. And that's not okay. In fact, that's a whole big bunch of bullshit. If Kurtis thinks he's gonna get away with screwing Bettie Big Boobs even as he woos me and whispers sweet nothings into my ear and tries to lure me into his bed and licks my lady-parts and begs me to save him and make him good, then he can go hug a root. I am Charlie Wilber's Daughter, after all.

Even more importantly for my destiny, though, Kurtis sleeping with Bettie Big Boobs *and* making a movie with her, porno or not, is an unacceptable combination. Kurtis is a weak-willed man with the disposition of a gosh-dang thermometer. At any given moment, I'd guess he's one good screw away from deciding that Bettie Big Boobs, not me, should star in the epic, mainstream feature he's been dreaming about making his whole life.

I suddenly have a horrifying thought. "Good lord, Kurtis Jackman. Did you buy that woman her necklace?"

He looks confused. "What are you talking about?"

"That heart-shaped necklace she was wearing." I touch the diamond cross with the big ol' diamond star that's looped around my neck—my most prized possession. "Tell me the truth right now. Was that heart-shaped necklace she's wearing a gift from you?"

Kurtis scoffs. "Are you crazy? She *works* for me." He rolls his eyes. "So now you think every woman who happens to be wearing a necklace must have got it from me? Should we go see if Mildred's wearing a necklace today, too—and ask her if I gave it to her?"

I don't know how to reply. Maybe he's got a point. Maybe I am getting a wee bit paranoid here. But who could blame me? Lately, I feel like I'm living in a pressure cooker and I'm about to blow. These past six months, keeping Kurtis interested in me while still avoiding consummating the Big Deed itself, has started to drive me certifiably insane. Even if I enjoy all our fooling around, which I do, and then some, it's lately gotten harder and harder keeping that man happy and coming back, while still demanding he keep his pecker firmly out of my drawers.

No matter how much I'm tempted to just lie back and enjoy myself, no matter what sweet nothings Kurtis might whisper in my ear or where his mouth and hands might land on my body to make my skin burst into flames and my crotch turn wet and warm and ache for him, or how much lately I just wanna open my legs and scream, "Just do it already, for the love of God!" I'm always thinking in the back of my brain, "My movie won't see the light of day once we do it." And since that movie's my rightful destiny, I can't give in to my urges. I just can't. I'm in a race against time to get my movie off the ground before I finally can't take it anymore and give in—or before Kurtis loses patience or interest in me.

And now, damn it all to hell, I've got this hiccup with Bettie Big Boobs to consider on top of everything else. I'm not sure what to do. Can I really expect a man like Kurtis—a porno king, for the love of all things holy—to stay *celibate* for six long months? It's one thing to demand he keep his love muscle out of me, but can I really expect him not to stick it somewhere else while he's waiting on me? Isn't that like asking a lion not to hunt a prairie dog now and again while he waits to bag his golden zebra?

I look into Kurtis' eyes. They're pleading with me to let the whole thing blow over. Damn. It boils my blood to say it, but I reckon I'm gonna have to look the other way while Kurtis bags himself a prairie dog, even if that prairie dog has hideously big boobs that make me want to vomit. But, believe me, I'm only gonna look the other way 'til I finally let Kurtis bag me, his golden zebra, because once Kurtis Jackman puts his one-hundred-percent-all-beef-thermometer inside me, he'd better forget about bagging anyone else ever again, especially some two-bit, big-boobed prairie dog with a heart-shaped pendant that doesn't deserve to lick my boots.

"Buttercup, there's nothing going on between Bettie and me," Kurtis says again. "She just works for me, that's all."

"Kurtis, I want to believe you so much," I say, "but it feels like you're trying to sell me a five-gallon hat for a ten-gallon head."

"*Believe me,*" he pleads, sweating like a whore in church. "She *works* for me, that's all."

I sigh deeply. "You two looked awfully comfy-cozy together when I first walked in." I squinch my eyes at him.

"We were talking business."

It doesn't take a genius to know he's lying like a no-legged dog. And, frankly, it hurts my heart. But so what? What good would it do me right now to call him out on his lies? And what if, by some miracle, I'm wrong? I scrunch my face into a pout. "Why are you making a movie with *her* and not with me?"

"Because I make adult films, honey. You know that."

"But why haven't you made *my* movie yet?"

Kurtis exhales in exasperation. "I've told you, Buttercup, a million times, there's a big difference between making an adult movie, which I can do in my sleep, and launching a mainstream feature. I need to get investors—"

"And that's another thing. Why on earth do you need investors, anyway? Just make the movie yourself. You're richer than Croesus."

He rolls his eyes. "I'm 'richer than Croesus,' whatever the hell that means, because I'm smart enough to get investors for my movies. I've told you. First I make you a centerfold star, and then I make you a movie star. It's a *process.* First things first, I need *investors* to make you a movie star. And to get investors, I need to raise your profile. Trust me, I know exactly what I'm doing. You need to be patient."

"I *am* being patient. But my patience won't last forever."

"Well, neither will mine." His tone has suddenly turned as cold as a banker's heart.

I glance up at his face and I'm surprised to see that his eyes are hard.

Oh crap.

I've known for quite a while that Kurtis has been slowly losing his mind with his pent-up desire for me, but this is the first time I've seen coldness flash in his eyes when he's looking at me. I reckon something's gotta give here, or else his unfulfilled desire might just start curling up into something different than passion—something angry and dark. Holy hell, it suddenly dawns on me clear as a bell—Kurtis Jackman isn't gonna make his non-porno-legitimate movie starring me until I sleep with him, not the other way around. I've been a damned fool.

I embrace Kurtis. "I know you've been incredibly patient, darlin', bless your heart," I say. "I swear I've never met a man with more honor or integrity in all my life." I repress a smirk—I mean, I'm saying the words "honor" and "integrity" to a porno-king, after all. "And, baby, when the time is right, I promise, I'm gonna give you something you'll never forget."

He presses into me and I can feel his one-eyed monster poking me something fierce. He takes a deep breath. "Something no other man's ever experienced," he says.

I let out a long exhale. "I just worry you're gonna lose interest in me when I finally give it to you."

He scoffs at me. "I could never lose interest in you, baby." He leans slightly back from our embrace and takes my face in his hands. "Because I love you, Buttercup."

My mouth hangs open.

"You didn't know that?"

I shake my head, stunned.

His eyes soften. "Oh, Buttercup, of course. I *love* you."

I truly don't know what to say. He *loves* me? My heart feels like a water balloon filled to bursting.

"You just have to trust me," Kurtis says. He drops his hands to my shoulders. "*In every way.*"

Well, there you go. The jig is up. I'm pretty sure the man just gave me an ultimatum. "When do you think you're gonna make my movie?" I ask, just in case I'm reading this situation wrong.

"Well, when do you think you're finally gonna trust me—*in every way?*"

Damn. I'm not reading this situation wrong. Kurtis has just laid his cards on the table and he's calling my bluff. No movie about Marilyn Monroe's gonna come *out* until Kurtis gets *in*. Inside me, that is. If this is a game of chicken, it's clear which of us is gonna have to swerve first—me. And I don't like it one little bit.

Chapter 17

17 Years Old
929 Days Before Killing Kurtis

It's late afternoon, and, having just finished a pretty enthusiastic kissing session under the big oak tree, Wesley and I are now lying on our backs on the ground, looking up at the sky.

"You know what I just figured out?" he asks.

I turn my head to look at him.

"We're fate," he says.

"What the heck are you talking about?" I ask.

"I just realized we're like *Princess Bride.*"

I look at him blankly—I have no idea what the heck he's talking about.

"*Princess Bride,*" he repeats, as if saying those two words a second time will suddenly make me understand. "Wesley and Buttercup," he adds.

"What the hell are you talking about, Wesley?"

"You haven't seen that movie?"

I shake my head. "I read my books," I say. "We didn't have a TV—and we certainly didn't have money growing on trees enough to spend on going to the cineplex."

"Shoot, you don't need money to go to the movies—you just sneak in."

"Well, anyway. I read my books."

"Well, *Princess Bride* you gotta see." His eyes are sparkling. "Wesley loves Buttercup and he'd do anything for her. She's his princess—just like you're mine. You and I are fate—I knew it the minute I saw you that first day. There are no coincidences."

I roll my eyes. I don't know where Wesley comes up with half the stuff he jabbers about. "Just kiss me, Wesley," I say. "And stop talking like a no-count fool."

Wesley complies, and we kiss for a solid fifteen minutes. When we're done, we lie on our backs again and look up at the sky between the branches of the big oak tree.

"Hey, you know what else I just figured out?" Wesley says, turning onto his side to look at me.

I turn my head toward him.

"We've had ourselves a fifty-six day kissing streak lately." His face brightens with a sudden epiphany. "I'm officially the Yankee Kisser." He chuckles.

I can't help but smile at his joke, even though I hate to give him the satisfaction. No one else in the entire world would understand why this joke is funny as all get out, but I do, because Wesley and I are stuck together in a special kind of "consistency" hell with Mr. Clements and Joe DiMaggio.

Mr. Clements is always talking about his boyhood idol, Joe DiMaggio—"The Yankee Clipper"—and about how "Joe DiMaggio's record-setting fifty-six-game hitting streak could teach us all a thing or two about *consistency*." Living with Mr. Clements means hearing about Joe DiMaggio just about every single day. Or, if not Joe, then Lou Gehrig, his other favorite player. Without fail, Mr. Clements goes on and on about Joe and Lou the most because, he says, those guys were the ones with record-setting streaks, the ones who really understood the meaning of "consistency."

At the supper table, Mr. Clements is always asking us kids, "How do you think Joltin' Joe got a hit, game after game?" And we kids always have to reply, "Consistency," for the umpteenth time. "Yep, *consistency*," Mr. Clements always says. "Remember that, kids. It's what's gonna get you everything good in life."

Every time Mr. Clements makes his Consistency Speech, it takes all my restraint not to say, *Well, Mr. Clements, if "consistency" is gonna buy me a lifetime of sitting on a couch in a group foster home, watching baseball on TV with a box of baseball cards on my lap, then I'll pass.* But, of course, I never say that.

Actually, I don't mind Mr. Clements talking about Joe DiMaggio in particular because Joe was married to Marilyn. But when Mr. Clements also goes on and on about Lou Gehrig, too, and, occasionally about Babe Ruth and a million other two-bit-never-heard-of-'em players, and insists on showing us his entire baseball-card collection, filled with endless photos of old-timey Yankees holding baseball bats, and goes on and on wondering how he ever wound up rotting away in West Texas, I just want to ram Mr. Clements' bald head into the brick wall behind the TV set.

It's funny, because the only baseball card I actually *want* to see, the one of The Yankee Clipper, Joe DiMaggio himself, Mr. Clements won't let us see. Two days ago, when I asked Mr. Clements to show us that "priceless" card, he said, "No, Charlene, Joe's gonna be my ticket to a golden retirement one day, so I've gotta keep him under lock and key in pristine condition." And then he patted my hand like I was just too feeble-minded to understand what "pristine condition" meant.

Oh man, did that little pat of my hand boil my blood.

So, yesterday, while everyone else was out at work and school and Mrs. Clements was at the market and I was all alone doing my home study, I put down my book, put on the rubber gloves from the kitchen sink, and sneaked into Mr. and Mrs. Clements' room. Sure enough, I found Mr. Clements' usual baseball-card collection in a big box next to his desk. But when I sifted through the box, I knew right quick those cards weren't his most prized ones—they were the ones he's always got with him when he's watching baseball on TV.

A little more snooping, though, and I found a small combination safe tucked away in the back of his closet, covered by a quilt. When I tried to open the safe, the door was locked and wouldn't budge. Just for the heck of it, I tried a few numbers on the combination lock—Mr. Clements' birthday, Mrs. Clements' birthday, the street address of the house—but no luck.

Wesley runs his fingers down my arm, dangerously close to my right boob, and I snap back to the present with him under the big oak tree. Wesley leans into me and presses his body against my thigh, and I can feel the hardness in his pants that tells me just how badly he's dying to touch my boob.

"Have you ever been to a baseball game?" Wesley asks, gazing at me.

I shake my head.

"I have," Wesley says. "Once, when I was really little, before I went to live with my grammy."

Unlike me, Wesley loves to talk about his childhood and anything else that happens to pop into his head. I don't mind, of course—I actually like listening to Wesley talk. The sound of his voice keeps me from feeling so lonely, I reckon.

I'm amazed at how good and kind Wesley's managed to remain after all he's been through in his life. Wesley once told me his momma was a teenager when she'd had him without so much as a nickel to buy a hummingbird on a string, and he never even knew his daddy. "When I was seven," Wesley explained, his tone matter-of-fact, "my momma hanged herself, and I went to live with my grammy. But when I was ten, Grammy died, so I had to come here."

And now, Wesley's at it again, telling me buckets and buckets about who-knows-what. "I'm gonna take you to a baseball game one day," he says, pressing his body into mine and stroking my hair. "I'm gonna take you everywhere, to see everything, Buttercup." I know Wesley's never really liked calling me Buttercup, but sweet ol' Wesley pretty much does anything I tell him to do. I swear, that boy lives to make me smile.

Wesley leans in for a kiss, and I give him one, happily—a good and long and enthusiastic one—and while we're kissing, his hand moves to my cheek and then to the base of my neck and finally starts working its way down my chest until he's just about to...

I swat his hand away and pull back from our kiss. "What the hell do you think you're doing, Wesley? You can't touch my boob."

Wesley's eyes light up at the word "boob." "Aw, I'd give anything to touch it," he moans, pressing that hard bulge in his pants into my thigh. "I just wanna touch it once. *Please.*"

I sit up and look him in the eye. The poor boy looks desperate.

It's not news to me that Wesley wants to do more than kiss me, of course. For months now, I've known he'd do just about anything to touch my boob, and other places, too. In fact, I'd be willing to bet poor Wesley would set his own hair on fire if it meant I'd let him touch my boob. But I can't. I'd like to say it's because he's so dang dopey (which is true) or because I don't want him touching my boob (not true). But neither is the reason.

The true reason I don't want Wesley touching my boob is that I like kissing him too much. In fact, I *love* kissing him. Kissing Wesley feels so good, it's like flying with a jetpack or sliding down a rainbow or some other stupid thing like riding a unicorn when I do it. When he's pressed against me and I feel that little bulge in his jeans grinding into me and pleading for more, lord have mercy, it's like I'm losing my mind. I've never felt so damned good in all my life as I do when I'm smashed against Wesley's skinny body, my lips against his, his tongue inside my mouth, that hardness in his pants making me moan and clutch him closer to me.

Kissing Wesley like that, feeling him stroke my hair, even just listening to him talk about movies or baseball games or whatnot, all of it makes my heart ache and my skin sizzle and my crotch throb and my face flush. And all that's just from *kissing* the damn boy.

If I let Wesley touch my boob, or, God help me, both of them at once, then I'm pretty sure I'd let Wesley do a whole lot more, too. In fact, I'm positive I would, and then some, because there's something about him I just can't resist. And, unlike my daddy, I'm not gonna let the entire trajectory of my life change with one little ejaculation. No, sir. I can't let anyone—not even sweet and good and dopey Wesley—keep me from going to Hollywood to find my daddy and fulfill my destiny to become a legendary movie star like Lana Turner and Marilyn Monroe, seen by audiences in cineplexes around the world. I am Charlie Wilber's Daughter. *Amen.* I'm gonna be somebody. I'll finally be free of this place in about seven months, and I've just got to keep Wesley from touching my boob, or anything else, 'til then.

"The thing is..." I say, choosing my words carefully, "I'm just not comfortable being touched like that... because..."

Wesley props up onto his elbow so he can look down onto my face. He looks concerned.

"The man my momma... murdered..." I continue slowly.

Wesley nods, encouraging me. Despite the calm expression he's managing, I know he's flipping out on the inside that I'm about to reveal some personal information to him after all this time.

"His name was Jeb. And Jeb was... a bad man," I say quietly. Wesley's face darkens with concern. "A very, very bad man," I continue, my voice thick with intensity. I look down, and tears begin to flood my eyes as I remember poor Jeb's contorted face right after he'd swallowed that first huge chunk of rat-poison cake. "And now... after all he did to me... I'm sorry, but I just can't stand for anyone to touch me like that ever again."

Wesley envelops me in a firm and fervent embrace—well, as best that skinny boy can manage with his scrawny arms, anyway. "Shhh," he soothes. "You don't have to talk about it. I'm the one who's sorry. You never have to do anything you aren't comfortable with. I'll wait. Forever if I have to. Destiny put us together as kids so we can be together our whole lives—so I could always take care of you, forever." He kisses my lips gently. "I'll wait forever if I have to."

I nuzzle into him. "He hurt me, Wesley. Real bad. And now, I just... I can't."

"Shhh," Wesley says again. "It's all right. That bastard's dead and gone now, Buttercup." He pulls back from me and looks me in the eyes. "He can never hurt you again. No one can ever hurt you again, 'cause I'm here now."

"I've never told anyone that before, Wesley. Only you."

Wesley pulls me into him again, this time even closer. "There, there," he says.

"Only you," I repeat. "I've only told you." He squeezes me even tighter.

It feels like jetpack-flying and rainbow-sliding and unicorn-riding all rolled into one to be in Wesley's arms, telling him my deepest, darkest secret, even if that particular secret doesn't happen to be remotely true this time. The whole situation makes me ache to tell Wesley my *real* deep, dark secret, just to see if maybe, when he hears it, he'll still want to kiss me and hold me and tell me his stories and touch my boob. I know I shouldn't give in to this temptation that's overtaking me right now, but I just can't resist.

"Wesley, there's something else I need to tell you," I whisper. I pull away from his embrace, sniffling. I look him square in the face, my jaw clenching. "There's something you need to know about me. Something bad."

He sits back, readying himself.

"Well, you know, Jeb hurt my momma and me... A lot." Wesley leans in, as if he's fixin' to comfort me yet again, but I put my hand up to stop him. "Until, finally, one day, my momma just snapped, and she said to me, 'That motherfucker's never gonna hurt us again.' And that's when she up and baked Jeb a rat-poison cake."

Wesley nods. Apparently, he's heard all the major plot points of this story before, probably from Mrs. Clements.

I pause. I shouldn't do this, but I'm going to, anyway. I just can't resist the opportunity to purge my soul and come clean, especially to someone as sweet and understanding as Wesley. "And the thing you need to know about me, Wesley,... is that... when my momma baked that cake filled with rat poison for Jeb, bless her heart..." Wesley nods, encouraging me. My skin is on fire. "When she baked that cake..." Electricity is coursing through my veins. This is it. I'm going to finally tell someone who I really am—and not just someone. *Wesley.*

Wesley nods, his eyes blazing.

"When my momma baked that cake that killed Jeb, *I helped her do it.*"

There, I said it. Well, partially, anyway—but that's good enough. *I killed Jeb. I baked the cake. It was me.* That's what I just said, isn't it? Because whether I helped Mother or did it all by myself, it's all the same thing, isn't it? *I did it.* Holy hell, what a weight off my shoulders to finally tell someone the semi-truth.

I let out a shaky breath and look into Wesley's eyes, searching for his acceptance—or rejection. And there's no doubt what's waiting for me there—acceptance without reservation.

Wesley brushes the hair out of my eyes and then kisses me with a whole new kind of fervor that takes my breath away. Hot damn, this kiss lights a whole new kind of fire inside me.

"I'm glad you did it," he proclaims after our kiss. His eyes are ablaze like nothing I've seen in them before. "That motherfucker deserved everything he got for what he did to you," he says. He puts his index finger under my chin. "And if anyone ever lays a finger on you again, the fucker's gonna have to answer to me."

Chapter 18

17 Years, 11 Months and 26 Days Old
745 Days Before Killing Kurtis

I sit straight up in my cot, suddenly jolting awake from a dream, and blurt, "Consistency." It's the wee hours of the morning and, once again, I've been dreaming about opening Mr. Clements' safe. For months now, I've been obsessed with figuring out the puzzle of that damned combination lock. Every chance I get, whenever I'm sure everyone else has left the house and isn't coming back for at least an hour, I sneak into Mr. and Mrs. Clements' room with kitchen gloves on my hands, and I try yet another set of numbers on that gosh-dang lock.

Last week, I thought I had it for sure: 05-04-03, the jersey numbers of Joe DiMaggio, Lou Gehrig, and Babe Ruth, respectively. When I first had the idea about the jersey numbers being the answer, it near about killed me to have to wait a whole two days for a foolproof time when everyone would be gone from the house so I could run up there and try the numbers. But, gosh dang it, much to my shock and dismay, those jersey numbers didn't work. I tried every combination and order I could think of for those three digits, and they still didn't work. Damn, damn, damn. And I'd been so sure, too.

But now, out of nowhere, I just figured out the answer in

my sleep. And now that I know the answer to the puzzle, I can't believe it took me this long to figure it out. Just now, Daddy came to me in my dream and, after laughing his big ol' whooping laugh, he chided me, "Buttercup, use your noggin. What's the answer to Mr. Clements' question?" When I looked at him dumbfounded, he rolled his eyes and added, "What's *always* the answer to Mr. Clements' question?"

Just like that, I knew the answer, after all these months of noodling the problem—*consistency.* Of course. What a big ol' *duh*. And, jeez, good thing I finally figured it out now—just in the nick of time—because my eighteenth birthday is in four little days.

When the sun finally comes up, I'm already dressed and ready for school an hour earlier than usual. Unlike other days, I'm dying to get my butt to school today so I can look up something in the school library. I just need to research one little piece of information, and then I'll have everything I need to open that safe door and hold that "priceless" Joe DiMaggio card in my *un*-pristine hand.

At school, right before history class, I bolt straight to the library and pull the *"F-G"* encyclopedia off the shelf. I only need to flip around for a minute to find the exact page I'm looking for: "Henry Louis 'Lou' Gehrig, American baseball player for the New York Yankees." I scan the entry, and, right quick, I see it, the answer that's been eluding me for months: *2,130.* Of course! Lou Gehrig set the record for most consecutive games by playing in *2,130* straight games. *Duh.* How did it take me this long to solve the puzzle?

When I get home from school, it's my lucky day. Nobody else is in the house—although I'm not entirely sure if someone might waltz through the front door any minute. Normally, unless I'm sure no one's gonna come home for a while, I wouldn't risk it, but, dang it, I just can't hold my horses. And, anyway, time is running out if I'm gonna get this damned card before I'm state-mandated to get the hell out of Dodge in four days. It's now or never.

I quietly pull the rubber gloves on my hands in the kitchen and then tiptoe up to Mr. and Mrs. Clements' room, holding my breath. I creep into the room without making a sound and float silently to the safe in the closet.

I crouch down in Mr. Clements' closet, remove the quilt from the top of the safe, and with shaking hands, turn the lock, first in tribute to Mr. Joseph Paul DiMaggio's hitting streak—and then in honor of Mr. Henry Louis Gehrig's consecutive games: *fifty-six* to the right; *twenty-one* to the left; and then *thirty* to the right. And even though I'm one hundred percent sure I've figured out the answer to the riddle, I nonetheless exhale in relief when the door springs right open, as easy as if I'd said, "Open *sesame*." I can't help but giggle with glee.

I'm about to peek inside the safe, but something makes me pause for a minute.

It's funny. After all these months of fixating on this conundrum, I almost don't want to know what's inside. How could the actual contents of the safe live up to the wondrous marvel it's become in my mind? But I reckon that's just the romantic in me talking. Of course, come hell or high water, I'm gonna look inside the safe. Maybe I'm just savoring the promise of the dream one last time, just in case the reality of it falls short somehow, as is so often the case in life.

I take a deep breath and reach inside.

There's a stack of papers.

Birth certificates. One for Mr. Clements. Oh, his name's Eugene. I don't think I knew that. And one for Mrs. Clements. Martha. I knew that. There's another birth certificate—and a death certificate right behind it from just two days later—for a baby, William Eugene Clements. Then there's yet another birth/death certificate combo for baby Martin Phillip Clements, but this time, the birth and death certificates are dated the same day. I reckon Mr. and Mrs. Clements didn't have a whole lot of luck in the baby department. Well, that's awfully sad—but I don't have time to think about it. I put all that crap back into the safe.

There's a deed of trust for the house and I put it back into the safe, too. Mr. and Mrs. Clements can keep their paper-deed to this hellhole, as far as I'm concerned. Good riddance.

A key. I turn it over in the palm of my hand. I can't tell what it's for, and I don't have time to figure it out. Too bad. That might have been an interesting mystery to solve. I put it back into the safe along with the papers.

And then, there it is, sitting in the palm of my hand—a baseball card for the one and only Joe DiMaggio, the Yankee Clipper himself, carefully wrapped in a clear, plastic sleeve. Honestly, it looks just like all the other baseball cards Mr. Clements has already shown us a million times, so I don't know why this one's so dang special. But, okay, I'll take his word for it. But, jeez, the way Mr. Clements talked about this Joe DiMaggio card all this time, I thought it'd be gold-plated or something.

I look at Joe's picture carefully. What the hell? He wasn't even good-looking! How the hell did *that* guy marry Marilyn Monroe? I shake my head in disbelief—wonders never cease. That's near-about as crazy as me marrying Wesley—except, of course, that Wesley's not and never will be a legendary baseball player, so I reckon comparing Wesley to Joe DiMaggio, and especially picturing myself marrying him one day is a felony-stupid thought.

I look at the remainder of the items in my hands. Well, I'll be damned. There's also a Lou Gehrig baseball card and a Babe Ruth, too.

I study the Lou Gehrig card. Holy heck, he sure was a looker—just about as handsome as my daddy. My chest tightens for just a minute. Thanks to these cards, I'm finally gonna find my daddy and fulfill my destiny to carry the torch lit by Lana and carried by Marilyn. A wave of emotion wells up inside me like a high tide lurching toward a full moon, but I stuff it down. Now's not the time to lose my head and get emotional and sloppy, not when my entire happiness hangs in the balance.

I quickly browse through the remaining stack of papers in my hand, just to be sure I'm not missing anything important, and, yep, sure enough, there are two more baseball cards for players named Mickey Mantle and Yogi Berra. These last two cards don't look to be in such good shape compared to the others, and I've never heard Mr. Clements mention either of these two guys, so they must not have been all that famous, but, wow, that Mickey Mantle sure was a handsome devil—woo-wee! Like a movie star, that one. Why didn't Marilyn cozy up to *that* golden boy? Now *that* would have been a pairing I could wrap my head around.

I look at the remaining stack of stuff. Looks like a bunch of receipts or something—nothing important. But there's an envelope, too—and when I open it, holy hell, there's a whole bunch of cash in there. *Five hundred big ones.* I'm shaking as I count out the bills.

I sit and think for a minute, crouching in Mr. Clements' closet with the small stack of cards and the cash in my hand. For the past few months, I've been so consumed with figuring out the combination to Mr. Clements' lock, I haven't put much thought into my exit strategy. Now that I know the combination and can open the safe any time I want, what's the rush? Throwing your rope out before making a loop ain't gonna catch the cow. Better to come up with a plan that will allow me to leave here with the Joe DiMaggio card *and* the money in my pocket *and* no one the wiser that it was little ol' me who swiped them. I certainly don't want the police coming after me—and I reckon I also don't want Mr. and Mrs. Clements to think ill of me after I'm gone.

It's settled, then. There's a time and a place for everything. And right now's just not the time. As quiet as the morgue, I put every last baseball card plus the envelope full of bills back into the safe and close the door. I rotate the lock a few times to the right, just to reset it, and cover the safe with the quilt.

Chapter 19

18 Years 7 Months Old
524 Days Before Killing Kurtis

"Oh, Kurtis," I say, laughing. He's standing behind me, covering my eyes with his hands. "You're so silly, baby."

"No peeking," Kurtis warns playfully. "Keep your eyes closed." He sounds like a little kid.

We're standing in Kurtis' enormous backyard in the warm, late-morning sunshine. He led me out here to give me yet another present. That man sure does love giving me gifts.

"Okay, okay, I'm not peeking," I say. I can hear the sound of trickling water nearby. What is that?

"Are you ready?" Kurtis shouts, his voice bursting with excitement.

"I'm ready, sugar."

"Open your eyes."

I do as I'm told.

Standing before me is a gigantic fountain with naked ladies and cherubs and even a little cupid with wings. I gasp. I can't believe my eyes. It was months ago that I told Kurtis "This house has everything 'cept a big fountain with naked ladies and cherubs and a little cupid with wings," and now, just look at what this man has gone and done.

"Well, what do you think?" Kurtis asks, smiling from ear to ear.

I open my mouth to speak, but nothing comes out. I shake my head, overwhelmed, and Kurtis laughs.

"Did you see?" Kurtis asks, pointing toward the base of the fountain.

I look where he's indicating—and, oh my goodness—there's a ring of buttercups encircling the base of the fountain. My heart zigs and zags inside my chest like a butterfly on a string. "Kurtis..." is all I manage to say as tears spring into my eyes. I fling myself into his arms. "This is the best gift I've ever gotten in my whole life," I choke out, resting my cheek on his broad shoulder.

Kurtis leans down and kisses me with such fervor my knees wobble underneath me—and then, much to my absolute shock, he gets down on his knee.

I gasp.

"Marry me, baby," Kurtis says, holding up a humongous diamond ring.

I've never seen anything so big and sparkly in all my life. And I've never seen Kurtis look so strikingly good-looking before, either.

"Will you marry me?" he asks, a huge, toothy grin lighting up his handsome face. "Come on, honey, be my queen."

Even through my tears, I can't help but smile at Kurtis' choice of words right there.

My brain feels like scrambled eggs right now. I never thought I'd *marry* Kurtis. I reckon I always pictured myself marrying Wesley, as silly as that sounds. All I ever intended with Kurtis was that he'd discover me like Lana Turner in the malt shop and put me in his Marilyn movie—I never imagined I'd find my happily ever after with the man.

But now, after all these months with no movie in sight and Kurtis' appetite for me reaching a breaking point—and after all the nice gifts he's given me, and how patient and gentle he's been with me, and how he tells me he loves me each and every day—I suddenly realize marrying Kurtis is the unavoidable ending to this story.

I shouldn't be surprised. Kurtis is a man, not a boy; of course, he's claiming what he wants. He's a man who loves me—a rich and powerful and handsome man who treats me like a queen and wants to make me a huge star. Holy hell, when I think of it like that, I suddenly realize Kurtis must be my Joe DiMaggio. He must be!

Sure, my heart always went pitter-pat when I kissed Wesley or listened to him talk about God-knows-what, it's true; and, sure, Wesley was always as sweet as can be to me, sweet as anyone has ever been to me my whole life long. But dreaming about winding up with Wesley's just plain stupid is what it is. He's a boy, not a man—a boy who couldn't rub two nickels together, even if he wanted to. How could I ever fulfill my sacred destiny with a boy like that?

And, anyway, I'd bet dollars to daffodils Wesley's forgotten all about me by now. Yes, sir, I'd bet the farm Wesley's already fallen head over heels with some girl back home (who's not nearly as pretty as me)—in which case I'd be a no-count fool to sit around dreaming about one day getting to lie naked in a real bed with Wesley and feel him sliding deep inside me as he whispers into my ear, "You're my princess bride."

I bite my lip, considering the situation, the fountain with naked ladies and cherubs and even a little cupid with wings trickling pleasantly in my ear. The thing I've got to ask myself is this: Do I want to make that legitimate Marilyn-movie starring me or not? Because, clearly, that's not gonna happen until I give myself to Kurtis in the most sacred of ways. And I can't do that unless I've pledged myself to him under God—because that's what I've been telling him for months now. Gosh dang it, I've got a chicken-and-egg situation here, and I'm the chicken who laid the gosh darned egg.

The huge grin on Kurtis' face is starting to wane. He's growing anxious.

Hot damn, Kurtis really is a handsome man, actually. I don't know why I didn't see it before. He's like a movie star, really. And he's been awfully good to me, he really has—and patient as the day is long. I really couldn't find a better husband than Kurtis, even if I tried.

Kurtis lowers the ring, his face darkening.

"Yes," I shout enthusiastically, pulling him up to a stand. Kurtis' face instantly lights up. "Silly man, of course I'll marry you. I was just in shock for a second there, marveling that a girl could ever get this lucky. Yes, baby, yes!"

He throws his head back and guffaws. "You had me sweating there for a second, baby!" He puts the rock on my finger and swings me around, laughing like a kid on Christmas morning. "Let's do it as soon as possible," he mumbles into my lips, kissing me over and over—and I know the "it" he's referring to isn't the marriage ceremony.

"Oh, sugar," I whisper. I return Kurtis' kiss and nuzzle my face into the crook of his neck.

Kurtis kisses the top of my head and laughs again, obviously overcome with glee. I smile at him, fully intending to join him in laughing—but I unexpectedly burst into big, soggy tears, instead.

"Oh, baby," Kurtis coos, clearly thinking I'm crying tears of joy. "I'm so happy, too."

I bury my head into Kurtis' shoulder to hide my tears from him, but all that makes me do is sob even harder into his chest. I've never really believed I'd see Wesley again, not really, but I reckon now that I've said yes to becoming Kurtis' wife, forever and ever, 'til death do us part, I know it for sure.

Chapter 20

17 Years, 11 Months and 27 Days Old
744 Days Before Killing Kurtis

"I still don't understand why I can't go with you," Wesley says. We're standing under the big oak tree at our usual meeting spot. I'm eager to lock lips, as usual, but he's so anxious about my imminent birthday and departure from the house in three days, he can't even relax enough to kiss me.

I sigh, exasperated. "Hells bells, Wesley. I already told you—you can't come with me. Now, enough about that, let's do some smooching."

He practically stomps his foot, he's so mad.

"Listen, Wesley. There's nothing I want more—"

"Then let me come. I've got to take care of you—you're my princess bride."

I take a step toward Wesley and grab both his hands. "Think, Wesley, think. Use your noggin." I pull him down to the ground to sit next to me under the big oak tree. "Wesley, you're still sixteen, only just about to turn seventeen next month. You've got a full *year* left before you age-out. If you leave the house now, they'll come looking for you. You'll be classified as a runaway. We don't want to be looking over our shoulders all the time, now do we? How're you gonna take care of me if you're constantly worried someone's gonna haul you back here?"

He grits his teeth.

"When we're finally together, I want us to be free as birds to do anything we want to do."

He looks away, thinking. I can tell my words are softening his resolve.

"Listen, Wesley." I put my hand up to his face and gently stroke his cheek. He tilts his face into my touch. "All I want in this whole world is to be with you," I say, "but we have to be patient. We two are good at that, at being patient, aren't we?"

He smiles. "We sure are." He rolls his eyes and runs his hand through his hair.

"You know the minute I age-out I'm heading to Hollywood to be discovered. If you're patient, if you wait 'til you age-out to come out to Hollywood, too, by the time you get out there, I'll already be a big star. I'll have a mansion all ready for us, with a swimming pool, and a tennis court, and a fountain with naked ladies and cherubs and a little cupid with wings."

Wesley laughs. "Well, all of that sounds good 'cept for the fountain—that part sounds kinda creepy."

No, it does not sound creepy, I think. *It sounds beautiful and fancy.* But I don't say what I'm thinking because Wesley looks so darned cute right now, I have no desire to argue with him.

Gosh dang it. What the heck am I gonna do about Wesley? I'd absolutely love for him to come live with me in my fancy mansion in Hollywood. This boy's had just about the worst life of anyone, and yet he's somehow managed to stay sweet as honey on a biscuit. I'd be tickled pink to watch him float without a care in the world on a raft in my pool—and lie naked with me in my bed at night—but the problem is I don't know how Daddy's gonna feel about getting an unexpected house guest after all this time.

I'm surprised how often I dream about Wesley coming to live with me in Hollywood. For the longest time, I thought I could never wind up with Wesley, because... well, *duh.* Goofy and Marilyn can't wind up together. And yet, when I saw that picture of Joe DiMaggio on that baseball card and started thinking about how Marilyn picked him when she could have had anyone, which means they must have made sense together somehow, I couldn't help thinking maybe Wesley and I make sense together somehow, too—that maybe, just maybe, despite appearances, Wesley's the salt that goes with my pepper in God's natural order of things.

But, even so, I've got another problem to consider here, too—and it's a doozy. Can I fulfill my sacred destiny if Wesley's tagging along with me in Hollywood? I just don't know for sure.

What I need right now is time. Time to get my butt out to Hollywood to get discovered. Time to find Daddy. Time to figure things out. I can't be expected to come up with answers to everything all at once, for cryin' out loud.

I focus my gaze back on Wesley. Poor, distracted, anxious Wesley. He's sitting here next to me, studying my face like he always does on account of me being so damned pretty. I pucker my lips as an invitation for him to kiss me, and he obliges, just like he always does. And when our lips meet, man, oh man, it's like electricity all over again, even after all this time. Kissing this scrawny boy makes my heart race faster than bad chili through a hound dog—although, come to think of it, Wesley's not quite as scrawny as he used to be. He's filled out quite a bit in the time I've known him, actually. When the heck did Wesley's shoulders get so broad?

I shake my head, re-focusing on the task at hand. "Wesley, listen to me," I say.

He stares at me with mocking, undivided attention.

I swat his shoulder. "Listen up. I've got an idea that will make it so that, if we're patient, we'll have it made in the shade like a Thanksgiving Day parade."

"Oh yeah? Tell me all about it—I'm all ears."

That's an understatement. Wesley might not be quite as scrawny as he used to be, I'll give him that, but those damned ears are still too big for that puppy-dog face of his, bless his heart.

"I've been thinking this through," I say. "The thing for us to do is swipe Mr. Clements' very best baseball cards, and we'll be set for life."

Wesley looks surprised.

"I can sell the cards in Hollywood," I continue, "and by the time you come out there in about a year, I'll have us already set up to live like a king and queen."

Wesley looks up to the sky, like he's praying to the Lord himself for patience. He sighs audibly. "Even if I wanted to follow this spiffy plan of yours, how the heck would we swipe Mr. Clements' best baseball cards? I mean, we don't even know where he keeps them or which ones they are—"

"Mrs. Clements let it slip to me the other day in the kitchen that he keeps the best ones in a steel safe in his closet, and she said there's a combination lock, and that it was Mr. Clements who set the numbers on the lock." I can't help but smile to myself. Even though I know I'm lying, my brain suddenly "remembers" Mrs. Clements and me, standing in the kitchen, peeling potatoes and talking about Mr. Clements' safe.

Wesley raises his eyebrows at me, but he doesn't speak.

"All we have to do," I continue, "is figure out Mr. Clements' numbers. Once we do that, we can sneak into his closet and steal his best cards right out from under him. Piece of cake."

"Mrs. Clements told you all that?"

"She sure did. You know how much she likes me. She was laughing about how paranoid Mr. Clements is that someone's gonna steal his cards—and then she got all worried that she told me and made me promise not to tell anyone."

"Well, that's no good, then. You can't steal the cards now. Mrs. Clements will remember she told you about the safe and think it was you who stole 'em."

I slap my forehead. "Oh, jeez. I didn't think of it that

way. Dang it." I shake my head. "Gosh, I wouldn't want the police coming after me, especially now that I'm gonna be an adult in three days. It'd be different if I were still a minor. I mean, if you steal something when you're a minor like *you*, the worst they can do is put you in juvenile detention—and that's no big deal, 'cause juvie's nothing more than a dorm room and they have to let you out the very minute you turn eighteen. But if they catch someone stealing *after* they're eighteen, like *me,* well, then they put 'em away into a maximum-security prison for a really long time." I let out a long sigh. "Darn it, Mr. Clements is always saying how he's gonna retire on those dang cards, so they must be worth a mint."

Wesley squints and twists his mouth. I know that look—it means he's thinking really hard, bless his heart.

"Dang," I say, "I really thought those cards could set us up for life. I'm sorry. I didn't think it through."

"Well, hang on," Wesley responds. "Just give me a minute to think on it."

"Okay," I say. "But how 'bout you kiss me while you're thinking on it?"

Wesley gives me a half-smile, clearly willing to oblige me. But before he can even lean into my face, I plant my lips right onto his and kiss the hell out of him (a happy surprise for the boy, I'm sure, since I almost always just sit back and let him have his way with my lips). The best way to describe Wesley's physical response to my unexpected gift is that it's like his entire body—head, limbs, torso, the whole thing—is gonna explode into a trillion pieces and then shoot into the sky like fireworks on the Fourth of July. But I want insurance here—I *need* to get those baseball cards so I can get my butt to Hollywood and find my daddy, and I don't want anyone the wiser it was me who did it, either—so I do something the poor boy's been yearning for and dreaming about since the very first minute he laid eyes on me. I grab his hand, remove it from my shoulder, and place it firmly on top of my right boob.

Man, oh man, if Wesley was gonna explode before that maneuver, now he's gonna skyrocket straight up into outer space and orbit the moon a few hundred times and then scatter across the galaxy into a trillion tiny stars. The minute Wesley's hand makes contact with my chest, he jolts and jerks like he's a june bug on a string. He slams his body against me, hard, almost hurting me, actually, and tackles me all the way to the ground, moaning loudly, all the while groping my boob like he's a blind man looking for a peanut in a bag of walnuts. And, oh my goodness, *I like it.* I like it a whole lot.

I wrap my legs around Wesley and press my pelvis into him, suddenly aching between my legs like nothing I've felt before. Oh lord, it's all I can do not to rip his pants off and see for myself what all this trajectory-changing ejaculation business is all about.

Wesley moans and so do I, as our kissing and the pulsing between my legs intensify. But, no, no, no! What on God's green earth am I doing? I've got to get a hold of myself—keep my eye on the prize. I've come too far to let one self-indulgent moment with Wesley change the entire trajectory of my life. I cannot forget, even for an instant, that I've got a destiny—a sacred destiny to pick up Lana and Marilyn's torch and carry it ever-farther into the catacombs of history. I've got to stay true to my destiny, even when every molecule of my stupid, disobedient body aches and screams and yearns to fuse with Wesley's, to open my legs and feel him plowing deep inside me. Oh lord, all of a sudden, it's like I've got a horrible itch and Wesley's the only one who can scratch it. This is not good.

I abruptly push Wesley off me and sit up, wiping my mouth with the back of my hand.

"No," Wesley begs. "Please, no."

I leap up and begin pacing around Wesley like a wild animal.

"Please," he says again, his voice cracking. He's grabbing at his crotch, his face twisted up like I just crushed his trouser-snake in a vise.

"Wesley," I choke out. "I wanna be with you so bad. But only when everything's situated, so we don't have to look over our shoulders. Please, Wesley, you've got to stay here until you age-out. If you come with me now, I'll be an adult, and you'll be a minor—and, oh my God." I put my hand over my mouth, the picture of a girl having a sudden epiphany. "If I get with you now, I'll be committing a *crime*. Oh no, Wesley, if I get with you now, when I'm eighteen and you're still a *minor,* we'd be doing something *illegal.*"

Wesley's crumpled on the ground in an undulating heap, looking like he's going to throw up. He lets out a mangled cry, like the pain is too much for him and finally grunts out, "*Please* come back over here."

"Wesley, if we cut off the dog's tail, we can't sew it back on." I put my hands up over my eyes. "Lord have mercy, I'm having flashbacks. *Horrible* flashbacks. It's just like with Jeb... only... now *I'm* the adult, and *you're* the kid. That's just not right, Wesley—we have to wait 'til we're *both* adults or I'm no better than Jeb. I couldn't live with myself like that." Tears squirt out of my eyes. Good lord, I hate lying to Wesley like this, I really do, but I've got no choice. I can't let him come with me to Hollywood yet. I just can't.

As I've been talking, Wesley's been hunched over on the ground, grabbing at his crotch like I just whacked him with a baseball bat, but, bless his heart, being that he *is* Wesley, after all, when I start crying buckets of tears, he jumps up and comforts me in my time of need. He wraps me in his arms—which, like his shoulders, I notice, aren't quite as scrawny as they used to be—and presses his body against mine. When he pulls back from our embrace, there's tenderness in his eyes. He wipes the tears running down my cheeks with his thumbs.

"I have an idea," he says quietly, his voice soothing. "Just leave everything to me."

"What are you gonna do?" I ask.

He smiles. "Just leave everything to me."

"Tell me."

He pauses a beat.

"Wesley, what in God's name are you gonna do?"

He smiles broadly. *"You* can't steal Mr. Clements' baseball cards, but *I* most certainly can." His eyes flash with pride at his big idea.

"What are you talking about?" I try to look confused.

"Mrs. Clements told *you* about the safe, right? But she didn't tell *me* about it. And she doesn't know we ever talk. She'd never guess in a million years you told me about the cards in the safe."

I arch my eyebrows, like, *Hey, there's a thought.*

"And, worst case, if I ever do get caught, well, all they can do is send me to juvie for a year, right?" His voice is suddenly edged with confidence. "And that's nothing but a dorm room, anyway."

"That's true." I pause. My goodness, this boy really does have a heart of gold.

"And juvie can't be any worse than this Godforsaken place, can it? I mean, what's the difference if I'm here or there?"

"Juvie might even be better than this hellhole," I say.

"It probably is," Wesley agrees.

I purse my lips, considering. I take a small step away from him, trying to process his big idea. "Well, that all makes a whole lot of sense. You're so smart, Wesley, so much smarter than me. I never would have thought of any of that."

He puffs out his chest, just a little bit. "Yeah, the more I think about it, this is a great idea." He nods emphatically, like he's made a decision. "You've got to be good and gone from the house before I do anything, so they'll never suspect you. After you've left the house for good, I'll steal the cards and leave them in a safe place for you to come and get them on the way to your bus. Hey, I'll leave them right here, under the oak tree, under this rock."

"Yeah, okay." I nod, letting the idea gain steam in my mind. "And I'll sell the cards in Hollywood, so no one around here will ever be able to trace them back to either of us." For this next part, I lower my voice to an intense, breathy whisper. "And when you finally come to Hollywood after you turn eighteen, I'll just be sitting there, laid out like a picnic supper for you." I give him a heated look, a look that unequivocally promises future carnal relations. "It'll be just the two of us, never looking over our shoulders, doing *whatever* we want to do." I lightly graze my hand across my boob, as if I'm imagining a delicious day about a year from now when it will be Wesley's hand doing the boob-grazing.

Wesley exhales loudly and closes his eyes.

"You just have to be patient and wait 'til you turn eighteen," I say. "That's the only thing you've gotta do."

He exhales again. "Okay." There's resolution in his voice. "I'll wait. I can wait as long as it takes, if it means being with you."

I step toward him. "Oh, Wesley, you really do take such good care of me."

"I told you, I'm gonna take care of you forever and ever. I always have and I always will."

"You know what? I truly believe that."

"Can I touch your boob again?"

"No, I had a moment of weakness, and I'm sorry about that. But we have to wait, considering you're a minor and all."

He sighs like a flea-ridden dog with mange.

"Just think, though, in about a year from now, you'll be able touch me and my boob—or both of 'em —every single day."

He swallows hard. He's actually trembling, the poor boy.

I swallow hard, too. I reckon I'm trembling, too. "Forever and ever," I add softly, my skin suddenly electrified at the thought.

The expression on Wesley's face is so tortured, I know it would be kindest for me not to say anything more. But, damn it all to hell, I just can't help myself. "In fact, when you're eighteen and you come out to Hollywood, I'll let you do *anything* you want to me. *I promise.*" I lick my lips and exhale.

Wesley shudders and closes his eyes.

Good lord, what am I doing? I've got to get my head back in the game and think about the task at hand. "But for now," I say, taking a deep breath, "let's try to figure out those numbers on that combination lock, okay?"

Wesley opens his eyes and stares at me, his face on fire. Damn. I've never seen him look quite like this before. It's as if he's turned into a man just now, right in front of me.

"Wesley," I breathe. A funny kind of throbbing has announced itself inside my panties.

He bites his lower lip.

There's a long beat. I've lost my train of thought. My face feels hot. "We'll make a list of our ideas on the numbers," I finally say. "And the day after I've left the house, you go up to that safe and try 'em out when no one's home."

It's clear Wesley's not listening to a word I say.

"Wesley?"

He lurches forward and wraps his body around mine. "Buttercup," he mumbles, nuzzling into my hair. He inhales deeply, squeezing me tight.

"Oh, Wesley," I say, hugging him back with all my might. "Time's gonna fly by, honey. You'll see."

"I'm gonna miss you," he replies, his voice breaking.

"Aw, come on now, Wesley. There's no time for this. We've gotta come up with our plan."

But Wesley doesn't pay me any mind, and thank goodness for that. All of a sudden, he's laying soft kisses all over my face—on my lips, cheeks, eyes, nose, and ears—until my head is spinning and my heart is squeezing. "I'm gonna be counting the minutes," he breathes.

"Aw, come on now, Wesley," I choke out. "Time's gonna fly."

Wesley's kissing my cheek, pressing himself against me, stroking my hair, and there's nothing I want more than to throw my arms around him and never let go. But I can't. "Wesley," I say, my knees wobbling. "Come on, honey. We've got to figure this out." Honestly, I could stay here forever with Wesley, just like this. But I've got a sacred destiny to fulfill, and that's more important than anything else.

Wesley pulls back, nodding.

I touch his cheek. "Okay?"

He nods.

"Let's figure this out."

Wesley wipes his eyes and nods.

"All right, then. Mrs. Clements said Mr. Clements' most valuable card is some guy named Yogi—not Joe DiMaggio, after all."

Wesley's mouth hangs open. "Not the Yankee Clipper?"

"Nope. She said Joe's his *favorite* card, but not the most *valuable* one. So don't put Yogi under the tree for me with the others, okay? Keep it hidden somewhere really good so that, when the time comes, you can use it to buy your bus ticket to Hollywood."

"Ah, good thinking, Buttercup."

"Maybe under your mattress?"

Wesley shakes his head. "I'll figure out a good place."

"Somewhere *good*," I say. The boy's as sweet as can be, but lord only knows what 'a good hiding place' means to him.

"Gotcha." He shoots me a beaming smile.

Dang it, when Wesley smiles at me like that, I feel like blurting, "Damn it all to hell—come with me!" But that dog won't hunt, and I know it. If Wesley's meant to join me in Hollywood one day, then that's what will happen, exactly as it should. I'll just have to let fate take the wheel on that. In the meantime, though, as hard as it is to leave Wesley behind to do my dirty work for me, I don't have a choice in the matter. Before I can even think about starting a new, happy life with Wesley out in Hollywood, I've got get our there and get discovered in a malt shop and find my daddy and get my mansion ready (if Daddy hasn't managed it quite yet), and just plain figure things out.

Chapter 21

17 Years, 11 Months, 29 Days Old
742 Days Before Killing Kurtis

When I arrive home from school, everyone is gone, as usual. Hallelujah. I'll officially turn eighteen at midnight tonight, eight hours and seventeen minutes from now. Before then, though, I've got a few things to take care of in the house.

I grab the rubber gloves from the kitchen sink and head up to Mr. and Mrs. Clements' room. I work quickly. I take a handful of baseball cards out of the big box that's sitting next to Mr. Clements' desk. I count out twenty cards—it doesn't matter which ones, the first twenty random cards will do. I creep into the closet, remove the quilt from the top of the safe, and open the lock. 56-21-30. I roll my eyes yet again at the simplicity of it and about how it took me so damned long to figure it out.

When I "brainstormed" numbers with Wesley yesterday, it was a delicious kind of fun leading him right to the edge of figuring out the correct numbers, asking him all the right leading questions and throwing out all the right wonderings so that finally, ever so slowly, Wesley "thought" of the combination himself without me ever having to say the actual numbers myself.

When Wesley comes up here tomorrow and opens the safe using the numbers he thought of "all by himself," he's going to think he's as smart as a hooty owl. I smile to myself. It warms my heart to think of Wesley feeling good about himself. He deserves at least that much after all he's been through in his life.

I reach into the safe and remove the envelope full of cash, plus Joe, Lou, and Babe. Just for the heck of it, I take Mickey Mantle, too, because, even though I've never heard of him before, I'm thinking I might want to look at his handsome face a time or two during the long bus ride out to California.

I remove the cash from the envelope and stuff the bills into my bra and then take those random twenty baseball cards from the big box, plus the Yogi Berra card, too, and slip them into the envelope that formerly held the cash. Last minute, I put twenty dollars into the envelope, too, and then I place the envelope inside the safe. Again, I smile thinking about the expression on Wesley's face when he opens the safe tomorrow. I wish I could be here to see it—I can only imagine how precious it's gonna be.

I close the safe, reset the combination lock, and cover it with the quilt; then I sneak downstairs, return the rubber gloves to the kitchen cabinet, pack my little suitcase with everything I own (which now includes some spiffy baseball cards and a whole lot of cash), and sit on the couch in the main room to wait for Mrs. Clements to return home so I can say a proper goodbye. I look at the clock. Mrs. Clements should be here any minute.

Poor Wesley. It pains me to think what might happen to him after I'm gone. I reckon when Mr. Clements notices his precious cards and money are missing, he's gonna tear this whole damned house apart. And when he finds that Yogi Berra card in whatever stupid place Wesley stashes it—because that boy could throw himself onto the ground and miss—it'll be off-to-juvie time for poor Wesley.

If by some miracle Mr. Clements *doesn't* find that Yogi card, which I sincerely hope turns out to be the case, I reckon Wesley might be up shit-creek without a paddle, anyway.

Because when Mr. Clements starts accusing people, and someone speculates out loud, "Hey, what about Charlene?" I'm guessing Wesley's gonna confess to being the thief. He'll swear he did the stealing alone, too, with no help from anyone else, least of all the girl who hardly ever spoke to him for the past two years.

Where are the damned cards? Mr. Clements will demand to know.

I'll never tell, Wesley will say—or, hell, maybe he'll say, *I hid 'em out by the big oak tree,* for all I know, because, why not? By then, he'll be snickering to himself that the envelope he stole from the safe is long gone, just like we planned. Of course, I'm not really gonna hang around here just to retrieve those twenty worthless cards and twenty bucks, but I reckon they'll be gone just the same. Because surely, some rag-tag kid at the bus station will be more than happy to treat himself to a short stack of baseball cards and an Andrew Jackson hidden under a rock, especially if a sweet-as-pie girl pays him another twenty bucks to retrieve them.

Gosh dang it, I hate doing this to Wesley, I really do, but I can't figure out how to get my butt to Hollywood without Joe DiMaggio paying my way. And I can't figure out another way to get that Joe card *and* keep Mr. Clements off my back at the same time. It hurts my heart to say goodbye to Wesley like this, especially leaving him holding the bag, but I've got no choice.

I can only hope Wesley somehow manages to dance between the raindrops and get off scot-free—and, actually, to increase the chances of that happening, I made Wesley promise over and over to wear the big yellow kitchen gloves when he opens Mr. Clements' safe. But if, on the other hand, Wesley gets discovered—which certainly isn't my hope— then at least I feel comfort knowing Wesley won't be stuck in juvie for too long before he comes to meet me at the Hollywood bus station, as we've planned.

I let out a long exhale and shift my position on the couch.

I sure did cry a river of tears saying goodbye to Wesley under the big oak tree early this morning, and so did he. I haven't squeezed someone that tight and cried that hard since saying goodbye to Daddy all those years ago. I was a damned blubbering mess.

This time, unlike three days ago, it was Wesley's turn to reassure me. "Time's gonna fly by," he said, kissing my cheeks and lips and eyes. "We'll be together again before you know it—and then we'll never be apart again."

All I could do was whimper.

"You got the meeting time and place memorized?" Wesley asked.

I nodded so hard I thought my head was gonna fling off my neck.

"Noon at the bus station in Hollywood, exactly two days after my eighteenth birthday," Wesley reminded me. "That's only three hundred and ninety-five days away. No sweat."

"Okay, Wesley," I cried. "I'll be there."

"But repeat it back to me," he insisted.

"Bus station in Hollywood. Two days after your eighteenth birthday. Exactly three hundred and ninety-five days from today. Noon."

"Promise you'll be there, Buttercup."

"I promise, Wesley. Of course." I kissed Wesley's soft lips to seal my promise.

The screen on the front door squeaks open, jolting me from my thoughts of Wesley, and Mrs. Clements waltzes into the room holding a bag of groceries. I stand up from the couch, hug her goodbye, and thank her for everything she's done for me. Mrs. Clements hugs me back and tells me to keep in touch. She sheds a tear, which makes me shed a couple of my own, too, but only because I'm thinking about poor Wesley again. And then, without further ado, like so many eighteen-year-olds who've aged-out of this place before me, I head out the front door of the group home with my little suitcase in my hand, and never look back.

Chapter 22

Hollywood, California, 1990

18 Years 5 Days Old
736 Days Before Killing Kurtis

The bus ride to Hollywood is interminable and insufferable and makes me want to murder more people, all at once, than I've ever wanted to murder in my whole life—and, for me, that's saying a lot. Each and every person who sits next to me on each and every leg of my long and tortuous ride across half the country bores me half to death with their life story and their hopes and dreams and whatever big opportunity is luring them all the way out to California.

Of course, even though I'm bored as hell, I smile politely and attentively during each and every conversation, and every one of my riding companions makes me promise to keep in touch in California. It just goes to show, yet again—everyone always wants the pretty people to like them.

The very first thing I do on Day One in Hollywood is plunk down an entire month's worth of rent on a little room above a liquor store, right on Sunset Boulevard, courtesy of Mr. Clements and his big wad of cash. To be perfectly honest, I'm not all that thrilled about the liquor store part of my living accommodations, but I'm most definitely pleased as punch about the Sunset Boulevard part of it. Regardless, it's what I can afford right now so there's no sense wishing things were any different. If wishes were horses, then beggars would ride.

The second thing I do, even before going up to my new room, is ask the guy at the front desk if I can take a look at his phonebook. When I open that book, I go right to "W," holding my breath, and scan the alphabetical listings all the way down to "W-i-l-b-e-r." But, dang it, it isn't there. *It isn't there.* The list of names goes right from "Wilber, Catherine F." to " Wilcox, Alexander." Shoot. I actually believed finding Daddy was going to be as simple as opening the phonebook, even after all these years.

I look up from the phonebook, lost in thought for a moment. Gosh, maybe Daddy's such a bigwig these days he doesn't want people knowing his phone number? That could be it. Or maybe Daddy just doesn't have a phone? All of a sudden, thinking of reasons why Daddy might not be listed in that big Los Angeles phonebook makes me nervous and anxious and almost verging on panic, so, I decide not to think about it for a few days.

I move along to the third thing on my "Day One in Hollywood" list: visiting Grauman's Chinese Theater on Hollywood Boulevard. The minute I arrive, I kneel down on the cold cement and lay my hands on top of the handprints of Lana and then Marilyn—and boy-howdy, when my modern-day flesh touches the exact spots where those legendary beauties pressed their flesh, I experience something that can only be described as a spiritual awakening.

I close my eyes and feel infused with a deep-in-my-bones understanding, a that's-just-the-way-it-is kind of certainty about my higher purpose on this earth. If I didn't know it before, I sure as heck know it now: I've been put on this earth to mesmerize people the way they did, only even more so—to carry their torch ever-farther into the catacombs of history. Yes, there's no doubt in my mind I'm meant to be seen by audiences in cineplexes all over the world.

With these deep thoughts bouncing around in my head on

my way back to my room, I pop into a twenty-four-hour drugstore on Hollywood Boulevard and buy myself a big bottle of "Light Blonde Number 5."

Back in my little room, after I've treated my hair with the smelly chemicals and then dried and styled my new blonde mane into a perfect tumble of waves, I stare at myself in the mirror for the whole rest of the night. I can't help but marvel at myself—I finally look like me.

Of course, changing my hair is only part one of what I've got to do. The next morning, Day Two in Hollywood, I head out to tackle the second.

I'm standing in front of a boxy, one-level building on Hollywood Boulevard. A large sign on the rooftop reads "Casanova Club" in big, swirling letters—and a neon sign flashing over the doorway says "Topless Cuties." Yep, this place will do as well as any other.

The burly man at the front door looks at me from head to toe. "You here for a job?"

"No, sir. I'm just here to browse," I say, smiling sweetly.

He pauses, apparently confused. "Browse what?"

"The girls."

His eyes brighten like I've said something naughty. "Well, well, well." He chuckles wolfishly. "Hmm. We don't normally allow ladies into the club... "

I make my eyes wide and pleading and pout my lips in disappointment, too.

"But I guess it couldn't hurt if you're just here to 'browse.'" He chuckles again. "I'll have to charge you, though, just like any other customer."

I nod my assent. "Thank you kindly, sir."

"That'll be ten dollars."

I lay the cash into the man's outstretched palm, snickering as I do. I'm sure Mr. Clements would be pleased as punch to know his nest egg just paid my way into a nudie bar.

When I step inside the door of the club, I stop just past

the entrance to let my eyes adjust in the dim light. There's a softly lit stage jutting out into the middle of the room, and two girls are gyrating around on top of it wearing nothing but teeny-tiny undies. The girl with honey-blonde hair has boobs even smaller than mine. She's dancing under a flashing sign that says, "Rhonda." I don't care about Rhonda. But the other girl, the one with long black hair and thick bangs whose sign flashes "Bettie," well, her balloon-sized boobs are just about bursting off her tiny frame like they're gonna pop off and zip around the room. Those boobs don't look very pleasant to own, I must say, and they're definitely not what I'm in the market to buy, but at least I know I'm in the right place.

My eyes adjust to the dark room until I can make out an array of tables and chairs filled with men, including some particularly attentive ones seated along the perimeter of the jutting stage, right at the girls' feet.

I've never seen practically naked girls prancing around before, and I don't quite know what to make of it. I've seen naked girls in my life, of course—nudie photographs of Marilyn Monroe and Jayne Mansfield in the biographies I've read about them, and also real-life girls without their clothes on, too, since I shared my room at the group home with at least three other girls at any given time. But these two topless girls on stage aren't frozen into seductive poses on a page, and they're not young girls quietly changing into nightgowns, either. No, these two girls are jiggling and writhing around onstage for the world to see, right in front of a crowd of shouting strangers. I'm sure if Daddy were here, he'd call the whole situation "small-minded."

And yet, small-minded or not, I can't stop looking at them and wondering a million things. Do these girls' daddies know what they're doing? And what are the girls thinking while they gyrate and writhe up there? Do they feel sort of silly, or even a little bit ashamed? Or are they just thinking la-la-la the entire time, the same as if they were playing a game of checkers or talking about the weather? Or, when they're up on that stage and those men are staring at them and craning their necks and hooting at them and practically slobbering all over the stage, do the girls actually *like* it?

"Are you here for a job?"

I turn to look at the source of the raspy voice. It's a short man with dark hair.

"The man at the door let me pay ten dollars to come in," I say. "I'm just here to browse."

The man frowns. "Browse? It's a gentleman's club, sweetheart. If you're not here to dance, you can't be here. Everyone's already asking me if you're a new girl."

"I just want to watch the dancers for a little while, sir—so I can find out what nudie-dancing's all about, maybe try to get up the nerve to do it myself." That last part's a flat-out lie. I have no intention whatsoever of dancing in my skivvies for a crowd of—what? —forty men who've never done a dang thing in their sad-sack lives to deserve a personal glimpse of my titties.

Why would I give this paltry group of men a gander at something no man has ever seen before? Unless each and every of the men in this club is the head of a movie studio, then I can't think of one thing that would persuade me to hop up there and jiggle my bits for them. My destiny is to inspire audiences in the tens of millions, not in the tens. Neither Lana nor Marilyn, or even Jayne, ever pranced around shaking their titties in a nudie bar, as far as I know, and I don't plan to, either. But, of course, I don't want to say any of this to Mr. Sourpuss because then he'll kick me out, and being here's the only way I can figure to get the information I need to advance one step closer to fulfilling my destiny.

I smile sweetly and say, "I'd really like to talk to the girl onstage with the long black hair and big boobs." I look down like I'm shy.

By the expression on the man's face, I can tell he likes it when I act shy—and he most certainly likes the idea of me getting up on that stage. "Okay, honey," Mr. Sourpuss says, "you can watch for just a little bit, learn what it's all about.

But you can't stand here where everyone can see you. You're too distracting." He pauses, apparently thinking. "And you can't talk to Bettie right now—you'll have to wait 'til after her shift."

"Yes, sir, I'll just sit over there in the corner and I won't bother a dead fly." I smile again, but this time I make sure my smile is particularly shy. Before the man can say anything else, I glide away from him and scoot myself into an empty booth in the far corner of the room.

The man seems to be contemplating something, but then he heads in the opposite direction and leaves me in peace.

The big-boobs/small-boobs duo leaves the stage and yet another pair of gyrating girls—this time a medium-boobs/medium-boobs duo—comes out. I can't tell if these two girls were born with their boobs, or if they bought them. The only girl I'm sure bought her boobs is the dark-haired girl with the bangs from earlier—Bettie with the big boobs.

While the second set of girls dances on stage, Bettie Big Boobs enters the seating area of the club through a door next to the stage, all her parts now covered by tassels and sequins and such. Bettie begins flirting with the men seated around the room—and within half a minute, even before I can get up the nerve to walk over there and talk to her, one of the men hands her a bill and disappears with her into a back room.

I leap up from my chair and head over to Mr. Sourpuss by the bar.

"Excuse me, sir?" I say.

He looks up at me, exasperated.

"Can I *pay* to talk to the dark-haired girl during her shift? I just saw a man give Bettie money to talk to her—they just went into that room together over there. Can I be next in line, please, sir?"

His exasperation turns into a chuckle. "Sure, honey. If you've got twenty bucks, you can *talk* to Bettie, too, same as anyone else. I'll let her know you're waiting on her."

Thanks to Mr. Clements, I'm a high roller these days, so

the twenty-dollar fee is no problem. Even after paying for my bus ticket and motel room and splurging on the ten-dollar entry fee for this club, I've still got about forty bucks left from Mr. Clements' wad of cash. And, of course, I've also still got Joe, Lou, and Babe hiding safely under my mattress in my room, too. Still, I must confess, at this rate of spending, I'm starting to feel like I'd better get discovered in a malt shop right quick. Hollywood doesn't come for free, and Mr. Clements' Scholarship Fund ain't gonna last forever.

After a few minutes, Mr. Sourpuss motions for me to follow him. He leads me through a door and into a small room with a couch where Bettie Big Boobs is already seated.

"Thanks, Johnny," she purrs.

Mr. Sourpuss winks at Bettie, and then smiles at me. "Five minutes," he says matter-of-factly. He leaves the room.

Bettie pats the couch next to her, her long, dark hair cascading down her shoulders. "Sit down, honey."

I sit down on the far end of the couch, pressing my knees together. I figured this method for getting information would be more reliable and expeditious than randomly opening the phonebook, but suddenly I'm not so sure.

Bettie looks amused. "What can I do for you, honey?"

Now that I see Bettie up close and personal, this girl looks worn out. She's not ugly, not at all, but up close, she's more tired-looking than she looked up on stage under all that fancy lighting. Of course, it's hard to concentrate on Bettie's face because her boobs are so dang big and staring at me at full attention. I glance down at her boobs in awe, but quickly pretend to be staring at the sparkling pendant around her neck.

"I... I just wanted to ask you the name of your doctor?" I say. "Your plastic surgery doctor? I'm new in town, and I'm gonna get myself—"

Bettie bursts out laughing and I abruptly stop talking.

"You paid twenty bucks to ask me the name of my *plastic surgeon*?"

I nod. Why is that funny? I'm not sure if I should smile

and laugh along with her, or make like I'm offended—so I just stare at her blankly.

"Honey, you don't have to *pay* me to tell you the name of my doctor. I would have told you that for free." She laughs again.

"Well, thank you." I join her laughter. "Aren't you sweet as pie?"

"It's Dr. *Ishikawa*, honey. He does *all* the girls."

"Dr. Who?"

"*Ishikawa*. I'll write it down for you."

"Can I pick whatever size I want?"

"Of course. He can give you extra big ones, like mine"— she shakes her huge chest at me—"or, you know, more natural ones, though I don't know why anyone would bother paying for fake boobs that look like real ones." She laughs again, and I join her again, even though I'm quite sure I want natural looking ones.

Bettie Big Boobs seems awfully comfortable sitting here without any clothes on, so I take this golden opportunity to stare at her chest. Honestly, her straining flesh makes me wince. I wish I didn't need new boobs at all, to tell you the truth, but my destiny requires blonde hair and big boobs, and my boobs aren't gonna sprout like Chia pets all by themselves.

"You know, you don't *need* to get yourself new boobs to work here," Bettie says. "Customers like girls in all shapes and sizes."

"Oh, I don't wanna work here," I explain. I raise my small chest with pride. "I'm an *actress*." It feels exciting to say that word out loud for the first time.

"Oh yeah?" She smirks. "Well, good for you, honey. So am I. But I gotta pay the rent, you know, so dancing's my day job."

This girl must think I'm a half-wit. She's not an *actress*. Real actresses don't prance around in their skivvies in nudie bars with boobs the size of melons. Yes, it's true that Marilyn and Jayne took nudie-cutie *photos* for a famous men's magazine, but that's because they knew those photos would be seen by thousands and thousands of adoring fans all at once—and not just twenty guys in a nudie bar on a Wednesday afternoon.

When I remain silent, Bettie adds, "Well, honey, if you ever *do* decide to work here, you can't go wrong getting yourself the biggest boobs your back can handle." She puts her hands under her boobs and smooshes them up toward her chin, making the heart-shaped pendant around her neck disappear into her cleavage. "My tips tripled after I got these babies."

This girl is pulling on my last nerve. "Well, thank you for the information," I say primly. I stand up from the couch. "I'm grateful." I smile at her, sweet as syrup. "Dr. Ishikawa, you said?"

"Yeah, he's not too far from here." She writes his name and address on a piece of paper for me. "Here you go, honey. Our time's up anyway. Gotta get back out there and get my rent paid." She winks.

I take the piece of paper from her and head out the door.

Back in the main room, I march straight for the front door, Dr. Ishikawa's name burning a hole in my purse. But just as I'm about to exit, Mr. Sourpuss catches up to me. "Wait," he commands.

I freeze. Am I in trouble?

"The whole time you were in there with Bettie, everyone was asking about you. You've already made quite an impression on them, just standing there in your clothes. Do me a favor, go talk to my boss. He gives me a little bonus when I send him a really good girl." He hands me a pre-printed card with a name and address on it. "Go see him, right away, and make sure you tell him Johnny from the club sent you."

"Well, thank you, Johnny, but I've decided I'm not interested in working here—"

"No, no." He laughs. "I mean, yeah, he owns this place, sure, but he's a real big shot. He's also got *Casanova Magazine* and a whole production company, too, and he's always on the look-out for girls who've got a little something special—"

"A production company?" I blurt. "You mean, like a *movie* production company?"

Mr. Sourpuss nods, grinning at me like the butcher's dog.

I look down at the card in my hand. "Kurtis Jackman," I read aloud. I've never heard the name before, but it sends a shiver down my spine. There's no doubt in my mind this Kurtis fellow is the one who's gonna discover me like Lana Turner in the malt shop. "Okay, Johnny, I'll go meet your Mr. Jackman tomorrow," I say. *Right after I pay a visit to Bettie's Dr. Ishikawa.*

Chapter 23

18 Years 10 Months Old
436 Days Before Killing Kurtis

I've enjoyed being Mrs. Kurtis Jackman more than I ever thought I would. I like living with Kurtis in our fancy mansion, lying around by our pool and shopping for more clothes and books than I could ever wear or read. But most of all, I adore giggling with Kurtis between the sheets about how gorgeous I am.

"I'm so pretty, you should look at me with a flashlight in the daytime," I coo to him when we're lying in bed, naked as jaybirds, and he just laughs and laughs.

"Tell me another one," he begs, stroking my face.

"I'm so good lookin', I bring a tear to a blind man's glass eye," I say, and Kurtis throws his head back and guffaws.

Kurtis sure does love it when I talk Texas. "Okay, now say one about me," Kurtis pleads. My husband likes to say we two are like Beauty and the Beast—and even though he's almost as good-lookin' as me, I always play along.

"You're so ugly, your cooties gotta close their eyes," I say.

Kurtis hoots loudly.

"If I had a dog as ugly as you, I'd shave his butt and make him walk backwards."

Kurtis whoops.

"You're so ugly, your momma used to take you with her everywhere she went, just so she didn't have to kiss you goodbye."

Kurtis laughs so hard, he grabs ahold of his sides.

"I've been to four county fairs, three goat ropin's, a clown rodeo and a hangin,' and I ain't never seen a face as ugly as yours," I say.

Now Kurtis howls so damned hard, I think he's gonna bust a spleen.

These are my favorite times with Kurtis, when we're lying naked in bed together, giggling and guffawing under our soft blankets. I especially love it when Kurtis sighs and touches my cheek like I'm a rare treasure—that's when I catch myself thinking I just might be the luckiest girl in the world.

Of course, laughing's not the only thing Kurtis and I do when we're in bed. In these past four months of marriage, my husband and I have had enough sex for fifty pornos, and then some. Kurtis loves to say we're "making up for lost time." Sometimes, the deed happens quicker than a knife fight in a phone booth, but that's okay—that just means Kurtis loves me so much his body can't stand it.

Lately, Kurtis has taken to calling himself "Kurtis the Great," like he's a grand conqueror and I'm an unexplored continent. Every time we do it, even after four whole months, Kurtis acts like he's getting away with stealing the Mona Lisa. Of course, Kurtis wants to try every single variation he can think of with me, and I always say, "Sure thing, sugar." I mean, heck, the man married me just to get with me, after all, so it's only fair to give him plenty of bang for his buck—especially when I've discovered I like the bang so damned much.

The only time sex with Kurtis was anything less than thoroughly enjoyable for me was our very first time. Kurtis was gentle and careful with me, actually, so that wasn't the problem. I reckon I just wasn't prepared for what happened the minute Kurtis' junk finally made its way inside me.

Everything leading up to that precise moment was moving along like a cherry pit through a greased goose, actually. Kurtis and I were mauling each other just like we'd gotten so good at doing before our wedded bliss (except we were finally the both of us naked as babies). "Oh my God," Kurtis kept saying to me, over and over, his voice ragged and strained, all the while stroking me between my legs and kissing me and licking me, too. Oh man, I was squirming and moaning and bucking like a bull at the rodeo, just aching for him to get inside me. When he finally climbed on top of me, his erection fixin' to skewer me like a kabob, I held my breath and closed my eyes and threw my head back, bracing myself for him to finally give me what I was dying for.

"You ready, baby?" he whispered in my ear, his voice trembling, and I could feel his erection poking at me, rapping on my front door.

"Yes," I breathed.

"I love you," he said into my ear—and then I felt him burrow himself deep, deep, deep inside me, so deep my eyes sprung open and bugged out of my head.

And that's when I yelped like Kurtis had stepped on my tail—not because Kurtis was hurting me (because he wasn't)—but because, right when Kurtis entered my *body*, Wesley entered my *mind*. And that's the story of how my mind got fucked for the first time along with my body.

An hour later, when Kurtis wanted an encore with his "little virgin bride"—and man, did his hard-on look ready to impale me that time—can you guess what happened again? Yep, there he was again—Wesley—popping into my head the second Kurtis' arrow hit my bull's-eye.

That whole second time while Kurtis was inside me, thrusting and groaning and telling me he loved me, I couldn't stop wondering what Wesley might look like naked and whether Wesley moving inside me would feel the same as Kurtis, whether he'd make me want to scream and groan and whimper, too—but maybe even more so? And the worst part of all was that, after we were done and lying together soaked in sweat, all I could think about was Wesley and wondering what it might be like to lie next to Wesley's naked, sweaty, scrawny body instead of Kurtis' big, brawny one. And that thought made me want to cry.

Luckily, though, after those first two times with Kurtis, and during the past four months of our happy marriage up until about eight minutes ago when we were going at it like rabbits for the umpteenth time, I've learned how to focus on Kurtis and nothing else and just enjoy the sizzling ride. What would be the point in doing otherwise?

Yep, once I figured out how to enjoy the husband I've got and stop wishing things could be different, I reckon that's when I finally found true happiness in this life. Because these past four months with my husband have been pure bliss, they really have—and not just in bed, either. I haven't even needed to nag Kurtis about my sacred destiny these past four months because my darling husband keeps bringing it up on his own.

And he's not just talking the talk, either; he's walking the walk. Last month, Kurtis finally released the *Casanova* special double issue with my full-frontal pictorial in it—and true to his word, my husband made me the centerfold, cover girl, *and* "Casanova Cutie," too—an unheard of trifecta in the Land of Perverts that, according to Kurtis, was gonna make the world take notice. Of course, my sweet porno-king husband was right as rain, yet again—that special issue with me on the cover beat the crap out of all prior *Casanova* sales records and made me an instantaneous "It" girl the world over, just like Kurtis had predicted.

I had no idea how many people "read" *Casanova*, or at least take a peek at it, but it turns out it's tons and tons—especially an unheard of special double issue like mine. The issue featured not only my cover shot and centerfold, but also a rehash of all my prior good-girl photos, too, *plus* an in-depth interview with me about my turn-ons and turn-offs, and a whole big thing on the back page about how I saved myself for marriage on account of my ultra-strict upbringing (next to a photo of me wearing a lacy, white negligee).

The day after the special double issue hit newsstands, Kurtis gazed into my eyes in bed and whispered, "The world's devouring you, baby—we're having record numbers." He cupped my face in his hands, looked deeply into my eyes, and kissed me—and when he pulled back from our kiss, his eyes were blazing. "The whole world loves you like I do," he said—and I actually felt myself swoon when he said it.

A couple days after that, when I was lounging by the pool reading my book and sucking on an Otter Pop, Kurtis came over, kissed my forehead, and said, "The whole world's losing their shit over you, baby. Our numbers are through the roof." I looked up from my book then, and he touched my cheek with his fingertip. "You're so fucking gorgeous," he whispered, his eyes on fire—and I felt my cheeks blaze a deep crimson.

And then, just yesterday, while we were sitting at the breakfast table, eating cream of wheat and reading the morning papers like an old married couple, Kurtis suddenly slammed down his spoon onto the table and blurted out, "You're so fucking gorgeous, it hurts to look directly at you—looking at you is like looking at the fucking sun." He smiled broadly then, so I knew it was a good kind of hurt he was talking about. "I'm gonna make you the biggest fucking star the world has ever seen," he added. "You can count on it." Well, that last one didn't just make me swoon, it soaked my panties clean through—mostly because I wasn't even wearing any lipstick when he said it.

In fact, the way Kurtis looked at me over his bowl of cream of wheat made me feel a pang in my *heart*—and not just in my panties—like nothing I've ever felt before. I'm not sure exactly what to call that pang-y feeling, but I wouldn't poke you in the eye and spit on you if you were of the mind to call it love. My husband might not be perfect, it's true—yes, I'm well aware I'm married to a porno-king, after all—but I reckon every dog's gotta have a flea or two, and a girl shouldn't throw the hound out with the pest.

Even if I originally married My Husband the Porno King as a means of fulfilling my sacred destiny, I reckon I've somehow managed to find a platinum-lined happily ever after with him despite myself. The very thought of how happy my life's unexpectedly turned out makes me wanna slap my own forehead and shout, "Ain't that the berries!" almost every single day.

I've been so happy with my sweet and gentle husband these past four months, in fact, I'm a whole new person. Nowadays, all I ever do is sing a happy tune and giggle and pinch myself all day long at my good fortune. Just the other day, Kurtis and I were in bed together after an especially toe-curling session in the sack, and Kurtis said, "Hey, honey, why'd you decide to get such small boobs?" He asked me the question like it was a "by the way" kind of query, like he was asking me something akin to, "Have you ever thought of trying *blue* eye shadow for a change?"—as if saying such a horrible thing about my beautiful boobies wasn't rightful justification for a wife to stab her husband in his chest and cram the cavity full of cornbread stuffing.

"I'll pay for bigger ones if you want to get 'em, baby," Kurtis added, probably thinking I was gonna squeal with delight.

"Well, bless your heart," I replied, smiling sweetly. "But I think my boobies are the perfect size for an *actress*." (I didn't have to add, "as opposed to a *stripper*" on account of that second half being implied.)

The thing that amazed me about the whole conversation was that, as much as my blood should have boiled when Kurtis made that unforgivable comment about my beautiful boobs, I didn't even want to jerk him bald for it. It was like I wasn't even me.

And that's when I knew that living in this fancy mansion and getting spicy-hot lovin' every single day from a husband who adores me, and hearing about how gorgeous I am (even without lipstick on), and how my husband's gonna make sure I'm seen by audiences in cineplexes all over the world has transformed me into the pure and good woman Kurtis thinks I am. It's true I've done a few bad things in the past (by necessity), but now, thanks to my newfound happiness with my husband, I've finally been able to put the past firmly behind me, cleanse my soul, and start anew.

The only teensy-weensy thing that's given me just the slightest bit of a peach-pit in my stomach these past four months is one tiny thing (and, really, it's hardly a thing at all, hardly even worth mentioning). But lately, maybe for the past month or so, it seems like Kurtis' passion for me has started to morph and twist into something I don't completely understand. When he's on top of me and giving it to me really good, really making me scream his name and beg him for mercy, he's lately taken to growling low and gravelly into my ear, "You're mine." And the strange part is that he says it over and over again, with each thrust of his body, and with such fierce intensity, it kinda makes my hair stand on end and my stomach flip upside-down.

I mean, I knew Kurtis would be passionate about me once I finally gave myself to him completely—but his zeal about me is beginning to feel like something different than passion. I just don't know what to call it, though. I expected Kurtis to become wrapped around my little finger when I finally became his virgin bride—and he most certainly did. What I didn't expect, though, is how, lately, having Kurtis wrapped around my little finger has started to feel an awful lot like having Kurtis' fingers wrapped around my slender neck.

Chapter 24

18 Years 10 Months Old
430 Days Before Killing Kurtis

"I've got a big surprise for you, baby," Kurtis says, bursting through the front door and bounding into the living room.

I look up from my book. Kurtis is always surprising me with fancy presents.

Kurtis bounds over to me on the couch and scoops me up like a rag doll. "I enrolled you in acting classes today, baby." He's smiling from ear to ear as if he thinks this news is gonna make me jump for joy.

I'm instantly prickly as a porcupine. My husband wants to send me to *school*?

"You're officially an acting student, baby," Kurtis continues. "Now all you need's a job as a waitress, and you'll be a true Angeleno." He laughs.

"You don't think I'm a good enough actress already?"

He scoffs. "Of course, I do. But let's be honest; you don't have any experience, honey—you know, in front of the camera, saying lines from a script. You're gonna need some experience before we can convince investors you can carry an entire movie all by yourself."

"*Whom* do we need to convince? I thought you believed in me, Kurtis."

"Of course, I believe in you. But you're green, honey.

And investors aren't gonna gamble big money on an unknown actress with zero experience."

"But why do we need investors, anyway? I still don't understand why you can't just pay for the movie yourself."

"Don't you worry your pretty little head about the business side of things, Buttercup," Kurtis says, as if I've got the IQ of a pollywog. "You just worry about being the star."

Well, damn, it's awfully hard to worry about being the star of a movie when there's no movie to star in. I'm suddenly angrier than a hornet. I push Kurtis away and leap up from the couch. "I'm a whisker away from having a hissy-fit with a tail on it, Kurtis Jackman."

Kurtis laughs, totally unfazed by my flash of anger. "The camera loves you, baby, obviously, and there's no doubt you're gonna light the screen on fire, but you still need acting classes to get comfortable saying scripted lines in front of a camera. That's just the way it is."

"Are acting classes like *school*? Where they try to make everyone standardized?" I ask. "Because I don't want some small-minded acting teacher trying to make me think like everybody else."

"No, no, no, it's just the opposite." Kurtis chuckles. "You don't know about acting classes?"

I shake my head, defiant. "Do they give out multiple-choice tests?"

Kurtis laughs and pulls me onto the couch again. "Come here, baby," Kurtis commands, guiding me onto his lap. I feel like a little girl visiting Santa. He smooths my hair away from my face and grins at me. "Even when Marilyn Monroe was already a big star, do you know what she did?"

I shake my head.

"She enrolled in acting classes," Kurtis explains. "Do you know why?"

I shake my head again.

"Because she wanted to learn how to be better. *All* great actors take acting classes, baby, all of 'em."

Well, this is news to me. "Are you sure, Kurtis?"

"Of course."

"Even Marilyn?"

"Especially Marilyn. It was a whole big thing—in all the papers and everything."

Relief and elation floods into me. Maybe Kurtis actually knows what he's talking about here, after all. I scrunch my mouth up, deep in thought.

Kurtis laughs and beep-beeps my nose. "Baby, the whole time Marilyn made that movie with Laurence Olivier, she had an acting coach."

I don't know what movie he's talking about. I haven't actually seen a whole lot of movies—I've just read a whole bunch of books about movie stars. But I believe him. "Well," I say, suddenly resolved, "I reckon I need an acting coach, then, honey—I need an acting coach right quick."

Kurtis chuckles.

All of a sudden, electricity is coursing through my veins. "Kurtis Jackman, you've got to get me my very own acting coach. *Pronto.*" I bounce up and down on his lap to emphasize my point.

"Hang on, honey. Calm down," Kurtis coos. "Go to some beginning acting classes, see what you think, and we'll figure things out from there."

I throw my arms around Kurtis' neck. If Marilyn went to acting lessons, then I'll do it, too. Hell, maybe I'll even learn a thing or two—you never know. If it turns out acting classes are full of small-minded, dumbass teachers telling me what I can and can't do—people who wanna turn me into a standardized drone who can't think her way out of a paper bag—well, then, I'll just smile like sunshine on a cloudy day and ignore them all.

"Now, baby, I want you to go to your classes every single day like a good girl and learn as much as possible, okay? This is gonna keep you busy and out of trouble all those long hours while I'm at work."

Well, hang on a minute. What kind of trouble does he think I'll get myself into? I'm about to ask that very question when Kurtis says, "I like knowing my wife's being a good preacher's daughter when I'm not around." I suddenly feel Kurtis' hardness poking up from his lap, right against my undies. He places his hands firmly on either side of my head, right at my temples and looks directly into my eyes. "A pretty girl with too much time on her hands can get too easily distracted." His eyes flash with a sudden hardness I don't understand.

I force a smile. Why am I feeling like a mouse in a trap right now? "You always do so much for me," I squeak out. "Thank you."

Kurtis presses his hands even harder against my temples for a strange, unsettling moment, causing my breathing to go shallow. Just as I'm about to panic, though, he releases my head and exhales. "You're a good girl," he mutters, his erection hard as a rock underneath me. "Let's make sure you stay that way." In a sudden movement, Kurtis throws me onto my back on the couch, reaches under my skirt, and yanks down my panties. "You're mine," he growls, entering me roughly. "And I'm gonna make you a. Huge. Fucking. Star."

Chapter 25

18 Years 11 Months Old
415 Days Before Killing Kurtis

I wake up with a start.

I've been dreaming of Daddy. In my dream, he told me exactly where to find him. And, gosh dang it, where he said to look is so obvious, I feel like a fool for not thinking of it sooner.

The whole time I've been in Hollywood, I've tried and tried to find Daddy as best I could on my own. When I first got here, I stupidly thought I'd just look him up in the phonebook and scoot on down to his fancy mansion and throw my arms around him and cry. When that didn't work out, my next idea was hiring a detective, but I couldn't figure out how to pay for one without Kurtis finding out—and letting Kurtis find out about my not-dead, not-Preacher of a daddy isn't an option.

After those two ideas for finding Daddy didn't work out, all I could think to do was scrutinize the passing faces on the sidewalk, wander down random streets in the Hollywood hills with the biggest mansions on them, and pop into every juke joint and diner I passed within two miles of Hollywood, asking after him. But no matter how many places I've popped into, I keep hearing the same thing: "Nope. Never heard of him."

It's been discouraging, to say the least, but I've never given up hope. I've always believed serendipity would lead me to my daddy, sooner or later. But, now, thanks to Daddy visiting me in my dream, I don't need serendipity—all I need is the yellow pages.

I pad downstairs to the kitchen where we keep the phonebooks.

I'm in luck. There's only one listing in the entire city where Daddy could possibly be, and it's just a ten-minute cab ride away. The thought that Daddy's been right under my nose this whole time, just ten minutes away, makes me groan in frustration. I want to slap myself silly for not figuring this out sooner.

A short ninety minutes later, I'm gussied up fit-to-kill and standing in front of a sign that reads, "Hollywood Putt-Putt-'n'-Stuff Mini Golf." This has got to be the place. I slam the cab door and take a deep breath. I wonder if Daddy will even recognize me. He's gonna be fit-to-be-tied when he sees what's become of his twelve-year-old little girl—his namesake and greatest invention.

"Pardon me, honey," I call to a young man trimming the hedges over by the pirate ship at hole nine. The guy continues his work, apparently not realizing I'm speaking to him. I walk right up close to the man, close enough for him to smell my pretty perfume, and tap him on his shoulder. "Excuse me?"

He straightens up and turns around, and it's immediately clear he likes what he sees. "Yes, miss?"

"Hello there, sir," I purr to the man, smiling. "I'm wondering if you can help me, please?" I stick out my boobs and jut my hip alluringly when I say this last part. Might as well give this young man something to fantasize about on cold, lonely nights.

He smiles broadly at me. "Sure."

That boy could eat corn on the cob through a picket fence with those teeth, but still, he's kind of cute. "Do you know where I can find Charlie Wilber, please?"

The man scratches his head. "Um. I'm not sure. But maybe go inside and ask Bob. He's the owner. He knows everybody."

I smile sweetly and wink. "Well, thank you so much, honey."

Inside, an old, craggy man is standing behind a counter, handing out golf clubs to a family. I wait behind the family, reminding myself to breathe. When the family finally leaves the counter, I step right up.

"How many golfers?" the old man asks.

My stomach drops into my feet. This is it. This man's gonna lead me to my daddy, after all this time and so many tears. The tornado of emotions swirling inside me is almost too much to bear. "I'm actually looking for someone?"

He raises his eyebrows, inviting more information.

My heart is thumping in my ears. When I finally see Daddy, I'm going to hug and kiss him and lay my cheek on his shoulder and look up into his movie-star-handsome face and pepper his entire face with kisses. After that, I'll twirl and twirl around so he can see me from every angle, showing him just how much I've grown up and filled out. He'll whistle and bellow, "Oooooweeeee! You're the most beautiful woman that ever did live, Buttercup." And then he'll ask if I've settled for anything less than the very best in this life, and I'll be so proud to tell him, "No, Daddy, I most certainly have not. I'm living in a fancy mansion with a fountain with naked ladies and cherubs and even a little cupid with wings, just like you always dreamed for me! I'm Charlie Wilber's Daughter, Daddy! I'm *somebody*!"

But then... *Why,* I suddenly wonder... Why didn't Daddy write to me again after that very first letter? Why didn't he come get me? Why didn't he invite me to live in his fancy mansion with him?

"Miss?"

I take a deep breath. Daddy will explain everything. There's no point in wondering about all of it when, in just a few short minutes, Daddy himself will be standing in front of me, telling me every last thing I've ever wanted to know about the past six and a half years. "Yes, sir, thank you. I'm looking for *Charlie Wilber.*" I say Daddy's name slowly and enunciate it perfectly. I don't want there to be any confusion about the name I'm saying. "He's my daddy."

The man looks surprised. "You're *Charlie Wilber's* daughter?"

Lord have mercy. I've been running all over hell's half acre looking for Daddy all this time, and this man just recognized his name! I can barely breathe. All I can manage is a bug-eyed nod.

The man shakes his head. "Charlie's not here."

Tears instantly well up in my eyes. This can't be happening.

"He used to be, though, but that was years ago."

My heart is racing even faster at that news. *Daddy was here.* I look down at the carpet beneath my shoes and imagine Daddy's shoes standing on this very spot.

"He used to come around practically every day, telling his stories, showing off his golf course designs, helping people get their balls unstuck from the chute, telling everyone exactly how to sink hole fourteen... " The man's face flashes annoyance. "Yeah, everyone knew Charlie," the man continues. "He's not the kind of guy you'd easily forget." He pauses.

I know he's got more to say, but for some reason he's not saying it. I'm trying to be patient, I really am, but I'm bursting.

I wait as long as I can stand it before shrieking at him like a hyena. "Well, for cryin' out loud, sir, where's my daddy *now?*" This man better stop going around his elbow to get to his thumb, or I'm gonna leap across this counter and knock his teeth down his throat 'til he spits 'em back out single file.

The man presses his lips together. "Well, I'm not sure if he's still over there anymore..." He bites his lip.

I look him in the eyes, my nostrils flaring. "*Where?*"

He continues, "Like I say, I'm not sure if he's still over there, but I'll tell you what I heard happened."

I nod, my heart in my throat.

When the man speaks again, it's to tell me exactly where to find Daddy. And when he does, I have to grip the counter with white knuckles so I don't crumple onto my knees and throw myself on the floor.

Chapter 26

Lancaster, California

18 Years 11 Months Old
412 Days Before Killing Kurtis

After my horrible bus ride out to Hollywood almost a year ago, I swore I'd never ride a bus again, but, of course, I should've known a girl can never say never. A year ago, I never thought I'd be married to a porno-king, either, so go figure. If riding another bus means getting to see my daddy, then I'll ride another bus. I'd ride a bus straight to Hades to see my daddy— I'd ride a *hundred* buses into the pits of hell and crawl on my hands and knees across hot coals over ten miles of bad road.

As the bus pulls away, it's hotter than bacon grease in a skillet and I'm standing in the middle of nowhere in front of a stark gray building surrounded by barbed-wire fences. I've never seen an actual prison before, and the sight of it curls my toes, especially when I think about Daddy being locked up inside there. A sign to my right says, "Visitor's Entrance," and I reckon that's the place I've got to go.

The guard at the visitor's entrance does an extremely thorough job of frisking me and frisking me again. But I don't mind. I can't imagine he's ever had the pleasure of touching anyone as pretty as me in his whole sad-sack life, and I'm glad to give him a happy memory.

The closer I get to the room labeled "Visitor's Lounge," the jumpier I get. Lord have mercy, I'm so jumpy, I'd have to thread a sewing machine while it's running on high. I just keep telling myself to breathe, but I feel dangerously close to passing out and sprawling onto the floor.

It's been close to seven years since I sat across from Daddy at the little table in our trailer and begged him to take me to Hollywood with him. Seven long years, and so much has happened since then. I've crammed a whole lifetime into these past few years, what with Jeb's cake, and Mr. Clements' baseball cards, and Wesley, and now my husband the porno-king. I'm a full-grown woman now, and a legendary beauty for the ages at that, just like Daddy always knew I'd be. But right now, despite all that's happened and who I've become, I suddenly feel like I'm twelve years old again, waiting at the mailbox for a second letter from Daddy that's never gonna come.

The Visitor's Room is a cement box with barred windows and cafeteria-style tables bolted to the floor. Every cough and footfall and murmur echoes and bounces in this room for days. "Wait here," a guard barks and I take a seat at one of the tables. When I drum my fingers on the table, I notice my diamond ring and wedding band on my hand. I take them off and quickly stow both rings in my pocketbook. I cross my legs at the ankles and uncross them, shaking like a cat at the dog pound.

A guard on the far side of the room yells, "Door open!"

There's a loud buzzing noise.

The heavy steel door at the far side of the room clanks open. I rise from my seat anxiously, just as a line of shackled inmates shuffles into the room. The first three men enter the room, and each of them connects with other visitors.

But then the fourth inmate shuffles into the room, and, holy hell, he's my daddy! Tears spring into my eyes. "Daddy," I breathe, but my voice catches in my throat.

Daddy surveys the room.

"Daddy," I shriek, finally gaining control of my voice. I wave my arms above my head, my knees buckling.

Daddy looks over at me. "Buttercup?"

That voice. It's as if I heard it just yesterday, tucking me into bed for the night. "It's me, Daddy!" Tears stream down my cheeks.

Daddy shuffles to me as quickly as his shackles will allow. "Well, I'll be damned."

I fling my arms around him and lose myself to wailing sobs. I can't control any part of myself. I can't control my crying. I can't control my limbs. Or voice. Lungs. Mind. Everything's higgledy-piggledy out of control. Every part of me is either racing, flying, choking, wracking, reeling, sobbing, melting, or spinning, or doing all of it at once. "Daddy!"

Daddy pulls away to look at me. "I can't believe it," he says. "Just look at you."

When I've imagined this moment a thousand times, I've pictured myself twirling around so Daddy could get a good look at how grown-up and beautiful I've become. I've pictured myself throwing my head back and laughing as he shouts, "Woo-weee, girl, you sure did grow up right!"

But now that I'm here, I can't control myself enough to twirl and pose. The only thing my body wants to do is hold Daddy tight. I throw my arms around him again and nuzzle my face into his neck. "Oh, Daddy." A strangled cry escapes my throat.

"Ssssh, honey, now. We don't have too much time here. Let's sit right down so you can tell me all about what you've been up to. Sshhhh, now, Buttercup, sit down and talk to me, honey."

I do as I'm told, sniffling and wiping the tears from my face.

"Look at your hair. Wooh!" he exclaims, shaking his head. "Last I saw you, you were no bigger than a popcorn fart, and now look at you. You're prettier than a picture, Charlene."

Charlene? Since when does Daddy call me Charlene? I haven't been called that since the group home. I recoil. Is this really Daddy?

"What's wrong, Buttercup? What is it?"

"Is it really you, Daddy? You're Charlie Wilber, right?" Suddenly, my head is spinning and I can't see straight. Daddy's so much shorter than I remember him. I thought he was gonna be at least as tall as Kurtis, maybe even taller, but he's short and his shoulders are narrow. I thought he'd be handsome and dapper like Kurtis, but he looks different than I remembered him. His face is so much harder than I remember it. And so much more wrinkled. He looks so much older than I remember him, too. Where's that playful twinkle in his eye? I thought he'd look more like Kurtis.

Daddy's mouth is hanging open.

"Are you my Daddy?" I repeat. "Charlie Wilber?"

"Of course, I am. What's got into you all of a sudden, honey?"

"I...I just can't believe I'm finally seeing you after all this time," I say. I suddenly feel like I'm sitting with a stranger. Why didn't he write me more than one letter? Why'd he leave me for so long without telling me where to find him? "Why are you here, Daddy?" I ask. "What happened?"

"Well," Daddy says. He rubs his face with his hand and his shackle clanks against the table. "I'm goddamned unlucky is what happened—I could fall into a barrel full of titties and come out sucking my thumb, that's what."

My stomach lurches. Was Daddy always this crass? And his drawl so thick? Every time I've thought about Daddy's voice all this time, I've always imagined him sounding like a movie star. "What happened, Daddy?" I whisper, holding back tears.

"Well, shit, that Mr. Moneybags wouldn't give me the time of day is what happened. I reckon he thought he was too high and mighty to hear me out about my mini-golf course designs. The bastard wouldn't even see me. I tried the polite way to get Mr. Moneybags' attention for a couple weeks, but then I decided to take the short way home, and I waited outside his house to talk to him, man to man. And when he came out, he just strutted past me, acting like his shit didn't stink, so I decided to teach that fucker some manners. A man can't strut around acting like he's higher than everybody else, I don't care if he wipes his ass with hundred-dollar bills, he's gotta have some manners and hear another man out. So I went over to that fucker's house and I wound up teaching him some much-needed manners, is what happened."

My heart sinks. Does this mean Daddy's gonna be in this Godforsaken place for the rest of his life? I remember what happened to that fuzzy black-and-white kitty when Daddy taught Jessica Santos some manners. "Did you *kill* him, Daddy?" I whisper.

Daddy laughs. "Naw, I didn't kill the motherfucker. I just taught him a thing or two. But he was a big fat pussy and screamed like a little girl 'til all his neighbors showed up and held me down and called the cops. And then Mr. Moneybags called his goddamned lawyers and they all said, 'Yes sir' and 'How high?' when he told them to jump, and just because I might've been holding a golf club when I taught him a thing or two, might've swung the golf club at his head just a time or two to scare him and maybe knock a few extra manners into him, everybody started saying I gave the man something more than a routine ass-whooping and started calling it 'aggravated assault' or some other shit I can't even remember. Which all just goes to show, Buttercup, if you're gonna beat the snot out of a sissified rich man, don't fucking do it where all his neighbors can hear you doing it."

I smile. I can't believe I ever doubted this man was my daddy when I first laid eyes on him. His face has wrinkled up some in these past seven years, and there's the tiniest bit of gray at his temples now, but even in his denim jumpsuit, he's still as handsome as a movie star. Yes, he's still my handsome, clever daddy—although, to tell you the truth, I'm awfully surprised to find out he wasn't clever enough not to get caught for what he did. If it were *me* teaching some rich guy some manners, I sure as hell wouldn't get caught like Daddy did, you can bet on that.

"Now, Buttercup, go ahead and tell me everything. I can't believe how much you've grown up. You look like a pin-up girl, for Chrissakes. Woo-wee! I've never seen anyone so beautiful in all my life."

"I'm a legendary beauty, aren't I?"

"You sure are. Now, tell me what you've been up to and what I've missed."

I start right from the beginning. I tell Daddy the "official" story of how Mother killed Jeb, since I've lately preferred telling myself the Horrible Night of Jeb's Murder never even happened, and Daddy squints at me like he doesn't believe a word I'm saying.

"If your momma ever had an idea in her head, it would die of loneliness," he says, "and you're telling me she rubbed *two* ideas together enough to bake a special cake like that?"

I glance over at the guards on the other side of the room.

"Buttercup?" He looks at me sideways. "You're telling me it was your *mother* who baked that cake?"

I pause. I don't like thinking about that night. It's been a long time since I had a nightmare about the Horrible Night of Jeb's Murder, and I'd like to keep it that way. But I can't resist. I lean forward and lower my head. "Well, the man *was* sleeping in *your bed,* Daddy," I whisper.

Daddy's face bursts into a huge grin. "I knew it." He nods, encouraging me to tell him more.

Suddenly, it dawns on me that conversations in the Visitor's Center might be recorded. I keep my voice low and my words vague. "He was talking about sending me to school, Daddy."

Daddy understands me well enough. He purses his lips. "And what'd you think about that?"

"I thought, 'Nobody tells Charlie Wilber's Daughter

what she can and can't do.'" My pulse is pounding in my ears. "Nobody."

Daddy's eyes are sparkling like diamonds. "That's my girl."

In careful whispers and vague descriptions, I go on to tell Daddy as much as I dare about my performance at the trial and how I had the jury eating out of the palm of my hand. I tell him about how my performance in front of the jury lit a fuse inside me and made me realize my life's sacred destiny to pick up Lana and Marilyn's torch and carry it ever-farther into the catacombs of history. And without mentioning Wesley or the baseball cards (because I'm not sure Daddy needs to know about Wesley and, regardless, I don't want to answer any questions about what happened to all that baseball-card money, anyway), I tell Daddy about the group home and how I waited to age-out before coming to Hollywood.

Without mentioning Kurtis' nudie club or magazine, I also tell Daddy about how I got discovered by a "rich movie producer named Kurtis" on just my second day in Hollywood and how Kurtis is just about on the verge of making an "epic" movie starring me. "Kurtis calls it a 'movie-homage' to Marilyn Monroe," I explain proudly. "I'm not quite sure yet if 'homage' means I'll be playing Marilyn herself, like it's a biography kind of movie, or if I'll be playing someone that makes you *think* of Marilyn, like an 'inspired by' kind of movie."

Daddy expresses unadulterated excitement.

I'm about to tell Daddy about how Kurtis signed me up for acting lessons, too, just like how Marilyn took them, but I think better of it. I wouldn't want Daddy thinking Kurtis is sending me to school to get brainwashed into thinking like everybody else.

"Kurtis hasn't settled on all the details of our movie yet," I continue, bursting with enthusiasm, "because he's still getting *investors* for our movie—because, Daddy, even if you're richer than Mansa Musa, you've still gotta have *investors* to make a real Hollywood movie; that's just the way it is in the movie business."

Daddy's taking in everything I'm saying with a wide smile and blazing eyes—and when I finish talking, he leans forward in his chair, right up close to me, the shackles around his wrists clanking onto the table between us, and says, "So, just how rich is this producer guy, Buttercup?"

"Oh, heck, he's got enough money to burn a wet mule."

Daddy grins from ear to ear. "That's good, Buttercup. That's real good."

Coming here today, I wasn't sure I was gonna tell Daddy about me being Kurtis' wife and all, but now, seeing the over-the-moon grin on Daddy's face, I know he'd be good and proud of me for marrying a man as rich as Kurtis. "And, Daddy, guess what?" I open my pocketbook and pull out my diamond ring and wedding band. "Kurtis is my husband."

Daddy's eyes smolder as he eyes the sparkling diamond in my hand.

When it's clear Daddy's not going to say anything, I continue. "And the funny thing is, this big fat diamond's not even why I love him." My eyes prick with tears. "He treats me good and fine, Daddy. He's a big movie producer, yes, and he says he's gonna make me a big star—that's all true—but the thing is, he's also sweet as can be and gentle with me." I feel my cheeks bursting into flames. "He's just the sweetest husband in the whole, wide world." I swallow hard. Right up 'til this very minute, hearing myself say these words out loud, I didn't realize just how much I love Kurtis.

Daddy's mouth has twisted into a crooked grin.

My heart is beating out of my chest. "Every single day, my husband tells me I'm the most gorgeous girl in the world." I swallow hard. "Every single day, he tells me he *loves* me." I feel a lump in my throat. I think that's the part that chokes me up the most—finally getting to hear someone tell me they love me every single day.

Daddy manages a big smile. "He treats you like Charlie Wilber's Daughter deserves to be treated?"

"Oh, yes, sir. He sure does. I didn't settle for anything

but the very best in this life, just like you taught me. I couldn't have found a better husband for myself if I'd looked the world over." I pause, considering my words. "Kurtis really loves me, Daddy. He really, really does." As these last words come out of my mouth, tears glisten in my eyes. It suddenly hits me like a ton of bricks that I've managed to make a good marriage for myself, totally by accident. Even if I started out wanting a husband who could make me a movie star, I've managed to wrangle a husband who can make me a movie star *and* love me to bits, too. "He's everything I've ever wanted."

Daddy shakes his head in amazement. "Buttercup, you've made me real proud."

I'm enjoying the look on Daddy's face so much, I figure I'll hit him with the grand finale. "And you know what else, Daddy? Kurtis and I live in a big ol' mansion. Our house is so big, you need a jetpack to go from one end to the other. Hell, we've even got a fountain with naked ladies and cherubs and a little cupid with wings." I feel like I'm gonna burst with pride.

I'm expecting Daddy to shout with excitement, but, instead, his face goes instantly dark like someone turned out the lights.

I'm not sure what I've said wrong. Daddy's face went straight from glowing to scowling in a heartbeat. "Daddy? What's wrong?" I gasp. "What'd I say?" My stomach has turned to knots.

Daddy shakes his head.

"Daddy?"

Daddy rubs his chin with his fingers, and the chain on his handcuff swings and clanks against the table. "I wanted to be the one to get you a fountain with naked ladies and cherubs and a little cupid with wings."

I can't believe my cotton pickin' ears. "Oh, Daddy, I don't care about the mansion. I *never* cared about the stupid mansion. Don't you know that?" My tears come fast and furious. "All I ever cared about was being with you." I'm having a hard time getting my words out. "Why'd you leave me, Daddy?" I choke out. "Why didn't you take me with you? I waited and waited for you, Daddy, for years and years, and you never came back for me."

"Oh, honey, I couldn't take you with me, you know that."

"I *don't* know that! Why'd you write to me only *once* in all that time? All I've done my whole life long is wait and wait for you, and you never came back for me like you promised! And you never even *wrote* to me, either! You never even called! Not even on a single birthday! Not once! Why?" I don't mean to do it, but I'm screaming loudly. The sound of my voice echoes in the sterile room. I look around, embarrassed, and notice a guard glaring at us. Daddy and I both smile lamely at him, trying to assure him we're doing just fine.

The guard's eyes linger on us for a long beat, but then he looks away.

"I didn't want to write to you until I had everything situated," Daddy whispers urgently, leaning into me. "I wanted to get you everything you deserved, all the best things in life. And then, when I got to this goddamned place, I didn't want you to see me like this." He motions vaguely to the surrounding Visitor's Room and his shackles clank loudly against the table again.

I exhale in extreme exasperation. I want to tell him he's been a fool, but Daddy's not the kind of man anyone should ever call a fool. "So are you ever gonna get out of here, then?" I ask quietly. My cheeks are hot.

"You bet I am. In exactly twelve months and twenty-nine days."

Relief floods my entire body. "Shoot, Daddy, that's nothing. I thought you were gonna be in here forever. You can bide your time anywhere for a year and change as easy as falling off a greasy log." I take a deep breath, relief softening every muscle in my body. "And when your time's up, you'll come live with me in my fancy mansion." Oh boy. The minute that last part about Daddy coming to live with me escapes my mouth, I instantly wonder how the hell I'm gonna deliver on that invitation, seeing as how Kurtis thinks my daddy the preacher man met his maker in an unfortunate encounter with a hippopotamus.

Daddy's face lights up. "Why, thank you, honey. I'll most certainly do that, Buttercup." He smiles broadly. "That sounds like a real good plan."

Chapter 27

19 Years 5 Days Old
375 Days Before Killing Kurtis

"Kurtis?" I holler as I waltz through our front door. I don't know why his car is in the driveway so early today. Kurtis is usually home much later than this. He knew I was going to acting class this afternoon and to get my hair done after that—and I didn't mention my hairdresser cancelled on me at the last minute. So how'd he know to come home early? Well, well, well, I reckon my horny husband's gonna get an unexpected treat from his sweet wife.

I've been bursting to see Kurtis all day, actually, because I've got some news that's gonna knock his socks off and bring a happy tear to his eye. This morning, right after he left for work, a real-life Hollywood agent called me out of the blue and invited me to be his client. Just like that. No audition needed. I've been bursting all day to tell Kurtis all about how that agent drooled over me right through the telephone line. "I saw your photos in *Casanova*," he gushed, "and wow, you're incredible. I'm sure I'll be able to get you as much work in this town as you could ever want."

"You're talking about me being in real movies, right? Not pornos?" I asked, practically hyperventilating.

"You bet," he assured me. And then he rattled off some of the movies his other clients have been in, and I just about fainted with joy.

"Kurtis?" I sing out, climbing the grand staircase in the foyer. "Where are you, sweetness?" I slowly unbutton the front of my dress as I climb. I'm gonna give my husband an extra special treat today, on account of me being in the best mood of my entire life.

There's no reply to my call, so I continue toward the master bedroom.

The minute I'm inside our room, I hear the shower running in the bathroom. I move toward the closed bathroom door, but before I get there, I notice the bed is undone. I'm certain I made the bed this morning after Kurtis left for the office, right before that agent-man called. Why is it undone now? The hairs on the back of my neck stand up and my stomach turns over. I lean down slowly over the bed and take a deep sniff. My stomach somersaults.

I smell sex.

My nostrils flaring, I peer at the bed closely.

There's a long black hair on my pillow.

I scramble back downstairs as quickly as possible, burst into the downstairs bathroom, and wretch into the toilet. When I'm done, I rinse my mouth under the faucet and march right through the front door, tears streaming down my cheeks, acid burning in my throat.

I tumble into my car—a sporty little thing Kurtis bought me for my nineteenth birthday—and I race down the street, careening right, then left, and left again, worming my way deep into our hoity-toity neighborhood in the hills. As I drive, I can't make out the road in front of me through the imaginary porno playing in front of my eyes—a porno starring Kurtis and Bettie, in which my husband is groping Bettie's enormous, sudsy boobs in our shower while he plows her from behind.

When I'm on a quiet street with nobody around, I park my car, turn off the ignition, roll up the windows, and scream at the tippy-top of my lungs. After a moment, my screams become wailing, shuddering sobs. After fifteen minutes, my sobs become hiccups and sad-sack sniffles. After yet another fifteen minutes, I'm tuckered out and completely mute.

I recline my seat all the way back and gaze glassy-eyed through the windshield of my car, silently fingering the diamond cross with the big ol' diamond star around my neck. Now the movie playing on repeat in my mind is Kurtis giving me my diamond-cross necklace in that cramped storage closet, promising to make me a star. For a moment, I imagine myself ripping my necklace off and throwing it in Kurtis' face, but even the thought of doing that makes me cry even harder. I love my necklace—and I'd sure hate to break the clasp. If I'm gonna break a clasp on a dang necklace, it ought to be the one around Bettie's gosh-dang neck, not mine.

I imagine myself bursting in on Kurtis and Bettie in the shower. I rip that damned heart-shaped necklace off Bettie's neck, throw it at Kurtis' horrified face, and stalk away. Kurtis scrambles to follow me out of the bathroom, drying himself off with a towel as he goes. "Baby, wait. I love you," he yells after me, his naked man-parts flopping to and fro as he hobbles after me. But I don't wait. I just keep marching.

Damn it all to hell. I don't like this movie any more than the other ones playing in my head. I don't want to leave Kurtis. I've loved having a happily ever after these past months with him. I've loved strutting around, wearing my necklace, feeling like somebody on this planet finally loves me bigger than a sky full of stars again, the way Daddy did all those years ago. Tears are streaming down my cheeks fast and furious. How could Kurtis do this to me? Haven't I been the perfect wife? I clutch the necklace around my neck and hang my head, my whimpers and sniffles filling the lonely silence of my car.

But wait. I lift my head. Did we get a new housekeeper with long black hair? Or, maybe, our housekeeper—whatever her name is, I can't remember—was sick today, and so her sister—a sister with long black hair—filled in for her? Well, Einstein, I immediately think, why did the long-haired-replacement-sister-housekeeper *unmake* the bed? Holy hell, is Kurtis screwing our maid's sister?

I slap my hands over my face and fall back into my car seat. No, Kurtis is not screwing our maid's long-haired sister— he's screwing Bettie Big Boobs. Just like he was doing before we ever got married. Just like he's been doing during our entire marriage—the whole time he's been making sweet love to me and telling me I'm gorgeous even without lipstick on. I lean forward, unclasp my necklace, and stare at it in my hand for several minutes, tears streaming down my cheeks.

The happy pang I've lately been feeling in my heart has twisted and curled into a dagger-sharp pain like nothing I've felt before. But wait. Maybe I'm jumping to hysterical conclusions here. Kurtis loves me, I know he does. I saw the way he looked at me over his cream of wheat the other day. That man had genuine love in his eyes. And, anyway, with all the sex-miles Kurtis and I have been logging these past months of our happy matrimony, he couldn't possibly have a single ejaculation left for Bettie Big Boobs or anyone else. Even if Kurtis *used* to screw Bettie before we got married, that doesn't mean he's *still* nailing her, considering the fact that he's so in love with me. I clutch my necklace to my chest and breathe deeply.

It doesn't make sense to go off half-cocked and leave Kurtis and our happy marriage and the promise of our movie until I know for sure what's going on. Maybe I'm letting my imagination run off with me. Maybe I'm letting jealousy get the better of me. Maybe I didn't make the bed this morning like I thought. Maybe Kurtis got one of Bettie's hairs on his shirt today at the club, or at his office when they were having a simple business meeting about her next porno, and maybe my poor husband came home sick, and he crawled right into bed in dire need of a nap, just shaking and burning up with a fever, my poor, sweet baby, and that long black hair rubbed right off his shirt and landed smack onto my pillow.

It just doesn't make a lick of sense that Kurtis would be

cheating on me. Why on earth would Kurtis go to all the trouble of sending me to acting classes and getting investors lined up for our movie and going on and on about making me a star and telling me I'm fucking gorgeous all the time, even without lipstick on, if he was just gonna turn around and screw a tramp like Bettie Big Boobs in our marital bed?

A certain kind of calmness washes over me. I think I've jumped the gun here, as I've been known to do a time or two. I half-smile at myself. I just need to cool my jets for a minute, that's all—stop overthinking things. I hate to say it about myself, but sometimes my big ol' brain can be my own worst enemy. Until I know for sure what's going on here, I shouldn't do anything rash that might derail my happy marriage or movie-star destiny.

I look at my watch. I've been reclined here in my car seat for over an hour. Right about now is when I would have been coming home from my hair appointment if it hadn't been cancelled. I raise my car seat to an upright position, put my necklace back on, turn the key in my ignition, and head home.

"Kurtis," I shout, waltzing through our front door, my heart in my mouth. "Are you here?"

I'm relieved when Kurtis saunters into the room from the kitchen, looking relaxed and happy to see me. "Hey, baby," he booms cheerfully. Yes, he most definitely looks bubbly-bright and bouncy-fresh as a lamb. This most certainly isn't a man who came home sick and in need of a nap. "Oh, your hair looks fantastic, baby," Kurtis says. He kisses me on the cheek, and I have to fight not to turn my cheek away from him.

"You like it?" I stutter, smoothing my hair with my hand. "I changed the color just slightly this time. Is it too light now, you think?"

"No, it's perfect. I *love* the new color. Get it this way every time, honey. It suits you."

"I will. Thank you."

I stare at Kurtis for a moment, swallowing hard. My

husband doesn't particularly look like a sheep-killing dog right now. But I can't be sure. "Well," I sigh, "I'm fixin' to change into something a little more comfortable upstairs. I'll be right back."

"Not so fast." He grabs me by my waist and pulls me into him, just like he always does. But this time—for the first time, ever—I push away.

Kurtis' face flashes confusion. "Everything okay, Buttercup?"

"Everything's just fine," I mumble. "I'm just tuckered out from acting class, is all."

"Oh yeah? How'd it go today?"

I squint at him, trying to read his face. Is he a lying sack of dung, or isn't he? "Today was a good class, actually," I finally say, still staring him down. "We learned all about tapping into our deepest, most honest feelings, and channeling them into an 'authentic' performance."

"Channeling your deepest, most honest feelings, huh? Like what?"

"Well, like deep-seated rage, for instance," I say, glaring at him with steely eyes.

Kurtis bursts out laughing—but I don't join him in laughing. What I've just said isn't even remotely funny.

"You're learning how to tap into your 'deep-seated feelings of rage,' are you?"

"Yes, I am," I huff. "And it's not a laughing matter, Kurtis Jackman. I'm learning my craft and that's a serious business. I'm an *instrument*." I shake my head to whip my hair out of my eyes. "I'm learning all about harnessing the entire *spectrum* of my emotional *range*—including, yes, deep-seated feelings of *rage*, which, believe me, I have in spades."

"Oh, I'd love to see your deep-seated rage, baby, hell yeah. Maybe you can give me a sample of some of that *rage* later tonight." He slaps my behind and I flinch in surprise. He laughs.

I smile thinly. "Well, I'm sure that can be arranged."

He clutches at me, but I pull myself away again. I just can't make heads or tails out of this situation right now. I need a little space to think. "I'll be right back," I say. "Just give me a second, would you?"

"Okay, okay," he says, laughing. "But don't take too long. Kurtis the Great's in the mood to explore a whole new continent tonight."

I try to smile at that, but my stomach's too queasy for smiling.

I walk upstairs to the master bedroom.

The bed is neatly re-made. My stomach flips over and my chest tightens.

I pull down the bed covers and peer closely at my pillowcase. The long, black hair isn't there.

"Buttercup!" Kurtis booms from downstairs. "Get your gorgeous ass down here, baby. I want to teach you something brand new."

I stand frozen to my spot for a moment, tilting my head and blinking like a cockatiel. Have I gone bullbat crazy?

"Coming," I yell down after a minute. I stand over the bed for a long piece more, trying to quiet the whirling thoughts in my head. I'm not sure what just happened. Is he a lying dog or isn't he? Am I crazy or aren't I?

"Buttercup!" Kurtis shouts again. "Come on, baby! I've been thinking about you all day long."

I don't know what to think, but I'm not gonna be able to figure it out right now. With a loud exhale, I turn on my heel and head downstairs.

Chapter 28

19 Years 6 Days Old
374 Days Before Killing Kurtis

"Hello, Mildred," I sing out as I strut into Kurtis' office at lunchtime. I know for a fact Kurtis plans to be on the set of his latest porno-masterpiece all day today, because that's all he talked about at breakfast this morning. "So nice to see you again."

"Mrs. Jackman," Mildred says curtly.

I smirk. I keep forgetting about that "Mrs. Jackman" thing. "I'm here to surprise my husband with an extra special kind of howdy-do," I say.

Mildred bristles. "I don't expect Mr. Jackman in the office today. Would you like me to call him and tell him you're here?"

"No, I know he's busy as a stump-tailed cow at fly time today, but he said he might be able to swing by the office at lunchtime for a little *quickie* with his sweet wife." I wink when I say the word "quickie" and Mildred recoils. "I'll just wait a piece," I continue, "and if he doesn't show, then I'll trot along." I sigh dreamily. "I just can't get enough of that handsome man of mine."

Mildred looks utterly repelled. "Why don't you make yourself comfortable?" She motions to a chair in the corner.

"Oh no, I'm fixin' to wait in Kurtis' office, naked as a

boiled chicken." I grin. "My husband loves getting buck-naked surprises from his sweet little wife."

"How lovely," Mildred croaks out.

Bless her heart. I imagine it can get downright off-putting working for a porno-king. I lean toward poor Mildred and whisper conspiratorially, "I reckon you'll want to take an extra long lunch today, honey."

Mildred stands, her lip curling. She sniffs once, picks up her pocketbook, and wordlessly walks out the front door.

Once I'm inside Kurtis' office, I dash around the room opening drawers and file cabinets, making like I'm Mata Hari on a secret mission. I'm not sure what I'm looking for exactly, but that doesn't stop me from investigating. I thumb through a stack of scripts on Kurtis' desk. *Eating Barbara. Boned with the Wind. Cathy Gets Creamed and Sugared.* It's all the usual Kurtis crap—nothing particularly interesting or concerning.

I lean back in Kurtis' chair and sigh deeply. What did I expect to find here? A note from Kurtis to Bettie saying, "I sure had fun secretly screwing you in the shower before my wife got home yesterday"? I roll my eyes at my own silliness and stand up to leave.

Just as I'm turning away from Kurtis' desk, though, I notice a notepad covered in scribbles. I tilt the pad toward me and squint at it, trying to make sense of Kurtis' chicken scratches all over it. Kurtis' handwriting is just like the man himself—big and all over the place—but, suddenly, one notation in the middle of the page grabs my attention like a ton of bricks: "Bettie Page True Story."

Bettie Page True Story?

My heart's thudding in my ears. What the heck does that mean? Does it have something to do with Bettie Big Boobs? I've always known Bettie Big Boobs' stage name is a riff on some real-life nudie-cutie named Bettie Page, but I've never seen or read about her. When I caught Kurtis and Bettie in a clinch six months ago in this very office, Kurtis said he was planning a Bettie Big Boobs porno. Was he telling the truth?

Does this little scrawl have something to do with that? Or, God forbid, is Kurtis planning something even more sinister—like a *legitimate* movie starring Bettie? Now my heart's pounding in my throat. It sure would help me to know when Kurtis made this little notation and whether his idea, whatever it is, has developed into something more than chicken scratches on a notepad.

I look at my watch. Damn. I don't have time to sit here and think about Bettie Page or whether Kurtis is making a Bettie Big Boobs porno or otherwise. Today might very well be the most important day of my life, because in exactly one hour, I've got my very first, genuine Hollywood-movie audition, thanks to that agent-man from yesterday who called again this morning and told me where to go.

"Do I need to learn any lines?" I squealed into the phone.

"No, honey, the less you talk the better," the agent-man replied. "Just show up looking sexy as hell. Oh, and make sure you wear a push-up bra."

I know Kurtis is gonna be tickled pink for me once I get the part—he'll probably act like a damned country fool, hooting and cheering and twirling me around—even if a small part of him might feel the teensiest bit ashamed when it's not him who winds up giving me my first starring role in Hollywood. I reckon Kurtis is gonna be so happy, he'll tell me to put on my prettiest dress so we can paint the town *and* the porch red.

"Can I help you?" the man behind the counter at the adult bookstore asks. He's standing in front of a large magazine rack, filled to bursting with every kind of flesh-porn-sex-industry "adult" rag there is. I've stopped in here on the way to my audition because I've just had the bright idea to give the director a signed copy of the special double issue *Casanova* with me on the cover and my centerfold on the inside. Dang it, I wish I'd thought to grab a couple copies when I was at Kurtis' office an hour ago, acting like a spy, but oh well.

"Two copies of *Casanova*," I say to the clerk.

The man smiles politely and grabs the magazines off the rack for me. The instant he holds them in his hand, he clearly makes the connection between the blonde bombshell on the cover and the blonde bombshell standing in front of him in the flesh. "Hey, that's *you*," he shouts.

"Yes, sir. The one and only—Buttercup Bouvier." To this day, it gives me unparalleled pleasure to say my movie star name out loud.

"Wow. These pictures are hot, hot, sizzling hot. I've certainly enjoyed them in the privacy of my apartment, if you know what I mean." He winks and my stomach cartwheels. "Hey, will you sign a copy for me?" He grabs a magazine off the rack and opens it to my centerfold in no time flat, like he already knows exactly what page it's on. I glance down at my naked boobs busting off the page and look away.

"I'd be delighted to sign it for you, sir," I say. "Thank you for your kind words." I sign the magazine and smile for a picture with him, too, and then I go right ahead and say hello and "how do you do" to the man's shaggy coworker who sprinted out of the back room when the first guy started hollering to him.

"Well, I've got to be going now," I say. "I've got to get myself to an important audition."

"Oh, well, good luck. I'm sure you'll do great."

"Thank you kindly." I turn toward the front door but then wheel back around on a sudden impulse. "Hey, do y'all happen to have anything on Bettie Page? A book or whatnot?"

"Oh yeah, we've got a whole Bettie Page section."

The man leads me to a corner of the store that's covered to bursting with Bettie Page calendars, posters, mugs and more.

I stare at everything, flabbergasted. No matter Bettie Page's pose or outfit in any given picture, or the angle or lighting of the particular photo, one fact is undeniable. Bettie Page is the smaller-boobed and prettier twin of Bettie Big Boobs. Holy shit on a stick, she's her gosh-dang spitting image.

"She was a goddess," the man says, ogling a Bettie Page calendar. "One of a kind."

I try to smile, but I can't make the edges of my mouth curl up. Seeing these pictures of the real Bettie Page suddenly makes me bone-certain that Kurtis' scribble about the "Bettie Page True Story" has something to do with Bettie Big Boobs. And, surely, that's a very, very bad thing.

Chapter 29

19 Years 1 Week Old
373 Days Before Killing Kurtis

"Who is he?" Kurtis booms at me.

I was just now fast asleep in our bed when the sound of Kurtis hollering at me has jolted me wide awake. I sit up in bed, my heart thumping out of my chest. What the hell?

My eyes adjust to the dark. Kurtis is drunker than Cooter Brown on a Saturday night. He's staggering around like he's been shot—or, more accurately, like he's been shot (multiple times) by Jack Daniels.

"Who is he?" Kurtis bellows again, his eyes bulging out of his sloppy face.

I have no idea what Kurtis is talking about. I've never once told him about my recent trips to see Daddy. How does he know? "Kurtis, hold your horses." I try to keep my voice calm and reassuring, but my heart is racing.

Kurtis lunges onto the bed and grasps my upper arms with his strong fingers. "Tell me!" he shouts, shaking me 'til my teeth rattle. *"Who is he?"*

My arms burn under Kurtis' fierce grip and my neck is whipping back and forth. "You're hurting me," I shriek.

"Well, you're fucking *killing* me." He lets out a mangled cry and tightens his grip on my arms. "Tell me!"

His vise-like grip is excruciating. I struggle to free

myself from his grasp, kicking and thrashing. "Let go of me, Kurtis! I don't know what you're talking about." Does he know about my visits to see Daddy? Since my first reunion with Daddy a month ago, I've gone back to the prison twice. How much does Kurtis know?

"Who is he?" Kurtis screams.

"Kurtis, let go of me." My thrashing intensifies, but I'm no physical match for Kurtis. If he wanted to, he could snap me in two as easily as breaking a Saltine cracker. "What are you talking about?" I shriek.

"Johnny saw you with him today," Kurtis screams.

Now I'm confused. "Johnny?" I sputter. "Johnny from the *club*? I wasn't with Johnny today."

Out of nowhere, Kurtis releases his fierce grip on me—but only so he can whack me across the side of the face. The impact knocks me flat onto the bed and takes my breath away. I instinctively cover my head with my arms. I've never been hit before. I'm stunned.

"Don't play games with me. Who *is* he?"

I stammer for a brief moment and finally gather myself enough to reply coherently. "I don't know what you're talking about!" This has to be some kind of big misunderstanding. This has to be a bad dream. I begin to sob.

Kurtis leaps up from the bed and staggers around the room, pacing. "Johnny saw you with a man at the Roosevelt Hotel today. What the fuck were you doing at the Roosevelt Hotel today with another man?"

Good lord, everything's crystal clear to me now. "Kurtis!" I shriek. "I went to an *audition* today—a real audition—and I got a cup of coffee afterwards with the *director* at the hotel just across the street—in the hotel *lobby,* Kurtis—just in the lobby—so we could sit and talk about the *movie*." My voice is quavering. The side of my face is throbbing and so are my arms where Kurtis grabbed me so hard. "I got the part, Kurtis—my first audition and I got the part! I was gonna tell you about it when you got home tonight, but I fell asleep before you got home."

Damn it all to hell, I left that audition today feeling finer than a frog's hair split four ways, just bursting to tell my husband about my good fortune. I wasn't thinking about Bettie Big Boobs or any stupid Bettie Page True Story; I didn't have a care in the world except to squeal to my husband, "Those investors are gonna be lining up now!" I waited up for Kurtis until well after midnight to share my good news with him, certain he was gonna be so happy he'd throw his hat over the windmill—but I fell asleep before he ever got home. And now here he is, hollering at me and smacking me around? Why the hell didn't he just ask me about my day instead of walloping me across the face? How did I go from shooting out the lights to getting the snot smacked out of me in a matter of hours?

Kurtis crawls onto the bed and reaches for me. I recoil. "Don't touch me," I hiss.

"I'm sorry, Buttercup—I'm drunk, baby. Oh God, I'm so drunk." He flops down onto the bed on his back. "What have you done to me, baby? You're driving me crazy. I've never been crazy like this before."

Is he saying it's *my* fault he hit me?

"I'm sorry, baby," he says. "Forgive me—it won't happen again."

"Fuck you, Kurtis!" I scream. I'm shaking with my rage.

Kurtis is suddenly all over me like white on rice, kissing the side of my face where he hit me. His lips are slimy and he reeks, just like Mother always did. I try to pull away from him.

"Shh, baby, I'm sorry."

I push him off me. "It was an *audition*, Kurtis—I'm an *actress.*"

"Okay, baby, you're an *actress*." He laughs.

Why is he laughing? That director sure thought I was an actress today. When I showed up at that audition and gave that director a signed copy of *Casanova* with my picture on the cover, he said, "Thank you so much—I'm a huge fan." And then, without even making me read lines from a script, he said, "You're the ultimate Dream Girl for my movie," and I thought I'd died and gone straight to heaven. Mind you, it's not actually a speaking part—I'll mainly be washing a car in a bikini and then changing clothes in a bedroom while some nerdy college boys peep at me through a window—but the whole movie's this comedy about these horny college boys plotting and scheming about me, their Dream Girl—in fact, the whole dang movie is called *Dream Girl*—so I reckon you could accurately say I'm the star of the whole picture.

Suddenly, a thought pings my brain like a pebble against a window. "The Roosevelt Hotel isn't anywhere near the Casanova Club. What the hell was Johnny doing at the Roosevelt Hotel today?"

"Watching you," Kurtis slurs.

Kurtis sent Johnny to *spy* on me? The hairs on the back of my neck stand up. Oh my God—what did Johnny see? I try to remember how much I flirted with that director as we sat there drinking our fancy cappuccinos. Did I reach over and touch his hand? Did I throw my head back and laugh at anything he said that was even remotely humorous? Did I bat my eyelashes and bite the tip of my finger? Holy crap. Yep. I did all of the above. What the hell did Johnny see? And how many other days has Johnny been watching me? Has Johnny seen me with Daddy? My mind is reeling.

"What do you mean, he was watching me?" I ask, trembling like a leaf.

"I like to know what my wife is up to while I'm at work."

I leap off the bed. "You don't trust me."

His anger flashes again. "I don't trust all the assholes slobbering all over my wife every fucking day, that's who I don't trust. You're my *wife*—you're *mine*. I can see how they look at you, baby, drooling all over you, staring at every inch of your body... They're all out there right now, sitting on the toilet with your photo, ogling your tits, jacking off and fantasizing about fucking you. It makes me crazy." He runs his fingers through his hair.

Well, this is some fucked up logic right here. I throw up my hands. "All those slobbering men out there have only seen me naked because you yourself put my nudie pictures in your gosh-dang magazine—*in a special double-edition featuring me!*"

"Yeah, tell me something I don't know. That's what's making me so crazy." He lets out a long exhale. "I've never been *married* before, Buttercup. I've never *loved* someone before. I didn't know how it'd feel to have men gawking at my wife's tits and ass and writing fan mail saying how much they want to fuck her." He grabs fistfuls of his hair. "I can't stand it."

Well, shut my mouth, I'm speechless. This man's lost his vertical hold.

Kurtis rubs his face and sighs.

Damn, I'm freezing standing here in the dark in nothing but my skimpy nightgown, but I'm afraid to move. A few minutes pass in silence.

"What's that director's name?" Kurtis finally asks. He seems to have calmed down.

"It was just an audition," I say. "A legitimate audition." I cross my arms over my chest, trying to warm myself. I'd been so cozy and peaceful in my sleep before Kurtis busted in and gave me a heart attack and a fucking black eye. I think I was even having a nice dream about Kurtis.

He sighs. "I believe you."

Well, isn't that sweet. He believes me.

"I *believe* you, baby," he persists. He pats the bed next to him, inviting me to join him. "Come on. Just tell me the director's name. I'm proud of you. I just want to make sure you're in good hands."

I'm skeptical and I'm sure my face shows it. Maybe Kurtis already knows the director's name and he's just testing me. Maybe this is a trap. But maybe, on the other hand, he's telling me the truth—and if I tell him who the director-guy is, Kurtis will understand how legitimate this movie really is. I don't see a downside to telling him the truth, so I tell Kurtis the director's name. "He's a real director, Kurtis," I add. "He went to film school and everything. He's never made a *porno* in his life." That last comment ought to sting. "Maybe you should talk to this director-guy about directing our Marilyn movie?"

Kurtis grunts. "Oh yeah, I'll talk to him, all right, you can bet on that." He pats the bed again. "Now get over here. I wanna show you how sorry I am."

My stomach turns over like a crank-engine. There's no doubt now that whatever happily ever after Kurtis and I had together these past six months of marriage just vanished into thin air. Poof. Gone. Like smoke from one of Kurtis' stinky cigars.

"Come on," Kurtis slurs. "Get into bed and let me show you how much I love you, baby."

I don't want Kurtis to touch me. If he's feeling lonely right now, then he can go fuck himself. Or Bettie Big Boobs, for all I care. "Like hell I will," I spit at him.

Without waiting for his reply, I march out of the room and down the hall to one of the guest bedrooms, my heart racing the whole time. I'm shaking. He could beat me senseless right now and there's nothing I could do about it. Without a weapon or some advanced planning, I'd never be able to defend myself against an enraged Kurtis—tonight made that fact abundantly clear.

My heart's clanging and banging right out of my chest as I sit on the edge of the guest bed. I'm quaking and quivering, listening for any sound in the hallway. The house is quiet as a stone—it doesn't sound like Kurtis is coming after me. Of course, it's possible he's creeping down the hall on his tiptoes right this very second, but I'm not sure Kurtis is capable of creeping on his tiptoes, or doing anything whatsoever requiring any form of subtlety.

I look around the room for something I could use as a weapon against Kurtis if he were to come into the bedroom. There's a lamp on the side table, but it's too big for me to handle. Why'd I pick this room to run into? I'm a dumbass. There's hardly anything in here. I'm a sitting duck. I listen intently again. My blood is pulsing in my ears, but, other than that, I hear nothing. I search the closet. There's nothing usable in there, either. Damn. I sit back down on the edge of the bed, trembling with shock and adrenaline. I can barely breathe.

Motherfucking-fuckity-fuck-fuck! How could that bastard hit me? Nobody hauls off and punches Charlie Wilber's Daughter! Nobody. I ought to leave this house right now and never look back. I don't need Kurtis Jackman anymore—I've got a starring role in a legitimate Hollywood movie with a director who went to film school and everything.

And yet... Before I let my pistol go off half-cocked, I need to think this through. After Kurtis' drunken outburst tonight, it's clear he's not going to let me waltz right out the front door of his mansion after six months of marriage with nothing but a gosh-it-was-nice-knowing-you pat on my back. Hell no, he won't. That man's gonna let me leave over my dead body.

And there's also the matter of the fancy "prenuptial agreement" Kurtis made me sign the day before our wedding. Thanks to that snappy little piece of paper, I won't have a pot to piss in if I leave Kurtis before our first wedding anniversary. And that's six long months away. If I leave now, I'll be leaving with nothing but my bouncy boobs and the clothes on my back. And that'd be a crying shame because this city ain't cheap and I already spent every last dime of my baseball card money on boobs and dresses before Kurtis started footing my bills.

And even though I don't give two squirts about Kurtis' stupid porno-money, I sure do love living in this fancy house and floating on a raft in the pool—and Daddy sure looked awfully excited about getting to live with me in a Hollywood mansion. One day I'm gonna buy my own mansion, of course, but I'm not sure exactly when I'm gonna be able to pull that off—all that director said about the Dream Girl movie was that he was gonna call me "really soon."

I grasp fistfuls of the bedspread underneath me, trying to contain my rage and hurt. Damn it all to hell, I've been a downright fool, imagining I'd found a happily ever after with some kind of knight in shining armor. For months now, I've been swooning over my husband like a pie-eyed ninny, and the whole time, it turns out I was sleeping with a gosh-dang monster. While I've been playing Happy Wife all these months, I've forgotten who I am and where I'm going—I've lost sight of my sacred destiny. I've just been sitting here, sweet as pie, smiling like a simpleton, letting Kurtis' lying and cheating ways roll right off me like water off a duck's back. Yes, indeed, I've been a goddamned duck—a googly-eyed, swooning, blushing, sexed-up, panties-on-fire *duck*.

Well, guess what, Kurtis Jackman? Fuck a duck. All bets are off. I'm me again. My arms burn where you squashed me with your fingers. My neck and jaw ache from how you shook me like a rag doll. The swelling on the side of my face is starting to budge up into my right eye. I'm all stove up, just about everywhere—I'm gonna need four gosh-dang Tylenols just to get a wink of sleep.

Holy hell. Nobody whacks the crap out of Charlie Wilber's Daughter. *Nobody.* Now that I know for sure my happily ever after with Kurtis has been blown to Kingdom Come, I've got no choice but to do the right thing here, even if it's not the easy thing to do. I've got to teach my husband some much needed manners. Yes, indeed, the time to kill a snake is when he raises his head.

I tiptoe back down the hall to the master bedroom.

Kurtis is passed out on our bed, flat on his back, sawing logs. I stand over him in the dark. I've got a thumping gizzard for a heart. Ice water in my veins. I could sneak down to the kitchen right now and grab the big butcher knife, the one

Kurtis used to carve that big, fat turkey last month, and ram it right into the middle of my husband's heaving chest.

I can feel the side of my face swelling up where Kurtis walloped me. My head is throbbing without mercy. My neck is already stiffening. Yes, indeed, my husband most certainly has earned himself a knife in the chest tonight.

And yet...

I know better than anyone how the police react to a dead husband: "The wife did it." And when they see that the wife's got a battered and bruised face, and finger marks on her arms, and add to the mix the fact that the dead husband's filthy rich and there's a pre-nup, too—not to mention the husband's probably had a whore on the side all along—well, you've got an open-and-shut case against the wife.

Of course, I'd cry big soggy tears on the witness stand and say I was defending myself. But the prosecution's expert would get up in front of the jury and say, "The angle of the entry wounds and the pooling of the blood suggest that the knife penetrated the victim's sternum while he was lying down." And then the prosecuting attorney would point her accusatory finger at me and say, "She expects us to believe she was *defending* herself with a butcher knife against a husband who was lying flat on his back in bed?" And that'd be it for me. They'd lock me up and throw away the key. I'd never get the chance to fulfill my destiny to carry Lana and Marilyn's torch because I'd be too busy whittling sticks into wooden bears and fishes in my ten-by-ten prison cell.

I stand over Kurtis for a good long while, wringing my hands, trying to figure out how to kill him tonight without getting caught.

Kurtis continues snoring, blissfully unaware that his life hangs in the balance.

A loud snore catches in Kurtis' nose. He coughs and rolls over onto his side. I instinctively hold my breath. When his breathing and snoring become rhythmic again, my body relaxes.

Yes, Kurtis needs killing. And badly. But even if I could figure out what to do with his body and clean up every last drop of blood tonight, I wouldn't get away with it. Not tonight, I wouldn't. Not when I'm covered in bruises. Not after only six months of marriage and a pre-nuptial agreement that makes it so I'm better off killing him than leaving him.

Damn.

I creep into the bathroom and quietly find the large Tylenol bottle in the crowded medicine cabinet. It's behind Kurtis' countless bottles of pills—pain pills, sleeping pills, hypertension pills, thyroid pills, antibiotics from a sinus infection. Jesus God, I'm married to a crusty old man.

I pad back into the guest bedroom and lie gingerly down on the bed, positioning my injuries so as to avoid pressing them painfully into the mattress.

I feel calm. I always feel a certain kind of peace when I'm gonna do the right thing. I don't need a husband telling me my boobs are too small or asking me where I've been or with *whom.* I don't need a husband who's screwing a stripper with boobs the size of melons, and I most certainly don't need a husband who spends his time doodling about some "Bettie Page True Story" when he should be spending every waking moment thinking about our Marilyn movie.

Even if my big plan for any given day is to lie around on a rubber raft in my big, fancy pool reading a Danielle Steele novel and sipping cherry Kool-Aid, or strolling down Rodeo Drive to buy myself a new dress, that's my own gosh-dang business, and nobody else's. Nobody's gonna tell me what I can and can't do, or where I can and can't go, or with *whom.* Nobody. Least of all Mr. Porno King Kurtis Jackman.

Because I am Charlie Wilber's Daughter, goddammit.

Despite my various aches and pains, sleep begins to overtake me. As I drift off, one recurring thought scrolls through my mind on an endless loop. *I am Charlie Wilber's Daughter.* Yes, sir. And one day very soon, Mr. Porno-King-Lying-Cheating-Bastard-Motherfucker-Sack-of-Shit-

Husband-of-Mine-Kurtis-Asshole-Jackman is gonna find out exactly what that means in regards to him.

I reckon my husband better start thinking about giving his heart to Jesus, 'cause his ass is mine.

Chapter 30

19 Years 1 Week 1 Day Old
372 Days Before Killing Kurtis

The light peeking through the blinds in the guest bedroom wakes me up. It's already close to noon. Oh lord, my head hurts. My neck hurts. My arms hurt. My jaw hurts. My right eye is throbbing and swollen like a banana fish.

I creep gingerly down the hall to the master bedroom. The house is quiet as the grave. I slowly peek my head into the room. Kurtis is passed out like a hobo.

I pad down to the kitchen and grab an ice pack from the freezer and sit myself down at the kitchen table, holding the ice pack over my right eye. It's throbbing like a son of a bitch.

I flip through the yellow pages and pick up the phone.

"Hollywood Flowers."

"Yes, hello," I say into the phone. "I'm calling from Mr. Jackman's office?"

"Oh yes, we'll have Mr. Jackman's usual roses-and-buttercups bouquet ready for pick-up this afternoon."

I'm calling to try to weasel some information out of the woman, of course, but she quickly gives up the ghost without me having to do a dang thing.

"And Mr. Jackman's other bouquet is just about to go out the door for delivery, too."

All at once, my heart squeezes in my chest and my

stomach lurches into my mouth. I've been such a fool to believe all of Kurtis' tin-can promises. Kurtis is a liar, through and through.

"Hello? Are you still there?" the woman asks.

"Uh, yes, ma'am. Sorry. That's wonderful. Um... I'm a temp here today. So Mr. Jackman just wanted me to double-check you've got the right spelling on the name for that delivery? For some reason, he's worried you'll get it wrong this time."

"Yes, don't worry, same as always—we've got 'Bettie' with an 'i-e' instead of a 'y' for the usual roses and tiger lilies."

Hearing the flower-lady say Bettie's name, knowing Kurtis orders the "usual" flowers for her the same way he orders the "usual" roses and buttercups for me every week, I'm feeling madder than a wet hen in a tote sack. There's no denying it now—Kurtis has been screwing Bettie our whole marriage, right under my nose. In my bed. In my shower. And he had the nerve to bash my face in because he thinks *I'm* cheating on *him*? Well, don't that just beat the band. Leave it to a cheater to think everyone else cheats.

"Thank you," I manage to the flower lady on the phone. "Oh, and let's just confirm the address for that delivery, too, just so I can tell Mr. Jackman I did?" My blood is boiling inside my veins.

"Sure." The florist confirms the address and I scribble it down.

It's not the address for the club. It must be Bettie's home address—a handy thing to know. "Yes, ma'am, that's it." I say brightly. "I don't know why he got all flustered about y'all getting that address right all of a sudden. I'll tell him it's the same as always." The florist chuckles and I join her. We two are sharing a laugh that says, *Oh, silly men!* "Well all right, then. Thank you."

Tears threaten to pool in my eyes, but I tilt my head back and take a deep breath. I'm a frog's hair away from a duck fit right now. But what did I expect? It serves me right—I lay down with a dog and got up with fleas. I should have known. The man told me he's bad, for cryin' out loud. I should have listened.

Well, under the circumstances, I reckon there's no doubt Kurtis deserves to die. I think any reasonable person would reach the same conclusion. But damn, damn, damn. If I'm gonna fly off the handle and stab Kurtis in our house, then I might as well just forget about the killing part and drive myself right over to the police station and turn myself in. Because that's just about how long it'll take for the police to come arrest me.

I dig my fingernails into the wood of the kitchen table. I want Kurtis dead. Dead and drained of all his blood. Dead and relieved of his vital organs, especially his favorite and most-used organ. But I'll be damned if I'm gonna go to prison for doing what's got to be done. Unlike Daddy, I'm not gonna get caught. I take a deep, steadying breath. What I need is a Jeb-Mother-type solution here, a neat and tidy two-for-one. This ain't my first rodeo, after all.

I reckon I'll just have to ignite a little slow-burning trouble in paradise for my dear husband and his trashy little prairie dog. I flip through the yellow pages and pick up the phone.

"Flowers by Judy."

"Why, hello, I'd like to order a big bouquet of flowers to be delivered tomorrow, first thing, if possible?" I'm doing my best to talk with a nondescript California accent.

"Is it a special occasion?"

"Yes, ma'am, my boss wants to make a special lady feel like a million bucks."

"Ah, well, then." Judy the flower-lady gives me her idea for a big bouquet of roses and peonies. "That's perfect," I say, "as long as y'all make it something that'll make her eyes pop out of her head." Shoot. I think I just said y'all. They don't say that out here. "Please make the card out to Bettie—that's Bettie with an 'i-e,' not a 'y'—and let's have the note say, 'Your heart is even more beautiful than the rest of you.' Sign it from 'Your Admirer.'" The florist makes a clucking sound that confirms her approval.

I give Judy the address of the Casanova Club, just to be sure the whole world witnesses the generosity of Bettie's secret admirer.

"We'll get that off tomorrow," the florist assures me.

"Thank you kindly," I say. "Hey, and while we're at it, let's do another bouquet—a gigantic one to another address. Just put together a whole mess of happy flowers." Dang it. That didn't sound very Californian, either. I give the woman my own address at the house. "And on the billing, my boss has a very important request. Don't divide up the charges for each bouquet—he doesn't want the charges to show he sent flowers over to the Casanova Club. Just mark both bouquets as one giant bouquet, delivered only to the second address— the residence." If Kurtis ever looks at the bills for the credit card he gave me and sees a charge from a flower shop, let him remember how I bought a whole bunch of pretty flowers to make our house smell good and pretty.

The florist chuckles. "We get asked to do that kind of thing a lot, actually. No problem."

"Thank you so much. Bye now."

I inhale deeply and close my eyes. Tears are threatening.

The ice in my ice pack has melted completely, but I'm too worn out to get up and refresh it. I put my cheek down on the cool kitchen table. I feel like I've got one wheel down and the axle dragging. I truly thought I'd found a happily ever after in this big house with Kurtis, against all odds.

A noise in the doorway makes me look up.

Good lord, Kurtis looks like he's been rode hard and hung up wet.

"Oh my God," he gasps. He lurches toward me like I'm a man overboard on the high seas. "Did I do that to you? Oh, baby. I'm so sorry."

I haven't looked in the mirror yet this morning. If I look half as bad as I feel, then I must look like road kill. Kurtis puts his finger under my chin and surveys my face. I jerk away from his touch. "Oh, Buttercup, I'm sorry."

Yeah, he's sorry. He was born sorry. "Sit down," I say, my tone as cold as my frozen heart.

"Baby, I—"

"Sit. Down." My voice leaves no room for disobedience. Kurtis sits.

"I didn't know you had a monster inside of you, Kurtis Jackman, but now I know. And, believe me, I'll never forget it."

Kurtis looks ashamed.

I pause to let my words sink in for a moment. "But I reckon everybody's got a monster inside of them, hidden somewhere."

A small flash of hope flickers across Kurtis' face.

"Believe it or not, I'm not fixin' to ask you to be anyone other than Kurtis Jackman, monster and all. But I've got one rule, and it's non-negotiable: you can't let your monster out on me ever again."

Kurtis makes to speak, but I continue.

"If booze unlocks your monster, then you'll stay dry as dirt around me. If you're not coming home to me on a particular night, then go ahead and get drunker than who shot John and beat up whoever else you please into the middle of next week looking both ways for Sunday—just as long as you don't lay a hand on me. Oh, gosh, that reminds me, I got you a little something yesterday when I was out... " I retrieve something from a nearby drawer and sit back down. "Here." I toss a calendar onto the table in front of him. "I thought you might like to look at the gen-u-ine article for a change, instead of your two-bit knock-off."

Kurtis' face drains of color. If I were to blow on him, he'd tump over.

"As I was saying, I don't care what you wanna do and with *whom*. I don't have a dog in the hunt if you wanna let your monster out on someone besides me—just as long as it's always on *someone* besides me." I motion to the smiling picture of Bettie Page on the table to give him an idea of who that "someone besides me" might be. "But with me, you'll behave every bit the good and devoted husband, you got that?"

"Baby, I—"

"Hush, please. I'm not quite finished yet and I'd appreciate you not interrupting me. This is an important bit of business I'm conducting and I don't want to lose my train of thought."

Kurtis nods. I'm sure it's killing him not to talk. That man thinks the sun comes up just to hear him crow.

"I reckon it makes you madder than a bishop kicking in a stained glass window to see how other men fall all over themselves when they lay their eyes on me. But what you've got to keep in mind is that I'm yours, baby, just like you always say. Every man's *fantasy* is your *reality,* spread-eagle and begging for it in your bed."

Kurtis' eyes light up.

"But if you ever, *ever* raise your hand to me again, I will leave you faster than a sneeze through a screen door. You can beg and plead and make promises and buy me flowers and diamonds, but I won't come back to you. And I'll never, ever change my mind."

"I'm sorry—" Kurtis begins again.

"Now, if you can't control your monster, if you don't think you can keep yourself from whacking me upside the head now and again, then I'll just go now. No hard feelings. And I don't want your money, neither. All I've ever wanted is you, Kurtis Jackman, right from day one... and our movie together. Good lord, how I want our movie! Because that movie's our shared dream, the thing that brought us together in the first place, the one thing that's gonna prove to me once and for all that you love me like you say you do." I stare at Kurtis, unblinking. "In fact, without you making our movie like you've promised to do, I'm not sure I can believe a goddamned word you say about anything at all."

There's silence as Kurtis processes what I'm saying.

"And God forbid you make a mainstream feature starring another girl... Wooh!" I glance down at the calendar on the table again. "I can't even imagine what I'd do." I shake off the alarming thought.

Kurtis suddenly looks like he was sent for and couldn't go.

I prompt him, "Well, then? What do you want to do here, husband?"

"I want to do whatever I have to do to keep you."

I knew he'd say that, of course, but I also know Kurtis Jackman won't be able to control his monster forever, any more than King Henry could control his. Luckily, though, I don't need forever. I just need to buy me some time to figure out my best strategy for killing him without getting my own head chopped off. Lord willing and the creek don't rise, after this little speech of mine, he'll think twice before hauling off and punching me for a good long while—long enough for me to get a good killing plan in place and, heck, maybe even long enough to get the man working extra hard on our movie. "I know you want me to stay, baby, but are you in agreement with the terms and conditions I've set forth?"

Kurtis grins, seemingly tickled by the formality of my language. I can tell he thinks I'm a silly little girl trying to act like a grownup, but I don't care. He needs to understand the seriousness of the agreement we're striking here.

"I want you on any terms and conditions." His grin broadens to a wide smile. I reckon he thinks I'm laugh-out-loud funny.

"Well, okay then." I try to grin back, but the effort hurts my face. I wince.

"Oh, honey, let me get you some ice."

"Thank you, darling. Aren't you just as sweet as pie."

And a lying, cheating, lower-than-a-gopher-hole, whacking-me-upside-the-head, mother-fucking piece-of-shit dead man, too.

Chapter 31

19 Years 2 Weeks Old
365 Days Before Killing Kurtis

For the past several days, even though all I've wanted to do is go straight to Daddy, I haven't stepped foot outside of my house. I can't let anyone see me bruised and battered. Whenever I finally send Kurtis to the Great Beyond, I don't want there to be a single witness who could ever say anything but that Kurtis and I were like two peas in a pod. I don't want a single witness to even whisper, "Maybe she killed him because he beat the shit out of her." Nope. From this day forward until Killing Kurtis Day, whenever that's gonna be—I still haven't come up with my foolproof plan yet—I'm gonna make damned sure the whole world, including Kurtis himself, thinks I worship the ground that sack of shit walks on. And when Mr. Kurtis Jackman finally meets his maker, I want everyone and anyone to say, "Good lord, she loved that man more than life itself."

Finally, today, after five long days of sitting around daydreaming about slitting Kurtis' throat and hacking off his private parts, my bruises have healed well enough to cover them up with clever makeup so I can go outside into the world again—specifically, to the Visitor's Center to see Daddy.

I look around, making sure there's no guard within earshot of Daddy and me. "There's something I've got to tell you, Daddy," I whisper urgently.

Daddy furrows his brow. "What's got your goose today, Buttercup?"

I glance over at the guards. "Do you think they record conversations here?" My voice is almost inaudible.

Daddy looks around the room slowly. When his eyes land on a ceiling-mounted video camera to our left, he nods his head at me and shrugs at the same time, as if to say, *I'm not sure, but I reckon so.*

"Daddy, listen to me close."

Daddy leans in.

I smile big and laugh so it looks to the guards like we're having a happy family reunion. "My husband? It turns out that man has no manners whatsoever—none at all. If I didn't have a boatload of makeup on my face right now, you'd be able to see all over my face just how bad my husband's manners really are."

Daddy clenches his jaw. He understands perfectly.

I nod slowly and match his clenched jaw with my own, the memory of Kurtis shaking me and whacking me across my face five days ago flitting across my mind. I touch my fingertips to my still-tender right eye in remembrance.

"It sounds like your husband needs to be acquainted with the idea he's married to Charlie Wilber's Daughter, huh?"

I nod. I knew my daddy would understand. "Remember how Jessica Santos bullied me? Remember what happened to her kitty?"

Daddy nods back at me. His jaw muscles are pulsing.

"I think my husband should wind up just like that kitty. Anything short of that, my husband just wouldn't fully understand who he's married to. Excuse me—to *whom* he's married." I glance at the guard across the room again, smiling and pretending to laugh at something Daddy's said to me.

"Yeah, it sure sounds like your husband needs to learn a thing or two."

I nod and glance around furtively. "How much longer 'til you get out of here, Daddy?"

"Eleven months and twenty-seven days."

"Well okay, then. What's today's date, Daddy?"

He tells me.

"All right. Exactly one year from today, Daddy, exactly one year to the very day, why don't you come over to my house and pay my husband a little visit, hmm? It'd be so nice for you two to get acquainted."

"That sounds mighty fine."

"Do you think you can remember the address of my house in Hollywood?"

"Does a fat dog fart?"

I slowly tell him my address and make him repeat it back to me twice.

"That's good, Daddy," I say. "Now, I should warn you, the day before you actually meet my husband, exactly a year from today *minus one day*, we won't be home. I'll make sure of it. But you come right into the house, anyway, through the *unlocked* back door, and you make yourself at home, okay? And the very next day, exactly a year from today, my dear husband will come back home without me, sometime before noon. I haven't decided why or how he'll come back home without me, but he will. And while the two of you are all alone together in the house, you just go right ahead and teach my husband a thing or two while I'm not there." I look around. "Teach him some much-needed manners."

Daddy nods, his eyes narrowed to slits.

"And when you're done, why don't you leave the house for a while? Hmm? After you've left, I'll come home in the afternoon. I'll call all the right people and tell everyone all the right things. And when the dust settles after a few days, we'll live together, just you and me, happily ever after in our fancy mansion, forevermore. We'll swim in our pool and watch movies in our home theater and lounge around by our fountain with the naked ladies and cherubs and the little cupid with wings."

Daddy's been listening intently as I speak. He nods slowly. "Sounds good."

I ask him to repeat my address again, and he does, slowly. I ask him to say the date he'll be coming to my empty house through the back door, and he complies. I exhale sharply, trying to control my racing heart. "I have full faith in you, Daddy."

"Nothing but the best for Charlie Wilber's daughter," he says, his voice steely.

I fist-pump the air, and Daddy and I smile at each other. After all this time, I'm still right on cue. "And for the next year, while you're biding your time in here, I'll be setting everything up on the outside so that a certain lady-friend of Kurtis' takes all the credit for teaching my husband some manners, instead of you. Oh, Daddy, this particular gal reminds me of Mother like you wouldn't believe."

"Is that right?"

"Yes, sir."

"Well, then, she must be a real peach."

"Oh, yes. This woman and my husband, they're just two peas in a pod." I lower my voice to the softest of whispers and add, "Two peas in a pod, a *bed*, a *shower*, and God knows where else when I'm not around." My lip snarls involuntarily for just a moment. "Just like I took such good care of Mother while you were away, I'm gonna take equally good care of this lady-friend of my husband's, too, bless her heart."

"Well, that's awfully sweet of you."

"Aw, Daddy, I'm so sweet, sugar don't even melt in my mouth."

Daddy grins at me.

"And another thing, since this nice lady's gonna take all the credit for teaching my husband some manners, I think it would be best if you taught him some *table* manners specifically? Because, honestly, bless his heart, my husband's just as crass as a big, fat pig."

Daddy looks confused.

"What I mean is that you should show my husband the proper way to use his fork and *knife*—because my husband's table manners are just deplorable, and I think it would be easiest to give this fine lady all the credit if you teach him table manners with a fork and *knife.*"

Daddy's eyes light up with understanding. "You betcha. I'll be sure to use all appropriate utensils when I talk to your husband. It'd be a crying shame for your sweet friend not to get all the recognition she deserves here."

"You're so right, Daddy. Thank you kindly."

"It'll be my pleasure. I'd do anything for you, Buttercup, you know that."

"I should warn you, though, Daddy—my husband's a pretty big man. And, sometimes he can be dumber than hammered owl shit. So you'll wanna use a really big utensil with him, just to be sure he totally gets the full extent of what you're teaching him. Otherwise, he might not get your *point.*"

Daddy smiles. "I'll use a nice, big utensil and make sure he gets my *point* and then some."

"I reckon you'll find everything you need in our kitchen, Daddy—I'll make sure everything's there for you. Just help yourself."

"Sounds good."

"You sure you understand everything?"

"Does a big black bear shit in the woods?" He grins broadly.

I reach out and throw my arms around Daddy's neck. "It's so nice to finally have my daddy back."

Daddy tries to hug me back, but his shackles get in the way.

"When you get out of here, promise you'll never leave me again," I whisper, holding back tears.

"Shh, I promise. Once I get out of here, we'll be together forever."

"Two minutes," a guard yells.

I begin to stand and say my goodbyes.

"Buttercup, wait a second."

I sit back down and look at Daddy expectantly.

"Now that we've settled on a time for me to come visit you and your husband, it makes no sense for you to keep coming here to the Visitor's Center, chatting up a storm for everyone and their mother's uncle to see..." He looks pointedly at the guard at the far side of the room and then up at that security camera mounted just below the ceiling. "While I bide my time here for the next year, how 'bout you do the same out there? An unforgettable girl like you shouldn't be hanging around a place like this, talking to a guy like me, anyhow."

My heart physically hurts to hear Daddy say these words, but my head knows he's right. As much as I want to visit Daddy every single week for the next twelve months, it's just too risky now that we're planning to send Kurtis over the Big Ridge. And now that I know Johnny the Dingleberry could be on my tail on any given day, I'm gonna have to be doubly careful about where I go and *whom* I see. Even this morning at the bus station, I looked high and low for Johnny for a good ten minutes before I felt sure I could safely board the bus for the prison.

"Okay, Daddy," I say. "I reckon you're right."

"Time!" the guard in the corner barks out.

Daddy rises up out of his seat.

"I love you, Daddy," I whisper, giving him one final hug. "Bigger than a sky full of stars."

"I love you, too, Buttercup," he replies, nuzzling into my hair. He puts his mouth right on my ear and mutters, "Nobody fucks with Charlie Wilber's Daughter. *Nobody.*"

Chapter 32

19 Years 3 Weeks Old
349 Days Before Killing Kurtis

"Well, hello, honey," I say to Kurtis when he strides through the front door. He hands me a big bouquet of flowers—red roses surrounded by buttercups—what a surprise. "Oh, how sweet," I say. "Thank you, sugar." Ever since Kurtis revealed the monster inside him, he's played Perfect Husband to a tee. And I've played Perfect Wife. Aren't we sweet?

Kurtis sits on the couch and I sit on his lap, just like I always do.

"Baby," Kurtis groans, clearly enjoying the feel of my body pressed against his lap, "what'd you do today?"

"You mean Johnny didn't tell you?"

Kurtis chuckles. "Johnny didn't check up on you today. He's got plenty to do at the club."

"Oh, well, if he *had* checked up on me, though, then you'd have known I got my hair done all pretty for you, and then I went to buy me the latest Nora Roberts book—I just love her." I smile at him. "Another exciting day in Hollywood."

Kurtis leans in to kiss me.

"Oh, by the way, someone called the house for you this afternoon." This is a lie. "A woman."

Kurtis looks suddenly anxious.

"She wouldn't give her name," I add.

"Oh yeah? What'd she say?"

"I could barely make out a thing she was saying on account of there being loud music in the background. The only thing I could make out for sure was she said she needed to see you right quick." This is all a big, fat lie, of course. No one called. But I'm enjoying the look of anxiety on Kurtis' face too much not to keep going. "Do you know what that's all about?"

Kurtis shakes his head. "Nope. I've got no idea what that's all about. You say she called the house?"

"Mmm hmm."

"Well, no. Hmm. I have no idea."

"That's strange. Must have been a crank call, then."

"Sure sounds like it."

"Hmmph." I wait a beat. "Did you get a chance to call that director of mine like you said you would?"

Kurtis exhales loudly. "Yeah, I did. He's not going to work out. I'm still lining up investors for our movie, anyway."

"Well, gosh, maybe if you got a real director like him on board, investors would fall in line."

"He's not gonna work out, Buttercup," he says, his voice edged with annoyance. "Just trust me."

So we're back to me having to *trust* him, huh? "Why won't the director work out? He's a real director, you know—he went to film school and everything."

"So you've told me. But I don't need him." He grins like he's got a secret. "I've decided to direct the movie myself."

My mouth hangs open.

"And I'm gonna write the screenplay, too."

Well, shut the front door.

"I've decided I don't need anyone else to make you a star. I'm gonna do it all by myself."

I can't think of a damned thing to say. Kurtis doesn't even write or direct his stupid pornos—and he thinks he can write and direct a legitimate, mainstream movie all by himself? Kurtis has explained to me a thousand times that he "produces" his pornos, which means he's the big man in charge, but everyone else—from the director to the actors to the costume lady (whatever that means for a porno)—works for him and does what he tells them to do. Does Kurtis even know how to do anything besides order other people around? My stomach's turning over like a tumbleweed in the desert. "Oh my," is all I finally manage to say.

"I'm not gonna let some guy direct *my* wife in my own movie," Kurtis says. "If anyone's gonna direct *my* wife, it's gonna be *me*." His eyes are blazing. "And, anyway, I'll get a better performance out of you than some hot-shot 'director' because I know you better than anyone, baby."

I don't know whether to laugh or cry at that last part. "Well, bless your heart" is all I choke out.

I slide off Kurtis' lap onto the couch, trying to figure out how to manage this situation. Is it time to accept defeat? Is my Marilyn movie a lost cause? Should I stop trying to squeeze blood out of a turnip? Maybe I should just forget about Happy Killing Kurtis Day and walk away right now. Maybe I should just be happy to be the Dream Girl and let bygones be bygones with Kurtis—no harm, no foul. But would Kurtis even let me walk away—or would he come after me?

"I've got it covered," Kurtis says, patting my thigh. "Don't worry your pretty little head about a thing."

"But, Kurtis, have you directed a movie before?"

"I might as well have."

"Have you ever written a script before?"

"Practically." He shrugs his shoulders.

I take a deep breath. "Kurtis, please just tell me the truth. Are you still planning to make our Marilyn movie?"

"Of course, I am. It's been my dream my whole life."

"But, I mean. You're still planning on making it, starring me?"

He looks earnest. "Of course, I am." He touches the

diamond star at the top of my cross. "You're my star, baby— my *wife*. Who else would I want to star in the movie of my dreams?" He flashes me his most charming smile—and, for a moment, believe it or not, even after all the walloping and cheating and lying, I actually feel my heart go pitter-pat.

"Really, Kurtis?"

"Of course."

"And you think it's gonna happen soon?"

"Yup. I should have everything in place any day now, and then we'll start pre-production like gangbusters."

"Really?"

"You bet."

My face bursts into a giddy smile. "Well, this is mighty exciting news," I say, elation flooding me. "Thank you so much, baby."

"Of course." He kisses my nose.

Well, butter my butt and call me a biscuit. Maybe I was a bit hasty when I arranged Killing Kurtis Day so quickly after he whacked me upside the head. Did I go off half-cocked? I reckon anyone could do a bad thing now and again—I most certainly have myself when circumstances have forced me— but does *doing* a bad thing necessarily make a person bad? I don't think so. Maybe Kurtis feels so bad about what he did to me, he's decided to recommit to our movie with renewed purpose. And maybe he's feeling so awful about hurting me, he's decided to be gentle and sweet toward me forevermore, just like he used to be before everything went to hell in a handbasket.

"So," Kurtis says emphatically, like he's making a point to change the subject, "have you been going to your acting classes like you're supposed to, baby?"

"Yes, sir," I say. In fact, I've been going to acting classes almost every day for the past three months and I've never adored anything so much in my entire life.

"Good. Stay nice and busy like a good girl so you don't get yourself into any trouble."

Well, here we go again. What kind of trouble is Kurtis worried I might get into? Drinking cappuccinos with a real-life Hollywood director who's been to film school and everything? Landing a starring role in a legitimate movie that's already got investors lined up? "I go to classes and workshops every single day, getting myself ready for our movie," I say proudly. "I'm taking my craft seriously because I'm gonna be a respected actress one day."

Kurtis bites his lip, clearly stifling a smile. "That's great, honey." He pats my knee. "You keep going to your classes and looking gorgeous and leave the rest to me."

I exhale in exasperation. "Well, I'm trying, Kurtis. But it sure seems to be taking a helluva long time to get our movie off the ground."

Kurtis lets out a sudden roar that makes me flinch. "Do you have any fucking idea how many things I'm juggling, all at once—how many mountains I move on a daily basis, how many projects I've got going, how much product I successfully deliver every single month through multiple channels? And now I've decided out of the generosity of my heart to write and direct and produce a movie for my wife who's never been in a movie in her entire life, along with everything else I've got going on, and all you can say is 'It's taking a helluva long time?' Give me a fucking break."

Without warning, he pushes me off him and storms out of the room, leaving me gaping like a wide-mouth bass on a hook.

Chapter 33

19 Years 1 Month Old
347 Days Before Killing Kurtis

The entire drive over to the bus station, and then as I walk from my parked car to the station entrance, I glance behind me, over and over again, searching for any sign that Johnny the Biscuit-Eating Bulldog is trailing me. It seems Johnny's nowhere to be seen, thankfully, but just to be on the safe side—because that man can be harder to get rid of than eczema—I take a slow loop around the block, twice, before taking off my wedding rings and walking into the station.

Three hundred and ninety-five days ago, Wesley and I swore we'd meet here today, two days after his eighteenth birthday, exactly at noon, and I'd never dream of leaving that poor boy hanging out to dry. I find a bench with a good view of the entire station and take a seat. I look at my watch. It's 11:45. My knees are jiggling with nerves.

I know I shouldn't be here. It's too big a risk to take, and I'm a dumbass for taking it. There's still eleven more months before it's time to send Kurtis to his last roundup in the sky, and I shouldn't be doing anything that even remotely suggests I'm not hopelessly devoted to my husband. But I can't help it. How would I ever find Wesley again after Kurtis is dead if I didn't show up today? And how would he ever find me, either, what with my new hair and boobs and name? I have no choice—I had to come, even if it's a horrifically bad idea.

229

And, anyway, there's no harm in me just sitting and talking with Wesley today, and that's all I'm going to do. I'm just going to say hello to him and tell him, "We can't be together any time soon, Wesley, and maybe not ever."

I can't imagine poor Wesley's going to take that news very well, but it can't be helped. My husband isn't the sort of man to share me, least of all with the only other man who's ever had the pleasure of kissing my lips, even if that "man" just happens to be a dopey, puppy-faced boy. After Kurtis takes his dirt nap, well, things might be different then, who knows? But there's no way to know about that right now. We'll just have to let fate take the wheel when the timing is right.

I look at my watch again. Noon. What's taking that boy so long to get here? I figured he'd be here early, chomping at the bit, to tell you the truth.

Gosh, it's gonna be nice to see that dopey boy again, I must admit. Truth be told, I've missed him something awful. Life out here in Los Angeles can make a girl feel as lonely as a pine tree in a parking lot. Now don't get me wrong, I'm used to being alone. That's all I've ever been my whole life. But there's a difference between being *alone* and feeling *lonely*, and most of the time, Hollywood makes me feel like the last pea at pea-time. First off, there's no good place to get books; all anyone ever cares about is watching movies around here. Also, nobody in Los Angeles ever stops to chat about how it's so gosh darned hot the hens are laying boiled eggs. Of course, I used to hate how people went on and on about the heat back home, but now, I kind of miss it.

I look around the bus station for a long beat. Still no Wesley.

The loneliest thing of all about living out here in Hollywood, though, the thing that makes me feel as lonely as a cloud, is living with Kurtis in that big house and finding Bettie's long, black hairs everywhere I turn. In my shower drain. On my couch. On my pillow. Damn it all to hell, feeling like a third wheel in my own home is enough to make me feel lonelier than the man in the lighthouse—not to mention fit-to-be-tied, too.

I look at my watch. 12:05. That boy's slower than molasses running uphill in the winter—what's taking him so long? If he moved any slower getting here, he'd have to walk backwards just to make any progress at all. Good lord, when I finally see that big-eared, scrawny-assed, puppy-faced boy, I'm gonna slap him silly for keeping me waiting—right after I give him a big ol' kiss on those delicious lips of his. Wooh! My heart's racing. Wesley's gonna foam at the mouth when he sees how gorgeous I've become in a year—he's gonna go so batshit-crazy at the sight of me, one of his marbles might just pop out his ear and roll across the floor.

I look around again, slowly scanning the scattered people milling around the station. Good lord, people hanging around a bus station on a Tuesday afternoon sure aren't what I'd call a bunch of lookers—I could hire half of 'em to haunt a house. I look at my watch again and tap my toe. *Where the hell is that scrawny-ass boy?*

It's not that I mind being alone. To the contrary, I'm happy as a clam at high tide when I'm floating all by myself in my pool, reading a good book and sucking on an Otter Pop. The problem is when Kurtis comes home and starts blabbering about some new scene from his latest porno or how he wants to open Casanova Clubs in New York and Tokyo—and all I can think about is whether he just came home from screwing Bettie. That's when I start to think about my ever-faithful Wesley and how we used to lie under the big oak tree together and talk about Lord-knows-what and kiss 'til our lips were swollen and sore. Those are the times when I feel so lonely, it feels like my heart is wilting like a cut flower.

By the time I boarded the bus for Hollywood, I'd told Wesley more about me than I'd ever told another living soul—a thousand times more than I've told Kurtis and more than I'd ever tell anyone else in a month of Sundays. Good lord, I even told Wesley about Jeb's cake! And the best part is he still wanted me.

My heart lurches with a sudden epiphany: Wesley *loves* me. He never said those exact words to me, but I suddenly know it's true. He loves me and he's going to take care of me forever and ever.

Wesley and I just fit. We just make sense. And it's always been that way. From the minute I walked through the front door of the group home, it seemed like I'd known Wesley my whole life, like we weren't so much as meeting each other, but reuniting. There was never a time when I felt like I needed to explain anything to him—he always just *understood*. Wesley never needed me to be anyone or anything besides the real me, no matter what. For cryin' out loud, that boy loved me even before I had my blonde hair and boobs! Before I wore a stitch of makeup! And even after he knew I served Jeb a big ol' slice of rat-poison cake! *Oh my goodness.* My heart is clanging in my ears. Wesley *loves* me—all of me—even the bad parts.

I touch the diamond cross around my neck and let my fingertips glide up to the diamond star at the top. I thought Kurtis loved me, but I was wrong. He only wants me because I'm so dang pretty—but Wesley wants me 'cause I'm so dang *me*. My eyes brim with sudden tears. I reach behind my neck, unclasp my necklace, and stuff it into my pocketbook.

Wesley would never lie to me or cheat on me. And he'd certainly never wallop me upside the head. That boy wouldn't harm a hair on my head—or anyone's, for that matter. He might be sharp as a mashed potato, it's true, but he's also sweet as the day is long. And that's why I love him.

Damn it all to hell. *I love* Wesley! It's true! I'm not gonna tell Wesley goodbye when I see him—I'm gonna tell him I love him and that I want to be with him forever and ever, starting today. I'm not gonna wait eleven whole months to start my new life with Wesley—hell no. Let the chips fall where they may, I'm gonna start my life with Wesley right this very minute.

I'll just walk right up to my husband and tell him we're through, that I don't love him and he can't have me anymore. And then I'll just walk away, my head held high, holding my darling Wesley's hand.

I reckon Kurtis will try to make me stay with promises of money and movies and cars and whatnot. But he can keep it all. I don't care about Kurtis' fancy mansion or anything else. Wesley and I could live in a mud hut and be happy, as long as we're together. And I don't need my Marilyn movie, either, even if Kurtis could get it off the ground after all this time, because I've got my *Dream Girl* movie now. When the world sees me as the Dream Girl, I'm gonna be a huge star—I'll have to beat directors off with a stick! I'm gonna make myself into a respected actress, all by myself, no thanks to Kurtis the Porno King, thank you very much.

Honestly, it's a relief to be thinking this way. I don't even want to kill Kurtis anymore. I really don't. Yes, he walloped me, it's true—which means he rightly deserves to get hacked into little tiny pieces and scattered throughout the bushes in the backyard. But all of a sudden, I wanna take the high road here and turn the page. All I want is to start a happy life with Wesley and that means washing the blood off my hands, once and for all. From here on out, I'm gonna be more like Wesley—good and pure and sweet.

I look at my watch. 12:27. Where the fuckity-fuck-fuck is Wesley, for fuck's sake? I'm bursting out of my skin to throw my arms around that scrawny boy's neck and tell him I've loved him all along, since the first time we locked lips on my cot all those years ago.

I let out a long sigh. I sure wish Wesley would show up already.

I'm feeling relieved about calling off Killing Kurtis Day, I really am; but I'm a bit apprehensive about it, too. Kurtis isn't the kind of man who's gonna say, "It was darned nice to meet you, honey; now go ahead and have a great life with your boyfriend." But I've just gotta have faith that Wesley and

I can figure out a happily ever after that doesn't involve carving my husband like a Thanksgiving Day turkey. Because Wesley and I love each other—bigger than a sky full of stars—and I just have to believe a love that big and pure and true, the kind of love I've read about in my books, can conquer any problem, big or small—even a problem as big and brawny, and jealous, as Kurtis Jackman.

Chapter 34

19 Years 3 Months Old
285 Days Before Killing Kurtis

Wesley not showing up at the bus station two months ago took the wind right out of my sails, to tell you the truth. I waited as long as I could on that bench at the station, as long as I dared, and when I couldn't wait another minute, I hightailed it to my three o'clock acting class, even though I just wanted to crawl into bed for a thousand weeks. It was a good thing I made it to my class, too, because midway through, Johnny the Fink popped into the theater to check up on me and then proceeded to glare at me all class long like a duck watching for june bugs on a pond. Bastard. I wouldn't spit up his ass if his guts were on fire. In that moment, gosh dang it, I hated Kurtis more than I ever thought my cold, dead heart could muster—but all I did anyway was wave and smile at Johnny, as usual, like I'm sweet as the powdered sugar on top of a jelly doughnut.

For a solid week after Wesley didn't come to the station, I was eating sorrow by the spoonful, every day, all day. I couldn't even raise my head and pretend to smile, not even for the sake of playing Perfect Wife. For days and days, I felt like I'd been eaten by a wolf and shit over a cliff.

Wouldn't you know it, it was during that horrible, heart-wrenching week my acting instructor decided to teach the class something every serious actor needs to know: how to cry on cue. "You've got to put yourself into your character's head and allow yourself to *feel* whatever they're feeling," he explained. "No holding back."

"But how can I feel what my character feels if I've never actually experienced the character's situation?" another student asked.

"Human emotion is universal, regardless of specific context," my instructor explained, smiling. "You can discover your character's emotional life by drawing on your own personal experiences. If your character has suffered a devastating loss, think about your own sorrow when you suffered a devastating loss in your own life. If your character feels abandoned, or betrayed, then think about how heartbroken you felt when someone abandoned or betrayed you."

And just like that, just sitting there in my seat listening to my instructor talk about sorrow and heartbreak, I burst into big, soggy tears. It wasn't even my turn to come onstage and do an exercise or anything like that; I was just sitting there, listening closely to what my instructor was saying, and then *bam!*—the cheese slid right off my cracker.

All of a sudden, all I could think about was Wesley's big-eared, puppy-dog face, and I lost myself to noisy, wracking sobs. Sitting on that bus-station bench for hours and hours, bursting at the seams to finally tell Wesley I love him, all I could think was, "My Wesley wouldn't let me down—no, sir, my Wesley *loves* me—he'll come." And then, by God, what did Wesley do? He let me down. Just like everyone always has. And that got me to thinking maybe Wesley never really loved me at all—and that thought just about did me in.

And then, thinking that Wesley might not have loved me made me think about Daddy—about all the years I waited and waited for him to come get me and he never did, about all the birthdays that came and went without so much as a card or a call from him, and all the times I went to the mailbox and waited on the postman to come, just hoping against hope he'd finally bring me one teeny-tiny little note from Daddy, anything at all to make me feel like maybe there was one person in the whole world who gave two shits if I lived or died.

And then, for no reason I can understand, I started thinking about how Jeb used to hug me and tell me he loved me like a daughter; how he taught me how to bake a cake, and even let me lick the spoon when we were done; how he was always trying to take me bowling or to the movies or to ice cream, but I always said no; and how, on that horrible night when I served poor Jeb that huge slice of cake, his eyes lit up and got kind of watery as he said, "Nobody's ever baked me a cake before."

Just when I thought I was all out of tears, I started thinking about how Mother always used to yell at me; how she did nothing but lie around on her dirty mattress, stinking of whiskey (until Jeb came along, anyway). I thought about how my whole life Mother never so much as told me she loved me, not even one time—and, in fact, once told me that having a baby had ruined her entire life. And, finally, I thought about how Mother wouldn't even look at me at trial after she figured out it was me who baked Jeb's cake.

Just when my tears started to dry up the tiniest bit, Kurtis' face leaped into my mind like a scalded cat and wouldn't leave, and I started thinking about how Kurtis was supposed to discover me like Lana Turner in the malt shop, but didn't; and how he said he loved me but walloped me upside the head, anyway—and plowed Bettie Big Boobs in our bed, to boot. I thought about how I was stupid enough to want to give Kurtis my virgin-heart along with my virgin-body, but he only wanted the latter.

And that's when I suddenly understood the truth like I'd been whacked upside the head with it: I'm completely alone in this world, without a single person to love me except audiences in cineplexes around the world. And that's when I realized being the Dream Girl in that legitimate director's movie is the only thing I care about in this life.

I felt a gentle arm wrap around my shoulder and squeeze me tight, and when I peeked through my wet fingers, I saw my silver-haired acting instructor smiling at me, his blue eyes twinkling. "It's okay, Buttercup," he said quietly in his deep, smooth voice. "Let it all out."

Later, when I'd calmed down a bit, my instructor said, "It seems like you've got a lot of life experience to draw from, huh?"

I half-smiled at him and shrugged, not knowing what to say.

"You've got a lot of talent," he said. "You're a true natural."

No one had ever said something nice like that to me before—and right then and there, I swear my insides started glowing like a firefly's butt. Just like that, I actually felt like smiling again, for the first time in forever. And that's why, when I walked past a pet store after class and spied the fuzziest little black-and-white ball of fur in the window, I didn't hesitate about going inside and pulling out my wallet and making that little cutie patootie my very own.

"What the hell is that?" Kurtis asked when I got home with my new purchase.

"This here's my new kitty," I answered matter-of-factly. "Wilber."

"Wilber? You mean, like the pig in *Charlotte's Web?*"

"Yup," I answered, since, obviously, I couldn't tell Kurtis I'd actually named my little kitty on account of me being Charlie Wilber's Daughter.

Oh, how my darling Wilber turned out to be my salvation. Thanks to him, I was able to get my mind right again and realize that things with Wesley had happened according to fate, even if Wesley not coming to the bus station felt like my heart being ripped out of my chest at the time. With the *Dream Girl* movie about to start filming any day now, I'm sure, and my career about to take off into the stratosphere, I realized I couldn't afford any distractions—even a distraction as sweet as Wesley.

Plus, when Wesley didn't come, I realized I'd been a fool for thinking I could ever just walk out on Kurtis. How the heck was I gonna do that, especially to start a new life with Wesley? Kurtis wasn't gonna just let me walk out the door. And Wesley and Kurtis being together in the same city, both of them alive, both of them wanting me, wouldn't have ended well. I reckon that situation would have been like lighting the fuse on a big ol' stick of dynamite and then leaning in to watch the whole thing go boom.

Nowadays, though, I've got my head on straight. I haven't made it down to the prison to tell Daddy just yet (on account of me being extra busy with "advanced-intermediate" acting classes), but I've decided once and for all to suck it up and make a happily ever after with Kurtis. It's what makes the most sense in the grand scheme of things. Killing a man is serious business and I've decided I'm done with it, once and for all. Lord knows I don't need to be giving myself nightmares again like I used to have about Jeb; and I most certainly don't wanna be looking over my shoulder for the police all the time, either.

And, anyway, Kurtis has been a good husband lately. Not only has he recently started talking about our Marilyn movie in earnest again, he's also been sweet as peaches about me getting to be the Dream Girl, too. In fact, I'd even go so far as to say he's as happy as can be about it.

Plus, Kurtis' monster hasn't come out again since that one horrible night, and the more I think about it, I reckon a man doing one bad thing doesn't necessarily make him a bad person overall. At the end of the day, what I've come to realize is this: as long I'm the Dream Girl, and working toward my sacred destiny, I can be happy, come hell or high water, even being married to Kurtis. All I've got to do is keep myself from going off half-cocked, that's all.

To keep myself on the straight and narrow, I've been keeping myself busier than a moth in a mitten at all times, attending as many acting classes as possible. Why not? My husband doesn't seem to mind paying for 'em, so I just keep on goin'. Because, as it turns out, even if you're a "natural," like me, there's still a lot to learn about acting, once you aim to learn it all. It might not seem like it from the outside, but acting's a lot more than just crying or laughing or looking pretty on cue—at least if you aim to do it right.

In fact, now that I've graduated to taking "advanced-intermediate" classes, I can see why Marilyn Monroe herself took acting classes even when she was already the biggest movie star in the world. Just like Marilyn did, I'm gonna keep studying and learning and practicing my craft—because, one day, I intend to do a helluva lot more in a movie than standing around in a bikini and washing a gosh-dang car.

For now, though, since washing a car in a bikini is what the Dream Girl role requires, I'm gonna give it my all. Yes, sir, I'm gonna learn as much as humanly possible in my acting classes so I can wash the heck out of that dang car in a manner authentically befitting my Dream Girl character. I've even come up with a whole back story for the Dream Girl, and I think doing all that hard work is really gonna help me authentically convey her emotions and motivations to a tee, even if I don't say a word.

Speaking of the *Dream Girl* movie, though, I must admit I've been wondering lately why that director-guy hasn't called me yet. At first, I thought maybe our answering machine at the house had somehow erased his message, so I tried calling *him* a few times. When I wasn't able to reach him, I left him Kurtis' office number so that, when he called back, Mildred could take a message for me. But he never called back. In fact, I haven't gotten a single phone call from a soul, not even that talent-agent guy who sent me to the Dream Girl audition in the first place, the one who said he could get me as much work in this town as I could ever want. And I can't figure out why.

Chapter 35

19 Years 4 Months Old
265 Days Before Killing Kurtis

I'm bone tired of waiting around for that director to call me. I've been waiting for something or other to happen my whole life, and I don't want to wait around anymore. Today, I'm taking matters into my own hands—I'm marching right into that director's office and asking him, point blank, "When the heck are we gonna start shooting my *Dream Girl* movie, sir?"

When I arrive at the director's office, he's not there.

"I'll wait," I tell his assistant.

"I don't know if he's coming in today."

"I'm the star of his movie," I explain, jutting my chin with pride. "I'm his Dream Girl."

His assistant lets me stay—but it feels like she's only doing it out of pity.

After a couple hours, that director sure enough walks right through the door, and when he sees me, his face turns bright red. "Oh, Buttercup," he says. "Hi."

"Hey-ah. I was wondering if I could have a word with you, please, sir?"

"Sure." He leads me into his dark and disheveled office, flips on the lights, and motions to a chair. "What can I do for you?"

"Well, sir, I just wanted to tell you how excited I am about making our movie together. I've been going to acting classes for quite some time now, and I'm really looking forward to showing you—"

"Your husband didn't tell you?" He looks mighty uncomfortable. When my face makes it clear I don't know what in tarnation he's talking about, he continues, "I'm sorry, but the Dream Girl part's been recast."

I don't want them to, but tears spring into my eyes. "But I... I've been taking acting classes like crazy and I've been learning—"

"We're already in pre-production with another actress."

"But, please," I beg, panic rising in my throat. "You said yourself I'm the perfect Dream Girl—you said I was born to play this part."

He shakes his head. "You *are* a dream girl—without a doubt—just not mine."

"But why? What happened?"

He swallows hard. "The part just got recast, that's all. It happens all the time in this town. I'm sorry."

I jump out of my seat and point my finger at him. "Now you listen here, Mister Big Stuff. You tell me right now *why* it got recast, or I'm gonna slap the shit outta you and then slap you for shittin'."

A genuine smile flashes across his face for just an instant but quickly turns to stone-face. "Why don't you ask your husband?"

I'm taken aback. I don't understand what he means. "I... I already did," I stutter. "He said he talked to you. And he didn't say a word about the part being *recast*. He said he talked to you about directing a movie he's making starring me, but he's still lining up investors, so..." At the flat-out derisive expression on the director's face, I hasten to add, "It's not a *porno,* if that's what you're thinking—it's a legitimate movie-homage to Marilyn Monroe, starring me." I puff out my chest.

He smirks. "I don't recall the conversation going quite the way you're describing it."

"I don't understand."

He shrugs.

"What are you saying to me?" I ask, my eyes bugging out.

"You should talk to your husband if you want details."

I sit back down in my chair and begin to sob in earnest. "Please, just tell me what he said."

He sighs and hands me a box of tissues. "It's just not going to work out, okay?" He pauses, considering what to say. "I'll just say that your husband feels extremely *protective* of you. He made it abundantly clear he's not in favor of you working on any film projects with any director—any other *man*—besides him. Period."

I stare at the director square in the face and clench my jaw. "My husband doesn't *own* me. I was born to play the Dream Girl and you know it. You can still make me the Dream Girl, whether he likes it or not."

He chuckles, but there's no joy in it. He sits next to me on the couch. "Actually, I didn't get the impression I *could* make the movie with you in it, or do just about anything else, for that matter, if I crossed your husband. And, you know, I really enjoy doing things like breathing and eating solid foods, so..."

I'm sure my face registers my complete and utter shock.

"So, yeah, I'm sorry, Buttercup, but I chose breathing and being able to eat a cheeseburger over casting you in my movie."

My heart physically hurts. I clutch my chest, trying to alleviate the pain. "But," I stammer. "*Please.*"

"Look, I'm sorry to be so blunt with you, but as great as you are—and you *are* great, and I wish you the best—there's a line a mile long of girls who can play the Dream Girl in my movie. So, yeah, I decided to recast the part to get your lunatic-husband out of my hair. It's as simple as that."

My head is spinning. I put my hands over my face as

tears squirt out of my eyes and cascade through my clamped fingers. "Please, please, please," I beg, even though I know it's no use.

I already knew deep down inside Kurtis wasn't going to lead me to my sacred destiny, after all. But now it turns out he's been actively and purposefully keeping me *away* from it.

That Dream Girl movie was the only thing I had left in this life.

And now I've got nothing.

No Marilyn movie.

No Dream Girl movie.

No husband who loves me.

No Wesley.

No platinum-lined happily ever after.

All of a sudden, a tornado of rage swirls up inside me. I want to head straight home and hurl an axe into my husband's back. But I won't do it. Because I'm way too smart to veer off the plan I've made with my daddy. I am Charlie Wilber's Daughter, after all, and that means I'm gonna let Daddy take care of things just like we've carefully arranged—no more waffling.

And after Kurtis is six feet under, I'll go right ahead and star in any movie I want. Hell, when Kurtis is wearing a pine overcoat, and I've inherited all of his filthy porno-money— and you can bet your sweet ass I'll get every last dirty cent of it—I'll be the *producer* of any movie I please. And I won't need any fucking *investors* to do it, either. I'm done relying on anyone else to deliver me to my destiny or make me happy in this life. I'm gonna start taking care of myself.

And that's a fact, Jack.

When I get home from my meeting with the director, Kurtis isn't home yet, which is a lucky thing because not hacking my husband to death and burying his myriad parts throughout our backyard landscaping would have been a tall order.

I sit at the kitchen table with my darling Wilber on my lap and pick up the phone.

"Flowers by Judy."

"Hello there, Judy." I've gotten much better at my California accent by now, thanks to my acting instructor. "It's Charlene, calling to order flowers for my boss again?"

"Oh, hello again. Will it be the usual two bouquets?"

"Yes, invoiced as one giant bouquet delivered to the residence."

"Got it."

"But this time let's make both bouquets twice as big as y'all have ever made them—no, three times as big—just make 'em jaw-droppers, inexcusably excessive, like it's a damn shame to spend that much money on something as stupid as flowers instead of feeding a third-world country."

Judy the flower-lady laughs. "Okay."

"And for the note on the one to Bettie this time, my boss wants to say, 'I love you forever, my angel. Love, Your Eternally Devoted Admirer.'"

"Oh my. She's gonna like that. The usual roses and peonies?"

"Yes, but why don't y'all add some forget-me-nots, too."

"Oh, that'd be nice."

"And how about some lavender?"

"Hmm," Judy-the-Flower-Lady says. "Not typical for a romantic bouquet. Lavender's usually interpreted to mean 'distrust.'"

I can feel my eyes darkening. "Hmm," I say. "Well, gosh. My boss doesn't seem to put much stock in all that flower mumbo jumbo—he just likes what he likes. And he says lavender is this girl's favorite color, so why don't we just humor him?"

"No problem."

"And for the other bouquet to the residence, how 'bout y'all send the biggest, most boastful, most obscenely beautiful bouquet you can imagine. My boss doesn't care what's in that one, as long as you make it magnificent and unwisely expensive and bursting with joy."

Judy-the-Flower-Lady laughs again. "I'll do that."

"Thank you so much."

"Anything on the card for the second bouquet? Sounds like a special occasion."

"Oh, it is," I reply. "But we'll just let the flowers do the talking. Talk is cheap.'"

"Ain't that the truth."

"Well, thank you. Bye-bye now."

I stroke Wilber's soft fur for a moment, trying to calm myself. "Happy Killing Kurtis Day can't come soon enough, can it, Wilber?" I whisper, and my darling kitty purrs loudly in agreement. I pick up Wilber and nuzzle my nose against his soft face.

No it cannot, Wilber says to me. *It most certainly cannot.*

COUNTDOWN TO KILLING KURTIS

Chapter 36

19 Years 6 Months Old
195 Days Before Killing Kurtis

I'm startled awake. Kurtis looms over me next to the bed. He smells like he just got squeezed out of a bartender's rag. His hair is falling into his eyes. I jerk to a sitting position, every hair on my body standing on edge. My breathing is instantly shallow.

"Kurtis," I squeak out. I squint to make out his hands in the dark. Does he have a weapon? No. His hands are balled into fists. Is he fixin' to punch me in the face? Or to spread open his hands and wrap them around my neck? How bad is this gonna be?

Kurtis breathes heavily through his mouth. He's so drunk, he can't tell if he's coming or going. "I let my monster out, baby," he grunts out. His voice doesn't sound like his.

I'm too scared to speak.

"I let it out," he shouts, slurring. "But not on you." He lunges forward to kiss me, puckering at me like some sort of cartoon villain. When Kurtis' lips land on mine, they feel like slimy rubber. "She's been fucking someone else—and whoever he is, he keeps sending her flowers. Flowers and flowers and... 'I love you forever.' She wouldn't tell me who she's fucking, so I let my monster out, baby, just like you said I should."

I jerk sideways and Kurtis' body falls and heaves onto the bed. Wilber jolts awake and skitters to the floor.

Earlier tonight, right before Kurtis went out to the club, I told him "a woman" had called the house again. "It's the same woman as the last few times," I said. "She never leaves her name—she just keeps saying she needs to talk to you, needs to see you. This time she kept cackling when she said your name. Do you think it's someone from the club, honey?"

Of course, none of this was true, as usual. These days, when it comes to Kurtis, if my lips are moving, I'm lying. But I keep prodding Kurtis because I reckon the more times he thinks Bettie's called over here, and the more times Johnny reports that Bettie's secret admirer has sent her yet another extravagant bouquet, then the more likely Kurtis will be inspired to drink himself into a frenzy and barrel down to the club and chew Bettie out, and probably in front of countless witnesses. The fact that Kurtis just went the extra mile and let his monster cream Bettie's corn, too? Well, that's just an extra nice fact for when Bettie's on trial for Kurtis' murder.

"She always swears she's not the one calling. But who else could it be?"

Lord, I've never seen Kurtis this drunk before. I take a deep breath to calm my nerves. I just have to remember, as scary as Kurtis is right now, it's all part of the plan. "You're right, baby," I squeak. "It's gotta be her." I breathe deeply, steadying myself. "You've done a good thing," I coo, trembling. I cautiously pick up one of his hands and study it. His knuckles are swollen. He must have whacked her good and hard. "You'd never let anyone play you for a fool, isn't that right?"

He jerks his hand away from mine, making me flinch. "She won't tell me who it is," he says. "I told her, 'I don't care who it is. Just tell me. I won't do anything, I swear.' But she won't tell me. She said, 'I don't know who it is.'"

"Of course she knows," I scoff. "A man keeps sending her flowers and she doesn't know who it is? That woman's trying to tell you a lizard's an alligator."

"She's a fucking liar," Kurtis growls.

I suddenly notice an unmistakable splatter of blood on Kurtis' blue shirt, right underneath his shoulder. It's a small splatter, but there's no question what it is. "It was good you let your monster out on her," I whisper, eyeing the blood splatter. It looks almost purple against the blue of Kurtis' shirt.

"I let my monster out, just like you said I could," Kurtis mumbles again, sounding like he's falling asleep.

"That's just fine."

"I don't deserve you," he mumbles.

Truer words were never spoken.

"You love me even though I have a monster inside me."

"That's right."

He scoots close to me on the bed, and snuggles up to me. He reeks.

"Is she dead?" I whisper.

"No! Of course not. I'm not a murderer, for Chrissakes."

"Are you sure?"

"She threw her shoe at me when I was leaving."

"Well, that'd be pretty hard for a dead woman to do."

Kurtis chuckles. "You always make me laugh, baby. That's why I love you."

"And that's why you can *never* let your monster out on me—"

"I know! You already said that. And it's killing me, believe me, because some times I just wanna..."

My hair stands on end.

"But I'm doing what you want, okay? So stop fucking nagging me about it all the time."

His voice went from "I don't deserve you" to "I want to bash your face in" in three seconds flat. Goosebumps have formed all over my body. I need a new tack. "It's just that it makes me hot as a summer revival when you let your monster out on someone else. I like knowing you do bad things, Kurtis, just as long as it's not to me. It makes me hotter than a burning stump to think about you being so brutal and forceful and manly... and making that woman pay for her lies."

Well, that does it. Without warning, he pulls down his pants and slams himself into me, a wild, ravenous beast—and, strangely, thinking about how he just walloped Bettie and made her pay for her lies, it's the first time I've enjoyed sex with Kurtis in a very long time.

COUNTDOWN TO KILLING KURTIS

Chapter 37

19 Years 10 Months Old
33 Days Before Killing Kurtis

My acting instructor approaches me right before class. "Hey, some guy was asking about you yesterday."

I'm instantly filled with dread. Was it Kurtis? Or maybe Johnny? I try to remember what I was doing yesterday. Was I supposed to be in class? My mind is reeling.

"He asked about you by a different name at first," my instructor adds.

Now my dread turns to panic. Did the police finally figure out it was me who baked Jeb's cake? Or that it was me who swiped Mr. Clements' cards?

"But then the guy said, 'Well, she might go by Buttercup'—so I figured he must have been looking for you." My instructor grins broadly. "How many Buttercups can there possibly be in all of Los Angeles, right?" He laughs, and so do I, even though my heart is leaping out of my chest. "Anyway, the guy begged for your phone number and address, but of course, I wouldn't give him anything. So, he asked me to give you this." He places a folded piece of paper in my hand.

"Thank you," I manage, my voice quavering.

"He talked funny just like you do, so I figured he was legit." He winks.

I'm breathless. Did Daddy get out of prison early for good behavior?

The moment my instructor walks away, I hastily unfold the note with trembling hands—and in familiar, crooked handwriting, I see the digits of a local phone number followed by the sweetest little word I ever did see: *Wesley.*

I bolt from my seat, intending to sprint to the phone booth in the parking lot, but then I see Johnny standing just inside the front door of the theater, staring at me like a bald eagle watching a creek.

Slowly, I sit back down. Goddamned Johnny. Goddamned Kurtis. I shoot Johnny a clipped wave that says, "It's *not* nice to see you."

Johnny smirks and takes a seat in the back.

All I want to do is run outside and call the number on that note, but I'm stuck here.

I spend the next hour watching my classmates perform short monologues and debate "motivation" and "objective" and "subtext" with respect to each one. Normally, I'm a Chatty Cathy during class—that's what happens when you find your higher calling in life, I reckon—but today, I'm distracted and mute. That note's burning a hole in my hand and making me short of breath.

When class is over, I amble up the aisle toward Johnny as if I've got nothing better to do than chitty-chat with him about the weather. "Hey there, Johnny," I say, coming to a languid stop in front of him. "Well, aren't you as welcome as an outhouse breeze. You enjoying yourself back here?"

He grins.

"You gonna tell Kurtis about all those monologues? I'm sure he'll be thrilled to hear about every last one."

"Kurtis likes to make sure you get to your classes in one piece. He worries about you driving a sports car, you being a new driver and all."

It's so like Kurtis to give me a hot rod as a present and then turn around and hawk over me because he thinks I'll drive it too fast. "Yes, I'm well aware of Kurtis' concern for my safety, bless his heart." I decide to use this opportunity to stir up Kurtis' monster a little bit, since Johnny will surely report back on everything I tell him. "I wonder if you can answer a question for me, Johnny?"

"I can try."

"Who's the woman from the club that keeps calling my house?"

"How do you know she's not calling to sell you a vacuum cleaner? Sales ladies can be awfully persistent."

Man, that Johnny's slicker than a slop jar. "Gosh, I never thought of that. Thanks. That must be it."

"My pleasure."

"This last time, though, she sounded especially angry. I'm certainly not gonna buy a vacuum cleaner from anyone who curses me out like that."

"What'd she say?"

I twist my mouth like I'm thinking. "Never mind. You're right. I'll just leave it alone. Just, please, keep an eye on Kurtis for me—make sure he's safe. This lady, whoever she is, she's got an axe to grind with Kurtis, and I'm worried about him."

Johnny laughs. "Don't worry, I'll protect Kurtis from some angry little girl, whoever she is."

I suppress a smirk. "Thanks, Johnny. I'm sure you will. Well, are you gonna keep me company for the rest of the day? Because I'll tell you what other thrilling activities I've got on tap: another acting class, this one about how to most effectively use props, and then I'm gonna buy myself a pretty dress at a new boutique I heard about on Melrose, and I just might stop and get my nails painted a sassy, bright red. Kurtis always likes it when I'm sassy." I wink.

"Gosh, I hate to miss all that. But it sounds like you've got the rest of your day well in hand without me." He tips his imaginary hat to me and waltzes out of the theater.

I poke my head out the front door and watch Johnny the Egg-Sucking Dog walk down the sidewalk 'til he's a tiny speck. The instant Johnny disappears from sight, I sprint into the nearby phone booth and place my call with shaking fingers.

"Sunset Motel," the voice on the other end of the line says.

"Wesley Miller, please."

"He left his key, so he must be out. Do you want to leave a message?"

"If he comes back in the next twenty minutes, tell him to stay put," I shout. And then I careen down to the motel in my little sports car, faster than green grass through a goose.

I'm sitting on a rickety metal chair in the foyer of a dilapidated motel, rocking back and forth like my skin is on fire. I'll wait here all day long if I have to—all night long. My whole life, if necessary. Because, God as my witness, I'm not leaving this place until I've laid eyes—and lips—and everything else—on my darling, sweet, faithful, honest, kindhearted Wesley.

I wait and wait. And I wait some more.

Wild horses couldn't drag me away this time. Come what may.

Finally, after what seems like forever and a day, the glass door of the tiny lobby swings open, and there he is. The love of my life.

Wesley.

Chapter 38

19 Years 11 Months Old
33 Days Before Killing Kurtis

When Wesley walks into the foyer of the shabby motel where I've been waiting for him for close to two hours, I bolt up from my chair like I've been zapped by an electric eel. "Wesley," I blurt.

The look on Wesley's face when he sees me is priceless. Actually, now that I'm getting a good look at him, it's Wesley's whole face that's priceless, not just the look on it. Lord have mercy, what's happened to Wesley's face? He's turned downright handsome. Where's my gawky, pimply, big-eared, puppy-faced boy? This here's a *man*—and a good-looking one, at that—a really, *really* good-lookin' man. And where'd Wesley's scrawny shoulders run off to? This here's a *broad-shouldered* man—with bulging biceps and a square jaw, too. My knees go weak.

"Charlene?" Wesley's obviously shell-shocked.

I nod profusely. My heart is thumping out of my chest.

Wesley just keeps standing there, staring at me, his mouth gaping open.

"Wesley, get your room key," I whisper. My cheeks are hot.

Wesley shakes his head like he can't believe his eyes. "I searched high and low for you and, now, finally—"

"Get your gosh-dang key," I say. My crotch has begun pulsing mercilessly.

"Holy shit," he mumbles. He hurriedly collects his key from the motel clerk, who flashes Wesley a congratulatory smile.

Wesley and I gallop together to his room, both of us bursting at the seams. Wesley opens the door and motions for me to enter first, which I do, and then he steps inside and closes the door behind him. In a flash, and without asking permission like he always used to do, Wesley scoops me into his strong arms and kisses the crap out of me, feverishly pressing his hardness against my hip.

I literally swoon when his tongue enters my mouth. I've never tasted anything as sweet as Wesley's lips and tongue, never smelled anything so good as his scent, never wanted something as much as to feel him sliding deep inside me.

"I can't believe you're here," Wesley says, pulling back to look at me. "I went to every place I could think to find you—and now you're finally here."

I laugh with glee. I can't remember feeling this happy in all my life.

"And you look like a movie star," Wesley says, clearly awestruck.

"Oh, Wesley. I *am* a movie star." I giggle at the look of wide-eyed astonishment on his face. *"Buttercup Bouvier."* I throw my hands up in the air like a magician's assistant.

He kisses me again. But this time, when he's done kissing my mouth, he kisses my cheeks, eyes, nose, forehead, and even my ears—all the while pressing his erection forcefully into my crotch.

"Oh, Wesley," I breathe, rubbing myself against his hard-on. My heart is racing.

I reach down and touch the bulge between us, aching for him, hungry for him, and suddenly, we both know the time for talking is done.

Wesley rips off his T-shirt and I gasp at the sight of him.

Great thundering Jesus. Wesley's chiseled body alone is enough to make me ooze onto the floor, but there's something else about Wesley that makes me literally whimper with desire: That boy's gotten himself tattooed—lord have mercy—*with my name.* "B-U-T-T-E-R-C-U-P," Wesley's tattoo proclaims across his chest, each letter intertwined with the stems and blooms of swirling, slithering buttercups.

Well, if that right there isn't enough to make a woman scream a man's name, I don't know what is. "Wesley," I purr, but I don't want words. I want action. I want him. I begin to take off my dress, but Wesley quickly assumes the job, ripping that sucker off me like it's on fire.

When he beholds the sight of my naked body, his eyes ignite like hot coals.

My skin feels like bacon sizzling in a skillet under his gaze.

In a flash, Wesley's clothes are on the floor along with mine, his arms are wrapped around me, and his lips are devouring mine. When his fingertips touch between my legs and slide into me, I cry out and my knees buckle. I grab his erection and he moans. He guides me urgently onto the creaky motel bed, onto my back, and I open my legs to him, moaning like a calf at his momma's slaughter. I've never ached like this before.

"Wesley," I whisper. "My Wesley."

Wesley groans as his body burrows into mine, and I groan, too. I wrap my arms around him and pull him into me with all my might.

For so long with Kurtis, I've wondered if having Wesley's body moving in and out of me might feel somehow different than Kurtis'—and now I've got my delicious answer: hell yes, it does. Good lord, holy hell, yes sir, it does. There's no doubt about it—making love to Wesley is an ejaculation that's gonna change the trajectory of my entire life. And then some.

I feel like my body's gonna explode and shatter into a

million tiny pieces with each kiss of Wesley's lips, each lick of his tongue, each thrust of his body into mine. Now that I'm finally making love to Wesley like I've been dreaming about doing for so long, I suddenly realize clear as day I never loved Kurtis, not even when we ate cream of wheat for breakfast and he told me I'm gorgeous without lipstick on. This whole time, my husband's been nothing but a square peg to my round hole—whereas Wesley's peg is round and hard and deep as the day is long. Yes, indeed.

Speaking of which, Wesley's thrusts are becoming intense and noisy. I grab at his butt and shove him into me even harder, aching for him to go deeper inside me than Kurtis ever did. When my body starts clenching and rippling from deep inside, squeezing against him in warm waves of pleasure, I can't help screaming and crying, too. The physical pleasure I'm feeling right now is like nothing I've felt before, but I don't think that's why I'm crying. I think my tears are flowing because I'm feeling completely happy for the first time in my entire life.

Even after Wesley and I have done the deed twice in one hour—and the second time, *hot damn,* that boy kissed and licked me into a goddamned frenzy—we still can't get enough of each other. He keeps staring at me, kissing every inch of me, licking my nipples, caressing every curve, and gently tracing hearts and curlicues onto my skin with his fingertips. And I can't stop touching Wesley, either—his bulging biceps and strong jaw and ripped abs and soft lips, and especially his muscled chest with my name on it.

"You're so *beautiful,"* Wesley mutters, his fingers swirling over my skin.

My heart squeezes. Kurtis has told me I'm gorgeous a thousand times, but hearing Wesley say I'm beautiful feels different—like he's talking about more than my bouncy boobs. And actually, speaking of my bouncy boobs, Wesley's clearly not impressed with them.

"When did you get these?" he asks, grazing his hand across my left nipple.

"Right when I got to Hollywood," I reply. "Why? You don't like 'em?"

"It's just that you didn't need 'em. Your boobs were perfect before."

I pout. "Well, I needed 'em to become an actress, Wesley. I had to comport with industry standards—I can't become a legendary actress without industry-comporting breasts." (I say "breasts" instead of "boobs" because I want Wesley to understand that my new boobies are classy.)

"They're awfully big, though," Wesley mumbles.

"No, they're not. They're *Monroes,* not *Mansfields.*"

Wesley looks at me like I'm speaking Greek.

"They're classy," I explain explicitly (because, clearly, my prior use of the word "breasts" didn't convey my meaning enough).

Wesley bursts out laughing.

Well, that does it. I'm instantly enraged.

I sit up in the bed and reach for my dress, aiming to march right out of this motel room like a prairie fire with a tailwind—I don't care how good-lookin' Wesley is nowadays—but Wesley grabs ahold of my arm and forces me to stay put.

"Hang on," he says, surprising me with how forceful his voice sounds.

I deign to look at him—and the minute I do, I melt. He's just so gosh-dang handsome, I couldn't stay mad at him if I tried.

"The whole time I was in jail," Wesley says evenly, his eyes blazing at me, "all I did every single night was dream about finally getting to touch your perfect boobs." He licks his lips. "And now, I'm finally, *finally* here with you, after all this time and all my dreaming, and it turns out you've switched 'em up on me." His mouth tilts up into a crooked grin. "That's all I'm sayin'."

My anger is long gone. "Aw, poor Wesley," I coo, stroking his broad chest. "I sure pulled the ol' switcheroo on you, didn't I?"

"You sure did." He pulls me into him for a kiss.

Suddenly, my brain realizes Wesley just said the word *jail*—that he was in *jail* dreaming about my boobs—and I pull away from our kiss. "You went to *jail*?" I ask. "Did Mr. Clements figure out it was you who stole the baseball cards?"

"No. Not at all. Our plan worked perfectly."

I let out a huge sigh of relief.

"First of all," he says, "you'll never believe what the code for the combination lock turned out to be." He tells me what numbers opened the safe and I slap my forehead in apparent disbelief.

"Well, aren't you clever, Wesley," I say, and his face lights up.

"It was you who got the envelope from under the rock, right?" he asks.

"Of course, it was. Just like we planned."

"I figured. Because when I went to check under the big oak tree, the envelope was gone. Hey, how'd you like me putting that extra twenty bucks in there for you?" He beams me a huge smile.

"That was a sweet surprise," I say, returning his smile. "You always were so good to me, Wesley."

His eyes sparkle at me. "I've told you, Buttercup—I'm *always* gonna take care of you. That's the way it's always been, and that's the way it'll always be." He winks.

I beam at him.

"The only part of the plan I changed at the last minute," Wesley continues, "was putting that Yogi Berra card under *Christopher's* mattress instead of mine." Christopher was a particularly dumbass kid back at the group home. If all his brains were dynamite, that boy couldn't blow his nose. "I figured it was better to put it there and let Christopher take the blame if the shit hit the fan than get greedy and keep the card for myself."

My, my, my, so Wesley's smarter than I gave him credit for—smarter and a helluva lot handsomer, too.

"And it's a good thing I did that, too," Wesley continues, "because when Mr. Clements finally opened the safe and found his cards gone, he turned the entire house all catawampus before any of us kids even got home from school yet. He found that card under Christopher's cot right quick and had the police just sitting and waiting to take him away the minute he got home from school. Man, they took that boy away just like *that*, no questions asked." He snaps his fingers.

"Oh, Wesley, thank God you did that. If you'd followed my stupid suggestion and put that Yogi card under your own mattress, they'd have taken you away instead of Christopher." I shudder at the horrible thought. "Thank goodness you didn't listen to my stupid idea."

Wesley taps his temple with his finger. "I've got brains for days, Charlene."

I don't even mind Wesley calling me Charlene. In fact, it's kind of nice for a change. I'd even go so far as to say it kind of turns me on to hear him call me by that name after all this time.

"And do you know what else that bastard Mr. Clements did?" Wesley says. "He lied and told the police there was five hundred dollars inside that safe, not twenty, just to make sure the police took Christopher away for good."

"Woo-wee!" I exclaim. "That Mr. Clements would steal the nickels off a dead man's eyes."

"You bet he would."

"So why were you in jail, then?"

He rolls his eyes at what he's about to say. "After they took Christopher away, a bunch of kids started talking about how they didn't think Christopher had enough brains to figure out the safe. And then that fucker Thomas, you remember him? He started telling everyone he thought it was *you* who stole the cards. He said he saw me and you under the big oak tree a million times and that you were just playing me for a fool."

I gasp.

"So I bashed his head in."

Oh my. An intense humming sensation suddenly courses through my body, zinging me in my most private places. This man right here was willing to do whatever he had to do to protect me—even something against his very nature. The thought makes my skin buzz like I'm gripping an electric fence. "Wesley," I breathe, and we kiss again, good and long. "Touch my boobs," I whisper, and he complies greedily. I reckon he'll learn to like my new boobs good enough.

I've never put a man's package in my mouth before, but I'm suddenly aching to do it for Wesley. And so, I do.

I always reckoned sucking on a man would feel like sucking on a warm Otter Pop—but, no, even with my eyes shut tight, there's no mistaking Wesley's smooth, pulsing meat-popsicle for a frozen treat. At my tongue's first taste of him, Wesley groans really loud, so I reckon I'm on the right track—and when I take all of him into my mouth, he makes a noise of surprise and delight that could send a herd of buffalo stampeding. When I finally muster the courage to suck on him like I'm coaxing the last dregs of a Slurpee through a straw, well, I reckon I've hit the mother lode because the boy starts grabbing at my hair and pushing himself into me like he's a fish getting fileted. And that's when it dawns on me—this right here is what men throughout the history of time have been willing to die for. Or kill. And the thought makes me hotter than a fresh-fucked fox in a forest fire.

I'm not sure, but it feels like Wesley's about to lose control of himself into my mouth, so I stop what I'm doing and climb on top of him. I'm not opposed to letting Wesley give me a mouthful of something to remember him by—in fact, I'm surprisingly eager to taste every last drop of him at some point in the near future—but I'm thinking that particular feat might be a tad ambitious for my first time at the rodeo. I reckon Wesley doesn't mind me changing course on him, though, because after only a few minutes of me riding him like a mad bull, he's jolting and bucking underneath me and I'm screaming his name as muscles deep inside me twist and warp and squeeze.

When we're good and done and both of us are marinating in each other's sweat, Wesley and I lie side-by-side, naked as jaybirds, touching each other's bodies, and chatting up a storm. I find out that poor Wesley sat in jail for almost eighteen months for smashing Thomas' head in—until well after he'd already turned eighteen. Who knew a judge could "try a minor as an adult?" I sure didn't.

When I tell Wesley I'm awfully sorry he had to go to jail and all—and when my eyes tear up because I really am heartbroken over it—he smiles at me in the most adorable way and says, "Aw, jail wasn't so bad. The food was pretty good, and I got myself some true-blue friends." When I commend his positive attitude but repeat that I'm so very sorry he had to get locked up for so long, especially on account of me, Wesley just shrugs his shoulders and says, "If a man can't run with the big dogs, he'd best stay under the porch."

I feel a thousand pounds lighter knowing why Wesley never showed up at the bus station ten months ago. It wasn't because he'd forgotten all about me, like I thought; it was because he was busy whittling sticks into wooden bears and fishes in his ten-by-ten-foot prison cell.

It's funny how everything happens for a reason. As it turned out, jail wound up doing Wesley some good. I reckon it was almost like a happy vacation for Wesley after living so many years in group-home hell. He wound up having some good meals and making friends, like he said. And even better than that, he became a real man with real muscles while he was there. Wooh-*wee*, did he ever!

And even more to the point of how things happen exactly as they're supposed to, thanks to Wesley being in jail for so long, there's only about five short weeks 'til Killing Kurtis Day. He couldn't have come back to me at a better time. All

I've got to do now is bide my time for thirty-three short little days, and then Wesley and I and his new muscles can be together, forever and ever—making love whenever we want— every which way we please—and we'll be filthy rich while we're doing it, to boot.

Chapter 39

19 Years 11 Months Old
33 Days Before Killing Kurtis

"You're *married?*" Wesley booms at me, his face a mixture of rage and devastation.

"Well, now, hold your horses, Wesley, and let me explain."

Wesley springs out of the bed and paces around the tiny motel room, mad as a wet panther. Even though he's angry and this probably isn't the right time to ogle the view, I can't help myself. Wooh-*wee*, after being with my old man of a husband all this time, it sure is nice to look at a young, good-lookin', virile man's chiseled body for a change. I reckon Wesley did his fair share of push-ups and sit-ups in jail, because he looks like he escaped from a museum.

"Do you have any idea how long I've waited for you?" Wesley booms, his chest heaving. "And you got *married?*" He grabs at his hair, overcome with fury and pain. "But you're my princess bride." Wesley's voice cracks at this last part, his face twisting and contorting with his heartbreak.

My heart is splitting in two. "When you didn't come to the bus station, Wesley, I thought you'd forgotten all about me. I thought you didn't love me anymore. You promised to take care of me forever and you didn't even show up."

"Because I was in *jail!*"

"But I didn't know that. And I was just heartbroken. I thought I was gonna curl up and die." Tears begin to flow. "I didn't even wanna *live* anymore without you." The tears come faster and bigger. "When you didn't come, I was just as lost as last year's Easter egg, Wesley. For weeks, I went to that bus station again and again and again, every single day, at exactly noon, just praying you'd show up." That last part's a lie—but I have to say it. I'll say whatever's got to be said not to lose my Wesley again. "When you didn't come, I felt so low, I couldn't jump off a dime. I felt so low, you couldn't lay a rug under me." That's the God's truth. "And then, oh, Wesley, I went to an audition when I was as low as could be, just feeling like a possum had trotted over my grave, and that's when I met a rich movie producer and he asked me out to lunch— and, well, you know how beautiful I am, Wesley." I say this last part like I'm chastising him for how beautiful I am.

Wesley's clutching feverishly at his chest like he's trying to claw his heart right out of his body—or maybe he's trying to rip his tattoo clean off his flesh.

"I couldn't help it if that rich movie producer fell in love with me at first sight," I continue. "And when he asked me to marry him, well, I figured nothing mattered, anyway. If I couldn't have you, if you didn't love me anymore, then what did it matter if I married him or anyone else? Or jumped off a bridge? It was all the same to me—marrying him and dying." I realize I've fudged the timeline of my marriage to Kurtis just a touch, but it's got to be done. Now that I've finally got my Wesley back, I'll be damned if I'm going to lose him over something as meaningless as exactly when I married Kurtis.

Wesley's face is twisted up like I've just slammed his pecker into a car door. He puts his hands over his face and lets out a deep sob.

"Wesley," I say. "Please, baby. Don't get yourself all worked up over nothing."

His hands remain over his face as his shoulders rack with sobs.

"Wesley," I say. My heart is shattering. I can't lose him again. I have to make him understand. "Marrying that movie producer was the same thing as setting myself down on the railroad tracks and waiting for the train to come," I say. But then I can't hold back my emotions anymore—I let out a long, tortured wail.

Wesley drops his hands from his face and rushes to me, quickly wrapping his muscled arms around me and kissing my tear-stained cheeks. "Shh," he soothes. "I understand."

"I don't love him, Wesley," I sob. "I've only ever loved you. I love you, Wesley. I've always loved you." This is the God's truth. "I love you bigger than a sky full of stars," I say, emotion flooding me. I've never said these special words to anyone but my daddy before now. But I sure as heck mean them about Wesley.

Wesley squeezes me hard. In all the times Wesley and I met and kissed under the big oak tree back home, I never once told him I loved him. And now, all in one magical afternoon, I've let him sleep with me (three times!—including sucking on his corndog, which ought to count for something, for crying out loud!), *and* I've told him I love him, too—bigger than a sky full of stars! Yes, okay, it turns out I happen to be married, that's true—but two out of three ain't too shabby.

"Don't go back," Wesley says fiercely. "Stay here with me."

I wipe my eyes. "I can't. Kurtis would kill me if I try to leave him." I'm pretty sure I'm telling the truth about that.

"I'll protect you."

"You don't know my husband. I married a very bad man—and a very rich one. You wouldn't be able to protect me from him forever. He'd find a way. He'd send his goons. As long as Kurtis is breathing, he's not gonna let another man have me." I shudder at the thought.

"Well, then," Wesley says matter-of-factly, "we'll just have to kill him, then."

At Wesley's words, I feel that delicious humming inside

my body again—an electricity that makes me feel as hot as the hinges of hell. "Funny you should say that, Wesley," I say.

I tell him all about the monster inside Kurtis—every last detail about how Kurtis walloped me—until Wesley's raring to barrel on down to my house and slit Kurtis' throat tonight.

"No, Wesley!" I shout at him. "Who do you think the police are gonna blame if you go ahead and kill my husband tonight? *Me.* The police always blame the dead guy's wife, especially if he's rich. And if the wife happens to have an airtight alibi—which I *don't,* by the way, since I've been here riding you like a mechanical bull for the past three hours—then they figure out right quick who the boyfriend is, and they arrest *him.*"

Wesley tries to argue with me, but I interrupt him.

"Who showed up to my acting class yesterday, looking for 'Buttercup' and talking with a Texas twang?"

He clenches his jaw.

"And who just sprinted into a seedy motel room together, laughing and cooing and gushing and practically jumping each other's bones right in front of the sleazy motel clerk?"

I can tell my words are making an impact on Wesley.

"Don't you see? We're doomed if we do a damned thing right now. And I swear to God, I'm not gonna get you back after all this time just to lose you forever."

Wesley looks defeated.

"But don't worry. I've got a plan that makes it so that in thirty-three short days, we'll be together forever and ever. We'll be able to do whatever we want, whenever we want, and we'll have more money than God while we're doing it."

For the first time ever, I tell Wesley about my daddy, and about how he's coming to pay Kurtis a visit in exactly thirty-three short little days. "You've got to think about the forest and not the trees here, honey. What's the point in killing Kurtis if it means one or both of us goes to prison forever? Let my daddy do this sweet thing for me—for *us.* There's nothing to connect Daddy to Kurtis. You just make sure you get yourself an alibi thirty-three days from now. Make sure you're somewhere where a lot of people can see you, so nobody ever thinks for a second it was you who made Kurtis trade his guitar for a harp. If we let my daddy take care of Kurtis, then you and I will be together forever and never have to look over our shoulders again."

I give Wesley all the cash I've got in my pocketbook, enough to cover rent for an entire week at this low-rent motel, and his eyes bug out at the sight of all that money.

When I ask him how he's been managing to pay for things so far, all Wesley says is, "You'd be surprised how many people leave their windows and doors unlocked."

"I'll bring you more cash in exactly a week," I assure him. And when he looks about to protest, I add, "It's what's left of the baseball card money. It's yours, anyway."

Wesley looks so proud of himself, I'm happy to tell him this lie about the baseball card money. Of course, I spent all that money eons ago on new boobs and clothes, but I'd hate for Wesley to think he went to all that trouble stealing Mr. Clements' baseball cards just so I could buy bouncy new boobs he doesn't even like.

Even though I've already spent the baseball card money, though, getting cash for Wesley won't be hard to do. Kurtis leaves more cash just lying around our house on any given day than Wesley's seen in his whole life. If there's one nice thing I can say about Kurtis—and one nice thing's pretty much the most I can manage these days—it's that he lets me have as much cash as I please to buy books and clothes and makeup and shoes and acting classes and whatnot. I could swipe a couple hundred dollars from around the house and bring it to Wesley, and Kurtis wouldn't miss that money any more than he'd miss a roll of toilet paper. "And when I bring you the baseball card money, we'll have another round or two in the sack, too. How does that sound?"

Wesley grins at that. "Mighty fine."

"Until then, just stay out of sight and trust me, okay?

And for cryin' out loud, don't come to my acting class ever again. Don't come anywhere near me. We have such a short amount of time to wait, and I've got to keep doing everything I always do, so he doesn't suspect anything—so the *police* don't suspect anything when Kurtis is finally six feet under. We don't wanna go off half-cocked here and cut off our nose to spite our face, okay?"

"I can't let you go back there if he's gonna lay a hand on you."

"Don't you worry about me, honey. There's someone else who's become Kurtis' favorite punching bag, lately. All I have to do is keep him trained on her for the next thirty-three days, and I'll be sittin' pretty."

Wesley's face goes dark and his eyes go hard. "Are you gonna sleep with him?"

"Oh, Wesley." I stroke Wesley's cheek to calm him down. "Kurtis is an old man—he's *thirty-six.*" I scoff. "Trust me, baby, Kurtis doesn't even have working parts anymore."

Chapter 40

Hollywood, California, 1992

20 Years 2 Weeks Old
1 Day Before Killing Kurtis

My head bangs against the hotel wall as Kurtis plows into me, groaning and grunting and sweating like a pig all the while. I can sense he's reaching his limit and can't hold out much longer, which suits me just fine. These days, all I ever pray for is that sex with Kurtis goes as quickly as possible. Now that I've tasted the pleasure of making love to Wesley, sex with Kurtis makes my stomach churn.

It's taken a Herculean effort on my part not to go down to that shabby motel every single day to roll around in the sheets with my Wesley. And whenever it's time for me to leave Wesley and go back home to my husband, it's like I put the most scrumptious piece of chocolate in my mouth, chewed it once, and spit it into the toilet. It makes no sense. But I've got to do it.

It's a testament to my strength of will and character that I've only sneaked off to see Wesley seven times in the last thirty-two days. All I keep telling myself, over and over again, is "Keep your eye on the prize, Charlene." And that's what's helped me stick with the game plan, even as I imagine Wesley and his taut muscles stretched out on that motel bed just a hop, skip and jump away. Johnny hasn't been following me lately—I reckon months of watching me read my books out at the pool, sitting in acting classes, or getting my hair primped and nails painted finally bored Johnny to tears and convinced Kurtis he can trust me (or that I'm too boring to worry about, anyway). But I don't want to get cocky and greedy, especially when I'm this close to the finish line. So, just to be on the safe side, I don't see Wesley even one-tenth as much as my body's aching and throbbing to do.

"Baby," Kurtis moans, his voice straining.

I turn my face into his ear, and I exhale sharply, making sure my breathing seems ragged and desperate, as if, despite my best efforts at maintaining my composure, I just can't control myself. Of course, my dear husband, only you bring out the wide-eyed little girl in me, the girl who believes in happily ever afters and soul mates. I roll my eyes, even as it bangs against the wall with a loud thud.

Damn it all to hell, Kurtis isn't finishing. What's taking so long? *Bang, bang, bang*. My head continues its assault on the wall of our hotel room.

"Oh, Kurtis," I whisper, taking great care to infuse my voice with breathless excitement. Actually, it's easy to make my voice sound like I'm genuinely turned on right now—all I have to do is think about making love to Wesley and it's easy as pie. That's what's called "method acting."

I wait.

Kurtis is *still* chugging right along, doing his thing—and moaning and grunting, as well—but undeniably hanging on. Hmmph. I try a few other well-worn tricks until, finally, thankfully, he's done. I let loose my trademark I'm-just-so-in-love-with-you sigh, the one I've perfected over the past year, and he collapses into me, glistening with sweat.

Kurtis becomes still and his body goes slack. "You're amazing," Kurtis says, looking into my eyes and grinning like a cow at milking time. "I love you, baby."

"I love you, too, Kurtis," I reply. And it's true. I *do* love

Kurtis—in the way you love someone who's lied to you for well over a year. In the way you love someone whose fingers on your skin make you gag. In the way you love someone who's whacked you so hard across the side of your face with his fist, it takes weeks for the bruise to completely go away, and shaken you so hard your teeth rattle, and squeezed your arms so hard, he's left deep bruises on your flesh in the perfect shape of his fingers. In the way you love someone who's been fucking a whore named Bettie, right under your nose and in your own bed for well over a year, if not longer, as if he doesn't already have the most loyal and beautiful wife in the world. In the way you love someone who's sabotaged your greatest chance at happiness by threatening a real director who went to film school and everything, even though you were born to be the Dream Girl in that director's movie and deserve that part more than anybody. In the way you love someone who's promised, over and over, to make a legitimate movie-homage to Marilyn Monroe, starring you—and not a porno, mind you, a *real* movie—and then just lollygagged and dragged his feet and second-guessed and sat around with his thumb up his ass until it's very obvious, without anyone having to say a damned word, that movie's never gonna happen.

Yes, indeed, I love Kurtis.

To death.

It's a real thrill—a turn-on, even, if I'm being honest—to be so close now, so very, very close, after waiting a tortuous year minus one day for fate to take the wheel and drive a freight train over Kurtis' lying, cheating ass. Being on the eve of Kurtis' one-way departure from planet earth, I feel somewhat hot and bothered, actually.

I suddenly kiss Kurtis' mouth with sincere enthusiasm, and he replies by plunging his tongue into mine. Being so close to killing Kurtis, realizing I'm only one day away from spending every night with sweet Wesley in my own bed and finally having the freedom to go to any audition I want and make any movie I want to make—finally getting to become the legendary actress I'm destined to be, *and* having Wesley by my side like my own Joe DiMaggio, too—is an aphrodisiac like nothing I've experienced before.

"Oh, baby," he murmurs. "Again?"

"Again," I mutter.

Might as well send the fucker off with a smile on his stupid, lying face.

Afterward, as Kurtis and I lie in the hotel bed together, I can't help but picture Daddy opening my back door (which I checked and re-checked was unlocked before Kurtis and I left the house this morning) and then imagining Daddy entering the house and saying, "Woo-wee!" as he takes in the fanciness of it. For just a moment, I'm sad I'm here and can't see Daddy's face light up when he sees my mansion for the first time—but I reckon not seeing Daddy's face when he enters his new home is a small price to pay to get to see Daddy's handsome face every single day for the rest of my happy life.

So far, everything's worked out from giddy-up to whoa according to what Daddy and I talked about a year ago, so there shouldn't be any surprises. Getting Kurtis out of the house with me on this little overnight trip turned out to be easy as pie. He was more than willing to spend a night with me in a fancy Beverly Hills hotel as his late twentieth birthday present to me. And, he was equally amenable to letting me spend some time in the hotel's spa tomorrow morning while he returns home to do God-knows-what.

"There's something I've got to tell you, Buttercup," Kurtis says, his voice tentative.

I turn my head on my pillow toward him.

"I... I don't think our Marilyn movie's gonna happen, after all."

I'm stone-faced.

"Investors think the idea of a movie-homage to Marilyn Monroe is overdone and clichéd."

Oh, for cryin' out loud. Kurtis sure has impeccable

timing, doesn't he? Of course, what he's saying to me isn't breaking news—but finally hearing these words out loud, especially on Killing Kurtis Eve, makes me hate my husband in a way I never imagined possible.

"They think a better idea might be a movie-homage to someone a little more mysterious and not as well known."

Gosh, who might this "more mysterious" and "not as well known" someone be? Bastard. Before this very moment, I couldn't have imagined Kurtis saying or doing anything to make me want him dead any more than I already do. But, damn, the man has gone and done the impossible.

Kurtis looks anxious.

"Have you done your best?" I ask.

Kurtis nods, wary.

"Then that's all I could ever ask of you."

Kurtis' face is the picture of pure astonishment.

I smile broadly. "We've got each other, and that's all we'll ever need."

Kurtis throws his arms around me and covers my face with kisses. "Oh my God, I don't deserve you, baby."

"That's a fact, Jack."

Kurtis laughs. He pulls back and looks into my eyes, his face awash in relief. "I was afraid you'd leave me when I told you."

"Well, then, I reckon you don't know me very well—I'm not going anywhere."

Kurtis pulls me into him and clutches me fiercely. "Never leave me, Buttercup," he begs. "You're the best thing that's ever happened to me in my whole, fucking, pathetic life." I'm surprised to realize he's suddenly choking back tears. "I can't live without you, baby."

"I'm not going anywhere," I repeat evenly.

"You promise?" He squeezes me tighter.

"May I be kicked to death by grasshoppers if it ain't the truth."

Kurtis lets out a chortle, sort of a chuckle and cry mixed

together, and then he presses his body even more fervently into mine. "I can't live without you," he whispers urgently.

"I promise you this, Kurtis Jackman: You won't ever live a day without me. Not a single day."

He kisses the top of my head and holds me close.

Good lord, I can't wait for tomorrow. I suddenly envision Daddy wandering through my house right this very minute, oohing and aahing at the splendor of it all, finding the butcher knives I laid out on the counter for him, and getting himself good and ready for Kurtis' grand entrance tomorrow morning. The very thought makes me tremble with excitement.

Kurtis squeezes me even tighter.

Motherfucking-fuckity-fuck-fuck, I've got to make sure Kurtis goes straight home from the hotel tomorrow morning to meet Daddy, exactly as planned. I'm gonna blow a gasket if Kurtis gets distracted and messes this up for me like he's messed up everything else I've ever wanted him to do.

"Now, listen here, honey. When I get home after the spa tomorrow, I'm gonna let you feel how nice those spa-ladies buffed and polished my body for you." Yes, I've got to make double-damn ironclad sure that Kurtis beelines his ass straight to our house tomorrow and doesn't make a detour to the office or the club or God knows where else. "And Kurtis, I've got a little present planned for you tomorrow." He's holding me right up against him so I tilt my face up to his. "You know that naughty thing you've been begging me to do?"

Kurtis' face lights up like dynamite.

"Well, tomorrow, that's exactly what I'm gonna let you do to me, right when I come home. How does noon sound, honey?"

Kurtis makes a lecherous sound.

"But if you make me wait on you, I might change my mind about letting you do it to me."

"Why wait 'til tomorrow when we're here tonight?" Kurtis presses into me and swoops in for a kiss.

I put my hand up to halt him. "Because I'm gonna be so

relaxed from going to the spa, it's the only way I'm gonna be able to go through with it, that's why. Do you wanna do the naughty thing or not?"

Kurtis smiles wolfishly. "I wanna do the naughty thing."

"Well, then you best get your ass into our bed and wait for me tomorrow by noon."

"Sure thing," he agrees.

Well, that was easy. Bastard. "What do I always say about the virtue of waiting for something you want, darlin'?"

"'The best things in life are always worth waiting for,'" Kurtis says, mimicking my speech pattern.

"It's the truth, honey. If you're good and patient today, then I promise at this time tomorrow you'll feel like you've died and gone straight to the place where the naughty little boys go."

Kurtis laughs. "You promise?"

"Oh, honey, yes, I do. I swear to God."

Chapter 41

20 Years 2 Weeks 1 Day Old
Killing Kurtis Day

I stop outside the front door of my house and catch my breath. This is it. I've waited a whole year to wish myself Happy Killing Kurtis Day and it's finally here. It feels like a dream. I turn the key in the door and step inside. The house is so quiet you could hear a mouse pissing on a ball of cotton.

I'm not exactly sure what to do. Should I holler for Kurtis and act immediately alarmed when he doesn't reply? Or should I call out to Daddy like a wise-ass, in case he stayed to say hello before having to duck out? No, this is no time to be a wise-ass. I've got to stay in character and use my method acting skills. Even when I'm all alone with my dead husband upstairs, I'm going to play every minute of this scene according to the script: I've just come home from spending hours in a luxurious spa (which multiple witnesses can confirm) and now I'm relaxed and happy as a gopher in soft dirt and looking forward to some red-hot lovin' with my darling husband.

I take a deep breath. It's show time. This will be my greatest performance to date. I slowly climb the grand staircase toward the second floor, inching closer and closer to freedom, my pulse pounding in my ears. With each step I take, my heart knocks harder and harder against my chest.

Soon, this house will be all mine. And Daddy and Wesley will live here with me. And I'll have more money than God. If I want to make a movie, then I will. If I want to star in a real director's movie, then I will. If I want to roll around in my bed with Wesley, then I will. If I wanna buy my daddy a jetpack and let him fly around my house, then that's exactly what I'll do. I'll do whatever I want to do, every single day of my life, and no one will be able to tell me what I can and can't do.

I'm at the top of the stairs. I tiptoe slowly toward the closed master bedroom door. There's not a sound in the house. My breathing is shallow. My head is spinning.

I open the master bedroom door. It creaks, breaking the deadly silence.

I peek my head into the room. Kurtis' body is lying on the bed. He's on his side, turned away from me and covered with a blanket except for his head. Daddy did such a neat and tidy job of things, it almost looks like Kurtis is just fast asleep and dreaming of me. I lick my lips in anticipation. I can't believe this is finally happening. I'm shaking like a hound dog trying to shit out a peach pit.

The fireplace in our bedroom is blazing with a roaring fire. That's strange. Why would Daddy turn on the fire?

I creep toward the bed, preparing to let out a bloodcurdling scream. So much adrenaline is coursing through my body, I can barely control myself from twitching.

I come to a halt right in front of Kurtis. His mouth is hanging open.

Adrenaline floods me, along with a healthy dose of elation—and, if I'm being honest, the tiniest sliver of regret, too. As much as I came to hate Kurtis at the bitter end, and understandably so, we actually did have some good times along the way. It was Kurtis who suggested I go to acting classes, after all, and I'll be forever grateful to him for that. Really, it's too bad things had to come to this. If I could have resolved things any differently, I swear to God I would have—

Wait just a goddamned minute—Kurtis' lip just *twitched*. This fucker is breathing. This fucker's alive!

Oh Sweet Jesus, this can't be happening.

I peek beneath the covers and I'm assaulted with the sight of Kurtis' naked body and flopping man-parts—and all of it with nary a scratch. With trembling hands, I replace the covers over Kurtis' body. Motherfucker! *Why is Kurtis alive right now?* Good lord, I've got to get out of here. Is Daddy hiding somewhere in the house with a butcher knife? I look at my watch. 1:30. The plan was for Daddy to kill Kurtis before noon. Why did Daddy wait? Should I leave and come back later?

Shit, shit, shit. I thought Kurtis would be buzzard bait by now. I was counting on it. I exhale loudly in my despair. Holy fucking shit on a stick.

Kurtis stirs and opens his eyes. "Buttercup," he mumbles, sounding particularly relaxed. "I fell asleep waiting for you." He smiles at me. "I'm all ready for you, baby." He lifts up the blanket to reveal that, yes, indeed, all his baby-making parts are instantly functioning exactly as God intended, and then some—contrary to what I told Wesley a month ago. "I was dreaming about getting that thank-you-present you promised me." He groans. "You know I'm not good at waiting, baby. Come on."

This can't be happening. I'm about to wretch.

"Come on," he repeats. "You promised. Get those pesky clothes off and get your ass into this bed. You're about to make Kurtis Jackman a *very* happy boy—a very happy, *naughty* boy."

Oh dear God. I'd put all my faith in Daddy. I'd thought if I did everything according to plan, Kurtis was as good as dead. It never occurred to me that Daddy would let me down. Panic rises in my chest. Is Daddy on his way right now? Did he get the date mixed up? Did he forget my address, no matter how many times I made him repeat it? Did he board the wrong bus? There are a thousand different ways Daddy could have gotten lost or fucked things up. My mind is racing. I've got to figure out what happened and set things back on course. Damn! I was counting on Kurtis dying today. Holy baby Jesus, I physically *need* Kurtis to curl up and die!

Get your mind right, Charlene, I say to myself. *Calm down.*

There's probably a very simple explanation for what went wrong—and no matter what it is, I'll figure it out lickety-split and make a Plan B. But in the meantime... I look down at Kurtis. He's grinning at me like a possum eating the shit out of a wire brush.

It's decision time. Fish or cut bait?

"Come on, baby," Kurtis says. "A promise is a promise."

I exhale. And then, even though it makes my stomach churn to do it, I peel off my clothes and slip into the goddamned bed.

Chapter 42

20 Years 2 Weeks 2 Days Old
Killing Kurtis Day + 1 Day

"What the fuck happened, Daddy?" I whisper urgently into the phone receiver. This time, the guards didn't allow me to visit Daddy in the Visitor's Center, but instead told me we'd have to chat through telephone receivers on either side of a thick Plexiglas barrier.

"Aw, Buttercup, I'm sorry about that, honey. I was really looking forward to teaching your husband some manners."

A quick call yesterday to the Department of Corrections confirmed that Daddy is, indeed, still housed in this Godforsaken place, but nobody would tell me why. So this morning, the minute Kurtis went off to one of his porno sets, or to the club, or to perform some other urgent porno-king business, I hopped into my fancy sports car and drove all the way out here to No Man's Land on a dime to find out what the hell happened yesterday.

"Why are you still in here, Daddy?" I whisper. "You were supposed to get out a few days ago and come visit me."

"Well, yeah, I was. But, funny thing about that, honey—my time in here got extended for a spell—"

"What do you mean your time in here got extended? They can't keep you in prison past your sentence. You've done your time."

"Well, yeah, I've done my time for teaching Mr. Moneybags a lesson, that's for sure. But, a couple months ago, I slashed a fucker in here with a shiv I made out of a glass shard—and he deserved every inch of it, believe me—and the Napoleon-types in here got their rocks off lording over me about it—so you know how that goes." He chuckles and shakes his head. "I sure gave that disrespecting bastard what he deserved, though." He flashes a toothy grin. "He didn't know whether to shit or go blind, so he just closed one eye and farted." He laughs.

For the first time in my whole life, I have this distinct thought: *My daddy's a dumbass.* "Damn it, Daddy," I whine. "What the hell?"

I can't believe this is happening. Thanks to Daddy's utter lack of impulse control, I've wasted an entire year of my life waiting for Killing Kurtis Day. And not only that, I wasted years and years before that, waiting for Daddy to come get me. Waiting for a second letter from him. Waiting to find him here in Hollywood. And this is how he repays me? By leaving me stranded and married to a good-for-nothing porno-king? My daddy's as useful to me as a goddamned ashtray on a motorcycle. I take a deep breath and exhale loudly. Well, now I know for certain—if a girl wants something done, she's got to do it herself. I'm done looking to any man to take care of my business. I'm gonna take care of things myself.

I feel overcome with a sudden urge to cry, but I swallow my tears. I don't have time for bellyaching and boohooing. It's time for me to pick my butt off my shoulders and come up with a new plan. And fast. I've just got to use the brains the Lord gave me. All the pieces of the puzzle are already in front of me; I know they are. I just have to reorder them. There's gotta be more than one way to break a bad dog from sucking eggs here. "Okay, Daddy, now you listen here," I say evenly. "You just remember the name *Kurtis Jackman,* okay?"

Daddy nods.

"*Kurtis Jackman.* You got that?"

Daddy nods again.

"If you can't pay a visit to Mr. Kurtis Jackman, I reckon he's just gonna have to pay a visit to you."

Chapter 43

20 Years 2 Weeks 4 Days Old
Killing Kurtis Day + 3 Days

When Kurtis comes home and sees my suitcases by the front door, his face contorts into instant alarm. Damn straight, Kurtis Jackman. You *should* be alarmed.

I summon big, soggy tears. It's not hard to do. All I have to do is think about how I'm supposed to be living in this big ol' house with Wesley by now, and how my daddy couldn't control his goddamned impulses for a few short months in order to help his sweet daughter out of a jam, and how I waited an entire *year* to kill my husband when I could have been using that precious time to come up with a foolproof plan that didn't involve relying on my flaming dumbass of a daddy.

"Kurtis Jackman!" I shriek maniacally. I make a big show of pulling off my rings and throwing them at him. "Kiss my go-to-hell, you son of a bitch!"

Kurtis' eyes are as wide as doorknobs.

"You can keep your diamonds, Kurtis. You can keep your fancy house and sports car and all your money, too. And you know what else you can do? *You can go fuck yourself.*"

I don't often use the f-word around Kurtis, since I've primed him all this time to think I'm sweet as peaches, and I don't like to cheapen the word by overusing it. But in this situation, no other word will do. I know I'm waving a slab of raw meat in front of a hungry lion right now, but I think I'm safe. As far as I know, Kurtis hasn't been drinking today, so that's the first good thing. And ever since Kurtis and I finally did that naughty thing he'd been begging me to do for quite some time (and which I swear gave me a mild case of post traumatic stress disorder after doing it), Kurtis has been happier than ol' Blue lying on the porch chewing on a catfish head. That's the second good thing. I reckon both of these good things have bought me a little leeway with my hungry lion today.

"What the... ?" Kurtis is thoroughly blindsided.

I make a dramatic turn and bound across the living room, finally crumpling onto the couch with my hands over my face, my shoulders racking with sobs. "How could you do this to me, Kurtis Jackman? After how much I've loved you? You're the only man I've ever loved—the only man who's ever been inside my sacred places—and now, you betray me like this?"

"What *happened*?" The intensity of Kurtis' voice matches my own. The man is rapidly coming undone with dread and anticipation. He bounds across the room and sits next to me on the couch, his face drenched in worry.

"Bettie from the club came to the house today," I seethe. "To the house!" Of course, it's not true. Bettie's never once called the house or come over or done any of the things I've repeatedly pinned on her, bless her heart.

Kurtis looks aghast. "She came *here?*"

"She said you *love* her, Kurtis. She said you've been sleeping with her the whole time we've been married—and in our *bed*." I choke on a sob. "She said I might as well move out now, because it's only a matter of time before this house is *hers*. She told me to get the fuck out of *her* house." I'm absolutely hysterical—or so it seems. "And, Kurtis, she said you're not making our Marilyn movie because you're making a 'Bettie Page True Story' movie, instead, starring *her*!"

The ironic thing about my little speech is that, lately,

Kurtis has been more devoted toward me than ever before. In addition to me doing that dirty-naughty thing he'd been fantasizing about for so long—which drove him crazier than I've ever seen him, by the way—I've also learned a helpful thing or two about how to please my husband through my recent love-making sessions with Wesley. All the hot sex I've been having with Wesley has made me realize what *true* sexual satisfaction feels like—and looks like—and I've lately been using my newfound discoveries to give Oscar-worthy performances in the sack. And, holy hell, Kurtis has been eating me up like a dog with kibble.

And so, even if Kurtis' interest in me had started waning just a touch in the months before Wesley showed up, his zeal-bordering-on-obsession for me is in full waxing-mode nowadays. The way things have been going lately, I can't imagine the man's had an ounce of desire leftover for Bettie Big Boobs or anyone else. And, anyway, regardless of all that, I also happen to know Kurtis couldn't get the "Bettie Page True Story" off the ground any more than our Marilyn movie, even if he tried, because my husband's not just a liar and a cheater, he's also a dumbass of epic proportions.

Kurtis runs his hand through his hair, obviously distraught. "Oh my God, Buttercup—"

"I'll hear your side of things, Kurtis Jackman, because, as your good and loyal wife, I owe you that. But if you *are* planning to toss me out and replace me with Bettie, and if you *are* making a Bettie Page movie starring your whore, then just tell me now so I can move along and mend my shattered heart as quickly as possible."

Kurtis springs up from the couch. He's a raging lion, but not toward me. I can see his monster already coming out. "Buttercup, please."

"Tell me the truth right now."

He exhales loudly. "Yes, okay, yes, I've always had this thing for Bettie Page—the *real* Bettie Page, not Bettie from the club—and I've always wanted to make a Bettie Page biopic one day." He shakes his head adamantly. "But not starring *Bettie*! Sure, I *might* have told Bettie about my Bettie Page biopic, just in passing, but I never promised to make her the *star* of it."

"Since when do you share your hopes and dreams with a two-bit stripper from the club?"

He opens his mouth to speak, but nothing comes out. Apparently, he can't come up with a plausible explanation.

"Oh my God," I gasp, clamping my hand over my mouth. "Bettie was telling the truth—about all of it." I leap up from the couch like I'm going to march out of the room.

"Wait! No! Listen!"

I stop and stand with my arms crossed. "Tell me the truth right now or I'm leaving you for good."

"I... I... " Kurtis stammers.

I turn to leave.

"Wait!"

I stop and stare, my chest heaving.

He closes his eyes for a beat, apparently mustering his courage. "Yes, I did have sex with Bettie." He opens his eyes. "But only a couple times."

He's so full of shit, his eyes are brown. I feign a look of devastation. "Here at the house?"

"No." He shakes his head furiously. "Never at the house."

This here's a man who'd beat you senseless and tell God you fell off a horse.

"I'm weak sometimes," Kurtis says. "I'm *bad.* We both know that." His eyes are pleading with me. "You told me I could do anything with anyone else, as long as I didn't raise a hand to you—and I've kept good on that."

I bite my lip. "Hmmph." My nostrils are flaring. "I did say all that, didn't I?"

He nods profusely.

I soften. "And I meant it."

Kurtis lets out the longest exhale of his life.

"As much as it hurts my heart to find out you'd rather sleep with someone that feels like throwing a hotdog down a hallway than make love to your sweet wife who's never been with another man, I reckon I'll just have to learn to live with it, if that's how you manage to keep your monster away from me."

Kurtis' entire body relaxes into palpable relief.

"It breaks my heart—it really does—but I'll just have to learn to move past the pain. Because I love you just that much."

"Oh, baby—" he begins, but I cut him off.

"But, even so, Bettie's crossed a line here today, Kurtis Jackman," I say.

Kurtis nods vigorously. "She sure as fuck has."

"She sure as *fuck* has," I repeat with intensity, and Kurtis' eyes blaze at my use of profanity. "She's *fucked* with the wrong wife," I say slowly, squinting at him. "Because you're *mine, Kurtis.*"

Kurtis' eyes ignite like Roman candles. He's never seen me exhibit jealousy before, and I reckon he likes it. Good. That makes my job much easier.

Much to Kurtis' obvious surprise, I begin to disrobe, slowly, never taking my eyes off him. I drop my clothes on the floor, step out of my panties, and move to him, wearing nothing but my pretty smile.

His chest is rising and falling like he's just finished running a hundred-yard dash. Without saying a word, I lick my lips, unzip and lower his pants, and drop to my knees in front of him. When I take his full length into my mouth, all the way to the back of my throat, Kurtis lets out a loud groan—and after just a few minutes of me working on him, his passion is quite obviously on the verge of boiling over.

When he growls like a grizzly bear and I feel him start rippling inside my mouth, I abruptly stop what I'm doing, push him onto the couch, and straddle him, taking him into me like a greased pig in a chute.

"Oh my God," Kurtis groans. "Oh my fucking God."

In the entire time we've been married, I've never once initiated sex with Kurtis, let alone sucked on his one-eyed jack. "I love you, baby," I purr, moving my body up and down on top of him.

Kurtis is beside himself. He throws his head back and growls.

"But I'm leaving you for good if you don't permanently fix this situation tonight. I don't care how much booze you need to drink to do it; I don't care *how* you're gonna do it—if you wanna squeeze the life out of that woman with your bare hands or slit her goddamned throat with a blade or slam her fucking head into a brick wall..."

As my movement becomes more and more intense, Kurtis begins furiously grabbing at me, his pleasure on the verge of erupting.

"However you decide to fix things, just make sure you prove to me in no uncertain terms that you choose your *wife* over your fucking *whore*," I say.

I grind my body into him with sudden emphasis and Kurtis makes a tortured sound. He grabs my butt and furiously guides my movement on top of him, and, much to my surprise, my body begins squeezing and clenching furiously from the inside out. Good lord, I'm about to boil over like an unwatched pot. I let out a long, deep moan. "You better let your monster out and show me how much you love me." Kurtis jolts and bucks underneath me. "You show her she *fucked* with the wrong wife." I can't hold out any longer. My body explodes with pleasure, seizing and clenching ferociously around Kurtis' hard-on, over and over.

"Oh my God," Kurtis says, his fingers digging into my back.

After a minute, when my pleasure has subsided and I've returned to my right mind, I see that Kurtis isn't quite finished yet—but he's damned close.

I lean down and press my lips against his ear. "You understand what you've got to do?"

He makes a sound like he's a bear caught in a steel trap.

"You understand what's expected of you?"

His entire body jerks and jolts with a massive release.

I sit up and wipe the sweat off my brow. *I'll take that as a yes.*

Chapter 44

20 Years 2 Weeks 4 Days Old
Killing Kurtis Day + 4 Days

I've been waiting up all night for Kurtis. For Pete's sake, dawn's an hour away—where the hell is he? How long does it take to kill someone once you've set your mind to it? For hours and hours, I've been pacing back and forth across the living room and jumping like a cricket every time I hear a noise.

Where *is* he?

Did I push him too hard? Did I show him too many of my cards? Is he coming back, or did he decide to ditch me for Bettie after all? All night long, I've been playing and replaying my earlier conversation with Kurtis over and over again in my mind, wondering if this whole time I've been a mad genius or a downright fool.

Finally, the front door opens just before sunrise, and Kurtis stumbles in, blitzed out of his mind and crying like a baby. Sweet Jesus, the man looks like he's recovering from an autopsy.

"Did you do it?" I gasp, barely able to get the words out. I take a good look at him from head to toe. I don't see anything but snot on his yellow shirt. Where's the blood on his shirt? Was he naked when he killed her? Did he strangle her to a bloodless death? Or did he simply fail to complete his assignment?

Kurtis scrunches up his face, wallowing in self-loathing. He mumbles something incoherent, followed by a slurred, "Don't leave me."

"Did you do it or not, Kurtis?" I can't read his sudden outpouring of emotion. Is he hysterical because he didn't do it—or because he *did*? I grab his hands. The knuckles on his right hand look red and swollen—or am I seeing what I want to see? "*Did you do it?*" I ask again, this time shrieking like a maniac.

Kurtis just keeps muttering, "Don't leave me," over and over, so I can only assume he's failed miserably. I throw his hand down. Damn it! I asked Kurtis to do one little thing for me—just one cotton pickin' little thing. I knew Kurtis was all broth and no beans, but this beats all. Now I know what my husband's made of—marshmallows and rainbows and goddamned roses surrounded by buttercups. The man's all hat and no cattle, a goddamned embarrassment. Yet again, if I want anything done, I've got to do it myself.

"Go upstairs," I say coldly. "I need time to think." Am I the only person on this entire planet with a little bit of backbone?

Kurtis doesn't move.

"Go upstairs!" I shout. "You've gotta sleep this off."

"Don't leave me," Kurtis sobs again, clutching at me. "I love you, Buttercup."

"Stop whining like a toddler begging for candy and go upstairs." I peel his hands off me.

Kurtis wobbles in place and stares at me with bloodshot eyes.

"Stop acting like a pussy-ass and get the fuck upstairs!" I shriek.

He lets out a muffled sob.

"Go!"

Kurtis turns and shuffles up the stairs.

I'm too wired to sleep. I pace the room furiously, trying to get my mind right. There are a thousand ways to kill someone if you set your mind to it, even if you're not half as brawny as Kurtis. I could sneak through Bettie's window tonight and hit her with a golf club while she sleeps. Or maybe go over there and slit her throat with a knife covered in Kurtis' fingerprints. Or I reckon I could go over there with a big bottle of champagne and a little pouch of rat poison and say, "Hi, Bettie. I've come to make peace!"

I shake my head. Damn. I don't know what to do. All I know is I can't wait another day to be with Wesley and begin fulfilling my sacred destiny. Shoot.

Regardless, though, I can't do whatever I'm going to do 'til the dark of night. Might as well get some rest now so I can clear my head and figure things out.

I begin climbing the staircase like I'm trudging through molasses. With each step I take, despair crashes down harder and harder on top of my head. Is it possible I'm *not* destined to be seen by audiences in cineplexes all over the world, after all? Or to lie naked in my own bed with the man I love? Am I destined for loneliness and heartbreak and nothing else, forevermore?

Up in the bedroom, Kurtis is passed out on the bed, naked and spread out on his belly like a cold picnic lunch. His bare butt looks like two ham hocks in a tow sack right now—I could vomit at the sight of it. There's a fire roaring in the fireplace. I stand close to the flames, letting the heat waft over my back as I stare at Kurtis' naked body on the bed. Tears form in my eyes. A scream of despair wants to escape my throat, but I stuff it down. For a moment, I stand stock still, staring at Kurtis, trying to figure out what the hell to do. But I just can't think clearly.

Jesus, I'm too damned young to feel this damned tired.

With a loud sigh, I pick up Kurtis' shirt off the ground and examine the pale yellow fabric, hoping against hope to find a telltale splatter of blood. But nope. I don't see a drop of blood anywhere. Not a single drop. I turn it over and over, looking for the faintest speck of blood, but there's nothing.

Surely, blood would be easy as pie to spot against the yellow of Kurtis' shirt. Is it possible he did the deed without getting blood on his shirt? Or did he just not do it at all?

I let out a long exhale.

Maybe it's time to give up on my sacred destiny.

Maybe it's time to admit defeat.

Maybe it's time to move on.

Wilber the cat jumps up onto the bed and I pick him up. He's soft and warm in my arms. He purrs loudly at my touch and I kiss the top of his head. "Oh, Wilber," I whisper—and suddenly every hair on my body stands on end. *I am Charlie Wilber's Daughter.* I don't admit defeat. I don't "move on." I've got a sacred destiny to fulfill and the sweetest man in the world waiting on me. It's time to get my butt off my shoulders.

I toss Wilber onto the bed.

What if I were to smash a pillow over Kurtis' drunk-ass face right now? It's possible the medical examiner might say Kurtis choked on his own drunken tongue, isn't it? Even if Kurtis is filthy rich and I stand to inherit all his money? Or what if I grab that big butcher knife from the kitchen and plunge it into my husband's back, right here and now, and carve him up like an Easter ham? I could say Kurtis came home, drunk and ornery, and beat the crap out of me. Yeah, I could say I had to kill the bastard to defend myself. *By plunging a butcher knife into his back while he was splayed out naked on the bed?* Gosh dang it, I'm losing my mind.

Fuck a duck. My give-a-shitter just broke. I don't care about being clever anymore; I just want my freedom, come hell or high water. I just want to be with Wesley. I can't wait another minute to start my new life with him. After I do this one more thing, I swear to God, I'm gonna be good and pure from here on out. I just have to do this one little thing, and then I'm gonna start fresh. I really am. I'll be as gentle and sweet as a newborn lamb.

I pick up a pillow from the empty side of the bed and move around toward Kurtis' sloppy face. My dear husband's gonna choke on his own drunken tongue tonight. The time for waffling and wringing my hands is done.

Oh lord, I'm shaking like a jackhammer on asphalt.

Is Kurtis drunk enough for this to work? Am I strong enough to press down as hard as needed? What if he wakes up when I've got the pillow over his face and starts pummeling me? Shoot, I don't care. I'll risk it. I've got to do something. I'm losing my mind.

I stand directly over Kurtis, holding the pillow, summoning my courage.

Dang it. It's now or never.

I place the pillow onto Kurtis' gaping face and press down with all my might, grunting with the effort, and, much to my relief, Kurtis doesn't even stir.

There's a loud commotion downstairs and a frantic knocking at the front door.

I freeze. Who could that be at this hour of the morning? And banging so loudly, too? Could my Wesley possibly be so foolish as to come here now?

There's another crashing knock.

I remove the pillow from Kurtis' face, my arms quivering.

Is it Bettie? After all the times I've lied about her calling and coming over to the house, did I tempt wicked fate?

There's more frantic knocking downstairs.

Damn it all to hell. I don't have time to kill my husband right now, though he's in dire need of killing. I take a deep breath. *Get a hold of yourself, Charlene.*

I look at Kurtis, spread out on the bed. He's not going anywhere. I'll do what needs to be done after I take care of whoever's knocking downstairs.

Suddenly, in the midst of all that frantic knocking, I hear a man's voice I don't recognize.

"Open up!" the voice shouts.

It's definitely not my Wesley. Who is that?

"Open up!" the voice shouts again. "It's the police!"

Chapter 45

20 Years 6 Months 4 Days Old
Killing Kurtis Day + 164 Days

"Ladies and gentlemen of the jury," the prosecutor begins. "The People of the State of California will prove to you beyond a reasonable doubt that Kurtis Jackman savagely beat and killed Elizabeth Franklin, known by her stage name as Bettie Paigette, in her apartment during the wee hours of the morning on the fifth of February."

I'm dressed to the nines, sitting in the front row of the peanut gallery. Woo-*wee*, I've never looked more gorgeous in all my life. First of all, my hair looks better than ever, and that's no exaggeration. It took some doing, but I've finally settled on the perfect shade of blonde for my skin tone—not too light to wash me out, but definitely blonde enough to turn every head when I walk into any room. And my costuming is also right on point, too. Given the seriousness of the situation and considering the influence of my strict upbringing, I'm wearing a tailored Chanel suit with mile-high, strappy heels (that last part to give the suit a little jolt of sex appeal), all of it accessorized by a certain sparkling star sitting atop a diamond cross around my neck—a small but unmistakable show of support for my wrongfully-accused husband. I'd hate for him to feel completely alone during this difficult and anxiety-producing time. Goodness gracious, I'm a loyal and kind wife—and a flat-out knockout, too.

On the way into court earlier, a horde of photographers surrounded me on the courthouse steps, snapping so many flashbulb pictures, I could barely see straight. "Buttercup," they all shouted at me at once. "Are you standing by your man?" "Look over here!" "Do you believe in your husband's innocence?" I covered my face with my hand like I didn't want the photographers to get a good shot of me—but of course I waited to do that until I was sure every last one of them had gotten a good shot of me.

"No comment," I demurred, puckering my lips just so. "I'd appreciate some privacy during this difficult time."

And now that I'm sitting in court, just behind the railing, I'm wringing my hands in my lap as doubt slowly descends upon me like an egg cracked over my head. Kurtis couldn't have done this horrible thing to that poor girl, bless her heart—could he? I just won't believe it. But... wait a minute—did he? Because, gosh, despite my desperate desire to believe in the innocence of my beloved porno-king husband, it sure doesn't look good for the man.

Apparently, I'm not gonna be called to the witness stand like I was at Mother's trial on account of something called the "marital privilege." It's probably for the best, though. My loyal and loving testimony ("I swear my husband never left my side that night!" "No, he's never laid a hand on me!") might have been a little too convincing (because when it comes to juries, you just never know, even when you're dealing with a defendant who's guilty as sin.) I'm not too worried about me not testifying, though—I reckon I can do plenty of damage from the front row of the peanut gallery, just the same.

"Can you describe Elizabeth Franklin's injuries for the jury?" the prosecutor asks his medical expert.

"The deceased suffered severely traumatic and fatal fractures to all regions of her skull, including her frontal, orbital, parietal, and occipital bones," the expert explains. "Injuries sustained were to the regions of her skull represented here, here, here, and here on this diagram." He points to a diagram showing the various bones of the head and face. "The fracture she sustained *here*, to her occipital orbit, caused her entire eye socket to collapse and her eyeball to dislodge from her head. This was the most devastating blow of all—probably the fatal one."

Oh my, my, my, how Kurtis loves to whack a woman upside the head. I glance at the jury. They're horrified—and, frankly, I just might be horrified right along with them. I needed Bettie to die, of course, but I never reckoned Kurtis would turn the poor girl's head into Hamburger Helper. Good lord. I actually feel sorry for the girl.

"Rhonda Kostopoulos," a fellow dancer at the club testifies when the prosecutor asks her name. "Yes, I've known Bettie—*knew* Bettie—for years. She was my friend." Rhonda chokes on that last word.

"Did Bettie ever say anything to you about being acquainted with the defendant, Kurtis Jackman?"

"Objection, hearsay," Kurtis' high-priced attorney says.

"Your Honor, it goes to foundation," the prosecutor declares.

"I'll allow it," the judge says.

I'm slightly confused by what that all means, but it seems the judge is letting Rhonda talk. That's good—because by the way Rhonda's glaring at Kurtis, I'm pretty sure she's planning to send my darling husband up the river.

"Well," Rhonda continues, "he was Bettie's boss at the club—and mine, too—so, of course, she knew him. But, yeah, she always referred to him as her 'boyfriend.'"

A low murmur ripples through the courtroom. I look down, the picture of humiliation.

"Did you ever observe Bettie and Mr. Jackman together?"

"Yeah, I saw them together at the club a thousand times."

"Literally, a *thousand* times—or is that a figure of speech?"

"Uh, yeah, I mean, you know, lots and lots of times." She shifts uncomfortably. "Not a thousand."

I can only see the back of Kurtis' head as he sits at the defense table, but his body language is stiff and cold as hell.

"Did you ever observe Mr. Jackman behaving violently toward Bettie?"

"Objection," Kurtis' attorney states calmly. "Inadmissible character evidence."

"Sustained," the judge says. He turns to Rhonda. "Do not answer that question."

The prosecutor regroups. "Did Bettie ever say anything to you about Mr. Jackman's proclivity for violence?"

"Objection," Kurtis' attorney says. "Hearsay. Inadmissible character evidence."

"Are you asking me if Kurtis *hit* her?" Rhonda asks, nodding furiously.

"Hold on a minute," the judge says to Rhonda, putting up a hand. "Don't say anything else."

"I'm not offering it for the truth of the matter asserted," the prosecutor explains. "It's a statement offered against a party that wrongfully caused the declarant's unavailability."

What the heck are those dang lawyers talking about? I wish they'd just speak English. Kurtis' fancy lawyer is making this a lot harder to pull off than Mother's baby-lawyer did all those years ago—a particular annoyance considering this time I'm working against someone who actually committed the dang crime.

The judge considers. "It's inadmissible character evidence. Objection sustained." He turns to Rhonda. "Do not answer that question."

Rhonda instantly assumes an expression that clearly says, "Well, that's fine, but he *did* hit her."

I shoot Rhonda a look that says, "He beat the crap out of me, too," and I'm certain at least a few of the jurors noticed this nonverbal exchange. Screw the lawyers. Rhonda and I will nail Kurtis to the cross, just the two of us girls, without having to say a damned thing.

The prosecutor rethinks his strategy. "Did you ever

observe Bettie with bruises or injuries?"

"Objection," Kurtis' lawyer says. "Your honor, it's irrelevant."

It's all I can do not to roll my eyes. I sure wish Kurtis' windbag-attorney would shut the hell up and let the woman speak.

"I'll allow it," the judge says. He turns to Rhonda the Stripper. "You can answer the question—but just that question specifically, without elaboration."

Rhonda nods at the judge and smiles. "Okay." She pauses, looking up. "Wait, what was the question again?"

A few journalists in the row behind me snicker. Well, that's just plain rude. How 'bout they try sitting up there in front of God and everyone and see how well they remember the dang questions? The poor girl is doing her best.

"Did you ever observe Bettie to have bruises or injuries?" the prosecutor asks.

"Yes, Bettie *always* had bruises," she says, like she's divulging a huge secret, and then she quickly adds, "but Bettie always said, 'There's nothing I can do about it—Kurtis signs my paychecks and pays my rent.'"

Kurtis' lawyer leaps out of his chair and throws up his hands. "Move to strike everything after 'yes' as non-responsive, Your Honor."

The judge shoots a scolding look at Rhonda, but she puffs out her chest and looks darned proud of herself. The judge looks at the jury. "Please disregard the latter portion of the witness' testimony about Mr. Jackman hitting Ms. Franklin and signing her paychecks and paying her rent, and limit your consideration to the fact that Ms. Franklin *had* the bruises, source of origin unknown."

I make a point of looking small and submissive in my seat. I reckon the tinier and more timid I look to the jury, the easier it will be for them to imagine Kurtis beating the crap out of me—and, therefore, Bettie, too.

The prosecutor says he's done asking Rhonda questions,

and Kurtis' attorney stands. I reckon it's his turn to try to dismantle Rhonda's testimony on cross-examination.

"You say Bettie told you Mr. Jackman was her *boyfriend*?" Kurtis' attorney asks.

"That's correct," Rhonda says.

"But he was her *boss* at the club, correct?"

"That's right."

"Did you ever observe them together?"

"All the time."

"At the club?"

"Yeah."

"Anywhere else?"

"Nope."

"Did you ever observe them having any one-on-one conversations?"

"All the time. Usually, he was pissed at her."

"Well, hang on. Did you ever overhear the content of their discussions?"

"Nope."

"Then you're just speculating when you say he was 'pissed at her,' aren't you?"

"Well, I could tell by his body language and his loud tone of voice that he was angry, even if I couldn't hear what he was saying." Rhonda shoots Kurtis a scathing look that clearly says she wouldn't walk across the street to piss on him if his hair was on fire.

"But you didn't *hear* what he was saying to her, right? For all you know, Kurtis and Bettie could have been having work-related conversations all those times, like about her being late to work, for example, correct?"

Rhonda looks at the lawyer like he's a maggot.

"Could you please answer the question?"

Rhonda clears her throat. "I suppose it's possible." She grits her teeth.

"Did Bettie ever mention any other *boyfriends* to you?"

Rhonda opens her mouth to speak.

"Objection," the prosecutor says. "Hearsay."

"Sustained," the judge says. "Do not answer that question."

Kurtis' attorney regroups. "Did you ever observe Kurtis behaving with particular *affection* toward Bettie?"

"Nope."

Kurtis' attorney flashes a smug smile. "Then what fact, other than what Bettie allegedly *told* you, supports your supposition that Kurtis was Bettie's 'boyfriend,' as you've previously testified?"

"Well, Bettie always said Kurtis was crazy-jealous when some other guy sent her flowers and—"

"Move to strike," Kurtis' attorney barks. "Hearsay, nonresponsive."

Good lord. Kurtis' attorney is pulling on my last nerve.

"Sustained." The judge turns to Rhonda. "The question is whether you've ever *observed* something with your own eyes that made you conclude Mr. Jackman was Ms. Franklin's boyfriend, not whether you heard a statement in that regard from Ms. Franklin."

Rhonda smiles politely at the judge and then turns her gaze back to Kurtis' attorney, her expression instantly hard. "Well, I walked in on them when they were fucking in the dressing room." The courtroom gasps. "That's what I *observed.*"

The entire courtroom begins murmuring all at once, and the judge demands order in the court. In a flash, I can feel every single eyeball in the courtroom on me. I try to give them nothing, even though a Kurtis-and-Bettie porno that makes my flesh crawl has just popped into my head. Even after all this time, it chaps my hide and hurts my heart to think Kurtis was nailing Bettie the whole time he was whispering sweet-nothings to me.

Kurtis' attorney clears his throat. "Well, hang on. You just said a minute ago you never observed Mr. Jackman behave with any particular *affection* toward Bettie."

"Yeah, that's right." Rhonda is stone-faced now.

There's a beat as Kurtis' attorney tries to make hide or hair of the situation. He shakes his head, not comprehending.

"When I walked in on them," Rhonda explains without further prompting, her tone exasperated, "Kurtis' behavior was anything but *affectionate*."

The entire jury adopts an expression of revulsion and so do I, but only fleetingly, just long enough for a couple of jurors to catch me—and then, just as quickly, I broadcast nonverbal solidarity with Rhonda, as if I understand better than anyone why she's characterizing sex with Kurtis as a decidedly *unaffectionate* act.

Kurtis turns to whisper something to his attorney, and even though I can only see Kurtis' face in profile, there's no mistaking the fury in his expression. I notice at least two jurors observing Kurtis' demeanor with disgust, and right then and there, I know Kurtis is toast. But, seeing as how this trial is funded by the taxpayers, and the prosecutor's probably worked long and hard getting all his ducks in a row, we've still got weeks to burn before the fat lady starts singing on this one.

Kurtis' secretary, Mildred, gets on the witness stand next, flashing Kurtis an apologetic look. "Yes," Mildred reluctantly answers the prosecutor, "I ordered flowers to be sent from Mr. Jackman to Bettie every single week.... Red roses and tiger lilies ... Yes, Bettie came to the office many times.... Yes, they stayed alone in his office with the door closed quite a few times—more times than I can count. No, the other dancers from the club never did that, just Bettie."

I try to make my face look humiliated but hopeful: Maybe my husband was just generously giving one of his employees pointers on her dance routines?

"Hmm," Mildred says, responding to the prosecutor's next question. "I started ordering flowers for Bettie... let's see...not too long after she began dancing at the club. So, hmm, I guess Kurtis sent Bettie flowers every week for about... two years or so?"

Two years? Holy hell.

Mildred looks at the prosecutor with pleading eyes, but nope, he's not even close to done with her. "Did you ever personally observe anything that led you to conclude Mr. Jackman had a *romantic* relationship with Miss Franklin?"

"Objection, calls for speculation," Kurtis' attorney says.

"Overruled. I'll allow it—as long as it's based on her personal observation."

"You mean something romantic I observed besides the fact that he was sending her flowers every week for two solid years?" Mildred asks.

"Yes," the prosecutor replies.

"And besides the fact that Bettie came to visit Mr. Jackman's office and they closed the door?"

"Besides that."

She closes her eyes for a long beat. "Yes. Mr. Jackman once asked me to buy Bettie a gift. A piece of jewelry."

My stomach clenches.

"What kind of jewelry?"

"A necklace."

My breathing turns shallow.

"A necklace with a heart on it—a pendant," Mildred adds. She glances at me apologetically. "A heart covered in diamonds."

I touch the diamond-covered cross on my neck, remembering how I cried tears of joy when Kurtis gave it to me in that cramped supply closet. Even after all this time and everything that's happened, I still feel like crying at the memory.

"Can you think of anything else you personally observed that made you think Mr. Jackman had a romantic relationship with Miss Franklin?"

Mildred looks like she's going to be sick.

The prosecutor stares her down. Clearly, he's got all day.

"Yes," Mildred finally answers. "There was one more thing."

"And what was that?" the prosecutor asks.

Mildred swallows hard. "I sometimes heard... um... *noises* from inside the office when Bettie was in there with Mr. Jackman."

The prosecutor can barely stifle his grin. "What kinds of noises?"

"Objection, calls for speculation," Kurtis' attorney says. "Irrelevant."

"Overruled."

Mildred shifts in her seat for the umpteenth time. "How does one describe a noise, really...?"

"Try," the prosecutor commands.

Mildred looks green. "Moaning, groaning, banging sounds, skin slapping, you know..."

"Noises consistent with two people having sex?"

"Objection," Kurtis' attorney says, leaping up from his chair. "Calls for speculation, Your Honor. This is ridiculous."

"I'll allow it," the judge says sternly. "*Overruled.*"

Kurtis' attorney sits back down, livid.

Mildred nods feebly. Her face looks downright squeamish, and I'm sure mine does, too.

"Is that a yes?" the prosecutor asks.

Mildred looks at Kurtis sheepishly. "Mmm hmm."

"Yes?"

"Yes."

Bastard.

"In the time period immediately leading up to Miss Franklin's death, did Mr. Jackman ever express any *anger* in regards to Miss Franklin?"

Kurtis' blowhard attorney objects for the hundredth time, this time on grounds of hearsay, cementing his title as the world's most annoying person, ever. Good lord, that man's pulling on my last nerve—he's got a ten-gallon mouth, big enough for ten rows of teeth.

"It goes to the defendant's state of mind," the prosecutor says smoothly, saving the day like the government-sponsored white knight he is.

"Overruled."

"Go ahead, please," the prosecutor says to Mildred.

"What was the question?" Mildred asks, her voice thin.

The prosecutor turns to the court reporter. "Would you read my question back, please?"

"'In the few months leading up to Miss Franklin's death, did Mr. Jackman ever express any anger in regards to Miss Franklin?'" the court reporter drones in a monotone.

"Um... yes," Mildred mumbles. "On several occasions during that time period, Mr. Jackman expressed... anger..." She shoots yet another apologetic look at Kurtis, and even from my viewpoint behind him, I can tell Kurtis is seething. "It seemed Bettie had received flowers at the club from someone besides Mr. Jackman, and he asked me if I'd sent Bettie a floral arrangement to the club. I told him, no, always to her apartment, and he seemed upset to think Bettie might have been romantically involved with someone else."

"Did Mr. Jackman say anything else?" the prosecutor asks Mildred.

"About what?"

"About him being upset Bettie had received a gift from someone besides him?"

"A *gift*? You mean anything? Not just those particular flowers?"

"Sure. Anything."

Mildred sighs. "Bettie received flowers from lots of different men, quite frequently, and jewelry, too. And, once, some guy even sent her a puppy with a big red bow on it. And Mr. Jackman expressed irritation about all of it. Quite frequently."

Oh my. I didn't see any of that coming. And here I thought I'd been stirring the soup all by myself.

"So," Mildred continues, "Mr. Jackman sometimes called different florists and jewelers, asking if a particular delivery for Bettie had come from them, but he never had any luck getting answers. So then he'd ask me to call around for him and see what I could find out." She shrugs.

"And did you?"

For a fleeting moment, the slightest hint of an eye-roll flickers across Mildred's face. "No."

"And why not?"

Mildred blinks slowly before answering. "Because it was my belief that florists and jewelers weren't gonna willingly tell me which customers of theirs had purchased gifts for a stripper at the Casanova Club."

There's a rustle of activity in the courtroom, and I use the opportunity to steal a quick glance at the jury. Several of them are nodding in apparent agreement with Mildred's logic.

And what am I doing right now? I'm letting out the longest exhale of my life. Holy hell, those dang flowers I sent to Bettie are gonna be the death of me. When I sent those suckers, I didn't know Kurtis was gonna be on trial for killing Bettie; I thought Bettie was gonna be on trial for killing Kurtis, in which case no one would have given two squirts what flowers Bettie might have received down at the club. I'd had no idea back then I'd be sitting here right now, listening to a prosecutor ask Kurtis' secretary about flowers sent to Bettie at the club.

Frankly, I've been wringing my hands for months about this whole flower thing. About three weeks ago, before the trial had even started, I got the scare of my life when Kurtis' attorney showed up during one of my visitations with Kurtis at the prison (because, to this day, I'm still Kurtis' good and loyal wife), and Kurtis started yelling at his attorney to send subpoenas "to every goddamned florist in the greater Los Angeles area" and "track down whoever was sending those fucking flowers to Bettie." Much to my relief, Kurtis' attorney just rolled his eyes at the suggestion. "They've got DNA evidence, Kurtis. Don't you understand?" the attorney said. "Hunting down every fucking flower shop in Los Angeles, just to *possibly* track down one of the *many* losers who sent Bettie a goddamned bouquet of flowers at one time or another isn't where we should be spending our fucking time and your fucking money. The woman shook her tits for a living in a fucking strip club—"

"Gentlemen's club," Kurtis seethes.

"Whatever. She was bound to have 'admirers.' But none of them had Bettie's DNA all over their shirt the night she was killed. None of them were seen going into her apartment a couple hours before she was found dead. Focus on what actually needs to be done here, Kurtis. We need to focus on ripping their experts new assholes, not figuring out who might have sent flowers to Bettie. All we'd be doing if we chase that rabbit is confirm you were consumed with jealousy—and that's a very bad thing to confirm." At that point in the conversation, Kurtis ran his hands through his hair and looked at me, sitting in the corner—and in that moment, the poor man looked so lost, so *broken*, I actually felt sorry for him.

Of course, it never even occurred to either one of those two geniuses that Bettie's secret admirer was sitting a few feet away, painting her nails a sassy, bright red. I swear I've never been so thankful to have men assume I'm a complete dumbass in all my life.

And as sorry as I was feeling for Kurtis in that moment, it nonetheless made me snicker just a little bit to think the one thing Kurtis wanted to know more than life was just sitting there under his nose the whole time on his credit card bills. But Kurtis never once paid any mind to the flowers I'd charged to his credit card, any more than he paid attention to any of the other stuff I'd bought with that dang card—dresses, purses, shoes, books, manicures, makeup, lingerie, champagne, Otter Pops, Slurpees, car washes, hair appointments, a tiny leather jacket for Wilber, and whatnot. I reckon Kurtis was particularly primed to ignore those flower charges because our house was always filled with pretty bouquets, sometimes bought by Kurtis himself—or, I reckon, *Mildred* herself—and other times bought by me "from Kurtis."

"You got me a whole mess of happy flowers again today,

husband," I used to say, pointing at some outrageously expensive arrangement I'd sent to myself.

"Wow. I have great taste in flowers, don't I?" he'd say, laughing.

"You sure do. Thank you kindly."

"My pleasure, baby. Whatever makes you happy."

And now, finally, after all these months of worrying those dang flowers might come back to bite me in the ass during Kurtis' trial, I can finally breathe a sigh of relief after hearing Mildred's testimony. I didn't know what Mildred was gonna say on the witness stand, and I'm about to flop out my chair with relief after hearing she didn't chase down those dang flowers sent to Bettie any more than Kurtis' high-priced lawyer did.

"Anything else?" the prosecutor asks Mildred on the witness stand.

"Anything else what?"

"Anything else Mr. Jackman might have said to you that expressed anger or upset toward Miss Franklin?"

"No. That's it." She glances at Kurtis, her expression once again full of remorse.

"Thank you. No further questions."

Kurtis' attorney stands up and proceeds to ask Mildred a bunch of questions, all of which are designed to allow Mildred to yammer about how generous and thoughtful Kurtis has been with her, which she does. For what seems like forever, Mildred goes on and on about Kurtis, making him sound like Santa Claus himself; and yet I reckon the woman's not exaggerating any of it. Because if there's one thing nice I can say about Kurtis Jackman, it's that he truly is a generous and thoughtful man (unless, of course, the thing you're wanting him to be generous and thoughtful about is making a Marilyn-Monroe-movie starring you).

Hearing Mildred talk about all the nice things Kurtis has done for her over the ten years she's worked for him, including putting Mildred's momma into a convalescent home on his dime (something that's news to me) makes me think about all the nice things Kurtis has done for me, too—like the time he surprised me with a fountain with naked ladies and cherubs and even a little cupid with wings. And the time he blindfolded me and brought me out to the driveway and gave me a fancy hot rod with a big red bow on it.

I look down at the humongous diamond ring on my finger, and just for a minute, I actually feel kind of sad things have worked out the way they have. Honestly, as I'm sitting here right now, I kind of wish maybe there'd been a way for me to just walk away from Kurtis and let bygones be bygones. But I reckon that's a crazy thought.

Finally, Mr. Blowhard is all done with poor Mildred, and she's allowed to slink off the hot seat, clutching her belly and looking as green as a tree frog as she does. As she's leaving the witness stand, I steal another quick glance at the jury. And, truth be told, a small piece of me feels a little bit sad to observe that, despite all the nice things Mildred just said about Kurtis, each and every one of them looks ready to relieve my husband of his treasured balls.

Now, Bettie's next-door neighbor in the apartment complex, a waitress, gets up on the witness stand. "Kathleen Wardenberg," she replies when asked her name.

"Ms. Wardenberg, did you notice anything unusual with respect to Bettie's apartment during the night of February fourth or the early morning hours of February fifth?" the prosecutor asks.

"Well, I was just coming up the walk from work and I saw *him*." She points at Kurtis. "He was banging on her door, yelling for her to let him in. He looked *agitated*, I'd say. I saw Bettie open her door and tell him to 'shut the fuck up,' and he went inside."

"Did you observe anything else that night with respect to Ms. Franklin?"

"Right after he went in there, I heard yelling coming from inside her apartment. Later, after it had quieted down, I was worried about her, so I went to check on her." Kathleen starts to cry. After grabbing a tissue and wiping her eyes, she explains how she was the unlucky one to find Bettie's mangled body—and oh my, it sure sounds like this poor girl discovered a gruesome scene.

Even as the jurors listen to Kathleen, I can feel them watching me. I reckon they're dying to know if it's dawning on me yet that, hey, I might be married to a merciless killer? I give them nothing, except that occasionally—and only occasionally—I try to look like a lost puppy (a Chanel suit- and diamond-cross-wearing, blonde bombshell of a lost puppy). It's not hard to do, actually—I reckon now and again sitting here in this trial, letting my mind wander, I might feel kind of like a lost-puppy for real.

Now it's Detective Randall's turn to sit on the witness stand. Wow, this detective's a good lookin' man—a different breed from the yahoo-detective with bushy eyebrows from Mother's trial.

The prosecutor holds up a clear plastic bag with a blue shirt inside.

"Yes, that's the shirt we retrieved from the defendant's home at the time of arrest," Detective Randall confirms. "We found it on the bedroom floor, adjacent to where the defendant was passed out... It was visibly splattered with blood just below the shoulder area, as these pictures demonstrate."

I must admit I feel kinda proud of myself about this one. It's amazing how much a girl can arrange in the forty-five seconds between when she hears the police at the door and when she opens it.

Next, the prosecutor holds up a clear bag with a pill bottle inside.

"Yes, that's a pill bottle prescribed to Kurtis Jackman," Detective Randall explains. "We found it in Elizabeth Franklin's apartment."

Good ol' Wesley. When I asked him to plant Kurtis' pill bottle in Bettie's apartment several hours before my "kill her or don't come home!" speech to Kurtis, Wesley was Johnny-on-the-spot. But that's Wesley for you. Loyal as the day is long.

The next witness is a forensic expert who works in the police lab.

"What were your findings, if any, regarding the blue shirt found at the scene?" the prosecutor asks, holding up the bag with Kurtis' shirt inside.

"My testing concluded with one-hundred-percent certainty," the expert responds, "that the small splatter of blood around the shoulder area belonged to Elizabeth Franklin."

"And did you make any other findings regarding the blue shirt?"

"Yes. Kurtis Jackman's DNA and hair were all over it. And there was also one long, black hair found on the shirt, as well, that did *not* belong to the defendant."

"Were you able to determine who the hair belonged to?" the prosecutor asks.

To whom, I think. *Were you able to determine to whom the hair belonged?* I haven't even been to law school and I know that's right.

"The long black hair belonged to Elizabeth Franklin, without a doubt."

It sure did. And it was so generous of Bettie to leave so many useful hair specimens lying around my house—on the couch, in the shower drain, in my bed. I look at the jury. If there were any holdouts on sending my husband to the Big House before now, there aren't any more.

As the trial unfolds day after day, detectives and lab technicians and neighbors and strippers and porn queens parade onto the witness stand in an endless stream, each of them efficiently pounding yet another nail into Kurtis' oversized coffin.

But the most interesting thing of all is how the trial begins to take on a life of its own in the media, separate and apart from the pesky question of Kurtis' guilt or innocence.

The accused is a porn king! His lawyer is a media whore! The prosecutor is a working stiff! The dead girl was the spitting image of Bettie Page! The world wants more, more, more—and, by golly, they always get it.

And guess what's at the eye of this media storm, week after glorious week? A strikingly beautiful blonde who dresses like a movie star and appears to be the dead girl's polar opposite in every way. Week after week, I sit in that courtroom looking loyal and beautiful, and, increasingly, if only slightly, unsure of my husband's innocence. And the world eats me up like a biscuit smothered in gravy.

It's hard to pin down exactly what's so alluring about me, but multiple writers and TV personalities try their best to explain it. One influential TV host comments that, in her opinion, I've managed to "float unscathed above the prurient fray." I like that one, even if I have to look up "prurient" in the dictionary when I first hear it.

Another pundit offers, "She's a nice girl swept up into a maelstrom of seediness and exploitation—a small town girl (with perfect skin), who followed her star to Hollywood only to find herself the embodiment of the American Dream gone haywire." That one gets picked up by all major media outlets from around the globe, and, over time, becomes somewhat of a calling card for me: I'm The American Dream Gone Haywire.

A common dialogue about me on talk shows goes something like this:

"She must have done porn—she's married to Kurtis Jackman, after all."

"No, by all accounts, she hasn't. In fact, from what Kurtis Jackman himself has bragged about, she was his virgin bride."

"Aw, come on," someone always says. "There's got to be a hidden Buttercup porno in a vault *somewhere*."

The world can't get enough of me, and the media is all too happy to keep feeding the beast. On any given day during the four-week trial, you can turn on your TV set and see me leaving or entering the courthouse, hounded by an army of photographers. Or video of me standing on the courthouse steps, thanking the world for their "love and support." If you like the late-night talk shows, well, you can get your fill of trial-related jokes during one host or another's opening monologue any night of the week (though never at my expense). And, of course, all you have to do to see my boobies flapping in the wind is flip the channels at any given time and you'd probably get an eyeful of them in my good-girl pictures (my *prurient* parts appropriately blacked-out for television).

Shoot, last week, there was even a Barbara Walters' primetime special about a list of ten fascinating people, and guess what? I was number seven on the list! Good ol' Barbara figured out my real name, I reckon from my marriage license (which initially made me shit a brick when I first found out about it); but, as it turned out, my hard life in Texas just made me all the more "fascinating."

"Buttercup never knew her father," Barbara erroneously reported in the short piece (though I really can't blame her, seeing as how Daddy was never listed on my birth certificate and Momma apparently refused to be interviewed, thank the Lord). "Buttercup's mother went to prison for killing the boyfriend who'd savagely abused her, and fifteen-year-old Charlene McEntire found herself adrift in the Texas foster care system."

It was right then in the piece that Mrs. Clements' smiling face appeared on-camera, looking mighty excited to be getting her fifteen minutes of fame. "Oh goodness, yes, Charlene was just the sweetest little thing you ever did see—just always had her nose in a book. Well-mannered, quiet, helpful 'round the house, just as shy as can be—goodness, she hardly ever said a word to anybody. She was just a fine, young, God-fearing girl. And, goodness, she was the prettiest little thing you ever did see, too; I used to tell her all the time, 'One day, Charlene, you're gonna have the world at your feet.'" At this point in the interview, Mrs. Clements furrowed her brow and looked mighty perturbed. "I must say, it broke my heart to discover she'd posed for those nudie pictures in that awful magazine, but knowing Charlene the way I do, I can tell you with one hundred-percent certainty that man forced her to do it."

At the end of the piece, Barbara looked straight into the camera and this is what she said: "When you look past the blonde hair and pin-up-girl body, past the salaciousness and titillation swirling around her, what do you see when you look at Buttercup Bouvier? Well, I'll tell you what I see: a little girl named Charlene McEntire who, after being dealt a horrible hand in life, picked herself up and reinvented herself, all in the name of pursuing her dreams. God speed, Buttercup."

Well, gosh. That was awfully nice of Barbara to say, wasn't it?

Barbara's piece about me being "fascinating" sure did make people like me a whole lot, or maybe just pity me. But either way, it was a good thing. But even better was how people felt about me after an article about the trial came out in a respected news magazine. "She's been studying acting intensely for over a year at the most prestigious acting school in Los Angeles," the article said about me (and, of course, I was over the moon to find out my acting school is considered "prestigious"). "Her instructor, an industry veteran with an impressive list of acting credits, said the following about her: *She's a true natural.*'"

Lord have mercy. Turn out the lights. That's what you call a game-changer, folks. When my instructor previously uttered those very same words to me in private, he made me believe in myself when I needed it most—something I'll be grateful for 'til the day I die. But when my instructor said those magical words to the entire population of planet earth in a respected news magazine, well, that saint of a man did something more than make people like or pity me. He made people believe in me the way he did—gosh dang it, he made them *respect* me. Without even one ejaculation, that man changed the entire trajectory of my life.

Before that article, I was already a *bona fide* international celebrity, thanks to the trial, but after my acting instructor's quote hit newsstands, I became a damned fine actress in the eyes of the world, too—a real student of acting who's working hard to learn her craft. On a dime, I became a respected and serious actress, and it was a dang dream come true.

Well, after that, I could do no wrong. I became a big ol' slice of cherry pie a la mode. Beef brisket at the barbeque. The jangle in everyone's spurs. Even now, three weeks since Kurtis' trial ended, the world still can't get enough of me. My face is splattered on the cover of at least one entertainment rag a day, and sometimes even two or three. Even before I've decided which talent agency in Hollywood may have the honor of representing me, movie scripts are already pouring in, including lots and lots where they'd even let me talk. I'm the world's beloved "Buttercup"—no last name even required. Yes, sir, I'm a gen-u-ine star.

I know things with Kurtis had their ups and downs—and, yes, my husband hit me and lied to me and cheated on me with his whore. But at the end of the day, I feel nothing but good feelings and gratitude toward the man. Because, despite the zigzagging way we got here, my husband did, in fact, deliver on his promise to me: he made me a star. And that's why I reckon I'll always feel a special kind of affection for Kurtis, regardless of all the bad blood I might have felt for him before. All's well that ends well.

Actually, I'm feeling so much affection for Kurtis lately, seeing as how everything's worked out so darned well, a small part of me is even sorry that jury decided to send him up the river. Of course, I know that's just the romantic in me talking—or maybe finally getting to be with Wesley out in the open has turned my heart good and pure and soft all the livelong day. But, really, in my deepest heart, I know that Kurtis getting shipped off to prison for the rest of his life is the only way his story could properly end. He did do the crime, after all; so I reckon he's got to do the time. That's just a little thing called *justice*, which is something I couldn't interfere with even if I wanted to—and something any Texan will tell you should *always* get served.

Chapter 46

Hollywood, California, 1992

20 Years Old
Killing Kurtis Day + 200 Days

"Will you grab me a coke, baby?" I holler. I'm floating in the pool on a raft, reading a screenplay in the glorious California sunshine. I'm feeling fat and sassy and fine as cream gravy. Life cannot get any sweeter than this.

"You bet," Wesley calls to me from inside—and a moment later, he's standing at the edge of the pool in his swim trunks, holding my drink, his chiseled muscles on full display.

I paddle over to the pool's edge and Wesley hands me my coke.

"Thank you, baby."

"Is that a good one?" He's referring to the script in my hand.

"Yeah, a really good one."

"What's it about?"

"Well, there's this really good-lookin' guy who fills out an application to a dating service, and the girl who reviews his application sends him an anonymous note that makes him wanna hunt her down. I'd play the girl's best friend."

Wesley looks unimpressed. "Sounds like a porno."

319

"Well, that's not the only script I'm considering. There are other ones, too." I exhale. "I've got so many to choose from, my head's spinning."

"Aw, you'll figure it out, baby. You always do."

"Yeah, I reckon I will." We share a smile. Wesley's always had such faith in me. Back when we were kids and I told him I was gonna get discovered like Lana Turner in the malt shop, he didn't doubt it for a second.

I lay the script facedown on my chest for a moment and close my eyes, drifting lazily across the surface of the pool, soaking in the sun and reveling in my good fortune. I'm free as a bird; my Wesley's here with me, and we can make love any time we like (and we sure do). I'm beautiful and young and talented and in love—and there's no one to tell me what I can and can't do.

I've finally found my platinum-lined happily ever after.

I continue floating for several minutes, slipping into a daydream, when the ringing of the telephone jolts me.

"I'll get it," Wesley says. He hops up from his lounge chair and grabs the phone. "Hello? Yes, she is. Who's calling, please?" Wesley's got the nicest manners—I just love that about him. "Just a minute, ma'am," he says into the phone.

"It's for you, baby. It's a woman from the government. She says it's important."

I paddle myself to the edge of the pool, careful not to splash my hair or makeup as I do, and gingerly crawl off the raft. I grab the phone from Wesley. "Hello?" I say.

"Mrs. Jackman?" the female voice asks.

I bristle. Who on earth would call me that?

"This is Sylvia Gonzalez from the Department of Corrections," the woman continues. "I'm very sorry to inform you, ma'am, your husband was killed at the prison today."

My mouth hangs open.

When I don't say anything, the woman forges right ahead. "He was stabbed by another inmate with a makeshift blade crafted out of a razor and a toothbrush."

I can't speak. My thoughts are racing like pigs at the fair.

"The perpetrator is currently unknown," the woman adds.

I'm surprised at how many things I'm thinking and feeling, all at once. On the one hand, I'm actually a touch sad to think Kurtis Jackman has drawn his last breath. The man wasn't *all* bad, after all, even if he was *mostly* bad. At the end of the day, he made me a star, just like he promised to do. I reckon time and happiness heals all wounds because, even after all those months of wishing Kurtis dead and relieved of his blood supply, I'm surprised to find myself saying a little prayer the poor man didn't suffer *too* much pain when he bled out.

On the other hand, however, I'm awfully grateful for the millions of dollars I just inherited from my dead husband— that ought to come in handy. And most of all, I'm feeling a special kind of elation to think my daddy finally, *finally* managed to do something sweet for me, after all this time. It's that last thought that chokes me up and brings a happy tear to my eye more than anything else, actually.

"I'm very sorry, ma'am," the woman says.

I reckon I'd better say something. "This is devastating news," I finally say. "Thank you for letting me know."

She tells me about some paperwork I've got to fill out on account of me being Kurtis' wife and we arrange for me to get Kurtis' personal effects.

"Goodbye, then," I say. "Thank you again."

I leap over to Wesley. He's lying on a lounge chair, sipping a soft drink and looking like sex on a stick. "Well la-de-dah, my daddy loves me," I coo. I shake my tail feathers in celebration.

"What was all that about?" Wesley asks.

"Ding dong, Kurtis is dead," I say.

"Oh," Wesley says, smiling broadly. He puts down his coke. "Sounds like it's time to celebrate."

"Pop the champagne, baby!" I say. "And buy yourself a brand new pair of boots!"

Wesley chuckles.

"I can't believe after all this time, my daddy finally came through for me," I say, suddenly choking up. "I'm so touched I could cry."

Wesley looks like he could cry right along with me. "The lady said it was your daddy who did it?"

"Oh, gosh, no," I say. "That's the best part—the fools have no idea who did it."

Wesley smiles broadly. "Imagine that."

I swat at Wesley's leg to make him scootch over in his lounge chair, and then I lie down right next to him, pressing my near-naked skin into his. "It sure is a delicious feeling having someone take such good care of me," I say, tracing the ridges in his abs with my fingertips.

Wesley's entire body stiffens. "Well, I take care of you."

I look up at him. Oh, damn. His feelings are hurt. "Well, hells bells, of course you do, Wesley—and you always have. I just meant it's nice to get such a sweet valentine from my daddy, considering how I've been waiting on him to do something nice for me my whole life." I run my fingertips over Wesley's muscular chest, across the letters of my name, and press myself into him again, trying to coax him away from his hurt feelings. But, dang it, no matter how much I caress him, Wesley still looks like he's got a burr under his saddle. I reckon I just haven't explained things well enough to him. "It's just that, up 'til now, my daddy's been as useful to me as a steering wheel on a mule," I explain, "and all I'm saying is that it feels extra special to have him finally come through for me, that's all." Tears flood my eyes and I wipe them away. "No one's ever given me a valentine quite like this before."

I can feel Wesley's body tense with anger, and I instantly realize my mistake. Shoot. Open mouth and insert foot. When Kurtis killed Bettie for me, he technically gave me the same sort of valentine Daddy just did. Dang it. I hate it when Kurtis' name comes up around Wesley. Wesley's always had a hole in his heart about Kurtis getting my virginity instead of him—and, then, on top of that, I know it rankles him to no end that Kurtis got to kill Bettie for me, too. Dang it. The last thing I'd ever want is for my Wesley to feel second fiddle to any man, least of all a lying, cheating monster like Kurtis. I kiss Wesley's soft lips, trying to seduce him into forgetting all about Kurtis, but his lips don't return my kiss. Dang it.

I've got to make Wesley understand how much I love him—that he's better than Kurtis ever was, that he's good and kind and loyal and sweet, exactly what I've always ached for my whole goddamned life, exactly what I always wanted Kurtis to be, but he never was. Wesley needs to understand I don't want a man who'd wallop me upside the head and lie and cheat. I don't want a man with a monster inside him who'd turn a woman's head into Spaghetti O's. Hell, Wesley has more character in his little pinky than Kurtis ever had in his entire, brawny body.

"Kurtis killing Bettie doesn't count as a *valentine*," I say, pressing myself into Wesley, "because I never *loved* Kurtis." Once again, I touch the tattooed letters of my name across Wesley's muscled chest. "This right here is the best valentine I've ever gotten, baby. Hands down."

Well, that does the trick. Wesley leans into me and kisses me full on the mouth.

"Oh, Wesley," I breathe. "I only love you—I've only ever loved you. Don't you know that?"

He nods and kisses me again, this time with even more heat.

"You've got me so hot, you could fry an egg on my belly," I whisper. "Come on, baby."

Wesley yanks my bikini bottoms down and slides his finger inside me, making me gasp. "You're mine now," he says, his voice intense.

"Of course, I am," I whisper. "He's dead and gone now, baby. It's just you and me." I kiss him and run my hands over his muscled arms and grind my pelvis into the hard bulge in his swimsuit. "Come on, baby," I purr, tugging on his swim trunks.

Wesley can't resist me anymore—he can never stay mad at me for long. He stands to pull off his swim trunks and when he lies back down with me, he pushes me roughly onto my back, pins my wrists above my head with his strong hands, and slides himself into me, as deeply as a man can go.

Oh my, he's taken my breath away.

"You're all mine now," he says, thrusting slowly in and out of me, staring into my eyes.

"Yes, Wesley, yes," I gasp out. "I'm yours."

"*I'm* the one who loves you. *I'm* the one who takes care of you. *Me.*"

My heart is racing. "Yes, Wesley. Yes."

"Not *him.*"

"Not him."

"*Me.*"

"You're the one, Wesley. You. The only one."

"Because you're *mine.*"

I glance down from Wesley's beautiful face to the letters of my name on his chest, mesmerized by the way they're sliding up and down on top of me with each ferocious thrust of his body. I'm on the verge of pure ecstasy.

"*Marry me,*" Wesley growls.

"Oh, Wesley," I breathe. My insides are beginning to erupt. He's ripping me in two and, damn, it feels good.

"Marry me," Wesley says again. "I want you to carry my name."

My insides erupt and explode all at once. "Yes," I choke out, my body convulsing with pleasure. "*Yes.*"

When I'm all done, Wesley's still going strong, so I put my lips against his ear. "I'm gonna be your wife," I whisper.

Wesley cries out and shudders with a forceful release, and then he lets go of my wrists and slides his hands to my face. He cups my cheeks tenderly in his palms and gazes into my eyes. "You're mine, Charlene—my princess bride." He kisses me gently. "And don't you ever forget it."

Chapter 47

Lancaster, California

20 Years Old
Killing Kurtis Day + 231 Days

All hell has broken loose. Two minutes ago, the guard who was frisking me blurted, "Oh my god! You're Buttercup!" and that's all she wrote. Every damned correctional officer and visitor in the entire prison converged on me like ants on a crumb, asking for my autograph, and I didn't have a choice but to smile and chat and sign every last scrap of paper shoved under my nose. Normally, I wouldn't mind the attention—I'd do anything for my fans—but today, I've got something pressing to do and I'm chomping at the bit to get to it.

It's true I could have had the nice folks at the prison mail me Kurtis' personal effects and forms that need signing, but, mad genius that I am, I figured I could use this errand as an excuse to see my daddy without anyone figuring out we're related. And I wouldn't have missed that golden opportunity for the world.

I haven't visited Daddy since he left me in the lurch on Killing Kurtis Day. Honestly, after Daddy left me hanging, I wasn't sure I'd ever want to see him again. But all that changed when he finally came through for me last month.

Goodness gracious, the minute I hung up the phone with that prison lady, I wanted to fly down here in my hot rod, throw my arms around Daddy's neck, and thank him from the bottom of my heart. But I couldn't. No way. Because now that I'm a famous and beloved celebrity the world over and well on my way to picking up the torch lit first by Lana and picked up by Marilyn and carrying it ever-farther into the catacombs of history, I can't ever do a damned thing that lets anyone find out I'm Charlie Wilber's Daughter. Christ Almighty, talk about something that would fuck up the trajectory of my entire life if anyone found out my daddy's name. Woo-wee, it sure turned out to be a lucky break after all that Daddy was never listed on my birth certificate. According to the world, I'm the daughter of "Father Unknown," which, as far as I'm concerned, means I'm the daughter of a preacher man who died in a tragic incident with a hippopotamus on a Godly mission to Africa.

I've been standing just inside the prison doors getting mobbed for half my life, smiling and giving every last guard and visitor my autograph, when one of the guards finally offers to escort me to the front office to handle my business.

"Sylvia," the guard says, handing me off to a woman behind a counter. "Look who's here."

Sylvia puts out her hand and introduces herself as Officer Gonzalez, the same woman who called me a month ago with the sad news of my husband's demise. "I'm very sorry for your loss, Mrs. Jackman," she says.

It takes all my strength of will and character not to correct this woman and say, "I'm not Mrs. Jackman anymore—I'm Mrs. *Miller* now." But I reckon now wouldn't be the time or place to share that particular piece of happy news. "Thank you," I reply, forcing myself to look appropriately sad and demure.

Officer Gonazalez pulls out the various forms needing my signature, which I dutifully sign, and then she grabs a small box filled with Kurtis' meaningless things. I sit down and poke through the paltry contents of the box for a few minutes, trying to feel some sort of emotion about the whole situation—but I don't. I'm Wesley's wife now—I belong to him—and I couldn't be happier about the way things have turned out. My life with Kurtis, along with all his lies and betrayals, seems like a distant memory.

Surprisingly, the only thing I'm feeling toward Kurtis as I sift through his box of belongings is gratitude. That's it. Kurtis was the man *whom* the Lord sent down to earth to deliver me to my sacred destiny, and he'll always have a place in my heart. It's true I've still got a ways to go before I'm carrying my torch into the catacombs of history, but I'm well on my way. And it was Kurtis who got me started down the road. Thanks to Kurtis killing Bettie, and the trial that made me famous, I've got almost everything I could ever dream about now—the only thing missing from my perfect picture is having my darling daddy by my side.

"Sylvia," I say, looking up from the box. "I was wondering if you could look someone up on your computer for me?"

Sylvia looks at me quizzically.

"There's an inmate here who's been sending me fan mail for a while now. He seems like a sweet enough fellow, actually, despite whatever he's done to get himself in here. And as long as I'm here today, I thought I might make this poor guy's day and pay him a quick visit? You know, give him an autographed photo to remember me by?"

"Wow. That's awfully nice of you," Sylvia says.

"It's a small thing to do to brighten the day of someone less fortunate," I reply. I motion to the prison around us. "I'm sure he'd appreciate someone showing him some kindness for a change."

Sylvia's face softens. "That's really kind of you." She takes a few steps over to a computer on the far side of the counter. "You're sure he's housed here?"

"I'm sure," I say. "He always puts this place as his return address on his letters."

LAUREN ROWE

Sylvia taps a few keys on her computer. "What's his name?"

"Charles Wilber," I say, and the minute the words escape my mouth, adrenaline floods me. I can't wait to see Daddy again. I'm dying to thank him for what he finally did for me, and I'm even more excited to tell him, "I *forgive* you." Because you know what they say—holding a grudge against someone is like taking poison and hoping the other person's gonna keel over.

It's gonna feel like riding a unicorn and sliding down a rainbow to say those powerful words of forgiveness to Daddy. And the best part is, when I say them, they're gonna be the God's truth. I *do* forgive Daddy—for every last thing. For leaving me in the trailer with Mother; for never writing me but that one time; for all the birthdays he missed and all the times I sat under the mailbox, just waiting for the postman to come; and even for making me wait a year to kill my husband when I could have come up with a Plan B in half the time. I forgive all of it. In fact, now that my life has turned out so well, I wouldn't have it any other way, just in case doing any of it differently would have changed how things ended up. I'm just that happy.

Speaking of which, I can't wait to tell Daddy about Wesley. Daddy's gonna be so proud to find out I've managed to marry my soul mate—the true love of my life—a man who treats me exactly the way Charlie Wilber's Daughter deserves to be treated, and then some. I look down at the wedding band on my finger and feel a wave of unadulterated joy wash over me. I'm married to the sweetest, sexiest, most loyal man in the world. Thanks to Wesley, my heart is bursting with love and kindness and forgiveness all the livelong day. And I'm ready to share all of it with Daddy.

"Hmm," Sylvia says. "I'm not finding a Charles Wilber. Looks like he's not housed here."

My heart skips a beat and my stomach clenches. "No, he is. I'm sure of it," I say. "Can you please check again, ma'am?"

Sylvia's staring at the screen. "No, he's not showing up in the prison population."

"Well..." My mouth is hanging open. "Was he transferred or something?"

"No, he'd show up in the system, even if he were at another facility." She twists her mouth, thinking. "Hang on. I'll check another database."

My heart's gonna burst out of my chest. This can't be happening. I've lost my daddy again? I'm about to throw a conniption fit.

"Ah, I found him."

I exhale. Oh, thank goodness. It was just a computer error. I can't help but chuckle in relief. Good lord, I almost went off half-cocked right there.

"Well, gosh, I'm sorry to tell you this, but it looks like Charles Wilber's dead."

I feel the color draining from my face. If I weren't already sitting down, my legs would give way underneath me. "What?" I ask feebly, tears pooling in my eyes.

Sylvia clicks a button on her computer. "Well, let's see what happened." She squints at the computer screen. "It says Charles Wilber was stabbed by another inmate last month. That's all it says." She shrugs. "Another one bites the dust."

A sob lurches out of my throat.

Sylvia's face turns bright red. "Oh, I'm sorry, Mrs. Jackman. I shouldn't have said that. That was insensitive of me." She grimaces. "I wasn't referring to your husband."

I shake my head, unable to reply. My heart is shattering and my head is spinning. Daddy died last month? Lord have mercy, Kurtis must have grabbed the knife from Daddy after Daddy stabbed him. There must have been a scuffle of some sort. I clutch my chest. *My husband and father killed each other!*

The prison lady shakes her head. "I'm so sorry."

Jesus lord, my daddy gave his life to finally do right by me. He died trying to make amends. He sacrificed his life for my happiness! I cover my face with my hands and let out the longest wail of my life. *My daddy was a goddamned saint.*

"I'm really, really sorry for your loss, Mrs. Jackman."

Chapter 48

20 Years Old
Killing Kurtis Day + 231 Days

Where the fuck is it? I'm positive I kept it in my underwear drawer, right underneath my necklace from Kurtis, but it's not here. And neither is my necklace from Kurtis, for that matter. My eyes are bugging out of my head. I've got to find that letter. I've opened every drawer in my dresser, but it's not there.

It takes all my might, but I yank the heavy dresser away from the wall, shrieking hysterically as I do. Maybe the letter somehow slipped out the back of the drawer and got wedged against the wall? But no, when I've finally gotten the dresser pulled out, there's nothing back there except a gosh-dang sock. *Where is it?*

I'm shattered with grief about my poor, sweet Daddy. The man gave his life to deliver me a happily ever after! The man made the ultimate sacrifice just so I would have the very best things in this life!

The whole drive back from the prison, all I could think about doing when I got home was lying on my bed with Wilber, clutching Daddy's letter to my heart, and sobbing my wretched eyes out. But now I'm home and the letter's nowhere to be found!

I'm turning into a certifiable maniac, opening every

drawer in my dresser a second and third time. I know I kept that letter in my underwear drawer. Where could it be? It's the only thing I have to remember my daddy by in the whole wide world.

I fly around my room, opening every drawer in my desk and nightstand, even my jewelry drawers—even the drawers where it couldn't possibly be. But it's nowhere. I fly into my closet and start rustling through my clothes and shoes, my mind racing and reeling. Where on earth could it be?

I careen back into my bedroom, panting. My heart feels like it's been stampeded by cattle and then chewed up by coyotes and shit into a ditch. I can't breathe. I need that letter! My daddy died to make things right with me—and now I want to lie on my bed and touch his swirling handwriting and read his sacred words and grieve 'til my eyes are swollen shut.

I am Charlie Wilber's Daughter and Charlie Wilber died trying to give me the very best things in this life. If I had his ashes, I'd scatter them into my fountain with the naked ladies and cherubs and little cupid with wings. The perfect tragedy of it all just shatters my heart.

Did I put the letter into Wesley's underwear drawer by mistake? Or did I leave it lying around recently and Wesley mistakenly put it away into one of his drawers? It makes no sense, but I start opening Wesley's drawers and throwing his clothes around the room. I'm grinding my teeth. My chest is heaving. Where the hell is it?

I race into Wesley's closet and rifle through his clothes, shoes, fishing gear, comic books. I'm about to leave when I glance up and notice a small box on the tippy-top shelf. I don't recall ever seeing that little blue box before—and the minute I see it, I stop dead in my tracks.

My Daddy's letter is inside that box. I can feel it in my simmering bones.

A strange calmness oozes over me as I suddenly realize exactly why Wesley took my daddy's letter from me: he's jealous my daddy got to kill Kurtis for me, instead of him.

He's jealous my daddy wound up giving me the greatest valentine of my life. He wanted to be the one who gave it to me.

Oh, how it hurts my heart to realize Wesley begrudges me finally getting something good and kind from my daddy, even though he knows I waited my whole life for it. Honestly, finding out Wesley isn't happy for me to finally get what I deserve is devastating news. I'm not sure I'll ever be able to forgive Wesley for such a horrifying betrayal, to be honest.

I race back into the bedroom, grab a chair from my desk, and drag it into the closet, just underneath where the box is sitting on the highest shelf. Damn it. Even standing atop that chair, I can't reach the box, so I grab a hanger and try again, maneuvering the hanger to poke and coax that dang box within reach of my outstretched fingers.

Once I finally have the box in my hot little hands, I grip it with white knuckles and sprint back into my bedroom, my heart raging in my ears. I sit on the edge of my bed, staring at the harbinger of doom in my hands, my cheeks flushed and my eyes bugging out.

Wilber jumps up onto my lap and I shoo him away. I love my kitty more than life, but I can't pay him any mind right now. My life's about to change, and probably not for the better. I know for a fact that when I open this box and see my daddy's letter inside, I'll never see Wesley in the same light again, and the thought makes me want to cry buckets.

Part of me doesn't want to know for sure what's inside the box—I'd rather just *suspect* Wesley's not happy for me than know it for sure.

But that's just the romantic in me talking. Come hell or high water, I'm gonna look inside the box.

Well, this is it.

I take a deep breath and open the box.

Chapter 49

20 Years Old
Killing Kurtis Day + 231 Days

Daddy's letter is sitting inside Wesley's little blue box. Damn it to hell. Now I know the truth.

Wesley wasn't happy for me when I got my special valentine from daddy—he's been pea-green with envy and spite this whole dang time. I thought Wesley was crying tears of joy along with me—and the whole time his tear ducts were squeezing out drops of jealousy. How am I ever gonna forgive Wesley for this betrayal? The man values his petty jealousy more than his wife's happiness. Dang it, that's a tough pill to swallow.

I shift the contents of the box around with my finger.

Well, damn. The necklace Kurtis gave me is in here, too, coiled up at the bottom—but that doesn't hurt my heart like Daddy's letter does. I reckon I can't blame Wesley for being jealous of Kurtis. After all, Kurtis got to be the first man ever to conquer my sacred places, and then he got to kill Bettie for me, too. I can't blame Wesley for feeling like a second banana there. Poor Wesley.

I poke around the box again. Besides Daddy's letter and Kurtis' necklace, there's also a green bandana, a white strip of plastic, a black comb, and something wrapped in white tissue paper at the bottom of it all. I reach into the box, intending to pull out the white-tissue-paper something, when a sound in the doorway makes me look up.

Wesley. He's standing in the doorframe, his arms bulging, his muscles taut, his eyes smoldering at me.

I open my mouth to speak, but nothing comes out.

Wesley raises his muscled arms and grips the doorframe, his eyes blazing. "You found it," he says. He nods toward the box.

I'm frozen in place, unable to breathe.

"Go ahead," he says. He crosses his muscled arms over his chest and leans against the doorjamb.

I grab ahold of the little square of folded tissue paper at the bottom of the box, and the minute I unfold the paper, the entire room warps and buckles around me. Holy Baby Jesus, I'm holding a heart-shaped pendant in my hand—a heart-shaped pendant covered in diamonds.

I look up at Wesley, stunned.

"That fucker hardly even touched her," Wesley says, his voice steely. "Kurtis barely gave that girl a scratch." He shakes his head in disgust. "Kurtis was a *coward*—yellow as mustard but without the bite. When that girl begged and cried and went all weepy on him, do you know what he did? *Nothing.* He went soft and couldn't finish the job. Not even to keep *you.*" Wesley's eyes have turned dark and hard as granite. "Kurtis left her to cry on her pillow with nothing more than a fucking black eye and a nosebleed." He narrows his eyes. "So I finished the job for him."

I can't wrap my head around what I'm hearing. It's not bad news, necessarily, to find out it was Wesley who killed Bettie for me—it's just mindboggling, is all. My sweet and gentle Wesley pulverized that girl 'til her eyeball popped out of her head?

Wesley makes a scoffing sound. "I went down there to plant that pill bottle like you asked—and then I hid in her closet and waited." His lip curls. "When Kurtis got there, I saw *everything.*" His eyes are as cold as a witch's titties in a brass bra. "*Every fucking thing,*" he says slowly.

LAUREN ROWE

Holy shit on a shingle. The way he just said that last bit made my stomach drop into my toes. Is Wesley implying he saw Kurtis having *sex* with Bettie that night? Oh lord. Yes, I do believe he is. Which would mean Wesley saw for himself how well Kurtis' man-parts actually functioned, contrary to what I'd told him. Oh, sweet Jesus. I can only imagine how watching Kurtis plow Bettie enraged my poor Wesley—I'm sure he figured out right quick just how well Kurtis had been plowing me, too.

"Wesley, come here," I say, my pulse pounding in my ears. "Come here, baby."

Wesley's eyes are dilated. He doesn't even look like himself right now.

"Come sit down on the bed, sugar," I say.

He waltzes into the room like a panther, his eyes flickering. When he reaches me, he grabs the necklace out of my hand and holds it up in front of my face. "*I'm* the one who takes care of you. *I'm* the one who did what had to be done." He's practically spitting the words at me. "*Me.* Not pussy-ass Kurtis. *Me.*"

My stomach is twisting. "Wesley," I breathe. I can see his monster coming out right before my eyes.

Wesley bends down and kisses me deeply, and the minute his tongue slides into my mouth, my crotch ignites. Wesley grips my shirt like he's trying to take it off, but I push him back. I'm turned on by this revelation, it's true, and making love to Wesley is the exact balm my grieving heart needs right now, but I'm too determined to uncover the truth about Wesley's green-eyed monster to jump into the sack just yet.

"I told you—I'm always gonna protect you," Wesley says, his jaw tight. "You need something to be done? I'll do it. Someone makes you cry? I'll make *them* cry. Someone lays so much as a *finger* on you, then they gotta to answer to me." His nostrils are flaring. He reaches into the box and pulls out the green bandana. "That fucker Thomas said it was you who

336

opened the safe? Well, he had to answer to me—with his goddamned head."

"Oh," I say.

Wesley reaches into the box again and pulls out the plastic comb. "That fucker Christopher kept jawing about how much he wanted to fuck you? How he was gonna take your virginity, whether you liked it or not? He said he was gonna stay behind from school one day when you were all alone doing your home study and give it to you good? Well, I guess I beat the crap out of him so hard he forgot all about that fucking idea right quick—and then, imagine that!—two weeks later, Mr. Clements' Yogi Berra card made its way under *Christopher's* fucking mattress." He clenches his jaw. "That fucker had to answer to me, too."

My entire body is tingling. "Wesley," I breathe. "Oh my."

Wesley reaches into the box and pulls out the diamond-cross necklace Kurtis gave me. "Oh, and this fucker takes the cake. He thought he could beat you up, when you're half his size and as sweet as the day is long? You were his goddamned *wife* and he thought he could treat you like that? Well, guess what? That fucker had to answer to *me*, too. He thought he was going to meet his maker, but he went to meet Wesley Miller, instead."

I furrow my brow with confusion. Wait just a cotton pickin' minute. Wesley's saying *he* killed Kurtis? Well, that's just plain crazy-talk. Kurtis was in prison when he died. It was Daddy who killed Kurtis for me. "Wesley," I say, shaking my head. But that's all I can muster to say.

"I'm sorry to have to tell you about this one," Wesley says, his face softening. "I would have liked to let you think your daddy finally came through for you." He exhales. "I know how happy it made you to think it."

I shake my head again. How on earth could Wesley have managed to kill Kurtis? It had to be Daddy. There's no other way. "But, Wesley, no. *Daddy* killed Kurtis, remember? I told

Daddy to be on the lookout for Kurtis Jackman. I told him, 'Remember the name *Kurtis Jackman*.'"

Wesley shakes his head. "No, honey. I'm sorry."

"But..." My brain feels like it's melting. "How could you possibly...?"

He can't suppress his grin. "I told you, I made some true-blue friends in jail." His grin widens into a beaming smile. "Those fellas in jail were nothing like the pussy-ass whiners at the group home, that's for sure—they were real men with honor and integrity, guys who know right from wrong. It's a brotherhood. I'd do anything for them, and they'd do the same for me." He chuckles. "And it certainly didn't hurt that you're my girl—you've got some pretty big fans on the inside." He winks.

My mind is reeling. I sit for a moment, shaking my head in disbelief. It feels like a knife in my heart to think Daddy wasn't the one who came through for me—but at the same time, it's like sliding down a rainbow to realize Wesley picked up Daddy's slack. And not just Daddy's slack—but Kurtis' too! Holy hot damn! My Wesley killed *both* Bettie and Kurtis for me. Ain't that the berries. Ha! Well, boy-howdy, Wesley truly is my knight in shining armor. "Oh, Wesley," I cry. "You've given me the best valentine ever." I throw my arms around him and attack him with kisses.

Now it makes perfect sense why Wesley stole Daddy's letter. He was just jealous Daddy was getting all the credit for killing Kurtis! Poor Wesley. Anyone would feel rankled to think they didn't get credit for killing their wife's husband. That's perfectly understandable. I lie back down onto the bed, inviting Wesley to ravage me. All this time I thought Wesley was a mouse, and it turns out he's a lion. My head is spinning and my crotch is throbbing. If all this doesn't turn a girl on, I don't know what would. "Wesley, make love to me," I say. I want him to make me scream so I can forget all about my shattered heart.

Wesley puts his hand between my legs and when he feels

how wet I am for him, he moans. Wilber jumps up onto the bed and I shoo him away. I love my kitty, but it's my pussy's turn to get stroked right now.

Wesley begins devouring me with kisses. His fingertips are making me squirm and moan. I'm feeling that filling-up-with-warm-Jell-O feeling between my legs.

"It was me who killed Kurtis," Wesley whispers into my ear, his fingers slipping in and out of me. "*Me*."

"Yes," I whisper. I'm feeling as hot as the hinges of hell. "You made him pay."

He pulls my underpants all the way off and starts unbuttoning the fly on his jeans 'til his erection springs out of his opened pants. "*I* made him pay. It was *me*. Your daddy was a pussy-ass. He never did a fucking thing for you his entire life."

Every hair on my body stands on end. I sit up. Wesley just said my daddy *was* a pussy-ass. But I haven't mentioned my daddy's demise.

"Don't waste your tears on your daddy," Wesley says, gently pushing me back so he can crawl on top of me and get inside.

I swat him off me and sit up again. I'm like a jack-in-the-box that just got cranked. It's suddenly occurring to me: If Daddy didn't kill Kurtis, then how the fuck could Kurtis have killed Daddy? I stare at Wesley, my eyes wide with horror. "Wesley?" I squeak out. "Who the fuck killed my Daddy?"

Wesley pushes on my shoulders again, aiming for me to lie back down so he can mount me, but I swat him away again and burst into tears. I throw my hands over my face, sobbing. "Wesley, no! Not my *daddy*!"

"Aw, shit." Wesley tugs on my arms, but I won't take my hands away from my face. "Come on, baby, don't do that," Wesley says. He pulls on my arms again. "Aw, come on, honey."

I shake my head. "My poor, poor Daddy," I murmur through my tears. I let out a pained wail.

"Aw, come on." He yanks on my arms with fortitude and then grabs my wrists, preventing me from covering my face again. "Look at me," he says firmly.

My eyes are closed. I shake my head.

"Look at me!"

His tone is so forceful, I feel compelled to obey. I open my teary eyes.

"You went on and on about 'Lah-de-dah my daddy loves me!' And 'I am Charlie Wilber's Daughter!' And all the while, your daddy didn't do shit for you! What did that pussy-ass ever do for you 'cept make you cry your whole damned life?"

I whimper.

"You should have ditched that sorry-ass loser years ago, but you just kept hanging on his every word and letting him make you cry."

I shake my head, my entire body quaking.

"Honey, I gave your daddy a fair shake, okay? He had plenty of time to prove himself. Kurtis had already been in the big house for well over a *month* by the time I went down there and had a little chat with a friend of a friend. A whole *month*, and your daddy hadn't yet made things right for you—after all the times he'd made you cry? Well, guess what. It was time for your daddy to answer to *me*."

I'm trembling with my horror. Wilber jumps onto the bed and I pull him onto my lap and clutch him fiercely.

"I'm not sorry for what I did, Charlene," Wesley says matter-of-factly. "It had to be done. You're not Charlie Wilber's Daughter anymore—you're Wesley Miller's Wife." His eyes are like laser beams. "*You're my princess bride.*"

I cannot for the life of me think of something to say. I hold Wilber close and nuzzle my face into his soft fur.

Wesley smiles. "I got a nice and tidy two-for-one for your husband and your daddy." He snaps his fingers. "Easy as pie."

I close my eyes tight and tears squirt down my cheeks.

Wesley tries to kiss me but I jerk away, squeezing Wilber in my arms. "No!" I scream. "No, Wesley!"

Wesley leaps off the bed and begins pacing around the room like a lunatic. "I had to do it, Charlene. Don't you understand?" His face morphs into pure anguish. "I never forgave myself for not being there to protect you when that fucker hurt you—I swore to myself I'd never let anyone hurt you again, no matter what. And I haven't broken that promise since."

I'm confused. Is he talking about the time Kurtis walloped me? That makes no sense. Wesley couldn't have protected me then—he was in jail.

Wesley shakes his head at my look of confusion and gesticulates like he can't come up with a word. "You know, the one who hurt you and your momma."

Oh my goodness, no. "*Jeb*?" I say, incredulous. "You're talking about *Jeb*?"

"That's it. *Jeb*." He's spitting bile when he says the name. "Jeb the Motherfucker. The minute you told me what he did to you, I swore to myself no man would ever make you cry again, not on my watch, no matter who he was." He literally spits at the ground. "Never again."

I bury my face in Wilber's soft fur as the image of poor Jeb convulsing on the ground slams into me. Poor, poor Jeb. I wish to God I'd never baked that gosh-dang rat-poison cake for that sweet man.

"It killed me knowing I wasn't there to help you when he hurt you—thinking about what he did to you made me crazy. And it was even worse thinking, if only Grammy hadn't died, I'd have been there all along, keeping you safe from him."

I feel like my brain's been unplugged from the wall. "Wesley, what the hell are you talking about?"

"If Grammy hadn't died, I'd have been there all along."

Wesley seems to think repeating this sentence has made everything clear, but I still don't have a clue what he's talking about.

He rolls his eyes. "Because then I wouldn't have had to leave you to go to the group home."

I feel like I've just been slammed with a rock upside the head. "Wesley," I say, my stomach doing jumping jacks. I pause as everything suddenly becomes clear to me. "Your grammy was *Mrs. Miller*?"

A smile unfurls across his face. "I knew from the minute you knocked on the door of our trailer, you were the only one for me, forever and ever—the most beautiful girl in the world."

My racing mind suddenly locks into place. "You're Mrs. Miller's dopey grandson?"

He nods.

"With the scruffy little dog?"

He looks as happy as a dog with two peters. "I knew you were my destiny the minute I laid eyes on you—you were the most beautiful girl I'd ever seen. And when you walked right through the front door of the group home all those years later, thank you Sweet Jesus, I knew it wasn't a coincidence. I knew it meant you were my destiny, and I was supposed to take care of you forever and ever, no matter what."

As Wesley's talking, I glance down at the box. There's still one item left inside. With a shaking hand, I reach inside and pull it out. It's a white strip of plastic—about six inches long and a quarter-inch wide, easy to bend. I'm not sure exactly what it is. I bend it this way and that for a moment, trying to make heads or tails of it. Over and over, I bend that plastic back and forth; until finally, by chance, I manipulate it into the shape of a tiny "O."

I clutch Wilber to me and gasp.

My stomach lurches violently at my sudden epiphany.

Wesley motions to the strip of plastic in my hand. "That Jessica Santos made you cry?"

"No, Wesley. *No.*"

"Well, then, I reckon I made *her* fucking cry, too."

This isn't a strip of plastic.

It's a teeny-tiny flea collar.

Epilogue

Hollywood, California

1996
24 Years Old

"Thank you," I say.

Tears are streaming down my perfectly made-up face. I'm laughing and crying at the same time, which is all right, though, because I wore waterproof mascara tonight.

"Thank y'all so much," I choke out, trying to catch my breath. Every single person in the entire theater, from top to bottom, is on their feet, showering me with a loud and raucous ovation. "Oh, goodness gracious, where to start?" I bring my manicured hand to my mouth, and it's noticeably shaking. "Well, first off, of course, I'd like to thank the Academy. This is a tremendous honor and a dream come true."

The theater begins the slow process of resuming their seats.

I wait a beat to make sure everyone has settled into their chairs—I don't want anyone to miss out on a single word I say.

"And, of course, I want to thank all the other nominees." I look pointedly at the other actresses, each of *whom* is sitting prettily in their seats and dressed to the nines. Each woman smiles broadly at me, pretending to be happy for me, bless

343

their hearts. "Y'all are so talented, and so deserving. It's an honor to hear my name mentioned in the same breath as yours." I wipe away a tear.

I look for Wesley's face in the third row.

The stage lights are shining in my eyes and Wesley's too far away to make out the expression on his face, but I reckon I can see his head. Holy shit on a shingle, if I don't get this "thank you" exactly right, if I don't go on and on in just the right way about how he always takes such good care of me, then I'm sure as heck gonna hear about it later tonight.

"And, of course," I begin, fixing my gaze on what I reckon is Wesley's head, "I've got to thank my precious valentine, my husband, Wesley." I shoot an adoring smile in Wesley's direction. "You always take such good care of me, baby. I'm the luckiest girl in the world to be your princess bride. Forever and ever."

I can't make out the details of Wesley's face right now, but I reckon he's smiling. Well, holy hell, he'd better be smiling, and not pouting and gritting his teeth about how I haven't thanked him enough for all he's done for me and I'm never grateful enough and *blah, blah, blah*. I've had about enough of that speech to last me a lifetime.

My chest is heaving.

I gaze out at the vast audience in the theater, catching my breath.

I reckon it's time to get my mind right and my butt off my shoulders and enjoy this special, one-of-a-kind moment. I can't worry about Wesley and what he might be thinking right now. This moment is about me and my sacred destiny. I'll deal with my husband and God knows what he's gonna say or do later. But I can say one thing for sure, now that I'm a legendary actress—now that I've carried Lana and Marilyn's torch into the catacombs of history—nobody's gonna tell me what I can and can't do, ever again. *Nobody*. Not even Wesley.

I take a deep breath.

I feel the eyes of the entire world staring at me right now.

I reckon I'd better give the people what they want.

I smile broadly at my audience in the theater and then flash a beaming smile into one of the many TV cameras pointed in my direction.

"Gosh, I feel like I'm riding a gravy train with biscuit wheels!" I say.

The audience laughs in unison. My goodness, how Californians love themselves a girl who talks Texas.

My blood is simmering down.

The audience's laughter is relaxing me.

"More than anything," I begin, "I just want to say this to anyone who might have a dream." I take another deep breath. "Dreams really *do* come true." The audience applauds. "When you know your sacred destiny, never let anyone tell you what you can and can't do."

There's more applause.

Music begins playing, signaling the end of my allotted time.

"Oh, gracious, hang on a minute," I gasp. I begin jumping up down and the audience chuckles at me. "I just want to say, if you want something, if you really, really want something, never, ever quit on your sacred destiny, no matter what." I'm shouting over the swelling music. "Just be consistent—*consistency* is key!"

There's a guy in the wings frantically motioning for me to come offstage now. I reckon I'd better go.

"Thank y'all, so much," I say, holding my golden statuette up high in the air. I blow the audience a kiss, and they applaud uproariously.

I begin gliding offstage, waving as I go.

My goodness, everyone loves me! I'm not The American Dream Gone Haywire anymore—I'm The American Dream Come True. *I am Charlie Wilber's Daughter.* I'm a role model—an inspiration. *I'm somebody.*

Yes, indeed, I'm living proof that a girl can have any

happily ever after she wants, anything at all, if only she puts her mind to it. Yes, sir, a big ol' brain can get a girl anything she wants in this life. Anything at all. Well, that and hard work. And having God-given talent sure doesn't hurt, either. Of course, it also helps move things along like a greased berry through a goose if a girl happens to be as pretty as a picture, too.

Well, like I always say, thank God I'm so gosh darned pretty.

About the Author

Lauren Rowe is the pen name of the USA Today bestselling author of The Club Trilogy, an erotic and suspenseful romance that's taken the genre by storm, and the twisting thriller Countdown to Killing Kurtis. Lauren lives in San Diego, California, where, in addition to writing books, she performs with her band, writes songs, and narrates audiobooks. Find out more about Lauren Rowe and her books and sign up for her emails at www.LaurenRoweBooks.com.

Lauren loves to hear from readers. Send an email from her website, follow Lauren on Twitter @laurenrowebooks and/or come by her Facebook page by seaching Facebook for "Lauren Rowe author" (or use this link: https://www.facebook.com/pages/Lauren-Rowe/1498285267074016).

Additional books by Lauren Rowe:

The bestselling The Club Trilogy, all books available:
The Club (The Club Trilogy Book 1)
The Reclamation (The Club Trilogy Book 2)
The Redemption (The Club Trilogy Book 3)

Acknowledgments

I need to thank so many people for helping me hone this crazy-ass story:

First, to the men in my life: My husband (who, after reading this book, said, and I quote, "Should I be sleeping with one eye open?"); Baby Cuz (who read this book and called me a "fucking savage," which, of course, is the best compliment any woman could ever receive); and, most of all, to my own sweet Daddy (who has read this book through every single draft and says it's his absolute favorite of anything I've written, even though I've yet again written yet another bastard father who bears absolutely no resemblance to him). You three men in my life have not only helped shape this book (which is so very precious to me), but even more importantly, you have helped shape *me* so very much. I love all three of you bigger than a sky full of stars.

To the gloriously twisted women in my life who read this book and loved Buttercup, even though, I reckon, she's a wee bit scary: Mom, Aunt Harriet, Lyn, Sophie, Nicki, and Lucy. You six loved this book and my darling Buttercup from the first page and gave me confidence to keep venturing out of my comfort zone and give free reign to the twisted voices inside my head. Without your encouragement, I'm not sure I would have written this book so honestly. Without you, I might very well have stopped short of revealing just how abnormal my brain can be. In particular, a special shout-out to my mom. Mom, you bear no resemblance whatsoever to Momma, I promise, other than the fact that you often pass out on a dirty mattress and piss yourself. Just kidding, Mom. You in particular were a huge voice of encouragement for this book and that meant the world to me. The fact that you got such a kick out of Buttercup right from the start, the fact that you loved her like I do, gave me confidence to be brave and reveal the depths of my socio-pathy to the entire world. Hey, Mom.

Think of it that way! You've spawned a sociopath! Aren't you proud?

Thank you to Stacy Carlson, Colleeny Roppé, and Heather Dinsdale. Your early insights into Buttercup were invaluable. You absolutely helped shape the direction of this novel, for the better, and I thank you so much. Stacy in particular, you have been with me every step of the way, psychoanalyzing Buttercup and helping me brainstorm, and I am so grateful. You made me earn it, girl, as I should. Thank you.

A superstar shout-out to Jessica McEntire, the Girl from Texas with the cutest accent I've ever heard. You figured me out, girl, when no one else did; and I'm grateful beyond words. I cannot thank you enough for all you've done in relation to this book, and beyond, from supplying me with endless authentic Texas sayings and slang, to sending me recordings of Buttercup's accent to help guide my audiobook narration and also hone Buttercup's "voice" on the page, too. And, most of all, I thank you for talking me off the ledge when I freaked out and thought no one would ever want to read this crazy-ass story. I truly cannot thank you enough for all you've done for me in relation to this book, so I did the one thing a writer can do to express utmost thanks: I gave Buttercup your name.

Huge thank you also to my devoted agents and friends, Jill Marr and Kevin Cleary for your early reads and input and encouragement, and also for always believing in me like you do, no matter which new direction I happen to go.

I'd also like to thank the following early readers who profoundly impacted the direction of this book and, in particular, gave me much-needed confidence to forge ahead and make *Countdown to Killing Kurtis* my follow-up release after *The Club Trilogy*: Joe Rossi (King Silverback), Elizabeth Robbins, Elmarie Pieterse, Kelly Wilson, and Keri Grammer. As you all know, I wasn't sure about putting out a psychological thriller after having found success in the genre of erotic/romantic suspense, but you all so enthusiastically encouraged me to follow my muse and not worry about genre, not worry about "rules" or "this is how you're supposed to it." You all really made a difference in my life and touched my heart. Thank you.

Melissa Saneholtz. Oh, woman. Thank you is not enough. Your suggestions, input, honesty, and support were invaluable to me. There are not enough words to express my gratitude. Thank you also to Sharon Goodman, too. You two ladies of Sassy Savvy Fabulous are rock stars of PR. I'm so lucky to work with you.

And last, but certainly not least, a special shout-out to my beloved army of Love Monkeys—the devoted and hilarious and wonderful fans of *The Club Trilogy*. Thank you for going along on this crazy journey with me. I love you. I adore you. I *lurve* you. I feel like I have gained a world of friends— literally. I can't thank you lovely people enough. You are so dear to me. xoxoxo Lauren

Made in the USA
San Bernardino, CA
15 June 2015